RISE TO FALL

By Gwendoline SK Terry

Danethrall Trilogy
Danethrall
Rise to Fall
Ashes Remain

RISE TO FALL

GWENDOLINE SK TERRY

TWO RAVENS PUBLISHING

Copyright © 2019 Gwendoline SK Terry

All rights reserved.

ISBN-13: 978-1-7339996-0-1

This is a work of fiction. Names, characters, places and incidents either are the products of the author's imagination or are used fictitiously. Any resemblance to actual persons, living or dead, businesses, companies, events or locales is entirely coincidental.

www.gskterry.com

Now all goes hard for me.
I see Hel, the goddess,
Foe to duplicity,
Waiting on the headland.
Nevertheless, joyfully,
With a jocund will
And a heart that fears nothing,
I await my death.

Sonatorrek
Egill Skallagrímsson

CONTENTS

PROLOGUE 1
CHAPTER ONE 6
CHAPTER TWO 23
CHAPTER THREE 39
CHAPTER FOUR 48
CHAPTER FIVE 58
CHAPTER SIX 67
CHAPTER SEVEN 80
CHAPTER EIGHT 100
CHAPTER NINE 112
CHAPTER TEN 123
CHAPTER ELEVEN 130
CHAPTER TWELVE.. 141
CHAPTER THIRTEEN 150
CHAPTER FOURTEEN 162
CHAPTER FIFTEEN 172
CHAPTER SIXTEEN 185
CHAPTER SEVENTEEN 197

- CHAPTER EIGHTEEN 211
- CHAPTER NINETEEN 233
- CHAPTER TWENTY 247
- CHAPTER TWENTY-ONE 265
- CHAPTER TWENTY-TWO 275
- CHAPTER TWENTY-THREE 286
- CHAPTER TWENTY-FOUR 299
- CHAPTER TWENTY-FIVE 311
- CHAPTER TWENTY-SIX 325
- CHAPTER TWENTY-SEVEN 344
- CHAPTER TWENTY-EIGHT 356
- CHAPTER TWENTY-NINE 365
- CHAPTER THIRTY 373
- CHAPTER THIRTY-ONE 394
- CHAPTER THIRTY-TWO 411
- CHAPTER THIRTY-THREE 423
- CHAPTER THIRTY-FOUR 439

RISE TO FALL

PROLOGUE

AROS, DENMARK
Spring, 880

IN THE SUMMER of 878, Vidar Alvarsson of Roskilde killed my husband, Jarl Erhardt Ketilsson of Aros, and took Erhardt's jarldom as his own. Vidar led a surprise attack against Aros and defeated the town with ease. Vidar had given the people there a choice, swear fealty to him or face the consequences. Many promised their loyalty to him, and those who refused were enslaved or killed, locked inside Erhardt's hall and burned alive.

I stared at the new hall before me, cradling my baby daughter in my arms. I followed every line of grain and every knot in the great hall's wide oak door, admired the fine iron ring pull and the long, thin iron strap hinges. The hall that had stood here before hadn't been half as fine as the one before me now.

This new hall was far bigger than all the longhouses in Aros. Like a longship flipped upside down, it was slightly oval shaped and built with planks from hundreds of oak trees. Posts were evenly spaced along the tall outer walls, tilted against the building to support it, with gorgeous images of animals, knotwork and scenes imagined from various tales carved into them. The entire hall was painted white with quicklime, from the posts to the walls, a vivid status symbol easily spotted from afar. Only the massive, sloping wood-shingled roof remained its warm, natural colour.

I had lived in the previous hall with my first husband, Jarl Erhardt, for five long years. Now the ashes of that hall, the only remnant of the building, were interspersed in the packed dirt floor of this grand new hall. Memories of my past life in Aros and my marriage to Erhardt flittered before my eyes, and a deep sigh of relief fell from my lips.

That chapter of my life was finally closed for good.

"Do you like it?" Vidar Alvarsson asked, appearing beside me.

Vidar rested his hand on the small of my back and I looked up at him. He gazed at me with bright, unblinking eyes, keen to hear my opinion on the new hall he had built for us and our children. I admired the beauty of Vidar's eyes, his irises were blue like ice, almost transparent in their paleness, rimmed with cerulean. They gleamed from his bronze skin like diamonds in sand.

"*Já*," I smiled. "I do."

"Shall we go in?"

I giggled at his eagerness and nodded.

"Young Birger, Sander, come my sons! Let me show you our new home!" Vidar called, and our two young blond sons dashed over to us, just as enthusiastic as their father.

We stepped into the hall and surveyed the interior. Young Birger and Sander, six and three years of age respectively, scurried about our new home, exploring every inch of it. Their bright blue eyes ogled the decorations and furniture, their little fingers touched every surface, probed every nook and cranny. Vidar even had the inside of our home painted white with quicklime, and gorgeous furs and pelts of bears, wolves and the like hung on the walls, alongside a collection of Vidar's beautifully painted and well-used round wooden shields.

A fire crackled and popped as it burned low in the long rectangular fire pit running the centre of the main room. The comforting yet pungent scent of smoke drifted from it, permeating the large space. I watched the small orange and gold flames flicker and dance, and the wood burn black and grey as the flames devoured it.

Mesmerised by the fire's dance and the quiet crackle of its song, the sound of my sons' laughter faded from my ears, the crunch of Vidar's footsteps on the hard dirt floor vanished, and even the soft sound of my daughter's breath as she slept in my arms disappeared.

I was apprehensive about returning to Aros. I wanted to stay in Roskilde for the rest of my life, but a jarl must rule his jarldom, and Aros now belonged to Vidar. Vidar had let me remain in Roskilde with our children, living in his parents' hall with his mother and father, while he rebuilt Aros and constructed this grand new hall for us, but now it was time for us to come to Aros, to stay and live and rule.

My heart yearned to return to Roskilde. Memories haunted me, shivers had skittered down my spine at the very mentioning of our move to Aros, and at night I would dream of my previous life there. Though I feared leaving Roskilde, feared moving back to the town I had been trapped in for so long, I would not be separated from Vidar again. I would live in Aros once more, but this time was different. This time I was with Vidar.

I turned my gaze to my husband, who was chasing after Young Birger with Sander atop his shoulders, the three of them laughing like madmen. I grinned at the sight of my husband and sons.

Yes, things were very different now. With Vidar at my side, I could go anywhere, do anything, and I would be safe and happy. Vidar had destroyed all evidence of my past life in Aros, he had done everything he could to erase any landmark that might remind me of the torturous five years I had lived here as the forced-wife of Jarl Erhardt Ketilsson.

Vidar would take on all the *jötnar* of Jötunheimr and all the gods of Asgard to protect our family. Vidar and I would never be separated again. He was my haven, he was my heart, he was my bliss. Deep inside me though, always a shadow in the back of my mind, I feared the end of my paradise.

In idyllic moments such as this, watching Vidar laugh and play with our children, I feared the end. In the wild laughter of our children as they played like wild cubs, feral and raucous; in the serene silence of every morning, wrapped in my husband's warm embrace; or when, in the darkness of night, we'd pant together, our flesh glistening with the sheen of sweat after loving one another wholly and completely … I always feared the end.

The end had not yet come, but that caused me to fear it more. The light of good fortune had never shone on me for long. I would find myself in the embrace of bliss, but always it would shatter. Since that fateful day when the Norsemen of Roskilde had sacked my village in the Kingdom of the East Angles and kidnapped me, a nine-year-old child, I realised peace did not last forever.

I had learned I would always rise to fall.

I thought of my family – my first family from the Kingdom of the East Angles. My life had been arduous, it had been simple and peaceful until the Norsemen of Roskilde had come. Fifteen years had passed since the Danes had attacked – since they'd murdered my family, burned my village and stolen me away to their land.

I couldn't remember my family's faces clearly anymore, but I had long since forgotten my guilt.

Birger Bloody Sword, the Dane who had kidnapped me, had saved me from death and adopted me. Birger had raised me and loved me as though I were his own flesh and blood. I had formed a love for him, and with that love came an overwhelming shame, as though I was betraying my Anglo-Saxon family by adoring him.

That shame had consumed me for so long, but I had risen from the ashes of my Anglo-Saxon life. I had risen and accepted my new life as a Dane.

Birger had died many years ago, and my heart ached for him as it had for my biological kin. I had not forgotten his face, though, and I had named my firstborn son after him. Roskilde became my home. I had found love with Vidar; I had found that much sought-after peace once again.

But I fell.

Serenity had not lasted long, and fate had me stolen away from Vidar soon after his and my engagement. Fate had tossed me like meat to the wolves; when Vidar had left for a few weeks to trade in the Danish town of Ribe, the town of Aros besieged Roskilde. Vidar's own mother, Freydis, had been coerced into marrying me off to Jarl Erhardt Ketilsson to end the feud between the two towns, and to save her son's life.

The feud had never really ended, of course. Jarl Erhardt had succeeded in taking Roskilde and controlling it. Most of the Roskilde townsmen and warriors had been fighting with the Great Army in Britain when Aros attacked, and the remaining townspeople had been outnumbered and powerless to fight against Aros. Those who tried to rise against Erhardt and his people were slain.

I was married to Jarl Erhardt for five years, beaten and raped by him. Erhardt had mockingly titled me 'Danethrall', but my Anglo-

Saxon weakness had long faded from my body, and inside me smouldered the courage to endure all he put me through. I found a way to survive my harrowing marriage; I had drawn strength from my prayers to the Norse goddess, Frigg, and learned to do things I never thought I could do ...

Only Vidar and I had known I carried his baby in my belly when Freydis had me married off to Erhardt. I was forced to raise Young Birger as Erhardt's son – had he known Young Birger was Vidar's, Erhardt would have exposed the child, tossed him into the wilderness at birth and left to him die.

Vidar and I had conceived our second son, Sander, during a chance meeting a few years into my marriage to Erhardt. Again, I had to lie, had to pretend Sander was Erhardt's – but not for long. A year after Sander's birth, the day had finally come when Vidar set me free. No sweeter kiss had come from Vidar's lips than on the day he came to me, drenched in my first husband's blood, announcing my first husband's death.

It had been two years since then. I had lived in peace since then. Vidar and I had welcomed our third child, our beautiful daughter Æsa, we had married and now ruled as Jarl and Jarlkona of Aros.

I watched Vidar direct our thralls as they carried in our trunks of belongings, Sander still sitting upon his shoulders and Young Birger held under his arm like a sack. I was ready to put the past behind me and start this new life, but I feared – no, I *knew* this happiness would not last forever. It was only a matter of time ...

As I stared at the fantastic hall before me, the hall that was mine and my husband's, and I shuddered. My past had proven I would rise to fall, and I had risen higher than I could have imagined. I knew my fall would be devastatingly immense.

CHAPTER ONE

AROS, DENMARK
Early Spring, 882

I SHIFTED MY daughter higher on my hip. I stood at the edge of a flat glade surrounded by forest and watched my husband and sons, who were a few feet away. Vidar was teaching our boys archery.

The snow had melted a few weeks ago, leaving the greenery of Aros dull and muddy. The sky was constantly overcast, with frequent showers. It had been mild as of late, and Aros had been swept in shrouds of fog and mist. Today was no different. Clouds filled the sky, heavy with the promise of rain and as grey as the blade of the utility knife that hung from my husband's belt. It was nearing evening time now and the sparse sunlight that slipped through the clouds was fading fast.

Vidar and our two sons stood in a row, each holding their own elm and horn bows, aiming through the grey light at a round, red-painted shield hung from a tree maybe a hundred paces in the distance. There were already a handful of arrows piercing the shield and a number more sticking into the ground beneath it.

Young Birger, our eldest son who had seen eight winters, took a step forward and nocked an arrow into place. The boys' bows were smaller than Vidar's but of equally fine quality. Young Birger drew the bowstring back until it kissed the tip of his nose and lips, and I smiled at the determination on his face.

As Young Birger aimed, he chewed his bottom lip, just like Vidar. The father and son were very like-minded; calm, quiet and hardly separated. Although he was only a boy, Young Birger was the epitome of Vidar, from his mannerisms to his appearance.

Sander, three years Young Birger's junior, may have looked like his father and brother, but he was not as composed as them. Sander was noisy, naughty and mischievously playful – and he delightfully brought out the joker in Vidar.

RISE TO FALL

The father and sons complemented each other in every aspect. Both of our sons took their features from their father, from their silky sheets of golden hair and their startling ice-blue eyes to their faded bronze skin. They were duplicates of Vidar.

I rubbed my large tummy with my free hand and the occupant inside me wiggled, sending jolts of discomfort through me. I wondered whether this child would resemble Vidar as well? Or would the child hold some of my features like Æsa? Our only daughter, Æsa, had inherited her pale flesh and amber eyes from me, but soft strands of straight, pale blonde hair cascaded from her head, identical to Vidar's mother Freydis's tresses.

"Don't aim with your bowstring drawn, Young Birger," I remarked. "Also, your legs are too far apart, and you keep moving your back foot between shots – your *faðir* isn't teaching you the importance of a consistent stance."

A smirk on his face and one eyebrow cocked, Vidar glanced over his shoulder at me. Young Birger lowered his bow. He and Sander glanced between us, their ice-blue eyes alight and wide, smiles brimming on their little faces.

"I'm not teaching him properly?" Vidar asked, amusement in his words.

"He can shoot an arrow well enough, but his stance is incorrect," I explained. "He would do better if his legs weren't open as wide and he kept his feet rooted in the same spot."

"His stance looks good to me."

"He stands with his legs too wide, and his back leg is sticking out too much. He needs his feet shoulder-width apart, no more – no less."

"He *is* standing shoulder-width apart."

"He needs to move his legs closer together, he's *too wide*."

"You're being pedantic, little fawn."

"You're a good shot, my love, but the difference between your leniency and my strict attention to detail is what makes me the better archer."

Vidar's jaw dropped, and his eyebrows shot up his forehead. Suddenly he doubled over in raucous laughter, and a furious blush burned on my cheeks.

"I *am* better at archery than you!" I barked.

"Your *móðir* thinks she can best me at archery." Vidar said to the boys, wiping his eyes with the heels of his hands.

"I don't think, I *know*." I remarked, shifting Æsa higher on my hip. "If you're going to teach our sons how to use a bow, you should at least teach them the correct way to stand."

"I've been shooting longer than you've been alive, little fawn," Vidar grinned, holding his bow out to me. "But by all means, show me where I'm wrong."

"Come fetch our daughter and I will."

Vidar sauntered over, holding a hand out to our darling Æsa. The two-year-old girl beamed at her father as he neared her.

"Your *mumie* thinks she's a better archer than me," Vidar cooed to her. "What do you think about that?"

Æsa giggled, covered her cheeks with her pudgy little hands and rocked side to side, her wispy ivory locks of hair tumbling into her face with every turn.

"*Já! Mumie, mumie, mumie!*" Æsa squealed.

"Ha!" I grinned victoriously, planting a noisy kiss onto my daughter's cheek, much to her delight.

"Unfair advantage – of course a daughter will side with her *móðir*." Vidar protested in mock offence.

"We will see if she's right, won't we?" I replied, curling my slender fingers around his bow.

It was a gorgeous bow made of elm, with reindeer antler on the tips. A small smile played at the corners of my lips as I admired the fine crafting of the weapon. Vidar had made it himself. He could craft all sorts of items from wood and bone – toys and trinkets to intricate chests and elegant bows like this.

Vidar took our squirming daughter from me, and she giggled wickedly as she clung to his cloak, her legs wrapped around his side. Æsa stopped giggling when she spotted her older brothers snickering behind us. She jabbered at them in a variety of pitches and sounds, with a few intelligible words in between. She wriggled to be free and gently Vidar lowered her to the ground. Immediately the small girl tottered off towards her siblings.

"I'll need arrows." I smiled coyly, stepping close to him.

RISE TO FALL

I rested my hand on Vidar's chest, gliding it lower down his body. Vidar rested his hands on either side of my swollen stomach and grazed his lips against mine as I pulled an arrow from the leather quiver hanging from his hip.

Our eyes locked and radiated so intensely with excitement, I could almost feel the heat burning between us. Vidar's smirk deepened, and he leaned closer offering me his lips once more. I brushed my lips against his, but before I could place a kiss upon them, he pulled away yet again.

"You're teasing me." I barked. "Are you afraid I'll beat you, *mighty Ullr*?"

"Show me your skill, Skaði." Vidar winked; his voice soft.

I scowled at him, turned on my heel and marched towards our sons. Vidar wasn't riled by my mocking comparison of him to Ullr the god of hunting, instead, he strolled along behind me, humming a light-hearted tune. Though we were just jesting with each other, I knew I was as skilled as the huntress goddess, Skaði, and I planned on proving it to Vidar.

"Alright," I said to the boys as Vidar took Æsa's hand and ushered her back to the tree line. "Your stance is an important part of archery. The stance I'm going to teach you is the easiest, and simple enough for you to reproduce – it's the best stance to learn when you're beginning. It will help you maintain your balance and keep your body steady as you shoot."

The smirks slipped from the boys' faces and they returned to their spots, an arm's length apart from each other.

"I want you to keep your body relaxed; align your feet – keep them shoulder-width apart – perpendicular to the target – your left foot forward." I explained, moving into position as I described it to them.

"Do as your *móðir* says." Vidar called to the boys.

I glared at him from over my shoulder. Vidar crossed his arms over his chest, the long sleeves of his blue tunic stretched over the swell of his muscles, that damn smirk fixed to his face. I stuck my tongue out at him before turning my attention back to our sons.

"Come, boys, stand as I do – it's not difficult." I barked.

The boys imitated me.

"Sander, your stance is beautiful, but I want your *left* foot forward, not your right. That's it, turn around – align your feet again – yes, that's it! Young Birger bring your back leg a little closer – a little more – *there*! Stay like that."

I nodded at them in approval, smiling at their forms. They had recreated my stance wonderfully – now all they had to do was practice it, so it would become a natural position for them to stand the moment a bow was in their hands.

Moving on from standing positions, I brought Vidar's bow up, gripping it with my left hand, and extended a finger to point at the shield in the distance

"Hold the bow in your non-dominant hand," I instructed though both boys were already doing so. "Raise the bow – your finger, wrist and arm should all be aligned and pointing at the target. It will feel a little odd at first," I added for five-year-old Sander's benefit. "But it will become comfortable to you in time."

Both boys shifted a little, making sure their fingers pointed at the shield, turning their faces to me when they were ready. I curled my finger back around the bow and nocked an arrow into place, gripping the string with the tips of three fingers, the arrow rested between my forefinger and middle finger.

"The arm that draws the string is an extension of the arrow. Keep the hand drawing the string in a straight line behind the arrow from your fingertips through your wrist, out to your elbow. Draw the string to the point when your middle finger touches the corner of your mouth – and do this *every time*. It will help you maintain a consistent draw length. To be a good archer, you need a combination of *consistent form*," I emphasised loudly, answered by a snort from Vidar. "And intense focus on your target.

"You must focus on the smallest point on your target and maintain that focus until after the arrow has struck. Focus on the target as you draw your bow. The moment your middle finger touches the corner of your mouth, release the arrow. Do *not* aim when your bow is at full draw. Do you understand?"

"*Já, móðir.*" The boys said in unison.

This was not their first archery lesson, in fact, Young Birger himself was a fair archer. The moment they had each seen their fourth winter, Vidar would take Young Birger and Sander with him on every hunt. He taught them archery, trapping, fishing with both nets and hook and line, and much more.

The boys had caught more prey with traps than they had with arrows – though Young Birger had shot a handful of birds or squirrels on each of the various hunting trips he had attended. Regardless, Young Birger and Sander were diligent in their learning and with time I was sure they would be fantastic archers. They were comfortable with their bows, though not at all refined, they paid careful attention to everything Vidar and I taught them.

When I was a child, I had been much the same.

My Anglo-Saxon father had taught my seven brothers' archery and swordplay, he had taken them hunting, and practised fighting with them. I pined after their knowledge, craved to learn what they did – their lessons were far more enjoyable than cooking, cleaning, making and mending clothes or spinning wool with my mother. My father had found my tantrums amusing, though my mother had not, but eventually my father allowed me to participate in my brother's lessons regardless of my mother's staunch disapproval.

Like a fish to water, I mastered archery with ease. I was a natural! I had quickly outshot the youngest of my brothers, Bryni and Oswin, much to their disdain, which of course increased my enjoyment. My father had been so proud of me – even my mother reluctantly admitted I was skilled.

It warmed my heart to see my sons gazing at me so attentively, absorbing all the knowledge I shared with them – just as I had with my father. I heard Æsa's shrill laugh in the background … Yes, when she saw her fourth winter, she would be here too, and learn archery and hunting alongside her brothers, just as I had.

"Come then, little fawn, show me your skill." Vidar heckled impatiently. "Then give me back my bow!"

I ignored my husband and stared at the red shield hanging from the tree. I drew the bow and –

Wait, what was that?

Amidst the brush and bracken behind the shield, I spied a dark patch of ashen-brown and a flash of light-grey. Was it foliage? Was it a shadow? Only that little square of colour was visible, but I was adamant it wasn't there before.

I took a chance. I stared at that patch, drew the bowstring back until my middle finger grazed the corner of my mouth, relaxed the back of my hand and released the bowstring. The arrow soared. My body froze, my hand still raised to my face, my eyes locked on that mysterious patch in the brush. The arrow sliced through the air, past the shield and pierced the square of colour. The moment my arrow struck, the colour vanished, and I dropped my hand.

"You missed, oh mighty Skaði! It seems Ullr is the better archer after all." Vidar teased, though there was surprise in his voice – I had never missed my target before, let alone one that was still and hanging from a tree.

"Don't be so sure." I grinned.

Vidar's bow still clutched in my hand, I dashed across the glade clutching my belly with my free hand, my children's confused voices calling after me. The grass was long and damp from the day's rain, and it slapped across my legs as I ran.

It took only a moment for me to reach the shield. I peeked behind it, eager to see what I had shot, but I couldn't see anything. I hooked the bow over my body and shoved through the bracken.

Only a short way into the clutch of trees and I found my shot. There, laying on the ground was an excellently sized stag. It had already shed one of its antlers, and the beams of its remaining antler were wide and long. It still had its grey-brown winter fur, but there was a ruddy hue to it, and its underside was a mixture of light-grey and creamy white. My arrow was sticking out of its side behind its front leg; a perfect shot, I had pierced its heart.

"What–" Vidar spotted my stag and his mouth dropped.

"*Mumie*! Look, deer!" Æsa exclaimed from her father's arms, pointing at the stag.

"It is." I grinned. "I didn't miss at all – I suppose Skaði truly is the better archer. What say you, Ullr?"

"Well done, my love," Vidar said sincerely, pressing a sweet kiss to my lips. "He's a very fine stag."

I leaned my head against Vidar's shoulder, as we admired my kill.

"How are we getting it home?" Young Birger asked abruptly.

Vidar and I glanced at each other blankly for a moment.

"Fetch Ebbe and Hallmundr, my sons." Vidar said. "They will help."

Young Birger and Sander nodded and tore away. As they bolted off on their mission, Vidar turned back to the stag and took a few steps closer to it.

"We will eat finely in a few days' time, and we will stock our cupboards well. There's a lot of meat on this." Vidar admired, yanking the arrow out of the stag with his free hand. He held the arrow out and twirled it, and Æsa giggled as she watched the feathers on the end of the arrow spin. "Maybe we'll even make something pretty from the antler for my lovely girl?"

"*Já!*" Æsa grinned.

"And for my beautiful wife." Vidar added, returning to my side and offering me the arrow.

"And we will have a delicious meal made for my wonderful children, and my handsome husband." I purred.

Vidar pulled me against him with his free hand, clasping me tight against his side. He kissed my head and as he did so, Æsa wrapped her arms around my neck. I took her, and Vidar knelt beside the stag, pulling his utility knife from its sheath.

"You shouldn't run when you're this far along with child, you know." Vidar commented as he heaved the great animal's front leg up to commence gutting it.

"*Hush*, mighty Ullr." I smiled, rolling my eyes.

***

I LEFT VIDAR to tend to my stag while I took Æsa home. Night had fallen by the time Vidar, our sons and Vidar's friends Ebbe and Hallmundr had arrived at the hall with the stag. Vidar had gutted it while Æsa and I had been at his side, and he had left the innards for nature to take. Other than the innards, the stag was still in one piece, skin and all.

The three men had taken the stag to a shed behind the hall to hang the animal for a day or so. We were now thankful for the cool spell of weather we were having – it was far from hunting season and we could not age the deer for long at all. Vidar, who despised the texture of venison when butchered straight after being killed, was adamant it would be fine to hang the stag for a day or so, but we wouldn't push it further in case the weather warmed.

Vidar had been right, the weather had stayed cool, and the storms of the night had come to rage into the day. A day and a half after I had killed the stag, the stiffness of death had subsided from its body, and I spent most of the day skinning and butchering the animal with Caterine, our house thrall, at my side.

Caterine and I first removed the stag's remaining antler for Vidar, then we skinned the animal while it hung and set aside the hide for tanning. After that, we set onto the long task of butchering. I had been lucky with this kill; the stag had a fair amount of meat on it considering it was the early days of spring.

We obtained a vast amount of meat from the stag – loins and tenderloins, roasts and steaks, shanks for stewing, and a mountain of scraps to dry. As we made our cuts, we trimmed away the fat, tendons and silver skin from the meat. We would render the fat down into tallow for baking, cooking and soap making.

We cut a portion of the shanks into cubes and set them aside to marinate in ale for a day – it would make us a fine dinner tomorrow evening, with mushrooms, carrots, potatoes and leeks. We separated the other cuts for drying, salting or smoking.

Every muscle in my body ached, my feet throbbed from standing for so long, and my legs were stiff. Night had fallen a while ago, the air had thickened, and dense cloud hid the moon and stars from sight. It was a lot of work for Caterine and me, but we finally had the stag meat set. We didn't eat deer all that often, and it wasn't the best time of year to be hunting it, but it was a grand stag – well worth the effort of preserving and preparing. I didn't regret killing it at all.

The rain that had been looming all day cascaded from the blackened sky, and I welcomed it. Caterine and I were soaked with blood and residue from the stag, sweat stuck our hair to our faces, and we stank of salt, smoke and carcass. As the downpour drenched us, I felt cleaner, cooler.

Caterine stumbled beside me, wincing at the sudden crack of thunder and flash of lightning. In my peripheral, I glimpsed her pale, timid face – she was so pretty, her features looked as though they'd been delicately painted on her porcelain flesh. Caterine was desperate to find shelter, but I didn't quicken my pace, I enjoyed the cool respite of the rain and the mild night air far too much.

"*Madame*, the storm." Caterine quaked.

"We're almost home, we'll be fine," I said. "Go ahead, if you'd like."

Just as brief as the lightning in the sky was the consideration to dash off ahead of me that flashed across Caterine's face. She stayed at my side, silently impatient and nervous, but with me all the same. I smiled and took her hand in mine.

"I truly don't mind; I just don't have the strength to run right now." I said warmly.

"We will get there when we get there." She said though dismay lined her words.

As fast as my heavily pregnant and exhausted body would take me, I finally staggered into the hall with Caterine behind me.

"Do you need my assistance?" Caterine asked.

"I'm fine, should I need help, I have Vidar." I answered.

Caterine nodded and disappeared into the kitchen.

"Well aren't you quite the sight to behold?" Vidar mused as I dropped myself into a chair across from him at the table.

"Oh, don't tease me – I'm not in the mood." I groaned, tossing my head back. "I need to bathe ... I need to sleep."

"You need to eat." Vidar added.

In the middle of the table was a plate of cheese, dried fruits and bread I assumed Vidar had been nibbling on over the course of the evening. Vidar rose from his chair, took the plate and placed it in front of me.

I smiled up at him in thanks and watched him cut a small chunk of cheese and stab it with the end of his knife. Carefully, he brought it to my mouth, and I pulled the cheese from the knife's tip with my teeth. I ate it gratefully, not realising how hungry I was until the pungent odour of the cheese drifted up my nostrils and the strong, delicious flavour danced on my tongue.

Vidar handed me the knife and rubbed my shoulders as I ate. He kneaded the knots from my tightened muscles, and a wave of gorgeous relief washed over me. I dropped the knife on the table top and paused mid-chew, so engulfed with relaxation. Vidar worked my shoulders, massaging my back and down my arms to my wrists, following this cycle thoroughly, my stiff joints and tense muscles popping and crackling in release. I swallowed hard and moaned, enjoying Vidar's firm and soothing touch.

"Where are the children?" I murmured.

It had taken me longer than I liked to admit, lost in the bliss of Vidar's tender doting, to realise that my children were nowhere to be seen.

"They're asleep already," Vidar said. "They all went to bed hours ago; it's late."

"Then why are you up?" I asked, struck with sudden guilt. As Vidar ran his fingertips over my chest, I touched his hands and turned around to face him. "You didn't need to stay up, I don't want you tired on my account."

"I couldn't sleep without you in bed with me." Vidar said, placing a kiss on my sweat dampened forehead.

"Ever the romantic, aren't you?" I grinned, though I was pleased to hear him say so.

"I don't know about that, but I do know I'm ready for bed now you're here." Vidar winked. "Let's get you clean so we can go to sleep."

I rolled my eyes at him. Caterine, still filthy and sodden, appeared with a deep bowl of steaming hot water in her hands and a small basket of soap and rags hanging from her arm. I thanked her as she placed the items on the table before me and shooed her off to clean herself up in the kitchen, giving her permission to eat and go to bed when she was done.

The moment her skirts whipped around the kitchen doorway, I unpinned the white kerchief from my hair and the brooches from my apron dress straps. With a sparkle in his eyes and an eager smirk on his face, Vidar watched me remove my sodden clothes. I shoved the wet garments into his hands with a wink and sauntered over to the bench closest to us. Naked, I laid upon a pile of soft furs on the bench and stretched out my leg, pointing to the bowl of water on the table with my toe.

Vidar chuckled for a moment, but he did as I indicated. He dropped my clothes on the chair, picked up the bowl and basket and brought them over. He placed them beside the bench and knelt on the dirt floor beside me.

Without a word, Vidar rolled up the sleeves of his tunic, revealing the tattoos etched in black upon his forearms. He dipped his hands into the hot water, soaping them and rinsing away the suds, his sight flickering between my impatient gaze and the bowl as he washed his hands, a smirk growing upon his handsome face. I poked him with my toe and, chuckling, Vidar took the rag and soaked it in the water. He wrung out the excess and delicately scrubbed my feet.

Vidar took his time, tenderly washing between each toe, up the arch of my petite foot, around the heel. Frissons of warmth tingled up my leg as he delicately, meticulously worked. He rinsed the soap from the rag and wiped the suds away, placing a kiss on the sole of my foot when his task was complete.

With identical methodical tending, he cleaned my other foot and kissed the sole, then moved to my lower legs, slowly and thoroughly washing away every ounce of dirt and sweat. Maybe I was consumed by the pleasure of being pampered, but my skin tingled and seemed to glow like polished ivory from his scrupulous care.

A warmth brewed inside me as Vidar brought the warm, damp rag over my thighs with a firm but mindful pressure. His ice-blue eyes bore into my amber ones as he inched the rag further up my inner thigh, and a sputtering sigh tumbled from my lips.

Vidar chuckled, and I felt my cheeks burn red. He brought his lips to mine and kissed me gently. I cupped his bearded jaw with one hand, the golden hairs soft like silk, and shivered as ripples of desire flashed through me as his tongue brushed against mine. Slowly, Vidar enclosed his hand around my arm while I held his jaw as we kissed, running his thumb of the sensitive inner flesh of my wrist, whilst dragging the damp rag delicately between my legs with his other hand.

All of a sudden, he broke our kiss and scrubbed my arm.

"You tease!" I cried out, glaring at him.

Vidar laughed heartily, which infuriated me further. He may have thought it was funny, but I hadn't at all.

"Ah, even when you're mad, little fawn, you're so beautiful." Vidar grinned, calming himself from his fit of laughter.

"I'm pleased you find my scowl so attractive – that's the only look you'll get from me for the rest of the night." I grumbled. "How dare you tease me so!"

"Let me make it up to you, little fawn."

Vidar dropped the rag into the bowl with a splash, still smirking at me, a chuckle falling from his lips every now and again. He rose, unbuckled his belt and tossed it to the ground, then pulled his tunic off and threw it on top of his belt.

The glower contorting my face relaxed as I watched Vidar undress. Only the smattering of silver in his golden beard and the few lines scattered across his face betrayed his age; Vidar had seen forty-three winters, but he remained as agile and strong as a man half his age. Broad and chiselled, Vidar exuded power and strength, his breathtakingly brawny body exquisitely sculpted from his life of battle, fighting and seafaring. I admired the planes and hollows of his body, the smooth lines of his limbs, the tautness of his stomach, the hardness of his muscles. Vidar's arms and legs were strong and strapping, his calloused hands were large and steady.

Upon Vidar's bronze flesh he proudly bore the silvery scars of many battles and dispersed across his body was his vast collection of tattoos, some recent, others aged and faded. Vidar's tattoos consisted of various beasts, figures and Norse knotwork patterns. Fabulously detailed, Yggdrasill, the great tree of life, was Vidar's largest and most grand tattoo, which he had etched into his flesh just a year ago, and it covered his entire back. Yggdrasill's luscious branches extended across Vidar's broad shoulders, its thick, mighty trunk ran down his spine, and its three roots reached across his lower back. Surrounding Yggdrasill were images of the creatures that live inside it, the squirrel Ratatoskr, Níðhöggr the dragon and his bitter enemy the nameless eagle, and the four stags named Dáinn, Dvalinn, Duneyrr and Duraþrór.

I smiled as Vidar bent to pull off his trousers. His bottom was plump and firm, and I blushed as I admired it, even though his body had belonged to me for so many years.

"What else are you going to do to apologise?" I asked, attempting to hold up my sulk as he laid beside me on the bench, resting his head on one of his hands.

Vidar ran the fingertips of his free hand over my chest and shoulders, and I arched my back as he drew his fingertips between my breasts.

"Wait and see." Vidar smirked, bringing me into a kiss.

Vidar cupped one of my breasts, squeezing it gently. He ran his thumb over my nipple, drawing it hard like a pebble before softly pinching it between his finger and thumb, sending sharp twinges of pleasure shooting through me. I purred as Vidar leaned over me, his soft golden tresses dancing on my body, and took my nipple lightly between his lips, flicking his tongue over it and sucking it, massaging my other breast with his hand.

I ran my hand down Vidar's body and reached between his legs. My heart skipped a beat as I held him, ran my hand along the whole length of him, applying gentle pressure as I did so. Vidar was hard, tantalisingly solid in my grip, and I couldn't help but smile smugly because *I* was the cause of his great arousal. Heavily pregnant, the stench of stag carcass and sweat mingling with the faint scent of lye soap and my feet swollen to double their usual size, my ego received a well-needed boost by Vidar's physical eagerness to enjoy my body.

Vidar's breath quickened, warm on my breast, and a quiet moan of pleasure slipped from his lips. I delighted in his enjoyment, he sucked on my nipple a little rougher as I increased my speed, and I grinned. Vidar Alvarsson, fearsome, bloodthirsty Norse warrior, mighty Jarl of Aros, not to mention the most handsome man I had ever laid eyes upon, was loyal and faithful and *mine*. Only I could satisfy him – even while stinking of a dead stag.

With a *smack!* of his lips, Vidar released my nipple and moved to the other, suckling it, squeezing my breast. I took his jaw in my hands and urged his lips to mine. Slowly I sat up, and Vidar sat up with me.

"Where are you going, little fawn?" Vidar whispered, his lips tickling mine while he spoke.

"Wait and see." I grinned.

I climbed over him awkwardly, holding my massive belly with one hand, but I didn't let my huge protruding bump dampen my eagerness to pleasure him. I knelt on the ground between his legs, holding his cock with both hands, taking it into my mouth and closing my lips around it.

A soft sigh of pleasure rolled from Vidar's throat. I peeked up at him, spotting his icy blue eyes glint while he watched me. With a blush upon my cheeks, I closed my eyes. My head bobbed up and down between Vidar's legs, my cheeks hollowing from the suction as I pleasured him. With a sneaky glance, I saw Vidar's eyes were closed and his head tilted up, pleasure rife upon his handsome face. Vidar moaned, deep and husky, leaning back on one hand to steady himself, tangling the fingers of his other in my hair. With one hand I cupped his balls, squeezing them gently, and with my other hand, I brushed my thumb along the ridge that ran down the underside of his cock, all while sucking him in a steady rhythm and constant speed.

It thrilled me that I could satisfy him, that my affection, my actions, my body was what Vidar desired above all other women – Vidar who was so important in the Norse world ... I drew almost a sense of power from it. Vidar, a man who ruled an entire town and various settlements surrounding Aros, who led armies to raid and battle, depended on *me* for his pleasure.

"I thought I was going to show you how sorry I am for teasing you?" Vidar said after a while, his breath quick and shallow.

"Would you like me to stop?" I asked innocently.

"*Nei*," Vidar smirked, smirking as he watched me draw my tongue over the full length of him. "But you should if you're going to let me apologise to you."

I giggled and let him pull me to my feet. Vidar kissed my huge, round belly, gripping my buttocks in his rough, calloused hands then dragged them over the back of my thighs. Gently he urged me to lay back down on the furs covering the bench. Vidar knelt on the floor where I had been moments ago, opened my legs and rested them over his shoulders.

Vidar kissed my inner thighs, the hairs of his beard tickling me. I hadn't realised I'd been holding my breath until he drew his warm, smooth tongue over me in one long, languid stroke and a deep sigh cascaded from my lips. Vidar drew his tongue over me again and again, gradually changing from long licks to drawing little circles with just the tip of his tongue. I grabbed fistfuls of the furs, gasping in shallow breaths as Vidar flicked his tongue up and down, rotating between the tip of his tongue and the full flatness of it, maintaining the perfect pressure between rough and tender.

The knowledge that Vidar craved physical gratification from only me was exciting, but the knowledge that Vidar craved to physically gratify *me* thrilled me even more so. I glanced down at him, his head buried between my thighs, his hands roaming over me, caressing me as he tended me, and I grinned smugly. Vidar Alvarsson, fearsome, bloodthirsty Norse warrior, the mighty Jarl of Aros, wanted to pleasure *me*, wanted to be the object of *my* desire, wanted to satisfy *me* in ways no other man could. Vidar Alvarsson could've had any woman in Denmark, but he wanted *me* – he had literally killed for me! Vidar's heart was mine and his body was mine, he had proven time and time again that he would do anything for me – and he always would.

My heart raced faster, and my palms moistened as heat rushed through my body. I squirmed, twitching with pleasure, and Vidar tightened his grip, pressing his tongue against me and lapping me with short, determined strokes. A pressure grew in the pit of my stomach and I couldn't help but arch my back high off the bed as that pressure grew, hot sparks shooting through me. Vidar pinned me in place by my hips as he eagerly led me to euphoria. The tingling pleasure grew into a storm, and with a sharp intake of breath I cried out; ecstasy crashed through me like a tidal wave, surging through my entire being.

Gasping and panting, I heard Vidar snicker between my legs, gazing up at me. *That damned smirk.* Even after all these years together, he delighted in satisfying me – just as much as I did in satisfying him. Never did he neglect my gratification, even after all these years – he would never rush to his own. No, Vidar wasn't a selfish lover, he was entirely the opposite, he denied himself his own gratification until I had first received mine.

"That was a great apology." I breathed.

"I'm not finished apologising yet."

Vidar's lips were damp, and I smelled the trace of my scent on him as we kissed before he pushed against my hip, urging me to turn over. I rolled onto my hands and knees; with one hand gripping my hip, Vidar took his cock and pressed it against me, easing it into me. We gasped in unison at the abrupt *give* as he entered me, the glorious rush as he slowly pushed further into me, my insides stretching to fit him. Impatient and yearning for the delectable feeling of having Vidar wholly inside me, I pressed back against him, forcing him to slide completely into me.

Oh! The glorious rush and delicious pressure of him filling me, his hips pressed against my buttocks, the front of his thighs against the back of mine! Though I hadn't felt empty before, there was a bizarre and incredible feeling of completeness with Vidar inside me. The waves of my previous orgasm still pulsated through me, but with Vidar inside me, a primal, animalistic need for more overwhelmed my body.

Vidar grabbed my hair, twisting it around his fist, his other hand squeezing my hip. His hips slammed onto my buttocks with loud fleshy thuds. My breasts slapped together, and my moans grew louder as Vidar increased his speed and force, thrusting faster and rougher, euphoria rising inside me once again, consuming me.

Vidar let go of my hair and gripped my hips with both hands. I gasped, cursing as ecstasy crashed through my body. Vidar didn't stop though, he pounded me quicker and quicker, his grip on my hips tightening, his nails stabbing into my skin. With a loud groan, Vidar's body shuddered, and his cock throbbed inside me as he released his own euphoria.

CHAPTER TWO

WE LAID IN rapture, panting and basking in the afterglow of our union. We held each other, tangled in each other's arms, our bodies pressed close although our skin was hot, sticky and slick with sweat. After a while, drifting between wake and slumber, Vidar peeled away from me and slipped off the bench. A small smile playing on his lips, his icy eyes locked on mine, Vidar wrung out the rag and tenderly continued to clean my body with the now cold water. Beaming, I closed my eyes and enjoyed his pampering.

My body delightfully clean from Vidar's methodical, wonderful bathing, Vidar massaged some scented oil, made from various flowers and herbs, over my flesh. At that moment, his large, rough hands were gliding over my belly, rubbing the sweet oil into me, and our fourth child was kicking up a storm inside me.

"He's a strong boy." Vidar grinned, pressing his hand against my belly to feel our child's activity.

"How do you know it's a boy?" I asked.

"I just do."

Vidar dripped a little more oil into his hands and massaged it over my ribs, breasts and chest. Our conversation slipped away as I drifted into a haze of tranquillity. I had almost fallen asleep by the time Vidar had finished. Sweetly and carefully, Vidar lifted me from the bench and carried me to our bed, stealthy as a cat so as not to wake our children.

My body encased in his, I fell asleep instantly and didn't stir even once during the night. And Vidar, my heart, my beloved husband, didn't wake me the following morning, choosing to let me wake when I felt the need to, and not a moment sooner.

It was midday by the time my eyes fluttered open, the grey light of yet another moody, dreary day pouring in from the smoke hole. I spent a long time stretching luxuriously in my bed, listening to the rain hammer down on the roof, before I decided to start my day. My swollen feet still throbbed from being on them for so long the day before, but I squeezed them into my leather boots and made my way to the main room of our hall, glowing still from the previous night with my husband.

"Sleep well?" Vidar asked, kissing me as I entered.

"*Já*, very." I purred, embracing him.

"I could tell from your snores – you were so loud, you almost drowned out the noise of the storm." Vidar teased.

I punched him playfully before I greeted each of our children, placing a kiss on their heads. Young Birger was carving away at a chunk of wood by the fire, barely breaking his concentration to acknowledge me with more than a mumbled "*Góðan morgin.*". Sander and Æsa squealed as they chased one another on the benches that lined the walls of our hall but paused to embrace me.

"*Mumie*!" Æsa exclaimed as I squeezed her.

"*Góðan morgin*, my loves." I smiled, watching the two children race along the benches again.

At the sound of my voice, Caterine appeared from the kitchen with a steaming bowl of water and a dry rag for me to clean my face and hands with. I sat beside Vidar and she placed the bowl in front of me. As I rinsed my hands and splashed the water over my face, Caterine brought me a late breakfast of hot porridge, honey and dried fruits.

"The storm was bad?" I asked, dabbing my face dry with the rag.

"Terrible," Vidar replied, watching me take a small bite of the sweet, creamy oats. "Young Birger and I went to the shipyard this morning to check on the fleet; luckily we've only lost one ship. The waves were too rough to retrieve any planks, but there may be some salvageable pieces washed up after it's calmed."

"Not a good day to sail." I commented.

"Only a man challenging the gods would set sail on a sea like this." Vidar said, dipping his finger into my bowl and stealing a scoop of my porridge.

"Hey!" I chided as he slurped the porridge from his finger.

"*Mmm*, delicious." Vidar winked. "Young Birger and I are going to the shipyard again, now you're awake. We need to moor as many ships on land as we can until this storm passes."

"How long do you think the storm will continue?"

"I'm not sure, I haven't seen a storm like this in many years." Vidar said. "Young Birger and I will be gone for a while, I want to check on the townspeople, in case the storm has damaged their homes."

I nodded in agreement and kissed my husband. He placed a hand on Young Birger's shoulder, indicating it was time to leave. They wrapped themselves in their cloaks before they stepped out of the hall and braved the raging weather outside. Their cloaks were hooded and made of goatskin, treated with beeswax and fish oil to keep them soft and waterproof.

After I finished my breakfast, Caterine retrieved a purse of pins and a comb from a chest in my bedroom, set to untangle the snarls from my unruly chestnut curls. She parted my long, thick hair into small sections, combing the sections and plaiting them, tying them back with thin leather thongs before she neatly pinned the plaits to my head.

As Caterine checked the front of my hair, tucking unruly curls back into place, I noticed dark puffy smudges beneath her eyes. She involuntarily shuddered as she explained she hadn't slept at all due to the storm.

I hadn't realised the extent of Caterine's fear of storms, though I suppose we hadn't owned her for long, and there hadn't been a storm of this magnitude in all the time we had owned her. As Vidar had said, he hadn't seen a storm this vicious in a long time.

We had bought Caterine a little more than a year ago when a thrall merchant had passed through Aros. Aros was located in the east of Denmark's Jutland peninsula in a luscious green valley on the northern shores of a fjord. Over the years of Vidar's jarldom, he had taken advantage of the town's excellent position and Aros had evolved into a rich, bustling trading centre.

Merchants from far across the world came to Aros to trade and sell their goods. From Dyflin in Ireland and the Danish-owned Jórvik in Britain came pottery, cups, glass beads and drinking glasses, leather goods, jewellery, weapons, cloth and chain mail. Some Norse traders would take iron, furs, timber, amber and soapstone to Constantinople and Baghdad and bring back silk, wine, Arabic silver, spices, fruit, fabric and so much more. The most profitable trade, however, was thralls. After raids and battles, the Norse would seize survivors, women, men and children, enslave them and take them to their lands.

I knew this all too well – the Danes of Roskilde had struck the Kingdom of the East Angles in Britain, my homeland, almost twenty years ago, when the sons of Ragnar Loðbrók led the Great Army to attack Britain. The Danes of Roskilde had killed my people, burned my village to ashes, and seized me and a handful of others as thralls.

I had been lucky though; I had been a child when the fierce warrior Birger Bloody Sword captured and adopted me. He had rescued me because of my uncanny likeness to his daughter, who had died years before he and his people attacked my homeland. Out of yearning for his beloved deceased daughter, Birger saved me, loved me, protected me. He spared me from thraldom and death.

I had known no other who had been as lucky as me.

I felt the deepest of sympathies towards slaves because of my close call to thraldom. I was kind to them, I befriended the ones closest to me, I refused to beat my thralls, and I fed them the same meals I would feed my family. Though I owned them, though they were forced into slavery, I tried to offer them the best life possible if I couldn't offer them guaranteed freedom.

Over a year ago, I had been visiting the market with my husband and children. Our house thrall had recently died from sickness in the middle of winter, and Vidar had decided we needed to buy another. Snow pellets lashed down from the silver sky onto the townspeople bustling through the market, shrouded in furs.

Æsa, a baby at the time, was swaddled in furs, strapped to my front and encased in my cloak to stave off the bitter cold of winter. Young Birger strode alongside his father and Sander darted between us, ever running off and getting into mischief.

"Where's Sander?" I cried out for what felt like the tenth time.

"That boy has a curious mind," Vidar commented – was that a hint of pride I heard in his voice? "He will be an adventurous man and travel to the furthest parts of the world, I'd wager."

"When Sander is a man, he can travel as far as he wants. Right now, he needs to stop getting lost." I snapped, glaring through the snow in search of our son.

"I'm sure he'll find us, don't fret so much, little fawn." Vidar said. "Ah, there's Herra Kaupmaðr."

Dressed garishly in a long, billowing tunic and trousers made of yellow silk from Asia, and a cloak made of hundreds of minx, ermine and sable pelts, was Herra Kaupmaðr. He wore otter skin gloves, and marten fur lined the top of his thick leather boots and the hems of his tunic and gloves. The long wiry hair that fell from his head was bleached saffron yellow, and his beard was orange like amber. Through the opening of his fur cloak, I could see a wide belt around his middle with various sized bags, tools and utility daggers hanging from it, and a large, ominous sealskin whip.

Herra Kaupmaðr, which meant 'Lord Merchant' in the Norse tongue, was an eclectic, nomadic old Swede, the most famous and richest merchant in the Norse lands. No one knew what Herra's real name was, he introduced himself to all with his pompous self-title, but admittedly he lived up to his name. Herra Kaupmaðr could find any item in the world – *anything*! – given time and ample payment. He surely was a lord among merchants. In fact, if he ever found a town to settle in, I'm sure Herra Kaupmaðr was rich enough to be a king.

Vidar made his way to Herra's elaborately decorated stall, where slaves stood on a large wooden platform in rags, iron collars around their necks, shivering violently in the bitter weather. Herra Kaupmaðr welcomed Vidar warmly, clapping his hand on my husband's shoulder.

"Jarl Vidar Alvarsson, what a joy and a pleasure it is to see you again! The Jarlkona is beautiful as ever if you don't mind my saying—" Herra bowed down low as he flattered me. "And how big your children are growing! Though, I thought you had another son?"

"Sander has run off again." Vidar smirked, and I rolled my eyes at the lightness of my husband's tone.

"Ah! A curious boy will grow into an adventurous man! He will be a grand traveller when he is grown, no?" Herra beamed, showing off his carved and brightly dyed teeth.

"That's what I said to my wife." Vidar grinned. At the sight of my dark scowl, Vidar cleared his throat and changed the subject. "We are in search of a new thrall."

"*Ah*! For the Jarl of Aros, I have only the best! I have new stock, a beautiful young thing from Francia, she would make a wonderful nursemaid; she has large breasts bursting with milk." Herra Kaupmaðr winked and chuckled wickedly.

"What of her child?" Vidar asked, his eyebrows raised.

"Don't worry, it died a week or so ago." Herra said carelessly. "If it isn't a nursemaid you're searching for, I have a number of sturdy males from the Slavic lands for any labour and field work. What are you looking for in particular?"

Herra reached up and wrapped his arm around Vidar's shoulders, leading my husband to view his 'stock'. Vidar was a tall man, and Herra Kaupmaðr was quite short. Vidar kindly slouched down to Herra Kaupmaðr's level, so the merchant could keep his arm wrapped around Vidar's shoulders. They made a humorous pair, the jarl and the merchant, but thanks to their high ranks no one would comment whether in jest or not.

I didn't follow Vidar and Herra. Instead, I glanced around in search of my son; Sander was nowhere to be seen, and I was beginning to panic.

"Sander!" I called. "Sander come here at once!"

"Do you want me to search for him, *móðir*?" Young Birger offered.

"*Nei*, I don't want you missing as well." I replied, kissing my son's forehead. "Did you see which direction he went?"

Young Birger shook his head.

"I can't shop for thralls while Sander is missing. Your *faðir* can browse, come with me – we're going to find Sander."

"Shall I tell *faðir*?" Young Birger asked.

"*Nei*." I shook my head, glaring at Vidar's back as he walked along the platform examining thralls. "He can stare at the Frankish thrall's breasts while we look for the *curious boy*." I grumbled quietly.

Together, Young Birger and I, with Æsa sleeping amidst my furs and cloak, took off in search of Sander. We combed the crowds, checked every stall and shop, explored the bay – maybe Sander had decided to play in one of the ships moored on the shore?

Nothing. Not a single sight of him.

Townspeople checked on me, concerned for their distressed jarlkona. I informed them of my missing son, and soon enough I had a group aiding my search.

Time passed, but still, no one had found Sander.

Young Birger and I returned to Herra Kaupmaðr's stand, which was surrounded by a huge mob of townspeople. I found Vidar, a frown on his lips and his brows knitted, his eyes wide and searching. When Vidar spotted me and our children, a wave of relief crashed over his face and softened his expression.

"Where did you run off to, little fawn?" Vidar asked, bringing me into his arms.

"I was looking for Sander," I said stiffly, pushing him away from me. "I knew his whereabouts didn't bother you, so I didn't think you'd care if I went to look for him."

Vidar stared at me through narrowed eyes for a moment and briefly chewed his bottom lip.

"Did you find him?" He asked, intelligently deciding not to argue with me.

"*Nei*, I haven't!" I snapped, tears brimming in my eyes.

"Let us search together." Vidar said, reaching out to embrace me again, but paused, obviously unsure if I would rebuff him again. "A thrall has fled the market stand, Herra is arranging a party right now to hunt for her. I'll have them look for Sander as well. Let's find our son."

I nodded, unable to speak in case my words would cause my tears to spill. Vidar kept his hand offered, and I grabbed it, gripping it tightly. He pulled me through the crowd, Young Birger right behind me, and we made our way to the platform where Herra Kaupmaðr stood commanding his mob.

"While your people search for your thrall, have them look for my son." Vidar ordered the merchant.

Herra nodded to his jarl.

"Sander Vidarsson is missing!" Herra boomed to his group. "Find the jarl's son! Bring him and the thrall here immediately!"

With that, the mob dispersed throughout the market, off to rake the town for my son and the thrall.

Minutes felt like hours. Where was Sander?

Vidar, Young Birger and I were combing the beach again, unable to stand around and wait in the marketplace. It was freezing on the shores; the bitter wind ripped over the waves and stung my face. Vidar, Young Birger and I were all red-cheeked and shivering.

"I will whip that boy when we find him." Vidar grumbled as we searched the shores again.

"And I will whip you for not looking for him sooner!" I scolded. *"He's a curious boy—"*

"Alright, Aveline!" Vidar snapped.

He leapt down from a merchant's *knarr* he had been searching and strode towards me, his face etched with guilt and frustration.

"I'm sorry," Vidar said, softer this time. "I should've taken his disappearance seriously. I'm sorry."

I stared down and watched Æsa blink and turn her head, peering at the surrounding scenery. It was horridly cold, but she was warm and cosy against me, protected from the weather. Vidar's shadow cast over me as he stood in front of me, still and quiet. I looked up at him, and he rested his forehead against mine.

"I'm sorry, too. I'm just worried—" I stopped as my voice shuddered.

"We will find him." Vidar whispered, kissing my forehead.

"Móðir – faðir!" Young Birger called some ways down the beach from us. "Look!"

Our oldest son pointed towards the waters where a bizarre creature crawled from the raging waves onto the beach. It was a woman! And in her arms, she carried a still, sodden brown creature. Young Birger ran to her, Vidar and I dashing up behind him. With a lurching step, the woman heaved herself out of the waters, clutching the animal against her chest, and collapsed onto the shore. Long tentacles of black, bedraggled hair stuck to her face, her skin was grey and tinged with blue, and she shivered viciously – visibly frozen to her core.

Vidar yanked off his fur cloak and wrapped the woman in it. She coughed and spluttered, fading in and out of consciousness. Vidar pulled the woman into his arms and briskly rubbed her back and arms, trying to generate warmth.

"*Móðir*!" Young Birger cried out, pointing at the woman's dog.

I stared at his horror-filled face and turned my gaze to the creature. It wasn't a dog–

"*L'enfant*!" The woman spluttered, choking up water as she attempted to point at the furs. "*L'enfant*!"

"Sander!" I gasped.

I cried out his name over and over, causing Æsa to wail in distress. So panicked, I ignored her, my heart racing painfully in my chest. I dropped to my knees and ripped the soaking fur away from the small figure on the sand.

It *was* Sander!

Oh! My beloved Sander! He was still, his chest didn't move! His golden hair clung to his face, his lips were blue, and his flesh was pale and grey from the cold. I pulled off my cloak, swathed my poor boy in it, and tried to pull him onto my lap.

"He's not moving, Vidar, *he's not moving*!" I howled.

Vidar thrust the half-drowned woman into Young Birger's arms and scooped up Sander's limp, slender body. He ripped the soaking clothes from our child and bundled him up in my fur cloak. My heart ached as I watched Sander flop lifelessly with every movement Vidar made.

"*Nei, nei, nei*!" I wept, gaping at my son.

Once Sander was bundled, Vidar held him against his chest, Sander's head slumped over his shoulder. Suddenly Vidar slapped Sander's back.

"What are you doing?!" I yelled, my eyes popping from my skull as I watched Vidar beating our son.

Vidar didn't answer. Over and over he slammed his open hand on Sander's back. I flinched with every slap that collided onto my four-year-old son. I clutched poor sobbing Æsa and wept into her hair, my body shuddering and shaking.

Suddenly, there was a rasping intake of breath.

I stared at Sander and Vidar. Sander took another hoarse breath and vomited out the water he had inhaled.

"He's alive!" Vidar exclaimed. "We must go back!"

With that, Vidar sprinted towards the town, our young son in his arms, alive – but barely. Between us, Young Birger and I carried the woman who had saved Sander's life, staggering up the shore to the marketplace.

"Get me furs!" Vidar bellowed as he barged through the crowd and shoved his way into the nearest building, an alehouse. "Make a fire!"

"My thrall!" Herra Kaupmaðr exclaimed as Young Birger and I stumbled into the marketplace, pointing a finger at the woman in Young Birger and my arms.

Immediately two of Herra's men dashed to us and snatched the woman away. They threw at Herra's feet and ripped her tunic from her. Herra pulled the whip from his belt, raised it high and lashed her. A sickening *crack!* rang through the air as the sealskin whip struck her soaking flesh; she shrieked in agony, high and shrill.

"What are you doing?" I screeched as Herra brought the whip up again.

"She escaped, Jarlkona, I must punish her." Herra Kaupmaðr explained with a look of confusion.

"She saved my son!"

"She ran from my stall–"

"If you want to keep selling your wares in Aros, Herra Kaupmaðr, you will stop arguing with me now!" I thundered. "I am the Jarlkona of Aros and I order you to stop beating this woman at once!"

But for the wind and the crashing of the waves in the background, the marketplace was silent, and every face stared at me. Even Æsa, still strapped to my torso, was shocked into silence by my raging outburst.

My heart raced as I glared at Herra Kaupmaðr. I had never used my title, jarlkona meaning 'jarl's wife', to force a townsperson to do my bidding in all the years I'd been jarlkona – whether married to Vidar, or to my first husband, Jarl Erhardt Ketilsson – but I felt a need to now. Herra Kaupmaðr needed reminding of my position, and of his place.

"What is her price?" I demanded.

"Three marks of silver," Herra Kaupmaðr replied. "But to apologise to you, my Jarlkona, I will sell her for–"

"I will pay you three marks of silver. Get one of your men to carry her to my hall." I growled. "I want her there *now*."

"Of course, Jarlkona."

Before Herra Kaupmaðr uttered another word, I stormed off to the alehouse I had seen Vidar carry Sander into.

Night had fallen by the time Sander had warmed and colour had returned to his flesh. He had stopped coughing and vomiting, and for hours he inhaled rapid, rasping breaths and hardly spoke – he just shuddered and shivered and breathed.

The owners of the alehouse had given us some of their son's dry clothes and furs to dress Sander in, and stew to feed him. Sander had sipped a little of the broth from the stew before we returned to our home, and Vidar had carried him the whole way to the hall.

When we were home, we found our new thrall asleep on the bench, still dressed in the rags we had found her in. I woke her, fed her and cleaned the deep wound that ripped across her back from Herra's whip, while Vidar settled our three children in the bedroom. Encased in blankets, with dry clothes on her back and food in her belly, I left Caterine to sleep by the fire. I finally retired to the sleeping area and found Vidar and all three of our children curled up asleep in his and my bed dressed in clean, dry nightclothes, Vidar's arms wrapped tightly around Sander.

I spent a lot of time teaching Caterine Norse. She had learned it quickly and even taught me a few phrases and words in François, her native language. Within a few months, between the pieces of information I'd gathered from Sander – who, at four years old, feared he might be punished for admitting what had happened – and the information in broken Norse I had garnered from the thrall, I managed to find out what had happened the day Sander had almost died.

Sander had run off to look at the ships, bored with traipsing through the marketplace. Caterine had seen him from the platform she was standing on and watched him dash towards the shore. He had clambered and climbed all over the ships and boats for a while when, suddenly, he fell.

At the sight of the small boy fall into the freezing, raging waves, Caterine had bolted away from the slave stand, knowing full well the punishment she would receive for doing so, but she couldn't let the child drown. When she reached the shore, Caterine lost sight of Sander. It had taken a while, but at last, she spotted his little blond head bobbing in the water and made out his muffled cries over the roaring waves. She dived into the water and swam to him, clutching him close to her when she reached him.

Taken by the sea, Caterine had struggled to get Sander and herself to safety. He had been conscious when she had found him, but by the time she had managed to get herself and Sander on the shore, he had inhaled too much water.

Thank all the gods in Asgard that Caterine had fled from Herra Kaupmaðr's slave stand to rescue my son, and that Vidar had dislodged the water from inside Sander's chest when he beat Sander's back.

I removed Caterine's slave collar that night, and I refused to cut her hair short as was the way thralls were meant to wear their hair. Herra had been wise to leave Caterine's gorgeous locks long before he sold her, and it explained the extortionate price he had charged me for her. Caterine was a very attractive woman, and her long thick ebony hair was a mantle of her beauty – a beauty of which she deserved to keep after risking her life to save my son.

Over a year had passed since that day. I had paid Herra Kaupmaðr his silver and had refused to visit his shop ever again – Vidar would make his purchases from Herra alone. I would never forgive the merchant for whipping the woman who had saved my son from death.

"If your chores are done, you may sleep for a while," I said to Caterine. "I will wake you in a few hours."

The Frankish thrall nodded her head and thanked me. She slipped off her shoes and crawled onto the bench nearest the fire and promptly fell asleep beneath the furs.

"Sander, Æsa, come here, it's time to practise the runes," I called. "We must be quiet so Caterine can rest."

***

THE STORM HAD raged throughout the day, and long into the night. By evening time, we sat at the table, the darkness of the hall punctured by the orange glow of cod liver oil lamps and the flames of the firepit, enjoying the delectable deer stew we had been looking forward to since I had killed the stag.

The storm bellowed and boomed outside. Poor Caterine flinched at every flash of lightning through the smokehole and cowered at every roar of thunder. This would be the second night the horrendous storm would rage, and I sympathised for the poor thrall.

Æsa had been fearful of the storm at first but had become accustomed to the noise thanks to it raging for so long. She still flinched at the flashes and thunder, but thankfully she had stopped wailing because of them now.

"*Mon Deu!*" Caterine gasped at a deafening crash of thunder.

"The storm is upon us." Vidar commented; his eyes cast upward.

I frowned at Vidar for a moment, my brows knitted. With every crack of thunder and the fierce pounding of the wind, the hall walls shook, and the shields hung upon them shuddered. The rain hammered down, and I wondered whether the roof would withstand the downpour. I thought of my sheep – would *they* withstand the fury of the storm? I shook my head; I would find out in the morning.

We kept most of our sheep on the mainland just outside of Aros, cared for by a farmer and his family We kept the ewes and lambs in a paddock behind our hall, and I had locked them away into their barn just before night had fallen. Norsemen normally penned livestock in their homes, but as Vidar and I were Jarl and Jarlkona of Aros, we could afford the luxury of a barn detached from our elegant hall.

"*Mumie*, I'm scared." Æsa whispered, crawling into my lap and wrapping her arms around my hugely protruding belly.

"Me too." Sander admitted, staring at me from across the table with his huge blue eyes.

"Come here," I beckoned, reaching out to my son.

Sander slid out of his chair and lunged into my arms.

"Be careful of your *móðir*'s belly, Sander." Vidar cautioned. "Your baby brother is in there."

Sander stared at Vidar without saying a word, clutching me tightly as a flash of lightning lit up the hall. The five-year-old hid his face into my dress, and little Æsa did the same.

"I have told you of the duel between Thor and Hrungnir, have I not, children?" Vidar asked suddenly, regarding Young Birger, Sander and Æsa in turn, a small smile turning up the corners of his lips. "One day, Hrungnir the *jötunn* invited the Allfather Odin to *Jötunheimr*. Odin rode his eight-legged horse, Sleipnir, to the realm of the *jötnar*, and when he arrived, he bet Hrungnir that Sleipnir could outrun any horse in *Jötunheimr*.

"Insulted, Hrungnir accepted Odin's challenge – he mounted his horse, Gullfaxi, and together the Allfather and the *jötunn* raced through air and water, mud and streams, over steep hills and thick woodland – until Hrungnir realised they had passed through the gates of Asgard.

"Hrungnir hadn't managed to surpass Odin. As he rode as fast as he could, Hrungnir passed by a group of gods who were drinking. They invited him to join them and Hrungnir accepted."

Vidar took a deep swig of his mead, then he stood and slowly stepped around the table to near his children.

"Hrungnir became drunk and belligerent – boasting he would kill all of the gods but for Freya and Sif, the wife of Thor." Vidar grinned, pretending to waver and stumble as he acted out his impression of a drunken Hrungnir, much to the children's amusement. "These beautiful goddesses, he exclaimed, he would carry back to *Jötunheimr*. Next, he boasted that he would drink every drop of ale in Asgard!"

RISE TO FALL

Vidar laughed, then drank down the rest of his mead, slamming his cup on the table.

"The gods grew tired of the *jötunn* and sent for Thor – who had been fighting *jötnar* elsewhere. Thor found the *jötunn* and gods and prepared to slay Hrungnir right then and there – but the *jötunn* accused Thor of being a coward for attempting to kill an unarmed man. He challenged Thor to a duel, and Thor accepted.

"Hrungnir arrived at the duel dressed in stone armour with a shield made of stone, and for his weapon, he brandished a huge whetstone!

"Suddenly lightning illuminated the sky, and thunder clapped above him, and the mighty Thor roared onto the battlefield!" Vidar exclaimed, and just as he spoke our hall lit up with the white flash of lightning and a clap of thunder exploded in the skies outside.

Vidar, the children and I glanced between each other and laughed at the coincidence.

"Thor is helping tell the tale." Young Birger chuckled.

"He is indeed." Vidar snickered. "Now, where was I? Ah, *já* – Thor roared into the battlefield, his orange hair blazing like fire from his head! He hurled his hammer – the powerful Mjölnir – at Hrungnir, and Hrungnir threw his whetstone at Thor! The whetstone exploded against Thor's forehead and shattered into pieces, causing flint to scatter upon the earth. And Thor's hammer struck Hrungnir's head and the *jötunn*'s head shattered!"

Young Birger, Sander and Æsa giggled and I couldn't help but chortle along with them. Vidar's icy eyes blazed as he told the tale. He beamed at his chuckling children – whatever worries they had previously, they certainly had no more.

"In the lands of the gods, my children, the mighty Thor fights the *jötnar*, and the storm is the proof of that. Every flash of lightning is Thor raising Mjölnir – so swift that lightning flashes through the sky–" Vidar grinned, swinging his hands into the air, as though he were lifting the hammer himself. "–And every roar of thunder is Thor bringing Mjölnir down upon a *jötunn*!"

The children giggled as Vidar slammed his imaginary hammer down, just as Thor would. Even Caterine and I giggled at Vidar's vivid commentary.

"With Mjölnir gripped in his fists, he cracks the powerful hammer upon *jötnar* skulls, *crack, crack, crack*!"

At the final *crack*, the door to our hall swung open, and there in the violent night stood a being as tall and broad as a giant from Vidar's tale!

"*Faðir*!" Screeched Æsa. "*Mumie*!"

Lightning flashed across the sky, briefly illuminating our surroundings with blue light. I gaped wide-eyed at the huge figure that filled our doorway, my heart racing inside my chest, the fair hairs on my arms standing on end, goosebumps erupting over my flesh.

The lightning flash lit up the *jötunn*'s face, and–

"Jan!"

CHAPTER THREE

JAN JÖTUNNSON, SON of Jarluf, stood drenched in the doorway, a small crew of men huddled behind his huge frame.

"Get inside!" I gasped.

Without the need of further invitation, Jan leaned down to avoid hitting his head on the doorframe and stepped through, his men scurrying in behind him.

Their rain-matted hair clung to their faces in sodden strips, and water streamed from their clothes, leaving small pools in the packed dirt floor as they hurried into my home. The men shivered violently, their visible flesh red-raw from the cold, howling wind and the icy rain.

"Jötunnson, my *bróðir*, what happened to you?" Vidar gaped, embracing his water-logged friend.

"Ægir travelled with us," Jan grumbled, returning Vidar's embrace just as tightly. It had been two years since the childhood friends had seen one another. "We sacrificed three rams on the shores of Roskilde before we set sail, but it wasn't enough it seems. Our ship survived Ægir's waves but Ran stole away a number of my crew."

Ægir, the *jötunn* of the sea, and his wife Ran were a notorious couple in the Norse belief. When Norsemen sailed and huge waves appeared, it was said to be caused by Ægir nearing their ships. Ægir was unforgiving and cruel and destroyed ships to seize the gold and treasure within them. The goddess Ran was known to be just as dangerous as her husband; she would catch sailors in her huge fishing net and drag them to the darkest depths of the sea to die.

"How many did you lose?" Vidar asked as he ushered Jan to our table.

"Three. There were only nine of us; we sailed a *byrðingr* here."

"Caterine, get stew for our guests, children it's time for bed." I ordered briskly, setting Sander onto the ground.

Caterine hurried to the kitchen while I shepherded my sons to the bedroom, Æsa clamped to my hip.

"But *mumie*, I want to meet the *jötunn*!" Sander whined as he reluctantly changed into his bedclothes.

"I'll introduce you to him tomorrow. For now, you must sleep."

"But–"

"Don't say 'but' to me again, Sander Vidarsson," I warned. "It is bedtime. You can meet Jan Jötunnson in the morning."

After a short while, I returned to the main room with a large pile of Vidar's clothes folded in my arms, my three children grudgingly tucked into bed. Jan and his crew were sitting at the table eating voraciously. Vidar was sitting beside Jan, his own bowl of deer stew quite forgotten as he listened to Jan and his men discuss their perilous voyage to Aros from.

"I hope these will do you all." I said anxiously, gazing at each of our guests' dripping faces.

"Let me help." Offered one of Jan's men. "*Þakka fyrir*, Jarlkona."

I smiled as he took the clothes from me and shared them among himself and his companions. Dark, puffy smudges hung beneath each man's bloodshot eyes; they were understandably exhausted. I held my stomach nervously, concerned by what had befallen Jan and his crew, so sympathetic for them. Three of their companions had sailed with them from Roskilde and now they lay at the bottom of the sea ...

The five remaining crewmen began stripping off their drenched attire right there in the main room. Caterine gasped and blushed fiercely at them. She turned on her heel and fled to the kitchen, much to the amusement of the men. Not as taken aback as my thrall, I did still feel my cheeks burn at the sight of the various stages of undress happening in front of me.

"Ale and mead." I muttered to myself and followed Caterine to the kitchen.

As I neared him, Jan Jötunnson rose from his chair.

"Aveline," Jan said warmly, holding his arms out to me. "Please don't pass me again without first embracing me. It has been too many years since I've held you!"

"Ever the silver-tongued devil, aren't you?" I grinned, throwing my arms around his waist.

Jan had always been a shameless flirt and an avid womaniser, but he was so charismatic he could always get himself out of trouble. I had met Jan many years ago when I was sixteen, and he was twenty-one. Vidar had arranged a dinner at his hall in Roskilde to introduce Jan to me as a suitor at the behest of my adoptive father, Birger Bloody Sword. Unbeknownst to me, at the end of that night, Jan had asked Vidar for permission to wed me, but Vidar had denied him, admitting to Jan that he himself wanted to marry me. Until Vidar finally admitted his love to me (which was long after my dinner with Jan), I had briefly considered marrying Jan.

Jan was grace and elegance blended with bloodthirst and battle skill; he was beauty and magnetism, and a true Danish warrior. He was one of the most handsome men I had ever seen; pale as the moon, with deep sapphire eyes that glinted with mischief, and a rose-coloured smile that exuded happiness and charm.

"I am called 'Jötunnson' because of my phenomenal height and strength – like an offspring of the *jötnar*." Jan had proudly explained to me in our first meeting.

Jan lived up to his name – he towered above every man he met. The Norse were much larger than Anglo-Saxons, and Vidar was tall for a Norseman, but Jan Jötunnson stood even taller – a head higher than Vidar at the very minimum. The top of my head reached just under Vidar's chin, whereas with Jan I stood many inches below his shoulder.

"The *jötnar* blood runs through both sides of my kin." Jan had also bragged.

Tall and broad, Jan was also fantastically muscled; I truly believed he did have *jötnar* blood running through his veins.

"And you, my Aveline, Jarlkona of Aros! With child again, I see?" Jan marvelled, holding my large, protruding tummy between his massive hands. "Vidar doesn't leave you alone for even a moment – does he chain you to his bed?"

From behind me, I heard Jan's crewmen snicker at his brazen jest.

"I go to my husband's bed willingly, and as often as he'll take me." I replied.

"Which is often, I'm sure. There is no man in any of the nine realms who would refuse to satisfy you; you're as beautiful as ever." Jan winked.

"I've missed you." I laughed, hugging Jan once again. "Tell me why you sailed here in such dreadful weather. You're welcome in Aros whenever you please, but why now? The last few nights have been vile."

The charming smile faltered on Jan's lips for a moment, and the playful glint vanished from his deep blue eyes.

"Once food is in our bellies, dry clothes on our backs and ale down our throats, then I will tell you." Jan said quietly.

"Your belly is full, Jan Jötunnson, and your dry clothes are on the table for you to change into." I said, raising an eyebrow at him. "I will fetch your drink, then you can begin."

***

JAN DID NOT begin his explanation until his crewmen finally gave in to their fatigue. Dressed in clean, dry clothing and wrapped in thick furs, the crewmen settled near the fire on the benches that lined the walls of the hall. Their bellies full of hot stew and strong ale to help them recover from their hellish journey, the five crewmen snored away peacefully.

Caterine stoked the fire in our large, rectangular fire pit until the scarlet and gold flames burned tall and bright, roaring with delicious warmth, the heat permeating the entire hall. But for the howl of the wind, it was quiet; the storm had passed us, and the rain had eased off for a while now.

Jan remained at the table beside Vidar, and the two men spoke to each other in low, hushed tones. Jan and his crewmen's wet clothing hung on drying racks around the fire, concealing Jan and Vidar from the sleeping crewmen and offering them some welcomed privacy. I meandered about the room, not wanting to interrupt them. My feet ached, and the child inside me kicked wildly, I yearned to rest but the night was not over yet. I paused at the doorway to the kitchen and glanced in at Caterine.

It was late and with food and drink on the table for Vidar, Jan and me if we wanted it, I had given Caterine permission to retire for the night. Averse to sharing the benches with the crewmen, she had bundled herself in furs and curled up on the dirt floor of the kitchen beside the low flames of the cooking fire pit.

I turned my gaze from my sleeping thrall to my husband and our friend. Vidar's bronze flesh glowed in the firelight, and Jan's alabaster skin glimmered. Both men wore neatly trimmed and finely maintained beards, a popular fashion amongst the Norsemen. Jan's beard fell to his sternum at its longest point, but for three plaits hanging from his chin, a style he had proudly worn since I had met him.

There was ten years difference between the companions, Vidar was the older of the two. They had known each other since childhood, they had chased women and drank together, raided and fought beside one another. They weren't tied together by blood, but they were brothers.

"Come sit with us, little fawn." Vidar called, noticing me and beckoning me to him with an outreached hand.

Immediately I went to Vidar and took his hand, and he pulled me onto his lap. Vidar wrapped his arms around me and kissed my shoulder before he turned back to Jan.

"Tell us why you're here, Jötunnson." Vidar urged softly.

"I suppose I shall." Jan smiled. "I cannot keep quiet for too long, *nei?*"

Jan ran his hand through his silky light brown tresses that cascaded far past his shoulder blades. He pursed his lips together and stared at the table top as though he was wondering where to begin.

"What's happened, Jan?" I pressed after a few more moments of silence.

"Thóra left me," Jan announced. "She took Thórvar. They're gone."

My jaw dropped. Thóra was Jan's wife; they had met at Vidar and my wedding and within a year of meeting, they were already married, and she was heavily pregnant with their first child. Their son, Thórvar, would be two-years-old by now.

Vidar squeezed me gently.

"Left? Where did they go?" I gaped.

"That's why I'm here," Jan said, a hint of bitterness in his tone. "I don't know where they are. Thóra took my son and left me without a word of where she's gone or why she's decided to leave."

"What happened, *bróðir*?" Vidar asked softly.

"I had been raiding the coast of Francia for three months, and when I returned, Thóra was gone." Jan shrugged. "I hadn't stepped foot in my home before a neighbour, Sigvin, dashed up to me to give me a message from my wife.

"The message Sigvin relayed to me was Thóra loved me, but she had to leave me. I would keep all our money, possessions and property, and she would not ask for a single thing, but she was taking our son. She said I was not to follow her, that she and Thórvar were well, but they would never come back."

Jan rubbed his bottom lip with his finger, his eyebrows creasing as they drew together, his eyes radiating with sadness and anger.

"I ran into my home and found my wife and son were indeed gone. Only Jakob, Burwenna and little Járnsaxa remained in the house."

Jakob was Jan's brother, eight years Jan's junior and was married to Burwenna, a dear friend of mine, an Anglo-Saxon who was once a thrall owned by my first husband. With Jarl Erhardt's death, I had given Burwenna and her sister Elda, who was also owned by Erhardt, their freedom. Jakob, Burwenna and their daughter Járnsaxa, and Jan, Thóra and Thórvar lived in the Jarlufson farm in Roskilde – Jan and Jakob's father, Jarluf, had passed away a few years ago, and their mother had died after birthing Jakob, long before I'd arrived in Denmark.

"Thóra had told neither Jakob nor Burwenna that she intended to leave me, let alone the reason why. In fact, it wasn't until the evening of the day Thóra had left that Sigvin was able to relay Thóra's message to Jakob and Burwenna. Jakob immediately organised a search party to find my wife and son, both on land and by sea, but to no avail. It was as if by magic, Thóra and Thórvar had disappeared." Jan said.

"What of her family?" Vidar questioned.

"I sent a message to Thóra's family, beseeching them for knowledge of her whereabouts, and begged them to notify me if she and our child appeared there. Her family claimed they didn't know where she or Thórvar was but agreed to notify me if that changed." Jan answered. He chuckled bitterly. "I haven't heard from them since."

"How long have they been missing?" I whispered.

"Six weeks," Jan replied with a deep sigh. "I spent a month scouring Roskilde and the surrounding areas trying to find her. I even travelled to Hedeby and paid a visit to her family, but she wasn't there – she wasn't in Hedeby at all.

"I couldn't give up my search though. I *had* to find them! So, I decided to come here to Aros and tell you of the situation and see if Thóra and Thórvar are here. I hastily assembled a crew, and we set sail immediately. We departed yesterday eve. I planned to be here just after noon, but the sea tossed us off course a few times."

A heavy silence settled over us. Vidar tangled his fingers in mine and stroked my hand with his thumb. I was thankful for Vidar's touch; it comforted me. Every sound was deafening; the snores from Jan's crew, the crackle of the fire, the creak of the hall as the wind battered it and whistled through the minute cracks in the walls and the smokeholes.

My heart ached for poor Jan. I dared to lift my gaze and look at him. Jan was still, staring at the table top, riddled with sadness.

"I knew the lives I was risking by sailing here, but it was too hard to stay in Roskilde without Thórvar and Thóra." Jan continued. "Once I'd organised a crew, we readied the *byrðingr*, sacrificed the rams and left. We took no belongings, just our weapons and ourselves.

"The waves raged like titans as lightning collided into the water, and thunder bellowed through the blackened sky. We sailed the night through, battling Thor's storm. Soon after we managed to get out of Roskilde Fjord, tossed and buffeted onwards, I became furious with Thóra for running away …

"She stole my son from me!

"My anger urged me on. I fought Ægir's waves, I fought Thor's storm. Even when morning time was soon to arrive, the sky didn't lighten but for the flashes of lightning slashing through it. The day passed, we were knocked off course many times, as I said earlier. But I wouldn't give in. I would find Thóra – I would get answers from her and I would get my son!"

Tears slipped down my cheeks. Jan had stopped talking abruptly, his breath shuddered as he inhaled, but when he exhaled his breath was steady. He fiddled with one of the plaits in his beard.

"Finally, Aros was lit up through the darkness by a huge, jagged fork of lightning. As the town met my bloodshot eyes, anger seething through my veins, I wept. Luckily my tears were hidden by the spray and the rain …" Jan released a breathy, humourless chuckle. "I-I realised I would never see my wife and son again. As furious with Thóra as I was, I loved her, I wanted her back. And more than anything, I wanted my son. I've lost so many children to death; I couldn't lose him, too …"

Jan cleared his throat. He grabbed his cup of ale from the table and tossed back the contents, then swiped the abandoned half-full cup that had belonged to one of his crewmen and drained the contents of that as well.

"I had known before I'd even stepped foot on the *byrðingr* that the chance of my wife hiding in the town ruled by my best friend was ridiculously unlikely – impossible, even. As my crewman and I struggled to moor our ship, I decided that I wouldn't return to Roskilde." Jan said, finally looking Vidar and me in the eyes. "So, Jarl Vidar Alvarsson of Aros, I'm here to ask your permission to live here, in Aros."

Vidar squeezed my hand briefly and shifted in his chair. I stood up immediately and moved aside for him, and he rose to his feet.

"My skaldic friend, why would you ask such a thing? Tragedy or not, you can live in Aros. By Odin, you can live here in my hall if that is your wish! As Aveline said, you are *always* welcome here." Vidar smiled.

A beaming grin broke across Jan's face.

"May I sleep in your bed, too?" Jan jested.

"It might get too crowded." Vidar smirked, offering his arm out to Jan. "You'll have your own bed, my friend, and you'll have your own wife. We *will* find Thóra, Jötunnson. I'll make sure of it."

"*Þakka fyrir, bróðir.*" Jan said.

Jan's playful demeanour fell away as quickly as it had appeared, instead, he gazed at Vidar with hope. He rose from his chair and took Vidar's proffered hand, and they clasped each other's arms for a moment, their eyes locked. Identical grins crept across their faces and they dropped each other's arms and embraced one another.

"*Þakka fyrir*, Vidar. Truly, *þakka fyrir.*" Jan whispered.

"I don't know how you survived this great storm without getting harmed, but I am *so* glad you did." I smiled through tears as Jan and Vidar released each other.

"As am I." Jan said, wrapping an arm around my shoulder and kissing the top of my head. "As am I."

CHAPTER FOUR

Summer, 883

NO CHRISTIAN HEAVEN could ever compare to the serenity and bliss of lying in bed with my husband, surrounded by our peacefully sleeping children. As I listened to the soothing sounds of their slumber, my thoughts drifted to poor Jan. It had been two years since his wife and son had disappeared, but still, there was no sign of them.

Over the first few months of Jan's arrival in Aros, Vidar had sent out various convoys to Roskilde, Hedeby, Ribe and Viborg to search for Jan's wife and young son. Should the convoys not find the mother and child there, they were ordered to search all the various towns, settlements and inhabited islands in between.

Jan's five crewmen had left Aros when the storm had dissipated and the waves had calmed, travelling with the convoy headed to Roskilde. Jan and his *byrðingr* remained in Aros. He had travelled with the Hedeby convoy to seek news from his wife's family there, but they still had not seen Thóra. Jan had returned crestfallen and more anxious than before. To draw Jan's mind from his missing wife and son even for a little while, Vidar swiftly settled Jan into his new life in Aros while they waited on news from the other convoys.

Vidar organised for Jan to live with and work for an elderly woman named Heimlaug Daðadóttir. Heimlaug's husband had died a handful of months before Jan's arrival and she had difficulty running her farm since her husband's death. Jan, already experienced in crop farming having been raised on a crop farm in Roskilde, was to run Heimlaug's farm and take her crops to market in return for lodging, food and a small portion of the farm's profits. Jan learned the farm's procedures quickly and managed the farm scrupulously, from overseeing crop planting, harvesting and rotation, and supervising the thralls to assuring Heimlaug the best revenues for her produce.

Needless to say, Heimlaug was more than happy at the arrangement. Though Jan had only lodged with Heimlaug for half a year, she had taken quite the maternal shine to him. Her only child, a son, had died in Britain when he had fought with the Great Army almost twenty years ago. The loss of her son had resonated through her terribly even after so many years, and the recent death of her husband had shaken her even further. Jan, ever the magnetic and cheerful man he was, offered her reprieve from her misery, as well as giving her much-needed aid with the farm.

"What are you thinking about, little fawn?" Vidar asked softly.

"Jan, his wife, his son …" I murmured, turning to him.

"Oh?" Vidar's ice-blue eyes twinkled in the pale morning light.

"I love you." I said, pressing a kiss against the soft flesh of his inner forearm.

"I love you, too." Vidar winked and brushed a stray chestnut curl from my face.

I took his hand and brought it to my lips and kissed each knuckle of his fingers. A peaceful quiet settled over us once more, but for the gentle sound of slumber that hummed around us, and the occasional rustle from the straw mattresses as sleeping bodies stirred upon them.

Still holding his hand in mine, I let my eyes roam around our bedroom, glancing over each of our children. I caught sight of dust particles dancing in the column of pale light that sliced through the centre of our bedroom from the small square smoke hole in the ceiling. I watched the dust flitter for what felt like an age, when the plump little form beside me squirmed.

Nestled between my husband and I was our youngest son, Einar, named after Vidar's older brother who had died many years ago before I'd even come to Denmark. I turned to my son and smiled; his soft, flawless porcelain skin seemed to glow in the early morning light. Einar had been born a little over a year ago, and a mass of tousled blond curls sprung from his little head – he had inherited my curls, though his hair was fair like Vidar's.

Gentle snores drifted from Einar's parted lips and I smiled again at the preciousness of him. I didn't want to wake him, but I couldn't stop myself from delicately pressing a kiss on his head. Einar had fallen asleep only moments ago; my breast was still bared from the deep 'V' opening of my shift, the glaze of his saliva gleaming on my nipple.

I heard Sander mumble in his sleep, retorting to an argument he was apparently having in his dream. Amused by Sander's sleep-talking, Vidar and I beamed at each other and giggled together.

Oh, Vidar's smile was wonderful! Vidar's lips curved into a warm smirk, deepening the lines of age that fanned from the outer corners of his eyes. His icy blue eyes were beautiful and sparkled with mischievousness and amusement. Even after thirteen years of romance and four years of marriage, Vidar's smirk and icy eyes still set my body aflame.

Hearing the muffled bustle of the thralls as they prepared breakfast in the kitchen on the opposite end of the hall, Vidar slipped his arm from underneath my neck with care and soundlessly rose from our bed to dress.

After a while I slid out of the bed without waking baby Einar. I stepped cautiously, glancing around the room in search of my clothing. As I wandered beneath it, I paused under the stream of light flowing in from the smoke hole and looked up towards the sky. It was to be a beautiful day; already the heat warmed my flesh deliciously. I closed my eyes and stood there, basking in the balmy sunlight, my sheer white shift draped over my body, my shoulders bared.

I felt Vidar's warm hands rest upon my hips.

"Your hair shines gold and red when the sunlight kisses it." Vidar admired.

A smile poured over my face as Vidar pulled my body against his. Wrapped in each other, Vidar glided one hand up my spine to the nape of my neck and ran his fingers through my chestnut curls. Through half-closed eyes, I caught his gaze, and we kissed.

Waves of goosebumps washed over my flesh; his full lips pressed against mine as faint as a whisper, and a shiver raced down my spine as his tongue grazed mine. I snaked my arms around him and squeezed his buttocks.

"You've been waiting to do that." Vidar smirked into our kiss.

"Oh, I have!" I admitted.

We giggled, and I rested my head against his chest, snuggling deeper into his embrace ...

The raucous cawing of a raven ripped me from my thoughts as it screeched over our heads. Vidar and I both peered up through the smokehole and saw the ink splotch of the raven marring the pristine sky. The cawing grew louder as the raven soared closer towards our hall.

"Huginn or Muninn, I wonder?" I muttered.

"It depends, what was going through your mind, little fawn – thought or memory?" Vidar winked.

"I want to stay here all day with you." I smiled. "But I need to dress, the whole house will wake soon."

"Just a while longer, little fawn, please?"

I beamed at Vidar and we tenderly kissed each other once again.

"I love you." Vidar whispered, his forehead rested against mine.

"I love y–"

"*Crrruck*!!"

Suddenly a black blur swooped through the smoke hole and whipped around the room, screeching out a shrill, ear-piercing cry.

"*Crrruck! Cruck, Crrruck!*"

"*Mumie, faðir*, what is that?!" Young Birger demanded, squinting with sleep-filled eyes at the ebony shape darting around the room.

"*Crrruck!*"

Einar wailed at the rude awakening. Three-year-old Æsa flashed us a panicked stare before the raven squawked again, and our terrified daughter pulled up her blanket over her head and hid. Sander, nestled in a cocoon of furs, was still fast asleep. His fair sweat dampened hair stuck to his brow, his cheeks were rosy, and loud snores still rumbled from his mouth.

"How can he sleep through this racket?" Vidar marvelled as he stared at our six-year-old son.

"I don't know!" I snapped as the raven continued to caw horrendously. I spotted my gown and unceremoniously yanked it on. "Vidar get that thing out of here!"

"Are you sure? I believe it's your friend." Vidar laughed as the damn bird flew over my head, catching a tangle of my loose curls with its sharp-clawed feet. "It's blind in one eye."

"Go away!" I roared at the raven as I lunged over to Einar. I scooped up the screaming child and held him tightly. "Get out, children! *Nú!*"

Young Birger leapt from his bed, lifted the snoring Sander and heaved him out of the bedroom. I staggered towards the door, ducking and dodging the irate raven. Laughing at me, Vidar scooped up the bundle that was Æsa, her blanket and all, and dashed out of the room after me. The raven continued to whiz around the bedchamber as we situated the groggy children onto the benches in the main room.

"*Góðan morgin*, and what's all this excitement?"

Through the hall doors stepped the tall, mighty form of Jan, his sapphire eyes twinkling with curiosity at the sight before him.

"Help him get that damned bird out of our bedroom!" I barked, rocking Einar in my arms as he continued to bawl hysterically.

Vidar and Jan swapped brief amused glances before Jan strode towards the bedroom doorway. Vidar lifted the curtains, when the raven suddenly swooped through and stabbed at Vidar's face with its short, arched, ebony beak. Cursing furiously, Vidar whipped his arm up to shield his face and ripped his utility knife from his belt with his other hand. The raven continued to attack him, and Vidar swiped and stabbed at the rotten bird in retaliation. The raven was far more successful than my husband. Vidar's forearm was a bloody mess, and the raven was unscathed. The bird ended its attack on Vidar and zoomed upwards, darting through the rafters of our hall, cawing nonstop.

I glanced around the room. Everyone gawped at the raven – but Vidar, who glared at it with rage rather than shock. The bird paused on a beam, almost camouflaged in the shadows, only a few feet away from the smoke hole.

We all held our breath. It was obvious the same thought was collectively passing through our minds: *fly away!* But, wish as hard as we might, our hopes were dashed as the bird plunged through the air – at Jan! Jan whipped up his arms to protect his face. Rather than swoop and dive in attack as it had at Vidar, the raven flapped in front of Jan, and perched on his raised forearm, digging its sharp claws deep into his flesh with an almighty caw.

"What in Hel's name are you?" Vidar scowled, glancing from his bleeding arm to the raven.

The raven glowered at us each in turn. With a sharp gasp, my legs gave way, and I dropped onto the bench as I spotted the raven's glossy white eye: Vidar was right – it was the half-blind raven!

Jan slowly stepped towards the doors, anxious to release the raven outside, but careful not to startle it into another vicious attack. The bird didn't fret as Jan moved, it maintained firm eye contact with me as Jan disappeared outside, and Young Birger leapt from the bench and slammed the doors shut behind him.

"Your friend doesn't like me, little fawn." Vidar remarked gruffly as Caterine appeared, pale-faced and wide-eyed, with a bowl of clean water and a rag in her quivering hands.

"It's never done that before," I said and wrapped an arm around Æsa, who snuggled next to me, still distressed by the raven's raucous appearance. "It's never attacked someone – usually it flies nearby or caws. I've never seen it attack."

"You've said the ravens appear before something happens?" Vidar asked, dabbing his arm with the dampened rag.

"*Já*, before a revelation … Or a death." I said weakly.

Vidar shrugged his shoulders and continued to dab at the wounds on his forearm.

"Whatever it is, the raven is trying to tell you *something*."

***

Late Autumn 883

I WATCHED YOUNG Birger, huddled on the floor by the fire, whittling a chunk of birch wood in his hands. With meticulous care, my son dragged his sharp utility knife across the wood, applying a precise amount of pressure, covering his lap in shavings. Though only months away from his tenth year of age, Young Birger was remarkably talented at woodwork.

"Hmm." Young Birger murmured.

He paused for a moment to inspect his creation, turning it at various angles, mentally scrutinising his work. With a mumbled noise of surprise, Young Birger realised he had nicked himself with his knife at some point, noticing a dribble of blood slowly slip down his thumb. He brought his thumb to his mouth and sucked the shallow wound for a few moments, then he continued his work.

Young Birger had been patiently working on this piece for a few days now. He had already shaved the bark off, begun curving the hull and hollowed out a few lengths in the centre. The birch wood was old and dried out, taken from the bottom of a log pile in the woodshed. It was tough to carve, but Young Birger wasn't perturbed by the difficulty at all.

He may not have his father's mischievous charm, in fact, Young Birger was a very quiet and somewhat stoic young man, but he was held in high esteem by the townsfolk of Aros due to his sharp mind and his hardworking and attentive nature.

What Young Birger lacked in skill, Vidar would provide and teach until his son was confident and satisfactorily competent. Vidar was a devoted and loving father to all his children, he was their loyal companion and dedicated teacher, yet I had never seen a bond as strong as his and Young Birger's.

From the moment he left the house after breakfast, Young Birger would work. He spent his days shadowing Vidar, assisting him with his duties, observing Vidar deal with town disputes and business, learning everything he needed for the day he would take Vidar's place as jarl. When Vidar would ask for his opinion on an issue, time after time Young Birger would pause thoughtfully for a moment, before eloquently offering a considerate and intelligent solution, much to Vidar's delight.

RISE TO FALL

Most of all, Young Birger enjoyed working at the shipyard. Young Birger spent a lot of time maintaining Storm-Serpent, Vidar's elegant *dreki*, dragon-headed warship. As well as tending to Storm-Serpent, alongside his father and many men of Aros, Young Birger helped build new ships, mend and repair broken ones, and maintain the existing fleet. Vidar would burst with pride as he watched his son pay pious attention to the ship makers and eagerly assist them with rarely a mistake – an ability most impressive for a boy of his age.

At the end of his busy days, when he had swallowed the last bite of dinner, Young Birger would sit down next to his basket of wood chunks and blocks and carve a new project or complete a previous one. Every now and again he would go out with other boys in the town, and he often played with his young siblings, but he devoted most of his leisure time to his woodwork.

"What's that?" Sander asked, plonking himself down beside his oldest brother.

"It will be a *dreki* like Storm-Serpent." Young Birger replied, not turning from his work.

"For me?" Sander pressed, sweetly smiling the way children do when attempting to manipulate their siblings.

"Do you want it?" Young Birger glanced at him from the corner of his eye, a smile forming on his lips.

"*Já!*"

"Then it's for you." Young Birger grinned.

Sander beamed and scooted closer to Young Birger, thanking him for another toy to play with. As Sander rambled on about toys and games, Young Birger listened and nodded and murmured when he needed to, but he did not look away from the longship he was carving.

It warmed my heart to see such closeness between my sons. Young Birger and Sander's closeness extended to their younger siblings, Æsa and Einar – the older boys would not whine nor complain when Æsa would demand to join in whatever they were doing, whether it was playing or work, and when Einar would cry, either boy would rush to him and sing to him or rock him in their arms.

Young Birger and Sander's patience and affectionate attentiveness towards their youngest sibling had influenced Æsa. My darling daughter was astute enough to realise how far she could take advantage of them (and almost anyone else for that fact) as the only female child, even at her young age. Of her many attributes, Æsa was headstrong, precocious and artful. She was demanding and inquisitive, but she was kind. Though she adored being doted on by her older brothers, she learned from them and treated Einar much how Young Birger and Sander treated her. From the moment Einar was born, she watched over him as her older brothers did her, to the point she had become somewhat of a mother hen.

I giggled and smiled at the curtains that hid the doorway to the sleeping area. A little while earlier, Æsa, lying on her bed beside Einar's cot, had sung to Einar and me as I nursed the young boy until he had fallen asleep in my arms, his belly blissfully full. I laid him down in his cot and snuggled with my daughter, who poked her hand through the rails of Einar's cot the moment he was inside it. Quietly, as I stroked her beautiful white-blonde hair, I recited different Norse tales until I realised that she, too, was asleep.

Vidar had made the cot for Æsa while I carried her in my belly. It was exquisitely carved, with images of animals and Frigga carved into it. The wooden cot had been finished with linseed oil mixed with cinnabar, giving it a gorgeous deep red colour. Now the cot was Einar's and would be used for all of our future children ...

With a sigh, I rose from my chair and fetched my black marten skin gloves and my fur cloak from a trunk placed against the far wall. I slipped the soft, warm gloves onto my slender fingers and turned to Caterine, who sat spinning near the fire.

"Caterine," I said to the thrall as I wrapped the thick cloak around my shoulders. "I'm going out for a little while, please mind the children."

"Will you require assistance, *madame*?" She asked, setting her spinning tools down to aid me with my cloak.

I held the heavy garment in place while Caterine pinned it closed with a large, shining silver brooch.

"*Nei*, I'll be fine on my own," I replied. "I won't be long."

"Should *mon maître* ask, where should I tell him you are?" Caterine asked.

"Out," I said. "Just tell him I am out."

CHAPTER FIVE

THE PROMISE OF winter chilled the air. The clusters of tall, arching trees dispersed throughout Aros had been stripped of their splendour by the changing season; only a few crisp scarlet and gold leaves remained clinging to the branches. A few birds chirruped and twittered upon the naked branches, and at the base of the greying trunks were bleak blankets of dry, wilted leaves, faded and drained of their colour, rustling noisily as the cold breeze disturbed them.

I hurried down the road away from the hall, headed towards the marketplace, my footsteps crunching on the hard dirt path. Vidar and my grand hall was situated in the heart of Aros, surrounded by the townspeople's homes and farms. At the edge of Aros, by the harbour, was the marketplace, ideally positioned for the merchants since they wouldn't have far to haul their wares. A little outside the shops was the healer's home, my destination.

Tendrils of smoke drifted into the dull silver sky, a coiling mass of charcoal snakes writhing over steel coloured clouds. I drew my cloak around me tighter as I entered the marketplace and luckily found it vacant, but for the hum of voices radiating from the alehouse. There were a few people out and about shopping, but not many to my relief. I wasn't keen to stop in the chilly streets and chat at that moment, and for the matter I wanted to discuss with Brynja I desired complete privacy.

Brynja's small longhouse, which doubled as both shop and home to Brynja, her three daughters, their husbands and their many children, came into view. I followed the dirt path that wound through Brynja's flower beds, the soil hardened from the growing cold. As I passed them, I reached out a gloved hand and dragged it over the skeletal and wilted remains of the herbs and medicinal flowers that had once blossomed in abundance before the cold arrived.

Some herbs in a couple of her beds retained their gorgeous colour and leaves but were becoming dormant in preparation for the fast-approaching winter. I noticed one large bed down the way, full of various types of mint, at least from what I see from how far away I was. The plants were overgrown and still bursting with their dark- to yellow-green colour.

"Brynja, are you home?" I called, rapping on her door with my gloved knuckles.

Without waiting for an answer, I pushed open her door and stuck my head into the room, where I found Brynja's seven grandchildren, between four and nine years of age, playing different games together – *noisily*.

"*Góðan aptan*, children." I grinned as I entered their home, their faces turning to stare at me. "Is your *amma* home?"

"*Velkomin*, Jarlkona!" Káta, Brynja the healer's eldest daughter, greeted.

Káta and Marta, the second of Brynja's daughters, rose from their seats at the opposite end of the fire, spinning tools and yarn in their hands, standing respectfully at my entrance. I hadn't noticed them until Káta had spoken, too distracted by the clutch of loud, playful children.

Bustling in from the kitchen came Nefja, the youngest of Brynja's daughters, with a thrall following behind her. They had been grinding herbs into powder by the looks of their hands, which were dusted with flecks of green, brown and grey.

"What can we do for you, Jarlkona?" Káta asked. "Svala, help the Jarlkona with her cloak." She added, waving her hand at the thrall, as I unpinned my brooch.

Svala, a small, slight thrall, dashed to me, wiping her hands on her apron, and took my cloak from my shoulders. I watched Marta hobble around the children, which wasn't quickly at all considering how heavily with child she was. Some of the children were hers, the others were her nieces and nephews, but she chided them all regardless, warning them to behave in a hushed, cautionary tone.

"Please, sit Jarlkona." Nefja said, politely beckoning me to sit on a comfortable looking chair beside the fire.

Appreciatively I sat on the plush, cushioned chair and pulled my gloves off, holding my hands to feel the warmth of the fire dance upon my palms and fingers. I glanced around the room, admiring the shields hung on the smoke-stained walls, and gazed at the multitude of herbs and plants hanging to dry from the beams and rafters, some in thin linen bags, others just bare bunches tied with string. The longhouse was filled with so many scents, pungent and sweet, musky and fragrant, from the drying plants.

"Is Brynja home?" I asked.

"*Já*, she is, Jarlkona – she's tending to some plants – I can send a thrall to fetch her for you." Marta said, returning to her chair as another thrall appeared with a tray carrying four deep steaming cups for the sisters and me.

I thanked the thrall as I accepted the cup and sipped the hot brew. The beverage was made of finely chopped apples and apple leaves simmered in water then sweetened with honey. A few chunks of apple and leaves still bobbed inside my cup. It was delicious, the sweetness of the honey had taken away the sharpness of the tart apples, and the heat of the drink warmed me through.

"There's no need, I can go to her," I said, standing. "Svala, my apologies, please get my cloak again."

Marta gaped at me, obviously wondering whether she should tell me to stay or whether she should let me wonder off in search of Brynja. The sisters glanced between themselves with identical expressions and I couldn't help but giggle at them.

"Worry not," I smiled. "I'd prefer to speak to Brynja alone, anyway. Let the children play again, and you–" I nodded at Marta's massive stomach. "Sit and rest. You mustn't overexert yourself in your state. How long until the child is due?"

"Any day now." Marta smiled, holding her belly.

"I'm delighted for you." I grinned as Nefja took my cup of the apple brew while Svala aided me with my cloak.

"I'll be delighted once this little one is born." Marta sighed, leaning back in her chair, rubbing her belly. "My whole body aches from carrying this child!"

"*Þakka fyrir*," I said, taking the cup back from Nefja. I turned back to Marta and smiled. "I felt the same way with all of mine. It will be worth it once he's born."

Marta grinned and nodded, resting her eyes upon the children playing across the room. Nefja held the door open for me, and I exited the home, following the dirt path to the garden behind the longhouse. I drifted through the flower beds and paused next to the large chicken pen in the centre of their land.

"*Heilar, hænsa*." I greeted the hens, watching the plump yellow and white birds skitter around their large enclosure, their heads bobbing, clucking noisily.

Suddenly a handsome black and white rooster darted out from behind the coop, cawing at me angrily.

"Ah, Gullinkambi, how do you do?" I mocked. "Aren't you meant to be in Valhalla?"

I stumbled back in surprise as the rooster charged at me, flapping his wings furiously.

"You're not Gullinkambi at all, are you? You're Hel's rooster!" I exclaimed. "Calm yourself, bird, *Ragnarök* isn't upon us yet!"

"He's protective of his flock." Chuckled a female voice behind me, giving me a start.

"Ah, Brynja, you surprised me, too!" I laughed, turning to the healer.

Brynja the healer grinned at me, the wrinkles deepening around her hooded eyes as she smiled. Her greying hair was hidden beneath a knotted white kerchief. Brynja stood as tall as me, bundled up in a long, heavy, brown fur cloak. The fingertips of her bare hands were stained with fresh dirt from pulling weeds. I had known Brynja for many years, she had even aided me with Einar's birth.

"My apologies." She smiled. "How are you, dear Jarlkona? I'm glad to see you. What brings you here today, and with no thrall, I see?"

"I'm in need of some advice, and you're the only one who can help me." I confided. "It's a personal matter, that I'd prefer to stay between you and me, only."

"Ah," Brynja nodded her head. "Of course. Whatever you entrust in me, I will keep it secret. Please, walk with me."

Together Brynja the healer and I ambled around her flower beds for a while, walking close together but not speaking. We strayed far from the house where even the clucking of the chickens was hardly audible, to a quaint little seating area near the end of her garden. A few aged yet sturdy wooden chairs were situated in a circle, surrounded by her flower beds, bushes and shrubs.

"I like to come here and think. It's quiet – I don't get bothered much." Brynja said, drawing her fur cloak tighter around her. "I love my grandchildren, but they can be *very* loud – and my daughters, as wonderful as they are, cluck about like hens when they spin – they're just as noisy as their children." She laughed.

"I can imagine – I only have four children, but sometimes they make so much noise, I swear the hall seems to shake from it all."

"So, my dear, how are you? How is your family?" Brynja asked after we finished giggling together.

"They are well, very well ... Vidar is at the shipyard working, the children are at home playing together ... Well, Young Birger and Sander are at least; Æsa and Einar were asleep when I left."

"And how is little Einar?"

"He is a handful." I laughed, taking a deep draught of the apple-water beverage, which had cooled considerably. "He is growing fast and eating constantly because of it – my breasts ache from his frequent feeding! The little monster is always on the move and getting into everywhere he shouldn't be."

"He does sound like a handful!" Brynja chuckled, a sparkle in her eyes. "Remind me before you leave, and I will give you a salve for your breasts ... *Já*, boys are terrible at that age, continuously eating and continuous trouble. My son was very much the same as Einar at that age – I remember it well, though it was almost twenty years ago. When Hraði started moving, things started breaking! He was quick, and he was handsy; far more wearisome than my daughters."

"How is Hraði now?" I smiled.

"He is doing well." Brynja smiled. "I miss him dearly, but he is doing fine. He has a lot of land and a fine house in Reykjarvík. I was so distraught when he married that Norwegian girl and announced before he'd even wed her that they were to move to Ísland, but all is well. He is happy, he is a wealthy man, and he is much better behaved than when he was a boy."

"I hope I won't have to wait until Einar is a man before he behaves." I sighed. "Brynja, I – I think I might be with child once again." I admitted abruptly.

"How wonderful!" The healer gasped, clapping her hands together – obviously not catching the hint of dismay in my voice.

"*Já*, wonderful ..." I said, not believing this situation to be a wonderful thing at all. "But – but that's why I'm here. I was wondering ... I – I want to know if there's a way I can *avoid* baring another child so soon ..." My voice trailed away.

The healer studied me for a moment, examining my face with her watery blue eyes. Her forehead puckered from her raised eyebrows, and her sagging jowls were emphasised by the frown that drew down the corners of her thin lips.

"Jarlkona, are you sure you're with child?" The healer asked. "It is *very* soon."

"*Já* – I've birthed four children; I think I know the symptoms by now," I said with a lopsided smile. "I'm sure you knew you were carrying Hraði sooner than you knew with your daughters – he was your youngest, wasn't he?"

"*Já, já.*" She nodded. "Mind my forwardness, Jarlkona, but I must ask – are you the only one who feeds Einar? Or do you have a nursemaid?"

"I have a nursemaid, Caterine, my thrall." I admitted.

As Herra Kaupmaðr had announced when he was selling Caterine, she did have ample, milk-filled breasts, and I had come to rely on Caterine to help me feed my two youngest children. Caterine had lost her own child to sickness less than a week before Vidar and I had purchased her, but her breasts had still swelled with milk. She was happy to be our nursemaid; she fed Æsa at her breast, and Einar too, though Æsa, at two years of age, was now weaned.

I had Caterine feed Einar while I gave lessons to my three older children. I taught them archery, reading and writing runes, and how to speak Ænglisc, the Anglo-Saxon language. They came with me while I tended to the sheep, and they helped milk and sheer them. I specifically taught Æsa spinning (when she was older, I would teach her to sew and weave), and she would help me make cheese from the sheep's milk.

Birthing Einar so soon after Æsa had taken such a toll on my body, my breasts ached constantly, my nipples had dried and cracked and throbbed with pain. Caterine would give me a much-needed break from feeding Einar and give my breasts a chance to heal.

"Then there is a good chance you *are* with child. That would explain it." The healer said, nodding to herself. "*Já*, you may have relied on your nursemaid too much. Have your menses returned since the birth?"

"*Já*, but it stopped maybe two months ago now." I explained.

"Then you have caught this pregnancy early."

Brynja stood up and shuffled over to a flower bed, where very tall, rickety, browned wild carrot stood. The wild carrot flowers had long since bloomed and gone, the long stems atop the plant had closed, forming a loose, tiny bird nest-like head that contained dried seeds.

Brynja undid the kerchief that hid her hair, and held all four corners of the fabric, forming a sling. She pulled a few heads from the browned plants and placed them into her kerchief.

"Does the jarl know of your suspicions?" She asked.

"*Nei*," I stammered. "I – I haven't told him, yet."

She stared at me wide-eyed before realisation washed over her face.

"Of course, of course." She said, nodding. "You want to avoid baring another child ... Well, I can make you a brew of pennyroyal you can drink now if you fear taking it home would inspire suspicion in the Jarl. The brew will provoke your menses and cast out the child, and no one will know. It *will* be painful and will make you horrendously sick, but it *will* work.

"But I beg your pardon, Jarlkona, I can only rid you of this child if you are sure it isn't the Jarl's. If this is the Jarl's child, I must have *his* permission. Without his permission, I risk a hefty punishment if it was discovered I gave you the brew—"

"The child I carry *is* the Jarl's." I interrupted, aghast at her suggestion. "I am searching for a way of avoiding baring another child *after* I have birthed this one – I do not seek to be rid of it!"

Brynja's mouth hung open, all colour drained from her aged face. She was obviously as mortified as me at her misunderstanding.

"Oh, Jarlkona, I see! I meant no offence—"

"Never mind." I barked, my cheeks burning from the blush upon them and my heart racing in my chest. "I intend to birth this child, *but* I do not wish to bear my husband another child for a few years afterwards, at least. I am so tired of carrying child after child. Can you help me, or not?"

"I can." She said with a smile, lifting the kerchief. "After the child is born, these seeds will keep you from baring another. Thoroughly chew and swallow a spoonful of wild carrot seeds, then drink a large cup of water or ale, within half a day after lying together, repeating the dosage at the same interval twice more. Do this once a week."

"Can't I just eat these seeds every day?" I asked, my blush heating intensely.

"Why would you need to?" Brynja asked, drawing her eyebrows together in confusion.

"The Jarl and I – we enjoy each other – *often*." I stammered, self-conscious at revealing such personal information.

Brynja gawped at me for a moment, before chortling at me, clutching her kerchief of seeds.

"Well, dear Jarlkona, I commend the Jarl for his virility and Freyr-like fertility! You're a very lucky woman." Brynja winked. "Unfortunately, the seeds would lose their potency if you took them so frequently. There are other options you could consider, however."

Brynja went back to the chairs, her kerchief of seeds held securely in her hands. I sat beside her in silence while she tied her kerchief into a bundle, knotting the corners together, careful not to spill even a single seed. I watched her, waiting with bated breath to hear these *other options*.

"You could chew the seeds daily for fourteen days, ten days after your menses begins." Brynja said finally. "Otherwise, another option would be to drink a decoction of chopped angelica root, pennyroyal and mugwort leaves, dried or fresh, simmered together in water. You must drink the brew whilst it's hot, once in the morning and once at night for five days, and your menses will come – if your menses comes sooner than five days, discontinue drinking the decoction immediately.

"The only other option is drinking a strong, hot cup of tansy tea – a handful of dried tansy boiled in water. Drink it in the evening and your menses will arrive the very next morning – should it not, drink one more cup of tansy tea and it will be there by nightfall. This method is the most assured, but you cannot drink more than two cups within a thirty-day period, otherwise, you risk losing your life.

"These methods are used to bring forth the menses … I warn you, though, if you are with child and don't realise it, they *will* expel the child from you."

"Thank you for your help," I said. "I don't know which I'll use, yet, but I have time to decide."

"You have plenty of time." Brynja agreed. "Please, tell me Jarlkona, why are you asking me this now, when you're so early with child, rather than after it's born?"

I shrugged my shoulders and raised my eyebrows.

"It doesn't hurt to be prepared." I replied.

"Of course not." She said with a distinctly dubious frown at my dismissive reply. "*Góðan dag* to you, Jarlkona. I warn you again, do not take *any* of these methods now, if you plan to keep the child inside you."

"I won't, and Brynja, please, not a word of this to anyone, not even my husband. I'll tell him when I'm ready."

RISE TO FALL
CHAPTER SIX

Early Spring, 884

I GLANCED UP at the rain hewn sky. From the smoke coloured clouds, the torrential downpour lashed down, heavy and constant. I shivered beneath the roof of the sheep shed, surrounded by the shuffling bodies of my many sheep. I braved a step forward, still under the shelter, and squinted upwards to examine the heavens.

Cold raindrops cascaded onto me, sliding down my face like tears, and I lowered my head, breathing a sigh of relief. Though months had passed, I found myself continually looking upwards, weary that the ominous raven might be soaring above me.

The raven's attack had been seven months ago, but every day I found myself glancing through the smokeholes of my home, combing the sky for the black smudge of the bird, always straining my ears for its raucous caw. I hadn't seen it since that summer morning ...

Vidar had been unconcerned with the possible implications of the raven's bizarre attack, but attached fishing nets to the smokeholes, should the bird ever decide to swoop in again. Jan, as superstitious as me, was apprehensive as to what the meaning behind the raven's attack might be, but after a few days of contemplation and observing the omen-free skies, he soon forgot his worries.

I hadn't.

"*Mumie?*" Æsa peeped. "What's wrong?"

"Nothing, darling," I said, turning to my daughter with a warm smile on my lips. "I'm just looking at the rain. It's heavy, isn't it?"

"It is!" The young girl exclaimed.

She tossed her long blonde hair behind her shoulders and waved her hands around in front of herself as she began an adorable, rambling tirade about the weather. Her fiery amber eyes were wide and sparkled with excitement as her description of the terrible weather grew more avid with every word that fell from her mouth. Her enthusiastic display of youthful knowledge lasted a good few minutes, and I nodded in agreement with her every syllable.

"—And all the rain could drown the crops and hurt the poor sheep's feet, and the cows' feet, and the horses' feet, and that wouldn't be good at *all*!" Æsa finished, shaking her head from side to side, her eyes bulging from their sockets at the severity of the situation she was describing.

"Oh, Æsa, you're so right!" I grinned and scooped her into my arms, her legs wrapped awkwardly around my largely protruding tummy. "You *do* know your weather."

"*Já*, I do." She agreed, her little face was so serious I couldn't stop myself from laughing.

"I am sure that the rain will stop, though." I smiled.

An unconvinced noise hummed from her throat, and her pale heart-shaped face looked dubious at my statement. I laughed again and sprinkled her soft pink cheeks with kisses until she giggled and squirmed in my arms.

"There is some good that comes from rain," I said, my daughter's forehead puckering in confusion. "Too much may be bad for the crops, but it *is* fun to play in!"

With that I stepped out of the sheep shed, my feet squelching in the mud, and stood out in the tempestuous weather with Æsa held in my arms. She squealed as the rain hammered down on her, laughing with me as we were soaked to the bone before I dashed back to the hall, smiles stuck to our faces.

"Oh, it is a bit wet out there!" I grinned, letting the hall door slam behind me.

I set Æsa down, her face bright pink from mirth as well as the vicious weather. Caterine rushed from the kitchen and saw Æsa and my bedraggled forms. Her slender mouth dropped, and her delicate eyebrows shot up her forehead.

"Caterine, please dry Æsa, and change her into clean clothing." I said to the thrall.

"*Oïl, madame*." The Frankish thrall replied, wrinkling her nose at my sodden form. "Would you like my assistance first?"

"I will help the Jarlkona change." Vidar smirked.

RISE TO FALL

Vidar eyed me amusedly as he rose from the bench, Einar fast asleep in his cot beside him, bundled in a nest of furs. As Vidar strode over to me, Caterine whisked Æsa off to the kitchen to bathe, and I noticed our other children were nowhere to be seen.

"Where are the boys?" I asked innocently.

"Jan took them out," Vidar said, reaching out to fiddle with one of the many beads that hung from the two brooches pinned to the straps of my dress. "And, as you can see, Einar is fast asleep."

As though he was trying to prove his father right, Einar emitted a rather loud and indelicate snort as he flopped onto his side in his sleep. Vidar and I giggled together before I took his hand and clasped it in my own.

"In that case, maybe we could go to the bedroom and you could help me change?" I suggested, batting my eyelashes.

I smiled at him and stepped backwards, enticing him towards the door to our bedroom.

"Of course, I'll assist you," Vidar smiled. "I don't know when Jan will return with the boys, we may not have much time together."

"We'll have enough." I winked, placing his hand on my hip.

We reached the doorway to the bedroom when Vidar pulled me against him and pressed his lips to mine. He parted his soft lips and slipped his tongue into my mouth, and I eagerly answered him with mine. Gently touching, grazing, I could taste the trace of sweet mead dancing on his tongue. Vidar's hands travelled over me, his fingertips drifted over my arms leaving a trail of goosebumps in their wake. Our kiss grew more urgent, more excited, more insistent. I pulled the leather thong from Vidar's hair and quickly untwined the plait of his golden locks, running my fingers through his long, silken tresses as his hands explored my body, lower and lower, squeezing my buttocks. Breathless, I broke our kiss for just a moment, giggling and gazing up at my husband, a smirk playing on his lips and fire burning in his icy eyes—

Jan, Young Birger and Sander burst through the front door, squealing and guffawing like madmen.

I groaned audibly and turned to scowl at Jan, furious by his inopportune arrival. The trio staggered into the room and dropped their wooden weapons to the floor, all panting and grinning, they hadn't noticed Vidar and me yet. Jan heaved himself into a chair and the young brothers collapsed into a pile together on the floor, laughing.

My selfish annoyance disappeared; I couldn't help but grin at the sight of them. Vidar reluctantly released me so I could whisk over to my boys. I scooped Sander up into my arms and placed a kiss on Young Birger's cheek.

"Mind your *móðir*'s stomach, Sander." Vidar said as Sander wriggled to free himself from my grip.

"*Mumie* – you're wet!" Sander cried out.

"So are you!" I remarked. "You've been fighting Jan and Young Birger in the rain!"

My six-year-old son ignored Vidar, and me and continued to squirm. I sighed, planted a noisy kiss on his cheek and released him.

"Come on, Young Birger, let's play!" Sander yelled as he charged through to the kitchen.

"Will you come, Jötunnson?" Young Birger asked, the weapons carried in his arms like a bundle of firewood.

"I will join you in a while." Jan puffed. "I must have an ale before I can continue!"

Young Birger shrugged his shoulders at Jan before he dashed off after his brother. The brothers ran through the kitchen where Caterine was bathing Æsa, and out the backdoor into the garden. We heard Caterine grumble in her native tongue as Æsa whined – she wanted to run outside and play with her brothers, she didn't want to have a *stupid* bath anymore.

"Jarlkona said you needed to be cleaned and put in dry clothes, so that is what will happen!" Caterine chided. "Now, hush child! Look up – I need to rinse your hair."

I smiled to myself as poor Caterine dealt with my daughter's tantrum – I felt sympathetic towards the thrall, Æsa was a very stubborn little girl. The moment she was cleaned and dressed in fresh clothing, I knew she would be out of that door and leaping into mud puddles with her brothers.

RISE TO FALL

"I raid, I fight, I battle, and I still have vigour enough afterwards to satisfy a woman the night through! Yet these two boys exhaust me when we play for just an hour!" Jan exclaimed.

Vidar and I glanced at each other and laughed at our friend. Vidar took a seat at the table with Jan, while I remained at the side of the room, where my boys had fled from, my hands rested on either side of my belly and my soaked clothing quite forgotten.

"My children are blessed with the stamina and energy of the gods." Vidar boasted.

"I miss the wildness of children filling my home." Jan sighed. "I remember when Burwenna and Jakob's second child, Johanna, turned two … It was as though she and Járnsaxa were each possessed by the spirit of Ratatoskr – they would scurry around the farm like that squirrel up Yggdrasil, chattering incessantly as they went."

"That sounds like our four." I commented, chuckling and passing a quick glance to my sleeping son.

"They do enjoy talking." Vidar commented, his eyebrows raised as he stared across the room.

I could tell from Vidar's stare he was reliving every bicker and squabble, every fit of squealing laughter, every noisy game. Since Æsa had learned to walk and talk, the hall would shake from the sheer volume of her. She and Einar would bicker and squeal, adding to the ear-piercing noise. Our older two boys were loud and chatty, but at least they would take their noise outside, no matter the weather.

A sly smile curled Vidar's lips as he turned his gaze to Jan.

"Do you remember when Alvar fostered me to your parents?" Vidar asked.

"I remember all the times my father would beat you and Jafnhárr for being so noisy." Jan grinned.

"I preferred your father beating us more than your mother," Vidar said with a shudder. "I feared Magga far more when she carried you in her belly! It didn't matter how far along she was, she was quick as lightning and strong as an ox – it was as though she turned into Thor when she was with child!"

Jan laughed.

"Oh *já*, she was *much* worse than Jarluf." Jan agreed. "She was vicious when she carried Jakob – I regretted for a long time that Jakob never knew our mother, but at least fate saved him from suffering a beating at her hand!"

My jaw dropped at Jan's insensitive joke, but he and Vidar didn't notice my reaction and snickered away.

"I think of her every time my children mutter or mope – how she would scold us for that! To this day, I don't understand how you can talk so much when she would punish us for our *ceaseless* talking."

"*You boys speak so much! Except, you don't!*" Jan quoted in a high-pitched mocking imitation of his mother's voice. "Jafnhárr said she would tell that to you and him every day – she certainly did to me! It makes sense now, but for the longest time, I didn't understand that phrase."

"I don't think you understand it now."

"I can't believe my parents fostered you for so long."

"It's not as though they had a choice." Vidar winked. "I was the *jarl's* son."

"Should I have been in my father's shoes, I would have broken my oath to the Jarl and handed you back to him."

The two laughed together again, and I took the moment to slip into the bedroom and change. Through the wall, I heard the men snicker and chatter as they reminisced. Their volume escalated, much like my children when they were overexcited.

My heart lurched as memories of my brothers trickled into my mind. I remembered when, after chores, Oswin, Bryni and I would run around our village playing, beating each other with swords or sticks, throwing balls between ourselves, or scare the poor livestock of our neighbours as wicked young children did.

Of my seven older brothers, Oswin and Bryni were closest in age to me. Sibbald was seven winters older than me and when he became engaged, he decided he was too grown up to play with me anymore. Beric was five years older than me and was much the same as Sibbald – he claimed he was too old to play with me, though he wasn't yet old enough to be engaged. My three oldest brothers, Kenrick, Sigbert and Dunstan, were all married, Dunstan had no children whereas Kenrick had three young sons and Sigbert had a daughter, by the time the Norsemen attacked, all those many years ago ...

I shook my head and sighed.

I missed my family, but I had not wept for them in many years. Every now and again there would be moments that would try to usher me into memory, but I evaded them as much as possible. I had lost my parents and brothers when I was only nine years old – so many years ago ... I couldn't let myself drown in self-pity, I had a new family to focus on.

When I returned to the main room, dressed in a dry gown, I found Vidar and Jan sat beside each other, nursing fresh ales brought to them by Caterine, who seemed to have lost her battle with Æsa. She smouldered with frustration and was damp and exhausted from fighting Æsa in the tub. My ears met with the sound of Æsa giggling with glee outside with Young Birger and Sander; the thrall's efforts had been wasted.

"What I would do for children of my own." Jan sighed dramatically, throwing himself backwards in the chair with his arms crossed behind his head. He watched Caterine as she bustled around the room, paying particular attention to her as she bent down to pick something up from the floor. "By the gods, I was blessed with handsomeness, charisma and great virility, but I was cursed to be childless!"

"*Childless*? What of your many bastards, Jötunnson?" Vidar raised an eyebrow and smirked at his friend.

With a short wave of his hand, Vidar beckoned me to him. I slipped onto his lap and he laced his arms around me, caressing my belly gently, his eyes still locked on Jan. A shiver ran down my spine at Vidar's question – we knew what had happened to some of Jan's bastard children. Many of Jan's children had been borne of thralls, and unfortunately, many of those children were dead.

"Of my bastards in Francia and England – if, I have any–" Jan said, winking at me. "They could be alive or dead – I do not know. And you already know my three bastards in Roskilde have been dead for years."

Jan lifted three fingers representing his dead bastard children from Roskilde. My heart broke for Jan as I watched him list them, staring defeated at his fingers, his confident smile depleting as he gazed at them. The children had died by the time Vidar and I were married; two had died in infancy and Jan's son, Jarðarr, had died soon after his third winter. The poor boy had been playing in Roskilde Fjord and had been taken away by a wave.

"I have no bastards here in Aros, alive or dead – *that I know of.*" Jan finished with a melancholic half-smile, staring at the three fingers. Slowly he lifted two more fingers. "And two legitimate children makes five ..."

I gazed at Einar, sleeping soundly in his cocoon of furs in his cot; comfortable, happy, safe. Through all the horrifying things I'd faced in my life – from the deaths of my Anglo-Saxon family and my Danish adoptive father Birger; to the beatings and rape I'd suffered from my first husband, Erhardt, and his right-hand man, Tarben the Beardless, all those years ago – in my maternal heart, none of these things could even scratch the surface of the agony of losing a child.

Unlike most women, I had never lost a baby, whereas most of the women I had met had lost at least one. Almost half of children born would die before they saw seven winters, a horrifying prospect with three of my children currently younger than seven.

But I had been lucky. The births of my four children had been relatively easy and all four of my children were healthy and lived. Jan's loss of every single child tore me apart ... I didn't know how he could keep smiling every day – there was no nightmare nor hell worse, in my maternal eyes, than watching your every child die.

"I have had a child borne from each of my marriages, and I had three bastards with three thralls ..." Jan smiled weakly, his voice thick as he stared at his hand, all five digits lifted to represent his children. "Of my five children I have lost them *all*. And for all I know, Thórvar could be dead too ... Every time I admit I have lost a child, it rips me apart. Five times – it's ... it's too much."

He shrugged his shoulders and released another deep sigh, finally closing his hand and dropping it onto the table.

"I understand," I whispered through tears. I reached out, took his hand and kissed it gently. "You were a good father, Jan. Your children loved you very much."

Jan squeezed my hand briefly and his smile grew slightly stronger at my words. Finally, he lifted his eyes and looked at Vidar and me.

"Not knowing where Thórvar or Thóra are; whether they are alive or dead; why Thóra chose to take my son and leave me ... it has maddened me every single day of the years they have been gone ..." Jan's voice trailed away, and he cleared his throat, unable to continue.

Jan and I still held each other's hands, but I couldn't tell if it was his hand trembling or mine. Tears slipped silently down my cheeks. I pitied Jan.

I had known Jan for many years. We first met when I was fifteen-years-old, and he was twenty. My adoptive father, Birger, had insisted I marry, to protect me from unwanted attention while he was away at war in Britain, and the added benefit of securing my position as a Danish woman, fully assimilated into the Danish culture, and thus receiving the legal and protective rights of a Danish woman.

Birger had Vidar arrange a meeting between Jan and me, offering Jan to me as a suitor. Jan and I had got along famously together, but he did not propose marriage to me at Vidar's request, due to Vidar's own want to marry me – something I had not known at the time.

Understandably, Jan had not divulged any of his marital histories to me when we first met – little had I known he had been widowed for two years already by that time. He was first married at sixteen and by eighteen, Jan was a widower; his wife had died birthing his son.

Over the nine years after his first wife's death, Jan laid with whores and thralls, and any woman he could charm into bed. He had fathered two daughters with two different thralls between the night of his and my first meeting and Vidar and my engagement announcement three years later, and both children had died soon after their births. Jan had conceived a son, Jarðarr, with a thrall, only a short while after Vidar and my engagement.

I had never met the child – he was dead by the time I returned to Roskilde. A few months after Vidar and I announced our engagement, Vidar left Roskilde for a few weeks to trade in a different city and in his absence, our town was attacked by Jarl Erhardt Ketilsson of Aros. Erhardt had forced Vidar's mother Freydis to marry me off to him as a peace-pledge under the threat he'd burn Aros to the ground, then he took me away to Aros …

Suddenly Æsa, Young Birger and Sander barged into the hall, filthy, red-faced, their sodden hair hanging from their heads like rats' tails. Their noise woke Einar with a start. The young boy wailed – I leapt from Vidar and rushed to the baby. I scooped him up and held him against my chest. As I shushed him, I gazed at my other children; Æsa was running around, Young Birger plopped himself down beside his wood basket and searched inside it for a project to continue with, while Sander set off for the kitchen in search of food and a drink from what I could tell of his banging about in there.

"I remember when Alvar and Freydis told me they were going to foster me to Jarluf and Magga." Vidar said brightly. "You weren't born yet, they only had Jafnhárr at the time, and they needed help on the farm. They didn't think they were able to have any more children."

I surveyed him, my brow knitted, a frown tugging at the corners of my mouth, unsure of why he suddenly mentioned this. I wondered where it was leading.

"I was excited … Jafnhárr was only two years younger than me, and he and I were such good friends." Vidar reminisced, his icy eyes twinkling. "I remember teasing my brother Einar – he was older and had to learn to be the next jarl. I obviously had the better end of the bargain since I had the chance to play with Jafnhárr rather than shadow my father.

"I had lived on Jarluf's farm for two years, by the time you were born, and I was furious! I thought I'd be returned to my parents because Jarluf and Magga finally had a second son."

"Ah, if only that had happened." Jan winked, sincerity returning to his smile.

"When you were four, you were finally enjoyable to be around – I remember all the tricks Jafnhárr and I would play on you!" Vidar smirked, snickering with Jan at the memories that flooded their minds. "Then Einar died, and my parents needed me back at the hall. I was heartbroken – not only had I lost my blood brother, but I was losing my foster brothers, too."

"I remember those days so clearly." Jan said with a sorrowful smile, identical to the one on Vidar's face.

"They were some of the best days of my life. I was so excited to live with Jafnhárr, I wasn't upset at all that my parents fostered me to Magga and Jarluf." Vidar said. "I'm so glad they did, for the unbreakable, lifelong friendship it created between you and me, and Jafnhárr and me."

"I am glad too." Jan smiled. "Jafnhárr was as well."

"You will have a son one day, Jötunnson," Vidar said softly. "A son who will live, who will grow into a man, who will honour you and fill you with pride."

"*Já*, one day." Jan's voice was distant and quiet. "Perhaps …"

***

VIDAR'S HAND CREPT under the blankets to my huge belly and he stroked it tenderly. I felt the child inside me move and kick against his hand.

"He's active tonight." Vidar chuckled as the baby inside me kicked Vidar's hand again.

"What makes you think it's a boy?" I said. "Maybe we will have another daughter."

"Is that what you want?" Vidar asked. "Another daughter?"

"I will love it whether it's a boy or girl, but I wouldn't mind having another daughter." I admitted.

"Then a girl it is." Vidar grinned. "What shall we call her?"

"Just like *that*, it's a girl?" I laughed. "What makes you think you can decide whether the child is a girl or a boy?"

"I will pray to the gods and tell them to give me a daughter," Vidar said, his tone somewhere between matter-of-fact and smugness. "They have given me what I've asked for many times now, why wouldn't they now?"

"I thought our fates were decided already?" I teased.

"They take special requests from the worthy." Vidar winked.

"Well, when you make our request for a daughter, could you ask them to stop blessing us with children for a while? I am *so* tired of carrying your children, especially so frequently." I sighed, shifting in the bed. "It's as though I am perpetually pregnant!"

"Really, little fawn?" Vidar asked.

The atmosphere grew tense. Warmth rose in my ears, my heart thudded in my chest and a wave of goosebumps crashed over my flesh.

"*Já*," I replied, meekly gazing up at him. "I – I am thankful for the luck we've had, so many children and all alive and well! But … I don't want another child so soon after this one, Vidar. Do you?"

Vidar was quiet. He stopped stroking my belly; his hand was still and heavy as it rested on my protruding stomach.

"The – the healer said there are decoctions and herbs she can give me to keep me from getting with child. They are effective, though not infallible, but they should work, at least for a time." I revealed.

"You've already spoken to Brynja?" Vidar asked, his eyebrows shooting up his forehead.

I nodded, though I did not intend to tell him how long ago I spoke with her unless he asked. But he didn't ask; Vidar was silent.

"She – she also said I depended on Caterine too often to help feed Einar, which is why I fell with child so quickly. She said I should feed the new baby from my breast frequently and not use a nursemaid at all – that should delay my menses, and, with one of her brews, I should be able to avoid bearing another child for a while."

Vidar chewed on his bottom lip, his eyebrows drawn together, as he thought. His silence was overwhelming – I wanted him to say something, but at the same time I was terrified of what he might say.

"Do you want another child?" I asked.

He didn't answer me – he continued to glare at the ceiling beams above our bed.

"Are you angry with me?" I whispered, timidly touching his hand with my fingertips.

"*Nei*, I'm not, little fawn," Vidar said, lacing his fingers with mine. "You have given me three sons – this will be our fifth child and I'm grateful, little fawn, I truly am. Of course, I want as many children as we can make together, but if you don't want anymore, then tomorrow we will talk to the gods. We will ask Frigg, Freya and Freyr to help you with your wish, and we will get the herbs from the healer after our daughter is born, but, little fawn ..."

Vidar's voice trailed off. I stared at him wide-eyed, my breath caught in my throat like a knot.

"B-but what, Vidar?"

"If her medicines don't work and you bear me another child ... I won't expose it – I won't expose *any* child of mine."

"I refuse to, as well." I rolled onto my side and cupped Vidar's jaw in my hand.

He turned to me and we kissed each other softly.

"Vidar?"

"*Mmm?*" He murmured.

"I may not want to have any more children in the near future, but I want the ones I have right now. I don't care whether it's expected of a jarl or not, I refuse to foster out my sons. Not even to Jan."

Vidar opened and closed his mouth, considering saying something but deciding against it.

"I understand, little fawn."

CHAPTER SEVEN

Autumn, 884

IT WAS THE final night of *Vetrnætr*, the yearly *blót* held for three days and three nights at the end of autumn. *Vetrnætr* celebrated the end of harvesting and the coming of winter, and honouring our ancestral spirits, specific gods and goddesses, and the spirits of the land.

Of the gods, we venerated the Vanir, such as the siblings Freya and Freyr, due to their association with fertility, as well as Skaði, goddess of winter and hunting. We also honoured some of the Æsir for their association with harvesting, agriculture and the fertility of the land, such as Thor and his wife Sif, and Iðunn, goddess of apples and fertility. We also thanked Ullr, god of hunting and archery.

On top of the many gods and goddess venerated at *Vetrnætr*, we also honoured the landvættir, the land-wights or spirits, due to their control over the weal of the land, for making the ground fertile and thrive.

On the first day of *Vetrnætr*, I, as the highest-ranking woman in Aros, had officiated the *blót*. I had called upon the gods and goddess, the landvættir and the spirits and thanked them for the fruitfulness of the land and for the bountiful harvest. I had hallowed the Last Sheaf which was left in the field it was harvested from as a gift of thanks to Odin.

We had also sacrificed a fine stallion to the gods. He had been tall, strong and muscular, the finest horse in the whole of Aros, and I had slit its throat. The horse suffered for just a moment before it collapsed to the ground. I had dipped the dried leaves of a branch into the blood that poured from the horse's neck and asperged the townsfolk. After the *blót*, the horse was butchered and put inside a massive cauldron that simmered in front of the hall, to be boiled ready for the feast that night.

At noon each day, we sacrificed to the gods and celebrated deep into the night afterwards. We slaughtered all the lame and old animals us didn't expect to make it through the coming winter. We butchered the animals' carcasses for their meat, most of which we salted, smoked or turned into sausage to store in preparation for the coming winter and the rest we boiled or roasted over fires for the townspeople of Aros to enjoy in the nightly feasts.

This evening was particularly raucous; after tonight the celebrating would end and tomorrow morning Aros would continue preparing for the fast-approaching winter. The hall teemed with people and overflowed with sound; it was filled with laughter and chattering, and the scarlet and gold fires in the pits roared gloriously hot.

There was dancing, feasting, singing. Men and children played games of skill, chance and ball games, women gossiped and giggled and skalds recited poems and tales. Music from lyres, bone flutes, goat horns and drums filled the air; the musicians from the *blót* were performing somewhere in the torch- and bonfire-lit night.

So many scents permeated my home; the pungent smoke as it drifted from the fire pits, the natural musky odour from the many bodies crowded inside, the tantalising bouquet of wine, beer, mead and ale, and the delicious aromas of meat, fish and vegetables cooked in a variety of delectable ways.

Upon the trestle tables, both inside the hall and outside, was an incredible array of food. Pork, horsemeat, poultry, oxen, beef and masses of fish were served, roasted, boiled and stewed. Platters of root vegetables that had been buttered or honey roasted; salads with a pleasantly sharp, almost bitter taste, and sweet fruit and nuts. Baked bread, fresh butter and cheese ... And upon the spits outside the hall was a fat boar and a sow slow roasting, their strong, mouth-watering smoky aroma streaming through the streets.

Vidar and my thralls bustled around the hall, greeting and chatting with our guests, who sat eating at tables or meandered about drinking. Many of our guests had brought their own thralls to aid them, nevertheless our three girls were run ragged.

We had purchased two more house thralls over the last few months; a Frank named Melisende and an Anglo-Saxon named

Rowena. Both girls were seventeen years of age, five years younger than Caterine. We had purchased the girls specifically for *Vetrnætr* and to help me with my children. Just over six months ago, I had given birth to Vidar and my fifth (and hopefully final) child, a beautiful daughter whom we named Alffinna.

Of our five children, Alffinna looked the most like me. Æsa, the oldest of our two daughters, and Einar, our youngest son, both had their father's fair hair (though Einar's strands were wildly curled like mine), but both children had my amber eyes. Young Birger and Sander held barely any resemblance to me, both boys were practically identical to Vidar. Little Alffinna, however, shared only the vaguest of features with her father – maybe her nose was like his? She had eyes the colour of fire, like mine; her flesh was pale and already springing for her little head was a mass of tousled chestnut curls – she was our only dark-haired child.

I was extremely thankful for the three thralls, though Vidar would take Young Birger and Sander with him to teach them to build and operate ships, fight, farm, raise livestock, trade and shadow him to learn what it was to be a jarl, I found myself overwhelmed by the five children.

The thralls aided me in wrestling my children into baths every *Laugardagr* – bath day, which happened once a week. They would mend or clean the children's ever-tearing, ever-dirty clothes, comb their hair, help me chase and catch the children should they run off, as well as the huge list of daily chores we all had to complete. I rarely used Caterine to feed little Alffinna, however.

Presently, I was sitting with my friends Guðrin, Domnall's wife, and Ebbe's wife Borghildr. Borghildr's lovely rosy cheeked daughter, Borgunna, was fast asleep on the bench beside her mother. Æsa was curled up sleepily on my lap and little Einar had fallen asleep hours ago and was lying down beneath a pile of furs in his cot in the sleeping area. Young Birger and Sander were off running around, their golden faces turned red with exhaustion and happiness as they dashed about with Domnall and Guðrin's red-haired son Yngvi, who was the same age as Young Birger, and Ebbe and Borghildr's three raven-haired boys.

RISE TO FALL

I glanced across the table at Jan, who held my youngest child in his arms. My baby daughter Alffinna was fast asleep, a string of drool leaking from her mouth onto Jan's sky-blue tunic. Jan didn't seem to mind, or he hadn't noticed yet. I saw his lips move and wondered if he was singing under his breath to her – something Jan would do every time he held my baby.

Though Jan seemed to be singing to Alffinna, he looked gloomy. Always happy to hold or play with my children, it was odd to see Jan looking so sullen while cuddling Alffinna. I tried to follow Jan's gaze and spotted a cluster of beautiful young women across the hall from him.

Ah, maybe he was tired of holding the baby and longing to hold someone else in his arms, instead.

"*Mumie*, I'm tired." Æsa whined, tugging on my sleeve.

"Alright little darling, let's get your sister and put you both to bed, shall we?" I said, kissing the top of her white-blonde head.

Æsa nodded, rubbing her eyes with her fists.

Borghildr and Guðrin bid sweet goodnights to Æsa, who nodded silently in acknowledgement. I took her hand and together we made our way to Jan.

"How lucky I am to have two of the most beautiful women in Aros approach me!" Jan exclaimed when he noticed us.

"I'm here to retrieve Alffinna." I smiled.

"I suppose you can have your daughter back." Jan winked, flashing me his warm grin. "Though, she *is* very comfortable."

"I see that." I giggled, wiping the drool from Alffinna's mouth with my finger.

Carefully Jan gave her to me, and I cradled the baby to my breast.

"Have you enjoyed your evening, Æsa?" Jan asked, stretching his arms out to her.

"I want to go to bed." Æsa grumbled, not moving a muscle.

I laughed at the seriousness of her tone and expression. Usually, she would have run to Jan, but not while she was sleepy. Æsa, a sweet and loving little girl, was an incredible grump when she was overtired.

"Then I will not keep you," Jan said kindly. "*Sof þú vel*, little Æsa."

"*Góða nótt*." Æsa grunted.

"Go and enjoy your evening." I smiled at Jan, tipping my head towards the group of women across the room. "I'm sorry I left you with Alffinna for so long."

"Don't apologise, I enjoyed her company. Besides, I was the one who took her from you." Jan winked. "I think I will fetch myself an ale and follow your advice, though."

I laughed as he turned to admire the women. I bid him goodnight, took Æsa's hand and whisked my daughters to the bedroom.

Without even changing into her nightclothes, Æsa flung herself into bed, curled up beneath her fur blankets and promptly fell asleep. From across the room, soft snores drifted into the air from Einar, who had been sleeping for a while. The moment I began to lay Alffinna down into the finely carved cot Vidar had made for our children years ago, the baby stirred and moaned.

"Hush, Alffinna, you'll wake your brother and sister." I chided softly, stroking her face with my fingertips.

Alffinna's drowsy whines quickly transformed into shrill cries. I hurriedly untied the front of my elegant wine-red dress, cooing hushed words of comfort to her as I did so, slipped out my breast and scooped up the wailing baby. With her small head cupped in my hand, I held her to my breast, and she clamped her little toothless mouth onto my nipple.

"Not so hard!" I yelped.

I pressed my hand down on my breast and tried to pull my nipple from Alffinna's mouth a little, to lessen the pain of her ravenous suckling. She groaned and grunted, her frustrated noises growing in volume. A curtain of my loose oiled and fragranced curls slipped forward over the little babe. Her tiny fist enclosed around a stray, and she tugged it furiously.

"Calm yourself, child." I grumbled, jerking my head to try to free my lock of hair from her grasp.

Her puckered forehead, tearful eyes and the red rising in her cheeks signalled she was about to bawl. I held my areola between my finger and thumb and angled my nipple into Alffinna's gaping mouth. Again, she latched, but this time it was painless. She released my hair, and I was able to sweep it behind my shoulder, releasing a sigh of relief as I did so.

I gazed down at her soft, porcelain face and ran a fingertip over her plump cheek. She gazed at me dreamily with those amber eyes she had inherited from me, the amber eyes I had inherited from my own mother. A quiet voice in the back of my mind spoke to me, a voice from the distant past. It was my father's voice – my Anglo-Saxon father.

"*You look just like your* móðir."

He had told me this many times; he last told me this on the eve of the Danes attack ... Did I still look like my mother? I hardly remembered her face, I hardly remembered any of my Anglo-Saxon family, but when I caught my reflection in the glassy face of water or staring back at me from shining steel, I would tilt my head this way and that and try to picture my mother's face over my own. Were our wide cheekbones the same? Did she have a button nose like mine, the same angular jawline? Or was it just identical amber eyes we shared? Sometimes I briefly remembered what she looked like, but doubt always struck me – was I remembering her face, or was I simply adding lines of age to the image of my own?

Alffinna's eyelids fluttered shut delicately, like butterfly wings, before closing completely. Her suckling slowed down, longs pauses appeared between each suckle and growing longer still as sleep swiftly stole her. The younger of my two daughters, the youngest of my five children, and the only child who had my eyes, my chestnut hair – the only child who shared her features solely with me.

"You look just like your *móðir*," I whispered to her in my native Ænglisc. "And you look just like your *ealdermoder*."

***

FINALLY, I HAD settled Alffinna into her bed, fast asleep, her belly full. While I cautiously laid some furs over the baby, careful not to wake her, Young Birger and Sander stumbled into the bedroom. I whipped a finger to my lips and glared at them – wordlessly commanding them to stay quiet. The boys nodded weakly to me, and, just like Æsa, they collapsed onto their beds, exhausted from the lateness of the night.

I stifled a giggle as I watched Young Birger tiredly bundle himself up into his blankets so there was nothing more than his fair, tousled locks to be seen. As I passed Einar, I paused and pulled his blanket further over him, his snores softly rising into the air. I monitored the fire briefly, it was low but exuded enough heat to keep the children warm.

Finally, I staggered into the main room of the hall, much sleepier entering it than when I had left. With inadvertently excellent timing, Caterine appeared before me just as I exited the sleeping area.

"Stay within earshot of the children. I've just fed Alffinna, and she's sleeping now, but should she awaken again, please feed her." I yawned and rested my hand on the crook of her arm. "If she stays sleeping, rotate watching the children with Melisende and Rowena so you each can have a short rest."

"Of course, *madame*." Caterine nodded. "Thank you."

I smiled and made my way back to the table where Vidar was sitting, laughing with Jan and his friends, Domnall, Ebbe and Hallmundr. Vidar's bronze cheeks held a rosy glow, and Ebbe's fair skin was outright pink; a sheen of sweat glazed each man's flesh, though Ebbe was perspiring much heavier than my husband.

"So, who won the contest?" I asked amusedly, dangling my hand over Vidar's shoulder.

"Obviously I did," Vidar smirked, grinning up at me, his cerulean and silver eyes glinting mischievously. "Old Ebbe can't run, we all know that."

"I can!" Ebbe protested. "You are the jarl – I *have* to let you win."

"I may be the jarl, but I am also your friend, Ebbe – for that you owe me a decent contest." Vidar winked, enclosing my hand in his.

"*Já, já.*" Ebbe replied, rolling his eyes and guzzling down the rest of his ale breathlessly.

I giggled at the pair and began to pull a chair out to sit on, but Vidar pulled me to his lap instead, wrapping his arms around me tightly. I clung to him, my arms around his neck, his flesh damp and warm. He leaned towards me and pressed his lips against mine. I delicately slipped my tongue into his mouth – his tongue was cold and sweet from the honey mead he had been drinking.

Vidar purred as I kissed him and squeezed me tighter. As cheers and whistles rang around us, Vidar smirked against my lips.

"It seems Vidar and Aveline will be performing for us tonight!" Ebbe laughed.

I rolled my eyes and faced Ebbe, a vibrant blush spread across my cheeks.

"Has your wife allowed you in her bed yet, Ebbe?" I asked innocently, leaning my head against Vidar's. "Or does she still refuse you? I thought I heard you say earlier that it's been half a season since you've enjoyed her – is that so?"

Ebbe smirked at me though his face was as red as my gown. Around us, Vidar, Jan, Hallmundr and our other companions boomed in amusement at Ebbe's misfortune.

"Never give the thrall that shares your bed a gift that should be your wife's." Ebbe advised, shrugging his shoulders before he took another deep gulp from his cup.

"Especially when your wife is Borghildr Hrafnkelsdóttir – whose jealousy is as mighty as her strength!" Domnall, a hulking, fiery red-headed Dane laughed, elbowing Ebbe in the arm.

Ebbe scoffed but still glanced over his shoulders in search of his wife, who was still far down the table. Borghildr and Guðrin were laughing together, their sons in various states of exhaustion, Ebbe and Borghildr's youngest son collapsed in Borghildr's lap sweating and guzzling watered down ale from polished cups.

"Fear not, Ebbe, I am just as jealous as you! I haven't kissed a woman like that in such a long time, either." Jan sighed melodramatically, answered by many a groan and eye-roll.

"What of those women from earlier?" I demanded.

"They were all married." Jan pouted.

"Since when has that stopped you?" Vidar commented.

The men snickered together, and I rolled my eyes again.

"When will you divorce that wretched husband of yours, Aveline?" Jan moaned. "What I'd do for a kiss like *that*!"

"I don't intend on ever divorcing him, unfortunately for you." I smiled, twining my fingers with Vidar's. "You must try harder to woo a woman – maybe find one who *isn't* married?"

Vidar, smiling smugly, kissed the knuckles of my fingers.

"You're a lucky man, Alvarsson. You're old and worn, yet still kisses you like that?" Jan said, throwing the remaining ale in his horn to the back of his throat.

"There are *many* things she does to me still, though I am an old man now." Vidar gloated, smirking at his friend.

"Shut your mouth, you braggart." Jan barked jokingly. "Oh Aveline, why did you choose him over me, all those years ago? I'm younger and far better looking than him. Why in all of Miðgarðr did *he* win you?"

"Well, to start with, I was the jarl's son." Vidar said, gazing at me with his big, beautiful blue eyes.

I slapped his forearm lightly in reply, insulted that he would suggest I'd married him for his position.

"You may have been the jarl's son, and richer than me, but they call me 'the Handsome' for a reason," Jan said. "Money, position, they don't matter – women still want an attractive man to fill their bed. Which leads me to repeat my question – why did you settle for *him*, Aveline, when you could have had *me*?"

"Vidar *is* incredibly handsome." I barked.

I gazed at Vidar for a moment and my expression softened. Suddenly a smirk lifted one corner of my lips and I cocked an eyebrow up at my husband.

"You're correct though, Jan," I said playfully. "I *could've* had you. In fact, I told Vidar I wanted to marry you at first, but he wouldn't allow it."

Vidar's jaw dropped before he laughed in disbelief that I'd outed him. I burst out laughing at him but rather than be irritated, he returned my smile with a sparkling one of his own.

"Vidar, you fiend – she should've been mine!" Jan gasped exaggeratedly.

"Not so, Jötunnson. I admitted my love for her, and she decided she didn't want to marry you after all." Vidar grinned, our eyes still locked.

RISE TO FALL

I pressed my forehead against Vidar's for only a moment, before placing a small kiss on his lips. I turned back to face Jan, who was pouting profusely like a child.

"Don't feel bad, Jan, it truly was a hard decision to make." I soothed.

"So hard, in fact, that you chose the wrong man to marry." Jan commented wickedly.

"Why should I have chosen you over Vidar?" I exclaimed. "But for the one evening we spent together at the hall which *Vidar* arranged, Jan Jarlufson, you *never* invited me to be alone with you; you *never* kissed me. Why would I wed you when you'd never wooed me? Vidar did – relentlessly, in fact. *That* is why I chose him. You may have been handsome and charming, but you didn't even try to convince me to marry you at all."

"That is where I was trapped, Aveline." Jan pointed out. "Should I have kept a vow to my friend, or break the vow and follow my heart?"

"Your heart? Be honest, man, you were following a *very* different body part!" Ebbe mocked.

"To make it up to you, *bróðir*, should Aveline allow it, and should I die before you, I give you permission to take my wife as yours, just as Vili and Ve took Frigg between them when Odin had gone and was assumed never to return." Vidar suggested.

"Aveline will deserve that, after so many years married to *you*." Jan scoffed. "I accept your offer!"

"I'm so pleased you both have decided *my* future for me." I said, scowling at the two men. "Perhaps I'd prefer to stay a widow or marry someone else? Someone of *my* choice, not someone of my husband's choosing."

"I did say *if you'd allow it*." Vidar said innocently.

Jan beamed mischievously at me, grabbed my hand and pulled me from Vidar's lap. He wrapped his arms around me, pinning my tiny frame against his giant body, and lowered his head so his lips were only a few inches from mine.

"If I kiss you now, would you run away with me? Would you leave that villainous husband of yours for me?" Jan asked, his voice as sweet as honey.

"I'm not dead yet!" Vidar said.

Jan and I burst out laughing and he released me. I tumbled back into Vidar's lap, and Vidar secured his arms around my waist once again.

"Have no fear, my love, there is no one I'd rather be with in this world but you." I promised, kissing his bearded cheek.

"And I, you, little fawn." Vidar smiled warmly.

"With all due respect Jarl and Jarlkona, you are both sickening." Jan said, picking up a stray cup of mead and draining it quickly.

"You're lucky you're my *bróðir*, Jötunnson, as brazen as you are." Vidar scoffed. "Had you been any other man, I would have beaten you for propositioning my wife – and right in front of me! – and I would have cleaved you in half the moment you took her from my lap!"

"Then it's a good thing I am Jan Jötunnson!" Jan said, bringing his empty cup in the air. "Now, as much as I'd like to watch you enjoy your wife, I am going to find more ale and a woman for myself to enjoy."

"A good plan, Jötunnson – maybe bedding a woman will relieve your frustration and calm you down." Hallmundr commented.

"There is only one way to find out. But first, to the ale!" Jan boomed, his cup still raised up high.

He turned his back on us and strode towards the kitchen.

"*Skål!*" Jan yelled as he pushed through the crowds.

Calls of '*skål*' thundered through the hall in reply to him.

"That man needs a woman." Hallmundr said, seriously this time, shaking his head at Jan's back as he walked away.

Vidar glared at Hallmundr.

"He *has* a woman, Hall. We just need to find where she has gone." Vidar replied.

"No disrespect, Jarl," Hallmundr said, eyebrows raised to the top of his stubbled head as he stroked his beard. "I only meant–"

"I know what you meant," Vidar interrupted. "But you're wrong. What he needs is his *wife*."

As Vidar brought his cup of mead to his lips, glowering at Hallmundr over the rim as he drank, I turned my gaze to Jan, watching him through the crowds.

RISE TO FALL

There was an odd tone to Jan's voice, a sadness, a bitter sorrow in the way he had said it was a good thing to be him. Even as he strode through the crowds towards the kitchen, I could almost see the heavy weight upon his shoulders that made him slouch just that little bit, that kept his face lowered to the ground rather than his head held high like before.

Jan stood in the kitchen's doorway alone, staring across the room. Yes, Jan could have any woman he laid his eyes upon, and, as Vidar had said, whether the women were married or not had never stopped him from pursuing a conquest in the past. Jan hadn't any luck with the group of women earlier because he *didn't* want them, not because he couldn't get them.

I heard the slam of the hall door as a few of our guests left, snapping me out of my thoughts. The slam seemed to snap Jan out of his, too; he drained his new cup and tossed it down on the kitchen table before striding through the hall and exiting through the great doors.

"Jan left. He didn't even say goodnight." I muttered under my breath.

"Did he have a woman on his arm?" Vidar chortled.

"*Nei*, he was alone."

"I'm sure he's alright, little fawn."

"Hmm." I frowned. "Well, I'm going to get some more pork. Do you want any?"

I kissed the curve of Vidar's cheekbone and felt the corner of his mouth rise into a smirk beneath my lips. Hidden by the table top, Vidar ran his hand over my leg and squeezed my thigh.

"You're as clear as glass, little fawn. He's a man; you *mustn't* mother him like this." Vidar advised lightly.

"I don't know what you're talking about." I huffed indignantly, standing up. "I'm going to get more food."

As I marched away from Vidar, he grabbed my hand. I glanced over my shoulder at him with narrowed eyes.

"If you see Jan, invite him to join us for one more drink."

I smiled at my husband and nodded.

Mead had warmed my cheeks and the heat from the fires and crowds had broken a sweat over my brow, but the night air was chilly and cooled me quickly. It was the dead of night, the moon was high in the sky, a gleaming ivory disc on black velvet.

I made my way to the spits where the remains of the pig carcasses hung, what little meat left on them kept warm over the low fires. As one of the townswomen cut some meat for me, I casually glanced around, absorbing the scenery and atmosphere. My eyes rested on the huge pile of wood that had been neatly stacked for the final stage of the celebration. Not long from now, this wood would become the great bonfire. Every other fire in Aros would be extinguished and families would take a flame from the great bonfire and light their own hearths, completing the celebration.

I turned my gaze to the happy townspeople. Women stood in clutches chatting and gossiping together, children dashed and laughed, playing games together, and a group of men were downing ale from huge horns, competing against each other to the cheers of their companions.

Across the way, a group of musicians were playing a beautiful song together, and through the various crowds, a group of young men in crudely made animal-face masks danced around, lacing through the other townspeople, occasionally whisking a pretty, young woman into a dance.

Suddenly, I noticed Jan's unmistakable silhouette vanish down one of the side streets in the distance. I gave my thanks to the woman who offered me a plate, hastily took it from her and scurried after Jan.

"Jan?" I called out. "Jan?"

He was gone.

I wandered further through the town, passed empty longhouses, harvested vegetable plots and wattle-fenced pens where livestock ambled. The cold breeze seemed to have blown away all the clouds and left the beautiful ornaments of the heavens clear for all to admire. Stars sparkled like silver and diamonds and the dark grey ribbons of smoke dancing from smokeholes were vivid against the black backdrop of the night. I couldn't, however, see Jan. I was sure he had slipped down this road …

Suddenly I stopped.

High-pitched, wailing screams pierced my ears. With my heart in my throat, I glanced around, trying to determine which direction the shrieks were coming from. Quickly I tracked the noise, dropping the plate of meat to the ground and ripping the utility knife from my belt as I ran.

I dashed passed a few more homesteads, turned left, and the screaming grew louder. I ran a little further down and there by a storage shed was Jan standing between a woman's legs, his trousers around his knees. Frozen in spot, I couldn't breathe, I couldn't blink, I wanted to run at them, wanted to pull him from her, but I couldn't. My body was suddenly too heavy to move. I watched him take her, her heartrending, despairing cries ripping through the night air. With a final thrust, Jan groaned, and his body shuddered. He paused for a moment and groaned before he staggered backwards and drunkenly pulled up his trousers.

The woman Jan had forced himself upon was lying on a crate on her belly, weeping into the sleeves of her gown. The skirts of her linen dress were hitched over her buttocks, her legs dangled open. Her flesh was as bright and pale as the stars. Anger, like an inferno, raged inside me at the sight of her as she slid off the crate and crumpled at Jan's feet, sobbing.

"*Jan?*"

Jan turned to face me as he buckled his trousers. With wide, terrified eyes I stared from Jan's gormless expression to the poor thing crying on the ground. I dropped my knife and rushed to her, yanking the brooch from my cloak and draping the garment over her.

"What did you do Jan?" I hissed.

"Calm yourself, she may have long hair and fancy clothes but she's just a thrall." Jan said flippantly. "Come on, let's go back to the hall. I feel better now – Hallmundr was right." He added with a chuckle.

"*How could you?*" I snarled.

Her body quaked violently so violently as she cried, her shaking seemed to reverberate through my body from the hand I had consolingly rested on her back. Her long, ebony tresses were a mess, cascaded in tangles over her face, which she hid with her hands.

"What's wrong with you, Aveline? You're acting as though you've never seen a man take a woman before." Jan mocked.

"You could've bedded any of those women in the hall!" I shrieked, tears filling my own eyes. "They were willing to share your bed! Why would you rape this girl when you could've had any of the others?"

The smile dropped from Jan's face. He stared at me silently; even the thrall had quietened.

"Why Jan? Why?"

"She looks like Thóra." Jan murmured pathetically.

My jaw dropped. Without so much as a glance at the woman or me, Jan turned and strode down the road, disappearing into the night.

"Look at me." I said softly to the thrall once Jan had disappeared.

Slowly the thrall lowered her hands and lifted her face. Yes, long ebony hair, a round, pale face and glittering light blue eyes; she could've been Thóra's twin.

"I'm so sorry," I whispered to her, grabbing a fistful of my skirts to wipe the tears and snot from her face. "What happened?"

"I – I went to fetch meat for my master." The thrall whispered, her voice broken by deep, wretched gasps as she tried to calm herself. "H-he came up to me a-and asked my name. H-he told me his a-and suddenly he whisked me d-down the streets to h-here and – and –"

"Ssh." I soothed. "What is your name? Who is your owner?"

"My name is Fríðr." She whispered. "I am owned by Magnus Geirsson."

Fríðr, 'beautiful'. An apt name for the thrall.

"Come, I'll make sure you get back to him safely."

Fríðr and I stumbled slowly through the dark. I picked up my utility knife as we passed it and left my cloak wrapped around Fríðr's shoulders.

RISE TO FALL

As we passed by the houses, I noticed that smoke didn't rise from the smokeholes anymore. The great bonfire would be lit soon.

When she and I reached the hall doors, Fríðr had stopped crying but her body still trembled. She slipped my cloak from her shoulders and gave it back to me meekly.

"The meat," Fríðr exclaimed suddenly. "I need to get master Magnus's food."

I nodded and accompanied her to the spits, my eyes darting through the crowd. With a plate of roasted pig in her hands, Fríðr and I entered the hall. I watched her return to her owner before I returned to Vidar.

"Did you find Jötunnson?" Vidar asked.

He stretched out his arms and yawned as I slipped into the chair beside him. The moment I was seated, Vidar wrapped an arm around my shoulders and pulled me against him, kissing the top of my head. I clung to his hand with both of mine and kissed it.

"I found him – briefly."

"Where is he?"

I shrugged my shoulders, scowling coldly at the hall door.

"I'm sure he's fine, little fawn," Vidar said, kissing me again. "I think it's time for the final stage of the *blót*, don't you?"

"*Já*, I suppose it is. I'll fetch the children." I agreed, reluctantly releasing him and standing up again.

I stumbled my way to the bedroom and found Rowena dozing on the floor beside Æsa's bed, their hands clasped loosely together. Æsa must've had a nightmare – she was plagued by nightmares multiple times a week, poor thing. Carefully I stepped over to the sleeping thrall and gently nudged her awake.

"*J-já*, Jarlkona?" Rowena gasped, scrambling to her feet.

"It's time to wake the children," I said softly in Ænglisc. "We light the great fire, then it will finally be time to sleep. Get Melisende and Caterine – I'll need help to carry the little ones."

"*Já* Jarlkona." Rowena nodded.

Soon enough, Vidar, the children, thralls and I were standing outside before the great well-organised stack of wood. Behind us, the townspeople eerily quiet around us, only the haunting sound of the musician's playing drifted through the air. Only one flame flickered in the whole of Aros – and that was the flame of the torch held in one of the elderly *goði*'s hands, a bowl of dark liquid in the other.

It was time.

The *goði* stepped forward and gave Vidar the bowl and torch while I passed the sleeping Alffinna to Rowena. The *goði* and I stood opposite each other, Vidar beside us. Delicately, the *goði* and dipped his fingertips into the bowl, coating them with the thick, gloopy liquid; blood from the slaughtered animals from the sacrifice earlier this day. I closed my eyes, and the *goði* wiped the cold blood over my face. The raw, acrid scent of the blood filled my nostrils as it dripped down my face and leaked down my neck. I opened my eyes, dipped my fingertips into the slime-like blood and wiped it over the *goði*'s eyes and cheeks. We nodded to each other and turned to Vidar, who offered me the torch. I accepted it and held it out before me, the flames reflected on my blood covered fingers. Vidar stepped back into the crowd, leaving the *goði* and I alone by the huge stack of wood.

"Hammer of Thor, hallow and hold this holy stead!"

As he called upon the mighty Thor, the *goði* stepped around the unlit bonfire, waving his hand in the sign of a hammer.

"Hail the Æsir! Hail the Vanir!
I bid you welcome, high ones,
Stand with us.

Hail the gods of the north,
We give honour to you, holy kin,
Our troth is true.

Hail the álfar! Hail the dísir!
We bid you welcome, honoured kin,
Stand with us.

RISE TO FALL

Hail the ancestors of our lines,
We give honour to you, worthy kin,
Our troth is true.

Hail the landvættir!
We bid you welcome.
Hail unseen ones, greetings I give,
Holy vættir, we give honour to you.
Stand with us."

The *goði*, his circle around the fire complete, returned to my side. It was my turn – I stepped forward and looked up to the sky, holding my arms out wide.

"We give praise to you, mighty Æsir and Vanir!
Landvættir, we thank you once more,
For keeping our lands fertile and rich.

Good spirits who keep Aros flourishing,
We thank you for the gifts
You bestow on us each day.

As you give us what is essential to our lives,
With the torch in my hand, I light the fire,
From which every hearth in Aros will be lit."

I brought the torch to the bonfire and slowly walked around it, pausing to light various spots. After a full cycle around the bonfire, each spot blazing satisfactorily, I stopped and stared at the flames as they grew mesmerisingly.

"After this night, the veil between our realms will wane,
And the dead will be free to roam our land.
Our roads will not belong to us,
But to trolls and the ghosts of the dead.
Upon the flames, we cast the bones of cattle,
To ward evil away from our land."

The fire quickly devoured the wood and tinder, flickering in the gentle breeze, and silver streams of smoke stretched to the stars from the tips of the growing flames. Townspeople slowly stepped forward with bones in their hands from the cattle that had been slaughtered in the past three days sacrifices. I lifted my hand in signal to my people, and they tossed the bones onto the fire in unison.

I paced around the fire once more, staring in awe at it, mesmerised by its dancing scarlet and gold flames. It crackled, hissed and popped as it grew, stretching its great arms of flame up high, its golden claws scratching the blackened sky.

Suddenly the fragrant aroma of rich wine filled my nostrils, engulfing me into a daze. Though I was so close to it, I couldn't feel the fire's warmth anymore. Instead, goosebumps had cropped up over my flesh and shivers streamed down my spine. Gripped in the eerie embrace of an inescapable stupor, immersed by the sweet scent and hypnotised by the flames, everything around me disappeared.

The townspeople faded from my vision. Even though I was surrounded by them, they became nothing more than shadows in the night. My voice quietened; I didn't call out as I had before. Instead, my words slipped from my lips and drifted through the air, dissipating like smoke. It was as though I was alone with the flames, the gods and the ghosts.

"After this night, the Wild Hunt will begin,
And alongside the restless ghosts,
And the spirits of those not yet born,
Mighty Odin will lead his host of dead to our realm.

Spirits of our kin, we honour you, we thank you.
We welcome you back to the land you once walked.
Your tales will be told, your deeds will be toasted,
We will tribute you and your accomplishments."

RISE TO FALL

I felt a hand close around my wrist, but I didn't turn to see who held it. Distantly the *goði*'s voice drifted to my ears, closing the ritual with the final thanks:

> "Hail the Æsir! Hail the Vanir!
> Hail the gods of the north!
> Hail the álfar! Hail the dísir!
> Hail the ancestors of our line!
> Hail the landvættir! We praise you all.
> Hail!"

"Hail!" The townspeople echoed.

Their voices rang loudly in my ears and rocked me out of the trance I was consumed by. It was as though I had fallen back into my body from a great height, my head spun, and my legs quivered.

I glanced around, alarmed, and found Vidar standing beside me, his hand curled around my wrist. Lit up by the glow of the fire, its orange light reflected in his eyes, Vidar stared at me. His eyebrows knit together, he chewed his bottom lip as he surveyed me. Slowly he reached out and took the burning torch from my hand and pulled me away from the fire.

In unspoken order, families took turns silently lighting their torches from the bonfire, before slowly proceeding back to their homes to light their hearths. Vidar, our children, thralls and I stood off to the side, watching our people in silence.

Heimlaug appeared and stepped towards the bonfire, lighting her torch alone. Jan was nowhere to be seen.

"Where is Jan?" Vidar muttered.

I didn't reply. I watched Magnus Geirsson appear with his family, lighting his torch from the bonfire. Cowered behind them was Fríðr, her eyes darting around the crowd.

"You're not worried about him, still?" Vidar teased quietly.

"*Nei*," I said humourlessly. "I'm not."

CHAPTER EIGHT

THE FISHING BOATS were all gradually coming in to dock, some already moored, rocking to-and-fro as fishermen hauled their full nets onto the shore. The fishing boats looked like scaled-down versions of merchants' *knarr* ships, with wide, deep hulls built to carry large amounts of cargo. With a smile on my face, I spotted Vidar, Young Birger and Sander's boat coming in – *was that Sander on the mast?!*

With baby Alffinna strapped to my front and Æsa and Einar's hands clutched tightly in mine, we walked a little closer. I squinted my eyes and stared at the little figure clinging to the mast – the golden hair shining white in the sunlight, his front darkened by shadow ... Yes, even shadowed, there was no doubt that was Sander. I rolled my lips and exhaled deeply through my nose, making a mental note to discuss sailing safety with Vidar later in the evening.

Under Vidar's lead, a large group had set out at dawn to go fishing, and Vidar had taken our eldest sons with him. The sun was lower in the sky now, noon had passed a few hours ago, and, from the looks of things, they had been quite successful during their day on the bay. They started hauling their nets from the boats, filled with mostly sea trout, but cod and a few flatfish, too.

The little figure I assumed to be my son slid down the mast and landed in Vidar's arms. His laughter pierced the air, noticeable even over the noise of the men dragging nets, the slopping sound of the fish, the wooden planks groaning as footsteps pounded on them, jolting the boats, the lapping of the waves. Yes, we would *definitely* be talking about sailing safety later on.

Æsa, Einar and I, with Caterine, stood at the edge of the shores, watching the men empty their moored boats, the pungent scent of fish filling the air. It wasn't unpleasant – not yet, at least – fish don't have an intense smell until they die, but later in the evening Aros would be overwhelmed with the ashy tang of smoke and the pungent odour of fish as women prepared them for storage.

"*Mumie, mumie,* look!" I heard Sander's faint voice calling over the noise.

Æsa, Einar and I hurried to Sander, the children giggling, Alffinna gurgling and her head turning this way and that. She was intrigued by the sounds though she couldn't see much beyond the furs covering her.

"I caught a huge fish!" Sander bragged.

"From upon the mast or were you on the boat's floor at the time?" I asked pointedly, raising an eyebrow at the boy.

The tips of his ears went pink but very matter-of-factly he replied, "From the boat's floor, of course, *móðir.*"

"He caught a huge sea trout!" Vidar said, disregarding my comment about the mast. "Biggest I've seen yet!"

"Oh, *já?*" I said.

"I took a hook, tied it to some rope with some bait, tossed it into the water and waited!" Sander bragged, breathing out a sigh of relief that I had let go of the mast climbing – for now. "It took the bait and tried to swim away, but I pulled it into the boat!"

"The fish almost dragged him into the water." Young Birger snickered. "I had to hold him while *faðir* helped him pull it in."

I laughed while Sander continued to grin proudly, his ears even redder than before.

"Can I see it?" I asked Sander.

"It's in that net over there!" Sander exclaimed, pointing to a net that Hallmundr and Domnall were dragging up the sands.

"You should go help them, then." Vidar said, pushing him towards the two men with a hand on the boy's shoulder.

Sander nodded and dashed over to the men, Young Birger following and quickly outrunning him. Each boy took a side and helped Hallmundr and Domnall pull the net, slimy fish squelching against slimy fish, the net full to bursting.

"We will eat well this winter." I smiled.

"We will indeed!" Vidar beamed, pressing a damp kiss to my lips, his face moist with sea spray.

"You might not, however. We'll have a word about safety later?"

"*Já*, little fawn," Vidar said quickly. "Of course – I must help with the nets now, though. I love you!"

Vidar pressed another hurried kiss against my lips, making me laugh and Alffinna squeal. He kissed the back of Alffinna's head, ruffled Einar's hair and stroked Æsa's cheek before jogging over the sands to the boats.

I stayed for a while, playing in the sand with the children until they grew cold and bored. Caterine offered to take the children back to the hall, her own porcelain face pink from the bitter breeze. Carefully I removed Alffinna and strapped her to Caterine, the babe sound asleep, and Einar and Æsa quite happily marched up the shore and back to the hall with Caterine.

I helped where possible, assisting a group of women and men dividing the fish, moderating disputes between townsfolk over said division of fish, and watching the haggling and bartering of the fresh fish sales. Sander made sure that his huge trout (and it truly was huge!) was kept in a crate, safely tucked away from view with the rest of the fish we'd be taking back to the hall.

"And it's done!" Vidar grinned, sweat dripping down his brow. "Hallmundr and Domnall are taking our crates home–"

"And I'm going with," Sander said, scowling at the men.

"They won't take your trout, Sander." Young Birger rolled his eyes.

"I don't care, I'm going with them," Sander argued.

"Go on then, they're leaving now." Vidar said.

Immediately the boys ran off after Domnall and Hallmundr.

"Care for a mead?" I asked, turning to Vidar.

"*Já*, I'd love one." Vidar beamed, wrapping his arm around me. "Maybe we can talk about Sander climbing up the mast?"

"Oh, little fawn!"

"Oh, *what?*"

Vidar rubbed his chin with his forefinger and thumb.

"Alright, little fawn. I apologise." Vidar smiled, his icy blue eyes twinkling as he gazed at me. "I inspired him; I was telling them of a time when Jan and I were boys and–"

"Oh." I interrupted, prickling at the mentioning of Jan's name. "Well, never mind."

"Little fawn?"

"It's alright – I was just teasing you," I said stiffly. "Come on, let's go to the alehouse."

***

WE SAT BESIDE the fire on the most comfortable chairs in the alehouse, Ebbe, Hallmundr and Domnall, who had come for a drink in the alehouse after dropping off our crates at the hall, were sitting with us. Sander and Young Birger had stayed at the hall, eagerly eating a bowl of hot stew Melisende had served them upon entering. Apparently, Sander had told the thralls he would be preparing his catch himself, to which the thralls had unsurely agreed.

Vidar and I had eaten at the alehouse, dining on a simple yet delicious meal of cabbage soup with sliced pork and crusty bread. Night had fallen, the patrons of the alehouse were getting rowdy and my breasts ached – it had been far too long since I had last fed Alffinna and I really needed to get home to her. Caterine no doubt had fed her in my absence, but I needed the relief.

"Jarl, before you go," Ebbe said. "Any word on Jan?"

I bristled at the mentioning of Jan's name. Vidar didn't seem to notice me stiffen, nor did he notice my grip tighten on his hand.

"Not yet," Vidar replied. "It's only been a couple weeks though, I'm sure he'll be back soon."

"Come on, let's go home." I pressed.

Vidar nodded, bid farewell to his friend and together we shuffled out of the alehouse together. I stumbled outside, paused and breathed deeply while Vidar closed the door behind us. The stench of body odour, pungent wood smoke and alcohol from the alehouse was replaced with the faint tang of the waters drifting through the brisk air. The sky was clear, the stars sparkled blindingly bright, and plumes of my breath drifted from my lips. It was lovely, the cold was welcomed. It had been so stifling in the alehouse, I felt free and able to breathe out in the cold night street.

I felt Vidar slip his hands under my hair and move it over my shoulders. He pulled me against his front and kissed my neck, stroking my sides with his hands.

"It's nice out here." I purred.

"It is." Vidar agreed.

"Let's go to the beach for a little while, then we'll go home."

Wrapped in each other's arms, we strolled down the beach, enjoying the sloshing sound of lapping waves as they rose and fell, the stars' and moon's reflections fractured on the rippling waters.

"I love the sea." Vidar said out of the blue, pausing to stare at the waters stretching out before us.

"It's beautiful." I agreed, leaning against him and admiring the view.

"When you're out on the ocean, you don't need to think. When you're on the ship, it's as though nothing matters but that exact moment. You focus on rowing and when the wind is good, we pull in the oars and lower the sails, and the wind propels us onwards. Then we just watch the waves sloshing around us. The only man having to think somewhat is the one operating the steering oar." Vidar's eyes were glossed over with thought, he didn't blink, he just stared out, remembering, his words slipping from his mouth almost absentmindedly. "I love sailing on windy days – I love listening to the thrum of the rigging as the wind wrenches it, the excitement of the boat heeling over as the sail fills with wind, and we speed over the waves … Being on the water gives you this infinite sense of peace, but it's thrilling, too."

"You're where Sander gets it from," I smirked.

"Sander's going to travel the world one day." Vidar mused, turning to me, his eyes wide and bright. "He'll discover new lands, new treasures, he'll win glory for himself, I'm sure of it. He exudes this ferocious enthusiasm on the water. Where Young Birger will be an exemplary ruler, Sander will be an extraordinary adventurer."

"Do you miss adventuring? You travelled a lot when you were younger, didn't you?" I asked.

"I practically lived on the sea," Vidar replied, sitting down on the sand. He grabbed my hand, and I curled up against him. "I've seen every inch of Denmark. I've travelled most of Norway, and I've visited Uppsalir in the land of the Swedes many times. I've sailed to Miklagarðr once, I've raided Frisia and all three kingdoms of Francia more times than I can count. I've been to Britain only once, but I've visited Dyflin a few times."

"You've seen the world, haven't you?"

"There's *so* much more left to see." Vidar sighed. "I'll never see it all in my lifetime, but I feel – *nei*, I *know*! – Sander will."

"I hope I get to see some of the world, too. I don't remember ever leaving my village when I lived in the East Angles, other than when Birger brought me to Roskilde." I said, an unexpected melancholy lining my words. "I've seen the few towns between Roskilde and Aros, and Frisia when we went raiding there last."

"You got over your sea-sickness." Vidar chuckled, squeezing me briefly.

"I did. It's terrifying being on the ocean, but you're right – it's beautiful, too."

"Do you miss the Kingdom of the East Angles?" Vidar asked.

"My heart used to ache for it when I first came here," I admitted. "But it's been twenty years … I've lived here longer than I ever lived in the East Angles."

There was that odd melancholy again.

"Alvar went to Britain so many times, I couldn't tell you the total," Vidar said. "In 865, when the Great Army sailed there to conquer, my *faðir* didn't want to settle in Britain, but when he arrived there, he began to change his mind."

Vidar's voice was soft, barely audible over the sound of the breeze and the rolling waves. He wasn't looking at me, he was gazing at the sky. I didn't say anything, didn't hassle him, just waited patiently for him to continue, a knot forming in my throat.

"Alvar said the lands were broad and vast. He said there were rich pastures as far as the eye can see, made of thick, luscious grass that was so bright a green, he had never seen such a colour." Vidar smiled dreamily. "He knew his people would be happy to settle in any of the Anglo-Saxon kingdoms, but the kings there were untrustworthy. He wanted to wait a few years until we had conquered more of Britain and established ourselves there rather than risk the lives of his people by settling immediately upon attacking them.

"There was a village settled by Danes in the East Angles, they were meant to be safe, but the Anglo-Saxons slaughtered them – men, women *and* children. No Dane was left alive. So, he waited and waited. Ultimately, I think he was torn though. His people would thrive in the East Angles – in any of the Anglo-Saxon kingdoms – but he loved Roskilde, it was his home."

"Roskilde *is* wonderful." I said softly.

"It is." Vidar sighed. "I love Aros now we've made it ours, I love Roskilde, but I'm interested to see Britain. Alvar spoke so highly of it – of the Kingdom of the East Angles especially; he said it was like walking into Fensalir – only he knew it wasn't, because of all the bloody Anglo-Saxons there."

I laughed at Vidar and saw his icy eyes sparkling.

"What's it like there, little fawn? Is it as beautiful as Alvar said?"

"I don't remember much," I admitted sadly. "I was so young when I left ... I can hardly remember a thing."

"Not a thing?" Vidar said, a whisper of disappointment in his tone, the sparks fading from his eyes.

"I remember," I said, thinking carefully and brushing my hair out of my face. "The marshes – Frigg would have been happy there, there were marshes everywhere ... We lived in a little village near a stream – I think there were only ten houses altogether, maybe less. There were lots of children there to play with though."

The sparks returned to Vidar's eyes, as memories trickled to the forefront of my mind. I chuckled at his excitement, admiring the innocence and interest radiating from his handsome face.

"We had sheep, lots of them, and there was always lots of work to do, but I loved playing with them – I had names for all our sheep."

"Ah, that explains why you have the habit of naming all of *our* livestock as well."

"They deserve to have names!" I argued.

"Even the ones we eat?"

"*Já*, even the ones we eat," I replied indignantly. "Would you like me to tell you about the East Angles or not?"

"I do, *já*, I'm sorry little fawn," Vidar said, kissing my forehead. "Please continue."

"Fine," I said, turning my gaze to the waves around us. It took me a few moments before I spoke again, trying to pull the remnants of memory from the shadowed crevasses of my mind, where they'd hidden all these years. "I remember I used to go to the stream to fetch water a few times a day, every day. It was hard, the bucket was always heavy, and I used to splash most of the water over myself on my walk home, which is why I had to fetch water so often ... I loved it though. I loved being on my own, I loved watching the birds and sometimes I'd even see a deer or two.

"I remember it used to rain a lot – I didn't like collecting water on those days. But I liked the peace, I liked daydreaming, though it was hard to fantasise with the rain pouring down on you." I giggled. "I liked helping my *modor* with our vegetable garden, I loved my fighting lessons with my *fæder* and brothers ... I remember visiting my brother Sigbert and his wife Alfwen. They lived a few houses away from ours; he lived with Alfwen and her parents, because her parents were old, and she was their only living child. Sigbert and Alfwen had a daughter together, Estrun ..."

I would never forget my last sighting of poor little Estrun, her sagging, waxen hand dripping blood; she was only a small child when she was slain by the Danes who attacked my village.

"But that's all I remember of home." I finished hastily.

"If you ever had the chance, would you go back?" Vidar asked.

I mulled his question over in my mind for what felt like an age. That question created a maelstrom of emotion raging inside me – I had never thought I'd see the Kingdom of the East Angles again, I never thought it a possibility.

"*Já* ... I think I would."

"I'll take you there one day, little fawn. I promise you."

We stayed on the beach for a while longer before the ache in breasts had turned to full-blown agony and milk was leaking through the front of my gown. With red cheeks (caused by embarrassment as much as the bitter breeze), I stood up and Vidar and I finally made our way back to the hall. Our feet slipped in the sand as we strode up the beach, finally reaching the hard dirt ground of the marketplace.

"Little fawn – I have another question." Vidar ventured.

"*Já?*"

"Why are you mad at Jan?"

Instantly my whole body stiffened. I wanted to tell Vidar the truth, I wanted to tell him I was furious at Jan for raping the thrall girl, Fríðr, but I couldn't. Raping a thrall was not against the law, in fact, it was quite an acceptable practice in the Norse world – thralls were viewed as nothing better than cattle, they were 'subhuman'. The Norsemen were not the only ones who raped their thralls, it was common everywhere, but I couldn't stand it. Being raped was worse than being beaten – physical wounds could heal, the emotional and mental damage caused by rape never would. Time would ease the suffering, but it would always be there, in the shadowed depths of the mind, that constant knowledge that someone had violated you, desecrated your body, stolen a piece of you that you could never get back ...

The alehouse doors slammed shut across the way from us where a man had noisily stumbled out with a thrall girl. She was young, she'd seen perhaps sixteen winters, maybe seventeen. He dragged her away from the alehouse to the shadowed alley beside it, pawing at her and drunkenly yowling like a cat over her cries, forcing her to go with him.

"*Stǫðva!*" I roared, sprinting across the marketplace, my skirts and cloak flying wildly behind me. "*Stǫðva*, you damned *bacraut*!"

By the time I'd reached them, the man had her pinned against the alehouse wall and had already ripped down the front of her gown, clutching one of her small naked breasts while clumsily trying to yank up her skirts with his other hand. The poor girl was trembling with fear, torn between attempting to pull his hand from her breast and pushing down her skirts.

"Open your legs or I'll beat you!" The man growled.

He stumbled over his own feet and fell against her; instantly she whipped her hands up and tried to push him off her. The poor thing didn't have a chance, she was small and slight, and he was so much larger than her. He pulled her skirts up over her hips, too drunk to even feel her fists pounding on his shoulders.

I ripped the utility knife from my belt, dashed over to him and pressed the sharp, pointed tip of the blade into his side. He froze.

"I said, *stoðva*." I snarled. "Release the girl, *vitskertr*."

"Who do you think you're talking to, *beiskaldi*?" He growled, slowly turning around to face me.

"I am Jarlkona Aveline. Who do you think you are to talk to *me* that way?"

It took all my power not to smirk as his face fell from fury to horror as he realised who I was. He reeked of ale, mead and sweat, but I stayed inches from him, my knife still pressed against his gut.

"My apologies, Jarlkona, I didn't realise it was you!" He gasped.

"Leave the thrall alone." I hissed.

"But Jarlkona—"

"You heard what the Jarlkona said." Vidar interrupted, appearing at the opening of the alleyway. "Leave the thrall alone, go home to your wife or go back to the alehouse and find someone you can pay to assist with your *needs*."

"But Jarl, she's a *thrall*." The man implored, staring at Vidar with confusion.

"Go home or go drink, make your choice, but you will not have this thrall." Vidar said firmly.

The man huffed before quickly giving in; he nodded to Vidar then stomped off towards the alehouse, his face red and his shoulders slumped.

"Thank you, Jarlkona!" The thrall gasped, her cheeks wet with tears.

"Where is your master?" I asked.

"I work here, usually I stay in the back and cook the food, but he crept in and grabbed me—"

"Go back inside and mend your clothes. Stay in the back, I don't think he'll bother you again."

The thrall nodded, pulled the front of her gown up to hide her breasts and scurried around the back of the alehouse, presumably to enter through the rear door.

"What's going on with you, little fawn?" Vidar asked slowly.

"What do you mean, *what's going on with me?*" I fumed, glaring at him. "He was trying to rape her! What's going on with *him?!*"

"Though we don't agree with it, there's nothing wrong with raping a thrall." Vidar pointed out cautiously.

"I knew you'd say that!" I snapped. "That's why I couldn't tell you about—"

I caught myself and stopped. I squeezed my eyes shut and hid my face with my hands, breathing deeply. Vidar cautiously stepped over to me and delicately held my shoulders, pulling me against him. I let him, needing the comfort that his embrace offered, but smouldering with anger, nonetheless.

"If you don't want to tell me why you're mad at Jan, you don't have to." Vidar said though I'm sure he could guess. "But know that Jötunnson is my dearest, most trustworthy friend, there isn't a malicious bone in his body. Whatever he did, he may not know it upsets you because he may not know it's wrong. Sometimes he doesn't think, he just acts. If you talk to him, he'll understand, he'll change, he'll stop, he'll apologise. Jötunnson is a good man."

My eyes burned with unshed tears.

"I know he is ... I know." I whispered. "I wish I didn't have to tell him, though – I wish he just knew, I wish all men did ... Raping a thrall *should* be wrong. Erhardt and Tarben saw me as a thrall – the *Danethrall* ..." A short, bitter laugh tumbled from my lips, but there was no humour in it. "Erhardt raped me over and over again, he didn't care – I was a thrall to him and there's nothing wrong with raping a thrall ..."

"The biggest regret in my life is not having been there to protect you, little fawn. I will never forgive myself for everything those wolves did to you but know I will *never* let anything like that happen to you again." Vidar said, taking me in his arms and pulling me against him.

"I know." I whispered.

"They're dead and will never hurt you again, little fawn."

After a while, we slowly made our way to the hall in silence. There had been something more I'd wanted to say to Vidar, but I couldn't ... When I watched Jan rape poor Fríðr, all the dreadful memories of my life in Aros as the wife of Erhardt Ketilsson came flooding back to me. Both Erhardt Ketilsson and Tarben the Beardless were dead, and I was glad of it. I would forever appreciate Vidar for killing them, but even though the two men were dead, the hurt they inflicted on me would never truly go away. When I saw Jan rape the thralls … He was just as bad as the men who had raped me. I didn't want to think that; I didn't want to compare or tar Jan with the same brush as Erhardt and Tarben the Beardless.

CHAPTER NINE

ALREADY A PHENOMENAL golden carpet of fallen leaves was forming on the ground of Aros, growing by the day. Many trees still wore their gilded crowns, but as the strong, bitter wind blew, another jewel would lose its grip upon a branch and flitter to the ground to rot.

The majesty and vibrancy of the trees were amplified by the thoroughly dreary and utterly grey surroundings. The ashen clouds were thick and heavy with rain, hanging so low from the sky I could almost reach out and touch them. I noticed a few boats and ships sailing away on the river that surrounded Aros, but when they reached a certain distance, the sky and sea seemed to merge into one steely abyss and the seafarers were swallowed by it, vanishing from sight.

"*Mumie*, look!" Einar exclaimed, pointing excitedly to the sea.

I peered in the direction he was aiming toward. There were four men hauling a *byrðingr* up the shore. I was surprised to see that one of the seafarers bore the weight of one side of the *byrðingr* on his own while the three other men shared the weight on the other side between them. The lone man was huge. Even from the distance, I saw he was broad in the shoulder, tall and well-muscled. He wore no furs even in this bitter climate, and what clothing he did wear was drenched and clung to his mighty frame. His dark sodden hair blustered about his head in the cold breeze, concealing his face.

"Wait," I said, holding my hand out to Caterine and my three youngest children.

We watched the men succeed in hauling the *byrðingr* safely to the shipyard, most probably for repairs. They would be staying a while it seemed …

"*Mon Deu*." Caterine admired, tilting her head as she watched them carry the *byrðingr*, a rosy glow lighting up her cheeks.

RISE TO FALL

"Let us greet the newcomers, shall we?" I offered, scooping Einar up into my arms.

"*Já!*" Einar and Æsa exclaimed in unison.

Caterine glanced at me nervously but followed me without question. Her gloved hands clutched baby Alffinna, who was strapped to her front in a bundle of furs. As we stumbled down the shore towards the shipyard, we saw the strangers heading up to the town. I squinted at the four men, trying to decipher their identities through their overgrown beards and the sodden locks of hair stuck to their red, weather-beaten faces.

As we grew closer to them, one of the men finally noticed us. He turned to his companions and pointed at us, and all four faces gazed our way. Lines of happiness formed at the edges of the tall man's sapphire eyes as a grin broke across his face, beaming through his bushy beard.

"Aveline!"

"*Mumie – jötunn!*" Einar exclaimed.

Upon sight of Jan, all resentment and anger I'd held towards him dissipated, so relieved to see him. At least a month had passed since *Vetrnætr* and we hadn't seen him at all in that time – he had left Aros without a word of where he was going, not even poor old Heimlaug had known. My fury towards him had subsided, exceeded by a growing worry and fear for his safety. Jan hadn't even told Vidar that he was leaving – and though Vidar had gently chided me for worrying, informing me that I was *insulting Jan's manliness* by fretting, I could tell in the last few days Vidar had become concerned, too.

Immediately Æsa and Einar sprinted to him. Jan opened his arms out wide and when the children collided into him, he embraced them, hurled them into the air and spun around in circles, squeezing them tightly. Caterine and I giggled along with my children; Æsa and Einar's laughter rang through the air contagiously.

"It's been weeks Jan!" I scolded, hugging my sodden friend after he set Æsa and Einar back onto their feet.

"I apologise, dear Jarlkona." Jan laughed.

"You just vanished in the middle of the night – no word of where you were going, not even a goodbye!" I barked, though I held onto him tightly.

"I wasn't sure you'd be thrilled to see me– you were awfully mad with me last time we spoke." Jan murmured as he pressed a brief kiss to the top of my head.

His words struck a deep chord inside me, and the image of him raping the thrall Fríðr flashed across my mind.

"Anyway, I thought I was a full-grown man, free to do his own will, but apparently I was wrong." Jan teased, his voice louder this time. "I will be sure to tell you my whereabouts next I venture out, *móðir*."

"Don't mock me Jan Jötunnson Jarlufson!" I chided, releasing him and glaring at him, my cheeks growing red at my children's poorly stifled giggles. "You sound just like Vidar."

"I'm sorry I worried you," Jan smiled. "Where is Vidar, anyway?"

"He's at the hall dealing with town disputes," I replied. "It was getting rather hectic in there, so the little ones and I decide to take a stroll along the bay."

"In this weather? It must be more than just hectic in there." Jan winked. "Perhaps we will wait a little longer before I make my presence known, then. To the alehouse?"

"*Já*, to Hel with being out here much longer," one of Jan's companions grumbled, briskly rubbing his hands together, which were red-raw from the cold. "I need a warm meal, a warm bed–"

"And perhaps a warm woman?" Suggested another companion, who had a lyre strapped over his back.

"I'm hoping she'll be the one warming my bed." The first man winked.

"Speaking of warm women, Caterine, do I not get to embrace you?" Jan asked shamelessly.

Caterine's beautiful face turned scarlet, her long thin eyebrows arched high upon her forehead and her lips formed a perfect 'O' at Jan's question. She eyed Jan up and down; he was thoroughly dishevelled from his travels, but his soaking clothes clung to him, displaying his prominent muscles and the smooth lines of his strong body. She didn't know what to do and shot a panicked glance at me. Before I could do or say anything, Jan opened his arms wide, ready to engulf her in his embrace.

"*L'enfant!*" Caterine gasped, holding her arms out to stop Jan from hugging her and squashing my young daughter.

"My Alffinna!" Jan cooed, gazing at her little face peeking happily through her camouflage of furs. He stroked her plump cheek gently and peeped at Caterine from beneath his long lashes. "Perhaps just a kiss, then?" He suggested to her.

"Wherever you have been, there were obviously no women there," I commented icily, placing a protective hand on the nook of Caterine's arm. "You'd have a better job wooing women if you washed first."

"The Jarlkona makes a good point." Jan sighed, lowering his arms. "I will bathe, then will you receive me warmly?"

Caterine spluttered something in her native Frankish tongue, her face still scarlet, lowering her eyes to the ground. Though I was far from proficient in François, I was sure I could make an accurate assessment of what she was saying from her embarrassed expression, her furious stammering and the generous amount of *Mon Dieu!*'s spilling from her lips.

Together, Jan, his three companions, Caterine, the children and I made our way to the alehouse in the market place. The large, aged building was bursting at the seams from the vast number of occupants inside; conversation hummed, like a hive of bees, punctured by booms of laughter. The air was thick with smoke, the musky stench of damp and body odour, and the delectable scent of stew cooking in the kitchen.

A table of patrons beside the fire noticed the jarl's wife, children and companions, and cleared a spot for us beside them. From across the crowded, smoky alehouse, Ebbe and Domnall's faces appeared, grinning from ear to ear. Ebbe spotted Jan and called out to him, causing quite the commotion of welcoming for him as others in the alehouse realised that Jötunnson had returned. Ebbe squeezed through the townspeople and made his way to us, a tall tankard of ale in hand and Domnall at his side.

"Where have you been, Jötunnson?" Ebbe demanded, taking a deep slug of his ale, before shoving it into Jan's hand.

"Here, there and everywhere." Jan beamed, slurping the ale. "First we feast! I cannot talk on an empty stomach; my friends and I are famished and cold!"

We ate and drank from the platters of exquisite dishes and beverages brought to us, and we conversed merrily with the other alehouse patrons. Alffinna, sat snuggly on my lap, reached and grabbed at everything upon the table. I quickly drew her attention from the hot meat and the knives strewn across the table top, to a beautiful little cherry wood cup given me by one of the alehouse-goers, which she gnawed on quite happily.

With thirst quenched and bellies filled, their clothes drying, Jan and his men's moods lifted. Einarr, one of Jan's small crew, pulled his lyre from his back and played it – beautifully, might I add – while Finnvarðr, another of Jan's men, sang along in deep, brooding tones, to the swooning adulation of a clutch of women who surrounded the two. Einar and Æsa bobbed along to the music, grinning and laughing.

Jan's other man, Lars, bolstered by sustenance and warmth, was in the middle of a rousing drinking game of verbal sparring, where the participants would take turns drinking before reciting a verse of poetry that disparaged their opponent's reputation and boosted their own.

Between Lars and his foe were many tankards of ale and mead covering the table top. Each man had a woman with him, Lars's woman was upon his lap, and his opponent's woman was curled up beside him, practically purring like a cat with cream.

It was Lars's turn in the game. Lars drank deeply from his tankard, his cheeks rosy, before reciting a damning poem. Caterine and I tried to clamp our hands over Æsa and Einar's ears, but they heard every booming word and cackled wickedly until they were red in the face and wheezing, much like the adults around them, so amused by Lars's horrifically lewd poem regarding his extensive list of conquests, which notably included his opponent's mother and sister.

"Caterine, come my heart, why don't we step outside, away from these cesspit-mouthed fiends?" Jan suggested, noticing the furious blush blazing on her face.

He wrapped his arm around her, holding her tightly against him, deepening the raging scarlet of her cheeks. Anger began to bubble in my stomach as Jan pinned Caterine against him – though I couldn't tell exactly whether she wanted to be in his arms or not.

"*Nei*, Jan–" I stopped abruptly.

Across the hall from us, I noticed a stranger sitting in the shadows with a cluster of men, peering through the crowds at our table. His face was mostly concealed by his long, lank hanging hair and his cohorts backs were turned to us, so I couldn't tell who they were either. I followed his glare and realised he was intently watching Jan and apparently growing angrier by the minute.

"Now I am clean and dry, perhaps you will give me that kiss from earlier?" Jan suggested, gazing at her amorously.

"*Mon Deu!*" Caterine gasped.

"Jan, *nei!*" I snapped.

Without further hesitation, Jan dipped Caterine and kiss her, much to the amusement of the crowd. I stared in horror at the pair but, frozen for just a moment of kissing him, Caterine moved to hold Jan's face between her hands and seemed to return his kiss amiably.

"Aveline! I wish to marry her!" Jan exclaimed, breaking their kiss breathlessly and drawing my attention from the stranger.

Caterine gazed up at Jan, touching her lips with a fingertip, her eyes half-open, her breath deep and racing.

"That is a discussion you must have with Vidar." I said uneasily as their lips crashed together once again.

Suddenly, a succession of slams shook the alehouse as the door banged shut, bouncing in its frame. Faces turned and commented, but most continued with their fun. I looked at the stranger's table and found it empty – the stranger and his gang were gone.

***

WE ARRIVED AT the hall just in time, for the clouds burst and rain cascaded from the skies the moment the hall doors closed behind us. Jan, Einarr and Finnvarðr, Caterine, the children and I left the alehouse for the hall, with Ebbe and Domnall accompanying us, while Lars, the victor of his competition, had stumbled somewhere with his woman to *celebrate* privately.

The crowd of townspeople in the hall had lessened but a small hoard remained. It seemed we had arrived just in time for the final dispute to be deliberated.

As I peered through the townspeople, I spotted Vidar sitting on his high-backed chair upon a platform in front of the crowd, Young Birger and Sander on either side of him. Sander, visibly bored, laid in the chair, his head lolling on one armrest, his legs hanging off the other. He was tossing a small leather ball into the air and catching it, a frown on his face. Young Birger, however, was still as a statue, listening to every word. Vidar was leaning forward in his chair, his arms rested on his lap, staring through narrowed eyes at the two men – one grey-haired, one blond – who stood directly in front of him, circled by the crowd.

"And what is this – you're fighting over a dead thrall?" Vidar asked, surveying the two men in turn.

"Ívarr killed my thrall – I demand retribution!" The grey-haired man exclaimed.

"Did you kill his thrall?" Vidar asked, turning to the blond man.

"I did." Ívarr admitted. "The–"

"Then by law, you must compensate me for killing him." The older man interrupted, beaming victoriously.

"I refuse, Klaus's thrall was fleeing!" Ívarr protested, shooting a furious glare at the grey-haired Klaus. "He was pulling a boat into the water! By law, I can slay a fleeing, thieving thrall – why should I be punished for executing my legal duty?"

"Executing is right – was he fleeing, or did you just *execute* him on the shore?" Klaus spat.

"Are you calling me a liar, old man?" Ívarr growled, glaring venomously from beneath his thick brows at Klaus.

"Are there any witnesses here?" Vidar interrupted. "Can anyone attest they saw the thrall stealing the boat in an attempt to flee?"

"*Já.*" Replied a handful of men in unison, stepping forward into the circle.

Vidar smiled briefly and somewhat insincerely at the witnesses, obviously frustrated over the men's petty argument.

"I am without a thrall thanks to—" Klaus began to argue, but Vidar silenced him with a short wave of his hand.

Vidar stared at Klaus and Ívarr for what seemed like an age. No one spoke, the air was tense. But for the muffled noise of people shifting where they stood, the hall was thick with silence.

"Young Birger, what say you?" Vidar said abruptly, turning to our eldest son, whose eyebrows shot up his forehead at his father's question. "This is a simple matter with a simple solution, and I want *you* to make the simple decision. So, what say you?"

Vidar tossed himself back in his chair, and all faces turned to stare at Young Birger. Even Sander righted himself in his chair and gawped at his brother. Young Birger thought silently for a moment. Nervously, he swallowed hard, but when he spoke, his voice was level and calm.

"It is within a Norseman's legal right to slay or punish a fleeing thrall, a thieving thrall or a thrall committing any wrongdoing." Young Birger said. "In fact, had Ívarr not killed the thrall and instead allowed him to run away, Klaus would have been without a thrall *and* he would have been held liable for the stolen boat and would owe the boat-owner compensation for it.

"In effect, Ívarr *saved* Klaus from owing the boat-owner, therefore he should certainly not be fined nor pay Klaus any compensation. Regardless of whether the thrall escaped or was slain, Klaus would be without a thrall; it was not Ívarr's fault the thrall fled, so Ívarr will not be punished at all."

Vidar grinned smugly at our eldest son, visibly brimming with gleeful pride at Young Birger's judgement. Ívarr the blond Norseman was just as pleased with Young Birger's verdict, grinning toothily at the disgruntled grey-haired Klaus.

"No insult to you or your son, Jarl Vidar, but he is not yet a man – surely he cannot decide on this matter?" Klaus said delicately.

"Young Birger is but weeks away from his tenth winter when he will be a man," Vidar said. "Besides, I concur with my son. What say you both, Klaus? Ívarr? Do either of you disagree with Young Birger *and my* decision?"

"*Nei.*" Ívarr grinned happily.

"*Nei.*" Klaus grumbled, red-faced, grudgingly shaking his head.

"Then the decision is made!" Vidar announced, clapping his hands together. "Ívarr will not be fined. That is all for today!"

Klaus immediately shoved through the crowds and stomped out of the hall into the rain. My group and I removed our furs and gave them to Melisende and Rowena, who hung them on drying racks around the fire as the crowd of townspeople slowly filtered out of the hall.

Jan, his two crewmen, Ebbe and Domnall approached Vidar, while Caterine returned the ravenous Alffinna to me, who promptly yanked on my gown in search of my breast. I cradled her with one arm, slipped my breast from the opening of my gown and offered her my nipple, while Æsa and Einar dashed off to their father, and the thralls scurried off to the kitchen. With Alffinna content, I slowly made my way to Vidar, Young Birger and Sander who were still sitting in their chairs on the platform.

"Jötunnson! You've returned!" Young Birger and Sander exclaimed in unison.

"I have, my boys!" Jan beamed, holding his arms out to my sons. "Well done, Young Birger, that was a wise ruling you made."

The boys leapt from their chairs and into Jan's arms, squeezing him tightly.

"Where have you been?" Vidar asked, embracing Jan after he set the boys down.

"I went to Hedeby, in search of news on my wife and my son." Jan revealed.

"Any luck?" Vidar's excitement immediately transformed into sober concern.

"They would be at my side had I any luck," Jan shrugged. "Still, no word; her family has no idea where they are."

"My sympathies." Vidar frowned.

"No matter." Jan dismissed, shaking his head. "Anyway, I see you've been busy. Have all the recent town disputes been so riveting and complex?"

The afternoon passed quickly, and the soothing peace of night finally settled upon Aros. Our three thralls spun wool beside the fire, Alffinna sat at their feet chewing on a wooden cat toy Vidar had carved for her. Einarr and Finnvarðr were sitting on the other side of the fire. Einarr idly plucked a tune on his lyre while Finnvarðr drunkenly hummed along, belching out a word or two, slumped drunkenly in his chair next to his friend.

Einar and Æsa were fast asleep in their beds, but Young Birger resisted the blissful embrace of sleep in favour of finishing his latest project – a fine statuette of the god Freyr to go with the collection of Norse god and goddess effigies he was making.

Sander and Vidar were play-fighting together. Vidar held Sander upside down his ankles, while Sander cackled, pink-cheeked, trying and failing to wiggle free from his father's grip. Jan heckled Sander playfully, poking him in the armpits or tickling the back of his knees. Domnall and Ebbe watched them, laughing and drinking from their cups.

Chuckling, Vidar carefully lowered Sander to the packed dirt floor and let the boy catch his breath. Vidar grabbed his cup and threw himself into the chair beside me at the table. Slouching backwards, he gulped down his mead, took my hand and kissed it, his lips damp from his drink.

"Does he always sing like that?" Vidar asked, tipping his head to Finnvarðr, whose wonderful singing voice had been addled beyond comprehension by the copious amount of mead and ale he had consumed.

"I think we may have broken him." Domnall snickered. "He's been drinking all day."

"He sang finely in the alehouse." I commented. "Oh! That reminds me; Vidar, have you received any visitors today?"

"*Nei*," my husband replied, frowning slightly. "Was I meant to?"

"There was a group of men I didn't recognise at the alehouse earlier," I explained. "One seemed awfully focussed on Jan."

"Perhaps he thought Jötunnson was pretty?" Ebbe teased.

"Maybe he fell in love with our handsome *jötunn*?" Einarr suggested, strumming a beautiful tune on the strings of his lyre.

"He looked rather angry to me." I said, rolling my eyes.

"Then perhaps Jötunnson slept with his wife?" Domnall winked.

"Perhaps he's jealous his wife slept with Jötunnson and he didn't?" Ebbe offered wickedly.

"Watch yourself," Jan warned playfully.

"It wasn't funny, it was alarming." I argued.

"Aveline, I appreciate your concern, but I am a man, I can look after myself." Jan pointed out, taking my hand and forcing me onto my feet. "You need to stop worrying!"

Einarr, grinning ear to ear, began a fabulous, jaunty melody on his lyre, which Finnvarðr peppered with hiccoughed verses describing beautiful women, energetic lovemaking and drinking, and Jan whisked me into a dance. I tried to return to my seat, reluctant to dance and unwilling to let go of my concerns, but Jan spun me around once, twice, three times, until I couldn't maintain the frown on my face any longer. I laughed, and so did our friends, and danced around the hall like an idiot with Jan.

"Vidar, you dastardly man, come rescue your wife!" I laughed, reaching out to Vidar.

"I would love to, little fawn, but my hands are full!" Vidar smirked, lifting Sander into the air.

"Young Birger come save your *móðir*!" I cried.

With a stifled grin and pink cheeks, my eldest son shook his head and distractedly tried to continue with his latest project.

"I'd release that man and put as much distance between you both as possible, if I were you, woman." A gruff voice growled from across the room. "Jan Jarlufson is a murderer!"

CHAPTER TEN

STANDING IN THE doorway was a muscled man of average height, his long ebony hair hung ragged and greasy over his shoulders. Through the tentacle-like locks that draped over his face, the danger sparking in his bright blue eyes was clear even at this distance. His overgrown beard was a nest of tangles and snares, and his clothes were soiled and filthy. Behind him were four of his cleaner compatriots, all wearing the same threatening expression. I recognised them all immediately, they were the strangers from the alehouse!

Quickly, Caterine scooped up Alffinna, protectively holding her against her chest. She leapt to her feet and slowly backed away.

"Who are you to tell this woman to run from me?" Jan asked.

Jan straightened his stance and let go of me, but for one of my hands which he held tightly.

"He may have a handsome face and honeyed tongue, but his cock is cursed, woman." The stranger continued, ignoring Jan.

Jan stared incredulously at him. Desperately I stared at Vidar, my heart hammering in my chest, and saw him glaring forebodingly at the man, his eyes glinting with danger. Silently, Vidar lowered Sander to the ground, and gently pushed him towards Melisende and Rowena, who hurried to the young children and held them.

"My cock is cursed?" Jan marvelled. "Cursed with grand size and ample girth, to be sure!"

Ebbe, Domnall, Finnvarðr and Einarr snickered at Jan's comment. The roaring firelight flickered across the stranger's eerily shadowed face as he continued to glare at Jan.

Vidar hadn't laughed either. He continued to watch the stranger; his lips drawn tightly together. Vidar was terrifyingly still, he remained slumped comfortably in his chair, but the alertness in his eyes betrayed him. He was a wildcat awaiting the perfect moment to pounce upon his prey.

"You've seen no more than thirty-three winters, Jan Jarlufson. How many wives have you married? How many have died?" The stranger snarled. "Though women admire your good looks, *Jan the Handsome*, none more will wed you in fear of death taking them. And those women who were daring – or stupid–" He tipped his head in Caterine's direction. "–Enough to marry you and share your bed – all of them are dead!"

Jan's fingers twitched as he scowled at the stranger, scrutinising every inch of him. His smile lingered on his face, but it was cold now, and anger swirled in his narrowed sapphire eyes.

"You know a lot about me, but I don't seem to know you," Jan said. "Tell me your name, stranger."

"You insult me with your forgetfulness, Jötunnson. I am Thorn Arnsteinson, brother of Thóra Arnsteinsdóttir." The man replied. "I watched you wed my younger sister before I set sail to Britain – I returned just weeks ago, to find you had killed her!"

The shocked faces of our companions stared at Jan. Vidar sat up in his chair and rested an arm on the tabletop. His hand dangled over the edge of the table, his fingertips subtly touching the hilt of his utility knife, which hung from his belt in its sheath.

"Thóra isn't dead – she left me." Jan growled through gritted teeth.

"And what of your previous wife?" Thorn remarked.

"My previous wife is none of your concern." Jan said. "Brother of my wife, I understand your sadness for losing Thóra, I felt the same sadness–"

"*Same sadness?*" Thorn scoffed. "A murderer doesn't feel the *same sadness* as the kin of his victim!"

"Victim? Thóra isn't dead, she disappeared!"

"A likely story for the coward who murdered his wife and child!"

With a swift swoop, Thorn's hand shot to his waist and drew his sword. He pointed the sharp, shining tip at Jan. Jan shoved me behind him quickly, hiding me behind his tall, broad frame. As Thorn pulled his sword, Vidar, Ebbe, Domnall, Einarr and Finnvarðr leapt to their feet.

"Enough!" Vidar roared. "Sheath your weapon!"

RISE TO FALL

Thorn's blue eyes, bloodshot and round as coins, darted towards Vidar. He made no attempt to sheath his sword but continued to point it at Jan. In one swift movement, Vidar stood abruptly, teeming with rage, sending his chair clattering across the platform. He stormed towards Thorn, yanking the utility knife from his belt and clasping it in his steady fist.

"I am Jarl Vidar Alvarsson of Aros!" Vidar seethed. "Who are you to enter my home, hurling insults in your wake, then point your sword at my wife and friend?"

Vidar stood in front of Thorn's sword, undaunted by the tip of the sharp blade held dangerously close to his neck. Vidar pointed his utility knife at Thorn. Though his weapon was minute compared to the stranger's, Vidar was unafraid.

There in Vidar's eyes was the telltale gleam of bloodlust.

Thorn and Vidar glowered at one another in silence and the hall was still but for the crackle and dance of the fire – not one person in my home dared even to breathe. The flames of the firepit reflected in Vidar's unblinking, icy eyes, mirroring the rage that boiled inside him.

"I said *sheath your weapon*." Though Vidar's voice was low and quiet, Thorn flinched at his words and slowly slid his sword back inside its wooden scabbard, scowling at my infuriated husband.

"Apologies, Jarl, I mean no harm to your wife," Thorn said stiffly. "I am here to take my vengeance on the man who murdered my sister and her child."

"Make camp for the night, Thorn Arnsteinson. I will hear your accusation in the three days." Vidar ordered.

"I cannot wait that long," Thorn hands clenched into shaking fists. "My sister has been dead for two years – she should have been avenged long ago! It's my *right* to take revenge upon this man!"

"You *will* wait," Vidar warned darkly. "Should you or any of your kin lay a hand on Jan Jarlufson before I hear your dispute in three days, then I will kill you all myself."

***

"YOUR BROTHER-IN-LAW is quite a fiery man." Vidar commented.

He scowled at the backs of Thorn and his men as they stormed into the night, leaving the hall door wide open behind them. Rowena crept to the door and bolted it shut.

"I hardly remember him," Jan said, staring at the closed door. "Like he said, I only met him once, at Thóra and my wedding. If I think hard enough, I remember seeing him, but I cannot recall saying a single word to him."

Noise gradually returned to the hall. Melisende, Rowena and Caterine ushered the children to bed, and our companions settled themselves back in their chairs, grunting about what had just transpired. I pulled my hand from Jan's grip and rushed to Vidar, throwing myself into his arms.

Vidar's chair had been picked up and set back in place, presumably by one of the thralls, and together we returned to the table, our hands clasped together. Vidar sat down and I tumbled into his lap. He secured his arms around me and pressed a kiss against my head.

"I hardly know the man, yet here he comes, after all these years, accusing me of murdering Thóra." Jan said, shaking his head in disbelief.

"Well, did you murder her?" Ebbe asked.

Vidar, Einarr, Finnvarðr, Jan and I glared at him.

"Of course not!" Jan exclaimed.

"Then why worry? This is a celebration!" Domnall grinned, offering Jan a cup of mead.

"Oh, how true, Domnall, why should I worry when he is just accusing me of *murdering my wife*?" Jan mocked, though he accepted the cup of mead and drank from it deeply.

"You say you didn't murder your wife, and I believe you. When the meeting occurs, your innocence will be proven. There is no need to lose a wink of sleep over some madman's outrageous claims." Domnall reasoned, stroking his thick red beard.

Ebbe, Einarr and Finnvarðr nodded and murmured in agreement.

"Should it come to it, you will have Thorn's blood," Vidar promised. "Domnall is right, worry not, Jötunnson. This *will* be settled in three days."

I gazed between Jan and Vidar. Vidar's icy eyes peeked over my shoulder, and Jan's sapphire eyes were locked unblinking with Vidar's. Wordlessly, they seemed to speak together, though their faces were blank, and their lips were drawn tightly shut. I shivered suddenly, goosebumps flooding my flesh.

"*Shh ...*" Vidar soothed, leaving a trail of kisses over my shoulder and neck, rubbing his hands over my arms.

"I need air." I whispered.

I rose abruptly from his lap, grabbed my cloak from the drying rack, and exited the hall before Vidar or anyone could say a word. In front of the closed doors, I hauled my cloak around my shoulders and marched off into the night.

I drew no comfort from Domnall and Vidar's reassurances to Jan. Thorn was venomous, he was certain Jan had murdered Thóra; would he really allow this to be settled with just a conversation? He hadn't been open to listening tonight, and teamed with his resentment towards waiting three more days, would he truly be willing to listen to Jan when the meeting came? Thorn Arnsteinson was quick to draw his sword and hesitant to sheath it. I truly believed he would have fought even Vidar to avenge his sister's 'death'.

Thóra and Thórvar's disappearance was certainly mysterious, and in truth, we didn't know if they were alive or dead, only that Thóra had chosen to leave Jan. We had sent out many convoys, many search parties, but had not received any knowledge of their whereabouts. I wondered whether her family were hiding her, but that didn't make sense; why would Thorn be so passionate about avenging her death if he knew where she was?

Thorn seemed convinced beyond a shadow of a doubt that Jan had killed Thóra and was adamant to exact his revenge – not something a brother would do if trying to hide his sister from her ex-husband. The wiser decision would be to keep quiet, not twist the knife in the wound, so to speak ...

Norsemen weren't known for lying, though. The Norse valued honour in the highest regard – if a Norseman wanted to kill another man for a slight, he would do so honestly and openly, for the sake of his honour. In fact, by law, a man who killed another under the cover of darkness and secrecy would be put to death for the murder; but a man who killed another in broad daylight with witnesses, exclaiming the reasons for his action, would only be fined for taking his foe's life.

I shuddered.

The darkness and loathing in Thorn's eyes had been terrifying. Thorn Arnsteinson intended to kill Jan, that much was sure. He would settle for nothing but Jan's blood.

I stopped.

Thorn's gruff, gravelly voice sounded ahead of me. His words carried indistinctly on the breeze, but his tone was angry and impatient. One of his companions spoke – I strained my ears, trying to make out their words, but to no avail. Whatever they were saying, I wouldn't be able to hear it from this distance. I sped up my steps, scarpering after them as quickly and quietly as possible.

An oil lamp or two still burned in the marketplace, outside some of the shop doorways, but most of the lamps had been put out. I saw Thorn and his gang's silhouettes headed towards the shore. I bolted behind one of the shops and crouched down to catch my breath.

My heart hammered, throbbing in my ears. Sweat dripped down my forehead and the palms of my shaking hands were damp. I yanked off my cloak, and, with a deep breath, I rose to my feet and peered through the night, trying to find Thorn and his men again.

The darkness was both a blessing and a curse. On one hand, it concealed me from Thorn and his gang; there were no fires or lamps burning on the shores, I would be safe from their sight. But on the other hand, though I appreciated the safety of the night, it was not easy to spot Thorn and his gang. The moon was hidden beneath heavy clouds, offering not even the slightest light to see them by.

RISE TO FALL

I stepped out of my hiding spot and slunk to the shoreline, cloak abandoned on the ground behind the shop. I strained my ears to hear them once more.

There! Over the sloshing of the cold waves, I heard a loud, deep laugh ahead of me and stole after them.

I stumbled blindly, following nothing but their voices and the occasional view of their dark silhouettes, I pursued them towards the waters. Their voices grew louder and louder until I froze suddenly – so close to them, now. I crouched down to the ground, spying orbs of light from burning torches ahead of me, lighting up their longship which bobbed on the waters ahead of me.

It was a *snekkja*, a small warship commonly used for raiding, and seated upon all twenty benches were men. The *snekkja* was not full – these ships carried just over forty men, but there was possibly twenty-five to thirty seated, not including Thorn and the four who had accompanied him into Aros. Not enough men to fill a *snekkja*, but plenty of men to fight.

Thorn and his gang climbed onto the *snekkja*, took their seats and together the men began to row, drawing the ship out of the bay. I watched them slowly row to the edge of the mainland where they moored the *snekkja*. Once moored, they disembarked and hauled their trunks onto the land. They were making camp.

***

I APPROACHED VIDAR, who had risen at my arrival, and slumped my body against his. He enveloped me in his arms, and I crumpled from his touch. Carefully Vidar sat back down, pulling me onto his lap. I melted into him, nestling my face into his shoulder, curling around him, yearning for the safety and reassurance of his body.

"Thorn and his men are setting up camp on the mainland."

Vidar kissed the top of my head.

"Worry not, little fawn," Vidar whispered. "This *will* be settled."

CHAPTER ELEVEN

LIKE A GLASSY cerulean snake, a river coiled around Aros, cutting it from the mainland which surrounded the town on three sides. Upon the flat and forested mainland across the river to the west, we grew fields of rye, barley and hay, watched over by the few families who lived there.

It was on the northern mainland where Thorn and his men camped, intelligently staying close to their *snekkja* and avoiding the longhouses that guarded our crops and hay fields. Once or twice, a small contingent of Thorn's men would venture into Aros to visit the alehouse or the marketplace, but not many and not often. Thorn Arnsteinson himself had not stepped foot in Aros since accusing Jan of murder at the hall.

Three days had passed quickly; today was the day Vidar would hear Thorn and settle this matter once and for all. Jan had sailed to Roskilde and back without any rest, bringing with him as many witnesses as possible, including his younger brother Jakob, to support him in his dispute with Thorn Arnsteinson.

I hardly slept the past few nights, so consumed with anxiety. I fondled the skirts of my gown, pleating the deep scarlet fabric, twisting it in my fingers. I eyed the fine material and my frown deepened – it was the finest gown I owned, my favourite dress, but today I couldn't stand it. It was red, like blood …

Should I wear this? I wondered as I examined it. *Am I tempting fate by wearing such a colour?*

With a shudder and a deep sigh, I smoothed my skirts and touched a hand to my hair. While Rowena had tended to my hair this morning, I could hardly sit still; my legs and hands shook, I had jerked this way and that at the slightest noise. Repeatedly she had plaited my hair, pinned it to my head then unpinned it and rearranged the plaits thanks to my fidgeting. Patiently she tweaked my hair through all my jittering. She plaited the locks that framed my face, drew them back and tied them tightly together with a skinny thong of leather at the back of my head, the rest of my hair left loose, curls of chestnut cascading to the small of my back.

Rowena had lined my upper and lower eyelids with black kohl, deepening and intensifying the amber shade of my eyes, and reddened my lips with a mixture of pressed cherries, blueberries, plum skins and honey. I was then adorned with a variety of silver trinkets, bracelets and rings, but as usual I had my turtle shell brooches with a string of beads hung between them pinned to the front of my gown, gifts from my late adoptive father Birger Bloody Sword – I wore them day in, day out, no matter the occasion, ever since he had gifted them to me when I was a child.

As the jarlkona, I was always well-dressed and ornamented with silver or gold – I was a breathing symbol of my husband's wealth, an important portrayal to those in the neighbouring settlements that swore fealty to Vidar. Ornately decked in finery, I was living proof their jarl was rich enough to protect their honour, security and prosperity, and could afford to reward them richly should they fight and raid alongside him. However, never would I be so finely attired for disputes between the karls, the freemen and landowners of the Norse society. I gazed at Vidar who sat still as a statue beside me, his shield tucked between our high-backed, ornately carved chairs, his sword propped behind his chair, hidden but close enough at hand should he need it.

Vidar's freshly washed hair was plaited back and bound with a leather thong, so long it reached below his shoulder blades. The back and sides of his head were cleanly shaven, baring the blue-black tattoos etched into his scalp. His eyes were also lined with the black kohl makeup, amplifying their icy paleness.

Vidar wore a royal blue long-sleeved tunic, hemmed with pale blue silk imported from Asia and embroidered with silver thread. He wore straight-legged grey linen trousers and his sturdy, thick black leather boots, and around his waist was his leather belt with a silver buckle, a money pouch, various tools and of course his trusty utility knife hanging from it. Vidar's wrists jangled with silver bands, silver rings glittered on his fingers, and around his neck hung a few silver chains. Dangling from one chain was a grand, intricately detailed pendant of Thor's hammer, Mjölnir.

Vidar knew of the platoon of men Thorn had brought with him and decided that he, our children and I, would be decked in finery as a point to Thorn Arnsteinson and his men – Jan had the Jarl of Aros, the Jarl's men and the Jarl's wealth supporting him. Despite Vidar's bias in favour of Jan Jötunnson, I knew Vidar would make a fair judgement on the dispute. He was an honourable man after all. But should Thorn Arnsteinson threaten my safety or the safety of any other townsperson in Aros, the Jarl of Aros had no qualms about slaying Thorn and every man he had brought with him.

I had rolled my eyes at the idea that a few nice garments and some sparkling jewellery would make such a point, but I appeased my husband, and the children and I were grandly adorned and arrayed, and my husband was happy.

"For a man who was so outraged to wait three more days, time does not seem to be an issue for him now," I muttered. "He's late."

Word of the strangers and Thorn's accusation of Jan had travelled around Aros and far beyond it quickly. Like churchgoers eagerly awaiting a bishop's sermon, it appeared as though every townsperson of Aros crammed inside the hall's four walls – the doors were wide open, and a sea of heads gawped in from outside, bobbing up and down to spy the happenings inside the hall.

Of course, nothing was happening.

Vidar and I sat in our tall, high-backed chairs upon one of the platforms, our children neatly seated beside us. With Alffinna in her arms, Caterine stood beside the children, white as a ghost, her lips drawn together so tightly I could hardly see them, and her long, skinny eyebrows were high upon her forehead in perfectly rounded arches. In front of us was Jan, standing with his sword strapped to his hip and a woollen cloak pinned over his shoulder, dark heavy bags hung beneath his bloodshot eyes.

Chattering buzzed around us, droning in a continuous hum. Every townsperson's face held the same expression, every whisper held the same words, *where is Thorn Arnsteinson?*

The whispering stopped so abruptly, my ears rang from the sudden silence. I hadn't realised how loud the murmuring had been. I followed the townspeople's gaze to the doors, where the sea of spectators parted to reveal Thorn, still filthy and greasy and dressed in the same dirty outfit he had appeared in days ago, his four usual companions and a good portion of his platoon behind him, storming down the dirt path towards the hall. No one spoke or even blinked as Thorn entered the Jarl of Aros's hall.

Thorn stood before us, a good arm's distance from Jan. He reeked of stale ale and the musky stench of sweat; it must have been some time since he had bathed last – since he'd last changed his clothes. Thorn's clothing was ragged and dirty, patches of grime stained his flesh and the stink emanating from him was repulsive. I rolled my lips together and flared my nostrils, attempting to maintain a respectable manner despite Thorn's abhorrent stench, but from the corner of my eye I saw a vast amount of townspeople, and unfortunately my children, wrinkle their noses or flinch in revulsion, commenting on Thorn's foul appearance and nauseating odour.

"I am Thorn Arnsteinson of Hedeby. Jan Jötunnson Jarlufson killed my sister, his *second* wife, Thóra Arnsteinsdóttir, and her child. I am here to claim my rightful vengeance upon him." Thorn announced.

Vidar surveyed him briefly, a line deepening between his furrowed brows as he scowled at the filthy man before him.

"What proof have you, Thorn Arnsteinson?" Vidar asked, his voice low and unnervingly calm.

"They are nowhere to be found," Thorn growled, a vein throbbing upon his sloping forehead from his instant anger.

"What proof have you that Jan Jarlufson killed your sister, Thorn Arnsteinson?" Vidar reiterated in the same quiet, eerily calm tone. "Do you have witnesses that can corroborate your claim?"

"My sister has been missing for two years." Thorn spat. "Had Thóra simply left Jarlufson, as he claimed, she would have returned to Hedeby, but she did not. She would have contacted her kin, but she did not. We have not heard from nor seen Thóra since she birthed her child four years ago!"

"Jan Jötunnson Jarlufson," Vidar said. His whole body seemed rooted in place but for his icy eyes that turned to Jan. "What say you?"

"Thorn Arnsteinson is wrong, I did not kill my wife, nor *our* child," Jan replied. "I was raiding the coast of Francia with a fleet from Roskilde when Thóra left me."

A growl rolled in Thorn's throat, but he was wise enough to keep his mouth shut and not speak out.

"What proof have you?" Vidar asked.

"I have over a hundred men of the town of Roskilde who can corroborate my whereabouts, for they were the ones I raided alongside." Jan declared, not caring to hide the smug tone in his voice. "I also have the word of Sigvin Eiriksdóttir, who was the last person to speak to my wife, Thóra, and whom Thóra left a message with, to give me on my return."

"Are any of Jan Jarlufson's witness here today?" Vidar asked, examining the crowd.

Immediately Jan's brother Jakob, ten men and a small woman with red hair, assumedly Sigvin, stepped forward.

"*Já.*" They declared.

"You have sailed from Roskilde to corroborate Jan Jarlufson's innocence?"

"*Já*, Jarl Vidar." The twelve nodded.

"This proves nothing!" Thorn snarled, his bloodshot blue eyes bulging from his sunken sockets. "How soon did you return to Roskilde after Thóra's disappearance, Jarlufson?"

Jan looked between Thorn and Vidar, who briefly nodded his head.

"A handful of days," Jan replied. "Yet more evidence I couldn't have killed my wife and child. As I keep saying, I wasn't even in Roskilde when she left me!"

"Did you search for her?" Thorn barked.

"I did!" Jan snapped. "I searched for her; my brother headed a search party looking for her as soon as he found her gone. We have searched–"

"A handful of days would have been more than enough time to find them." Thorn hissed, a bitter smile slithering across his face.

"Do you think I'm stupid enough to believe so many *skilled hunters and warriors* couldn't track a woman and her young child? Whether they fled by boat, by horse or by foot you would have found them! And I believe you did – and I believe you slew them in retaliation for her leaving you!"

"I did no such thing!" Jan roared, his hand whipping to the hilt of his sword.

"Where is my sister?" Thorn snarled, wrapping his fingers around the grip of his own sword, dirt caked beneath his overgrown nails.

"Do *not* unsheathe your weapons," Vidar warned them both. "Neither of you will draw blood in my hall. There is no proof that Jan killed Thóra Arnsteinsdóttir–"

"He did! I know in my gut and the marrow of my bones he did!" Thorn shouted.

"Perhaps you're so overwhelmed by your disgusting stench you can't think straight." Jan sneered. "Bathe and clean yourself and you may see things clearer. You look and smell like a shit-covered pig!"

"I have taken an oath to not wash until I find my sister! And what of you, Jan Jötunnson? You claimed to feel the *same sadness* as me over the loss of your wife and son, yet the moment I arrived in Aros, I found you with your tongue rammed down a whore's throat!" Thorn thundered, jerking his head to Caterine, who flinched at Thorn's abrupt movement towards her. "I left my own wife and children to search for Thóra, but what of you? You searched for a short while, then found yourself a new woman to shove your cock into! That doesn't sound like the *same sadness* to me! If you felt the *same sadness*, you would spend every waking moment looking for your wife, but instead, you are here laughing and dancing and getting your cock wet by a thrall whore!"

Jan ripped his sword from his scabbard and swung the blade at Thorn in a huge, swift arch–

"That's enough!" Vidar bellowed.

Jan stopped, his sword inches from Thorn's throat. The gold and orange flames of the firepit reflected in the shining metal surface of Jan's sharp blade. Thorn didn't even flinch.

"Neither of you will draw blood in my hall!"

Every man, woman and child inside the hall were still. Every face was ashen, gawping at Vidar, the fire and danger blazing in his icy eyes accentuated by the slather of black kohl framing them. Cold fingers of fear ran down my spine and with a shiver I tore my eyes from my husband's terrifying expression and found Thorn's men amongst the townspeople, gripping their weapons and shields.

"Not only is Thorn Arnsteinson falsely accusing me of killing my wife, but he stands before me insulting my honour!" Jan seethed.

"You have no honour, you villain!" Thorn hissed.

Jan's sword hand twitched. It was obvious Jan was using every ounce of willpower to restrain himself from slaying Thorn where he stood.

"Enough!" Vidar commanded. He gripped the arms of his chairs. An exasperated, breathy laugh fell from his lips, but there was no smile upon his face and his eyes glowed with fury. "Neither of you have any evidence – not Thorn to prove his accusation, nor Jan to defend against it. All you both have is hearsay! How am I meant to exact fair justice on a claim that cannot be proven or disproven?"

With a collective gasp, all eyes popped open wide and turned from the Jarl of Aros to gawp at the platform beside him. Young Birger had risen to his feet. He cleared his throat and swallowed deeply. His brows were furrowed, and he stared at Vidar bravely, scowling deeply to hide the obvious nervousness that drained his golden skin of its usual glow. Young Birger stepped forward beside his father and rested his pale blue eyes upon Jan and Thorn.

"There is no evidence to support either of their arguments, though of the two, I believe Jan has the stronger claim." Young Birger said, his voice shaking slightly as he spoke.

I balled my hands into fists on my lap at the sight of Thorn; he glared daggers at Young Birger. Young Birger didn't quail under Thorn's glower, thank the gods, instead he cleared his throat again, and his words came out stronger and steadier.

"I suggest they settle this matter through *hólmganga*. Jan Jötunnson Jarlufson and Thorn Arnsteinson are both intent to fight one another, and so they should be allowed. They will fight until one draws the first blood, then their dispute will be over. They can then turn their efforts to finding Thóra and the child rather than wasting their energy arguing over it here."

Every jaw dropped at the boldness and audacity of Vidar and my eldest son. My heart stopped, and my breath knotted in my throat from surprise and yet Young Birger was right, it was the obvious and best way to settle Thorn and Jan's dispute, at least for now.

"I agree," Vidar replied, a tiny smile curling the corners of his lips, pride exuding from him as he gazed briefly at our eldest son. "Jötunnson, Arnsteinson, you are both intent to spill each other's blood, so you will. What say you both?"

"*Já.*" They exclaimed, eagerly and in unison.

"In seven days, you will meet in front of my hall at midday. As Arnsteinson has accused Jötunnson of murder, so Arnsteinson is the challenger. Should his blood spill first, Arnsteinson will receive no compensation. Should Jötunnson's blood spill first, as the insulted party he will be forced to pay Arnsteinson a *hólmlausn* of three marks of silver." Vidar said. "You are allowed three shields and two swords each, and a man each to hold your shields for you. The moment blood spills, the fighting will end.

"Should Jötunnson not arrive for the *hólmganga* but Arnsteinson does, then Jötunnson will be branded a *níðingr* and can no longer swear a legal oath or hear witness for man nor woman.

"Should Arnsteinson not arrive for the *hólmganga* but Jötunnson does, then Arnsteinson will be branded a *níðingr* and outlawed from Aros and Roskilde. Far worse is a man too cowardly to maintain an insult he has hurled than a man too cowardly to defend against it.

"Do you agree to the terms, Jötunnson, Arnsteinson?"

Jan and Thorn nodded, and Jan slowly sheathed his sword.

"Then it is settled. You have seven days to prepare yourselves."

***

SWEAT STREAMED DOWN every inch of my body, my flesh blazed with heat and I panted with exhaustion. As I caught my breath, I gazed down at the weapons in my sweat-drenched hands. In my right, the gorgeous sword Vidar had made for me a few years ago, and in my left was one of Vidar's battle-hardy shields.

Tapered slightly at the end, my sword was light, swift-striking and made of high-quality steel. The hilt was made of antler and decorating the three-lobed pommel and the crossguard was beautiful intricate silver knotwork. My gaze travelled down the bevelled channel of the blood groove that ran down the middle of the sharp, double-edged blade. The blood groove's purpose was practical, it lightened the blade and helped balance it, no matter what the dark name for it implied.

Unlike Vidar's swords, which had all tasted generations worth of blood, my sword had never bitten through human flesh. It hadn't even earned a name.

After the death of Jarl Erhardt Ketilsson, my first husband, Vidar and I had vowed to each other to never be separated again. When Vidar travelled to the settlements and territories loyal to him, I was at his side; when Vidar left for raids, I would be there with him, always. No matter the danger, we kept our vow. A year after Æsa's birth, Vidar had organised a raid along the Frisian coast – a common raiding route. It was the first raid and battle he had planned since he had led the people of Roskilde to rise against Jarl Erhardt.

Before we set for the raid, Vidar gifted me this fine sword, sparing no expense in its creation. It would be an heirloom, as all swords were due to their expensive and precious nature, but I was determined to fight alongside my husband and proudly wield my beautiful weapon. I had not seen battle though; Vidar had convinced me to stay back while the seasoned warriors led the attack and so my sword's thirst for blood was left unquenched.

With a roar, I lunged at my target, a tall, fat tree trunk, slamming my circular wooden shield against it before bringing my sword around and slashing into it. Chips of bark splintered from the trunk and cut through the air from the mighty gash. As quickly as I had attacked, I pulled back, readying myself to strike again. I held my shield in front of me, lifted my sword above my head and charged–

"What's bothering you, little fawn?"

Surprised by Vidar's sudden question, I stumbled and fell to the ground.

"Why would you distract me?" I snapped, embarrassedly scrambling to my feet.

"I'm sorry." Vidar smiled, striding over to me.

I shirked away from his outstretched hand and turned my sight back to the tree trunk.

"What do you want?" I barked.

"I'm worried about you," Vidar said calmly. "Something's upset you."

"What makes you think that?" I asked, charging at the tree and striking it once, twice, three times.

"I can't think of anything that tree has done to deserve such treatment unless you are just taking your temper out on it." Vidar smirked, watching me with a mixture of amusement and pride.

Admittedly, I wasn't bad, but I wasn't at all the best with a blade; I excelled with archery more than with the sword. Dedicatedly, I practised with the blade, intent on becoming proficient with it. It was also, as Vidar recognised, an excellent way of relieving anger or stress.

"What's bothering you, little fawn?" Vidar pressed. "You've been out here for hours, every evening for the past four days. I haven't seen you practise this hard – *ever*, in fact. What's wrong, my love?"

I threw my sword and shield to the ground. Across the way, the fjord glittered in the fading sunlight. I strode to the water's edge and knelt beside it, reaching in and taking handfuls of the chilled liquid to splash over my face and rinse the sweat from my hands. My joints popped and cracked; my body ached. I pulled my leather boots from my throbbing feet, lifted my skirts and dipped my feet into the water. A deep sigh of pleasure rolled from my throat as the icy coldness soothed them. Winter may have been just around the corner, but my body blazed like a pyre and the chill of the water was delicious and welcomed.

"Little fawn–"

"The *hólmganga*." I confessed.

"Ah," Vidar said, gently lowering himself beside me. He took my dripping hand and kissed it. "Why are you worried about that? Jötunnson can take care of himself."

"Can he? Thorn didn't even flinch when Jan swung his sword to his throat. He didn't dodge it or draw his own weapon or anything. He wasn't afraid – he wasn't afraid to be hit, to die or anything – he was completely unafraid."

"Then this will be a worthy dual for Jötunnson. Save for me, I don't know anyone who could give Jötunnson a decent fight." Vidar winked.

"But–"

"If Jötunnson loses, then he loses. He will have to deal with the consequences of agreeing to and losing a *hólmganga*." Vidar shrugged.

I glared at him with disbelief. He was so flippant when it was Jan Jötunnson's life at stake – Jan Jötunnson, Vidar's closest and dearest friend!

"I appreciate your worry for him, you're a good friend to him, little fawn. But there's nothing I can do – and even if there was, I wouldn't do a thing. They have agreed to the *hólmganga*, it is set. It'll be worse for Jötunnson if he backs out." Vidar warned. "This is a dual of honour, and Jötunnson *must* fight it – you know this. Little fawn, Jötunnson is one of the greatest warriors I've had the honour of fighting alongside, and between him and Thorn, Jötunnson has size and youth on his side as well as battle experience and talent."

"Thorn isn't that old, maybe only a handful of years older than you. *And* you've never seen Thorn fight." I pointed out. "What if he is a better fighter than Jan?"

"Then Jan will lose." Vidar said.

"Vidar, Thorn *isn't* going to stop at drawing blood! Thorn won't listen to reason about Thóra's disappearance and he doesn't want to listen – he wants to kill Jan!"

"Then Jan will die an honourable death," Vidar said quietly, his eyes settled on the fjord twinkling before us. "And I will avenge him."

CHAPTER TWELVE

A CROWD HAD already formed in the marketplace, around the *hólmgöngustaðir* where Jan and Thorn were to have their *hólmganga*. Almost every townsperson of Aros was in attendance, and many families from allegiant settlements were, too. Though *hólmganga* usually took place on small deserted islands (the word itself literally meant 'going to the island'), there were no small deserted islands near the coast of Aros, so the centre of the marketplace was cordoned off for the duel.

The *hólmgöngustaðir* consisted of a large beige cloak about five *ells* square, with loops at each of the four corners, staked to the ground using wide-headed pegs. Three sets of furrows were cut into the ground framing the cloak, each about a foot apart and at the outer four corners were *höslur* posts with ropes tied to them. It was inside these posts and upon the cloak that Jan and Thorn would fight.

Vidar, the children, the thralls and I approached the *hólmgöngustaðir*. I tried to remain as outwardly calm as Vidar, but inside me raged a storm of anxiety. When I awoke that morning, Vidar had concernedly commented on how pale and sickly I looked. I was as nauseous as I looked. Vidar tried to convince me to stay home in bed, but I had to go. Though I feared the *hólmganga*, I had to attend it; I had to support Jan. I couldn't just stay home and worry over the duel's outcome – I had to see it for myself; I had to see Jan win!

The crowd parted for Vidar, the children and me to stand at the front and view the duel unobscured. Alffinna squirmed in my arms, I chided her softly and rearranged her, so she could look outward. She glanced around, just like my four other children. They had seen *hólmganga* take place before, but this was the first time we had seen one of our dear friends participate in one.

Dressed in charcoal trousers and a tunic of forest green, white hems embroidered with golden thread, Vidar wore his sword at his hip, his light-grey wolf-skin cloak fastened over one shoulder so his weapon was readily available should he need it.

The children wore blues and golds, and I had scolded Melisende when I saw her dressing Alffinna in red. There was to be nothing red worn today – I had even refused to let them redden my cheeks and lips. No, I did not want to see red today. The red of Jan's blood would be enough.

I was dressed in black.

"Look, there's Jötunnson." Vidar murmured, pointing to the alehouse.

I watched Jan exit the alehouse, helmet upon his head and two short swords in his hands, one tied to his wrist with a leather thong, and his shield tied over his back. He wore his usual dazzling pearly grin and a tunic the same sapphire colour of his eyes. Ebbe, Domnall, Einarr, Finnvarðr and Lars, who was carrying two extra shields for Jan to use during the dual, walked with him. Together, the men came to stand with us on the west side of the *hólmgöngustaðir*. Of all the gods in Asgard, I hoped Jan hadn't drunk too much before his fight.

"Will you gift me a kiss, for good luck?" Jan asked Caterine, winking at her.

The Francian thrall grasped Jan's face and pressed a long, sweet kiss to his lips. Jan's eyes grew wide with surprise and his cheeks pinkened with pleasure at her tender touch.

"Jarlkona, are you well?" Rowena whispered. "Your flesh is the same colour as ash!"

"*Oïl*, you're much paler than this morning. Are you sure you should not return to the hall?" Melisende said.

"I'm fine, *þakka fyrir*." I replied firmly, my eyes trained on Thorn.

From the shore Thorn came, helmet upon his head and two short swords in his hands, one tied to his wrist with a leather thong, and his shield slung over his back. His usual four men marched beside him, one carrying two extra shields for Thorn to use during the duel.

Behind the five Hedeby men, were the twenty-five or so others that had sailed with them. The fleet of men trudged up the beach in grey and black, like a storm cloud borne of the sea. As Thorn and his favourite four came to the edge of the *hólmgöngustaðir*, the others stopped at the outskirts of the marketplace. They all had shields and weapons in their hands.

"You are not a man's equal and not a man at heart!" Thorn roared at Jan from across the *hólmgöngustaðir*.

"I am as much a man as you!" Jan replied.

The traditional *hólmganga* phrases spoken, both men made their way into the centre of the *hólmgöngustaðir*, ready to fight one another.

"Before the dual commences, first we must recite the *hólmgangulog*," Vidar said loudly, eyeing the men at the shoreline. "Each man is allowed two swords, both only one *ell* long–"

At this, Hallmundr and Ebbe strode over to Jan and Lars. Hallmundr took Jan's blades in turn and measured them against his arm, ascertaining the blade was no bigger than the distance from his elbow to his wrist, an *ell* in length. Once confirmed, they made their way to Thorn and his shield-bearer to measure Thorn's blades, the men scowling at each other during the process.

"–And each man is allowed three shields and a shield-bearer." Vidar said. "When all three shields are broken, he must rely solely on his weapons. Each man will strike the other with a single blow in turn, starting with the insulted party.

"Each man must stand his ground. Should either man step a foot outside of the *höslur*, then it will be called 'he yields ground' and is a mark of a *níðingr*. Should both feet exit the *höslur* then it will be 'he flees' and he will be branded a *níðingr* and will be the defeated.

"The moment blood is spilt upon the cloak, the duel will end, and he whose blood spilt will be the defeated and will pay the winner a *hólmlausn* of three marks of silver. The *hólmganga* should *not* end in death," Vidar said, specifically glaring at Thorn. "But if it is so, then the survivor will be granted the defeated man's every belonging and the slain man's kin are forbidden from seeking compensation and *wergild*."

Thorn scowled acidly at Jan, and Jan smirked back. They nodded and murmured "*Já*." to Vidar, both eager to fight one another.

"Then let the *hólmganga* commence."

Deep, throaty caws rang through the sky like the tolling of church bells. I peered above and there was the sharp black silhouette of the raven I feared. I couldn't see its eye, but I knew in the pit of my stomach it was the blind raven. I gripped Alffinna tightly, my arms wrapped around her protectively, my heart pounding in my throat.

The raven circled high above; there would be death today.

Jan, as the insulted party, was allowed the first blow. He lifted his sword and brought it down upon Thorn, who blocked it smartly with his shield and shoved forward against the blade, causing Jan to stagger back before he swung his own sword at Jan's side. Swiftly, Jan blocked Thorn's blade with his shield.

Jan and Thorn's eyes were locked, and their mouths widened into grins as they paced around the *hólmgöngustaðir*, not turning their backs nor even blinking. There was no happiness in their smiles; they were two wolves baring their fangs.

Neither Thorn nor Jan possessed the eerie blaze of blood lust in their eyes like Vidar did when he beheld an enemy, but both Jan and Thorn had the darkness of hatred swirling in their eyes, and with each heavy strike they landed upon each other's shield, their determination to kill each other grew ever more apparent.

Neither man was fighting just to wound.

The men swung harder, faster. Iron collided with wood, shield crashed against shield, blade clanged against blade. Blow after blow, strike after strike, each man pounded upon the other's shield. Experienced *hólmgangumenn*, and those who had watched them, knew the best way to win was to destroy his opponent's shields as quickly as possible, which was exactly what Jan and Thorn were trying to do.

Destroying the shields deprived their opponent of their best defence and deprived them of their shield-bearer as well, though neither Thorn's shield-bearer nor Lars, Jan's shield-bearer, had been able to do much to aid their partners, due to the incredible speed both men fought and swung.

Thorn charged at Jan, who managed to dodge his attack. Thorn stumbled to a stop, trying to slow down in time so he wouldn't pass the first border of the cloak.

RISE TO FALL

Thorn made it.

He turned just in time to lift his shield and defend Jan's blow, as Jan brought his sword down upon Thorn's shield. Immediately a huge rend cracked through the centre of the shield, spraying shards of wood from his strike.

Jan smirked at Thorn, pleased with his blow – he was almost down one shield already! Thorn chuckled darkly, eyeing the deep crack in his shield, both men's arms shaking from the pressure of their opponent pushing against them. Thorn roared, swung his sword and smashed it against Jan's shield in a flash of *berserkr*-like fury. A gasp tore through the crowd and Thorn's men cheered as Jan's shield shattered.

My stomach sank. How did he do that? Thorn destroyed Jan's shield in one hit!

The smirk quickly disappeared from Jan's face as he slowly backed away from Thorn and threw the remnants of his shield to the ground. Lars tossed Jan his second shield, which Jan skillfully caught with one hand, slipping his arm through the handle on the back and holding the grip tightly. Once ready, Jan and Thorn circled each other again, a nerve-wracking dance before the attack.

Jan managed another swing and landed it on Thorn's shield, shattering it. Again, they separated, and Thorn was tossed another shield and swiftly attacked Jan, who parried the blow with his sword. My heart ricocheted in my chest as I watched them battle.

With blow after blow, both Jan and Thorn quickly destroyed each other's shields. Unfortunately, Jan had become shield-less first, much to Thorn and his men's delight. It was Jan's turn now, he raised his sword and slammed it down upon Thorn's final shield, breaking it apart, but the tip of Jan's blade caught the iron boss in the centre of Thorn's shield, and his blade shattered into pieces.

The crowd leapt backwards to avoid the shards of flying metal slicing through the air. I stumbled backwards but luckily Vidar grabbed me by the crook of the arm before I fell to the ground. He took Alffinna from me and gave her to the jaw dropped Caterine, who barely tore her eyes from the fight. Vidar held me as I trembled, but I didn't take my eyes from the fight.

Jan only had one sword now, but Thorn Arnsteinson had two. Jan had height on his side, I kept telling myself, he's younger than Thorn, he can defeat him. *Oh Týr, let Jan defeat him!*

Clothes ripped, shields and a blade destroyed, Thorn had even managed to chop off a lock of Jan's hair, but no blood had been spilt. Thorn cackled gleefully, holding a sword in each hand, but Jan smiled back at him, holding his arm out as though carrying an invisible shield, his sword high, poised ready for Thorn's attack.

Thorn lunged, swinging his swords wildly, and Jan somehow managed to manoeuvre each swing, parrying the two blades with his single one, veering and swerving, rolling and jumping, twisting and turning. Thorn slashed at Jan, who dived out the way, rolling over the dirt ground, almost slipping over the first border. Jan whipped his sword up and thankfully blocked Thorn's attack, as Thorn tried to slam both blades in unison upon Jan,

The noise of metal on metal was deafening!

Holding the hilt of his sword with both hands, Jan managed to shove Thorn backwards and leapt to his feet. Thorn swung one sword at Jan's hip, but Jan blocked it. Struggling against each other, pushing against one another's blades, Thorn lifted his second sword and, with a wide arch, brought it down upon Jan with all his might.

Women screamed, men roared, but Thorn's mighty strike did not slash through Jan's flesh – Jan caught Thorn's attack, seizing Thorn's wrist while bringing his knee up into Thorn's stomach. As the warrior staggered back, Jan kicked Thorn squarely in the chest with the strength of a horse, sending Thorn flying backwards, over the ropes tied to the *höslur* posts, and landing in a crumpled heap at Vidar and my feet.

We leapt backwards before Thorn could crash into us; Rowena pulled Einar and Æsa away, Melisende grabbed Sander by the shoulder and yanked him back with her, Caterine jumped to the side, clutching Alffinna.

"Thorn Arnsteinson is defeated!" Vidar roared, grinning from ear to ear at Thorn panting and red-faced front of us.

"This little feud is over now." Jan declared as he exited the *hólmgöngustaðir* and approached Thorn, who got to his feet, fuming still. "I defeated you and shamed you in front of all these people for nothing, brother-in-law – you are now outlawed from Roskilde and Aros for nothing! I did not kill Thóra, nor our child! But I propose that together you and I can work to find them if you are willing."

"You liar!" Thorn roared, overwhelmed with fury. "You *vámr*! You *níðingr*! Still you lie!"

"Thorn, by Odin's beard, you *fífl*! You're so consumed by your ridiculous theory you won't hear reason!"

"You speak no reason or truth, Jan Jarlufson! I will avenge my sister's death – I will avenge her child!" Thorn snarled, lifting his sword in front of him. "I will avenge them with the blood of your whore!"

"I didn't kill Thora and Thórvar–" Jan bellowed, panic crashing over his face as Thorn spun around and swung his sword at Caterine. "*Nei*! Don't touch her!"

But it was too late.

Caterine's scream ripped through the air as Thorn sword struck her. The sharp blade slit through her neck and across her chest–

"Alffinna!" I screamed, my baby daughter's ear-piercing cries ringing out.

Caterine fell to the ground, a look of shock frozen to her beautiful, blood-spattered face, my young daughter still clasped in her arms. Caterine's blood gushed from her throat and chest, cascading over my baby who howled, her cries growing gurgled from Caterine's blood pouring into her mouth. I lunged to them and tore my daughter from my dead thrall's arms.

"What name did you say?" Thorn demanded, eyes round as coins and he reeled around to gape at Jan. "What is the name of the child?"

"Thórvar, your sister and my son!" Jan snarled.

"Thórvar?" Thorn gasped.

"Vidar!" I shrieked, cradling Alffinna in my arms, her cries faltering. "He cut her! He cut Alffinna's throat!"

There upon the delicate flesh of my young daughter's neck was a deep, hideous gash, gushing blood. Vomit filled my throat, tears streamed from my eyes and dripped onto her little face. With a trembling hand, I tried to cover her wound, seal it and stop it from bleeding, begging my baby to stay alive. Alffinna writhed in pain inside my arms, her little fingers and tiny fingernails clawing and scratching at my hand. Alffinna's amber eyes glared at me, round as coins, full of horror, and a soft wheeze murmured from her throat. Pain exploded inside my chest like I had been struck by a battering ram as I felt my heart fall to pieces.

Suddenly, she was motionless.

No breath or sound fell from her lips.

Alffinna was dead.

"He killed my baby!" I screeched.

Vidar lunged at Thorn, quick as lightning, silent as the night, and grabbed his neck. Thorn dropped his weapons, whipping his hands to Vidar's, clawing at them, trying to pull them from him. Thorn's eyes bulged from their sockets in shock as Vidar's fingers tightened around his throat. Thorn's face turned a hideous scarlet and purple, his breath came in rasping spurts, and saliva oozed from his mouth

"You have failed to avenge your sister!" Vidar seethed. "But you have succeeded in striking a feud between your family and mine! I will not fail as you have – I will avenge my daughter! I will not rest until every member of your kin is dead!"

A series of pops and cracks sounded from Thorn's neck. Thorn's hands suddenly dropped to his sides, limp, and the stench of his shit ripped through the air. Vidar dropped Thorn's lifeless body to the ground, disgusted. He ripped his sword from his scabbard and aimed it at the men on the outskirts of the marketplace.

"Come forward, kin of Thorn Arnsteinson!" Vidar thundered, eyeing the men with rage. They raised their weapons and shields and stepped forward. "Come meet your deaths!"

For a moment, Vidar and my eyes locked, both our hearts ripped from our chests. The fury on his face softened to sorrow as his gaze dropped to our dead daughter. He bit his lip, turned back to Thorn's kin, who sprinted towards us. Fierce animosity contorted his face once more, and Vidar charged towards the four men on the east side of the *hólmgöngustaðir*, a gust of air blowing me from the speed at which he ran. I clung to my young daughter's dead body with an iron-tight grip, caring not for the chaos erupting around me. Rowena scooped Einar into her arms, and Melisende lifted Æsa and grabbed Sander's shoulder.

In the corner of my eye, I saw Young Birger's fingers wrap around the hilt of the sword Thorn had used to kill Caterine and Alffinna, the blade still dripping with their blood. Melisende cried out his name, but dashed towards the battle, following his father, snatching a stray shield as he ran.

I stared after him and opened my mouth to call him back, but no words came out; only a long, aching shriek.

CHAPTER THIRTEEN

"*MUMIE*, CAN I see her?" Æsa asked timidly, her voice no louder than a whisper, as she slowly crept through the darkness towards me.

Still as a statue, as though Alffinna and I were carved from stone, a permanent effigy of a grieving mother and her lifeless babe, I didn't move a muscle as Æsa approached me. She peered over my arms at her dead little sister, who was still drenched in her own blood and Caterine's, her flesh cold and her limbs growing stiff. I had been sitting here in my high-backed chair for hours in the dark of the hall, the fire ignored as slowly it died.

Sander and Einar were lying in their beds, but I knew they weren't asleep. We were enveloped by night, but the blissful embrace of sleep wouldn't cradle us tonight. Rowena and Melisende's weeping drifted from the kitchen in muffled waves, and I didn't know where Vidar and Young Birger were.

Æsa slowly reached out and stroked Alffinna's cheek with her fingertip. She dragged her finger down her face, to the wound on her neck, quickly pulling her finger away as she touched a small patch of blood that had not dried yet, the coldness surprising her. Dried blood caked the soft creases of Alffinna's neck; the wound had stopped pouring many hours ago. I hadn't any idea if there was even any blood left inside Alffinna's body.

In fact, as I stared at my baby with aching eyes, though she seemed familiar, though she resembled my Alffinna, it was as though I was holding a child I'd never seen before. Alffinna's amber eyes would glisten and sparkle, but there was no light shining in the eyes of the child I held. Alffinna would gurgle and squeal constantly, but the child I held was silent. Alffinna would wreathe and wriggle in my arms, always tugging at my gown, constantly desperate for nourishment, but the child I held was still.

Alffinna's flesh was warm and pure and pale like porcelain, alight with a rosy glow, but the skin of the child I held was cold and grey.

Æsa wiped the blood onto the front of her dress and turned back to her sister. She leaned forward and pressed a soft kiss to the baby's cheek, red flecks of dried blood transferred to her lips, before scampering back to the sleeping area. I heard her crawl into bed with Sander, who held her and shushed her with a voice broken by grief.

I didn't know how long had passed by the time Vidar and Young Birger returned. The sounds of weeping had long since disappeared, I heard the rustle of the straw as my children shifted in their beds, but no one entered the main room. No one came near the grieving mother and her lifeless babe.

I lifted my eyes to my husband and son. Without saying a word, Vidar shut the doors behind himself and Young Birger, their bodies dripping with their enemies' blood. Young Birger glanced at me briefly, tossed Thorn's blood-drenched sword to the ground and stole into the kitchen to wash the blood from himself. Vidar carefully laid his sword and shield upon the table and crossed the room to fetch a few new logs of firewood, his hands scarlet, like he was wearing red gloves. As he stoked the fire back to life, Vidar finally looked at me.

"Aveline," Vidar murmured.

"Am I not your *little fawn* anymore?" I whispered.

"You are, forever and always." Vidar replied softly.

I made no comment or reply, I remained curled in my chair, unmoving, watching him through half-opened eyes. Vidar's head dropped, and he stalked off to the kitchen. I turned my eyes back to my baby and listened to the splash of water as he cleaned his hands in a bucket of water in the kitchen. When he returned, Vidar's hands and face were clean of blood, the hairs around his temple were damp, and he crouched down in front of me.

"I killed Thorn and all but one of his men."

"Am I meant to be pleased?" I replied coldly, stroking Alffinna's still face.

"I avenged Alffinna." Vidar whispered, an almost undetectable tone of pleading shadowing his words.

"Did Thorn's death bring my daughter back to life?"

"*Nei—*"

"Then I do not care."

Vidar rested his hands upon my knees, and his touch sent waves of ice crashing through my body. I shuddered violently and glared at him. My gaze didn't soften though his expression brought fresh tears to my eyes and pangs of guilt and sorrow ripped through me. Etched upon his face was the greatest sadness I'd ever seen.

"Let me hold my daughter." Vidar begged quietly.

Every fibre of my being refused to move; I didn't want to give my daughter to him. I wanted to stay here forever and rot with her in my arms. But the grief that radiated from Vidar's face, the anguish that aged him, that deepened every line and weighed down the corners of his lips in a despaired frown I'd never seen before from the lips that usually smirked and smiled … My grip on my daughter lessened and I allowed Vidar to take her from me.

Delicately, as though she was made of glass, Vidar cupped her little head in his hand, his other hand spread out beneath her back, and took her from me. Vidar tucked her neatly against his body and carefully rearranged her, moving her head to the crook of his arm, her little body cradled by his forearm. Gently he rested his other hand on her chest, using a finger to press down a fold of cloth that covered her chin, so he could gaze upon her face clearly.

The cold air rushed over my body, filling the place where Alffinna had lain, a screaming acknowledgement that my arms were empty, that my baby was gone from me. More than anything, I wanted to rip my baby from Vidar's arms and hold her again, curl up in the chair and stare at her again.

But I didn't take her.

Alffinna was Vidar's daughter, too.

Vidar pressed a kiss against her forehead and, for the first time in the fourteen years I had known him, I watched him weep. Tears streamed from his ice coloured eyes and trickled upon her, as he gazed upon her lifeless form.

"I'm sorry." Vidar whispered breathily.

I didn't know whether he was talking to Alffinna or me. His body shook and delicately he wiped his tears from her face.

"I'm sorry I didn't protect you ... I'm sorry I didn't protect our daughter."

Vidar was talking to both of us and I didn't say a word in reply; no word to comfort him, no word to console, no word to accept his apology. I remained silent and let the moments slip away painfully; I let his words hang in the air. Even if I had words to speak to him, I had no voice to say them anymore, sadness had stripped me of speech and left me hollow and empty of feeling, but for the dismal melancholy that whirled inside me.

Vidar collapsed to his knees as his grief grew greater, his tears fell heavier, and his body shuddered more violently. Slowly I slipped from my chair and kneeled beside him, leaning my head against his arm. His hand was resting on Alffinna's chest again, and I placed my hand upon it. Vidar twined his fingers with mine, and there we stayed, engulfed in our misery, weeping together, holding each other and our dead daughter, until the cold morning light streamed through the smokehole and shone on us like a spotlight illuminating our sorrow.

***

GENTLY I DRIPPED warm water from a cup, over Alffinna's face. It slid down her smooth forehead, down her soft cheeks, and a few droplets were caught in her long chestnut eyelashes, like tears. Her tiny body seemed so frail in comparison to when life flowed through her. Alffinna's head rested on my palm, the rest of her body sat in a small wooden tub of water as I bathed her for her funeral.

It had been three days since Alffinna and Caterine were killed.

The morning after their deaths, Rowena, Melisende and I had set to clean Alffinna and Caterine's bodies of the blood that stained them. We had stripped them of their filthy, soiled clothes, laid their bodies in wooden tubs on the floor and scrubbed the dried blood and dirt from them, turning the water red.

"What would you have me do with their clothes?" Melisende asked softly, holding Caterine and Alffinna's filthy garments against her chest.

"Leave them there," I said, tilting my head towards an empty chair. "I'll sort them out later."

After Caterine and Alffinna were bathed, we anointed their bodies with fragrant oils, to overpower the stench of death exuding from their stiff forms. We dressed them in clean, fresh clothes, plaited Caterine's hair and pinned it to her head and wrapped her body in a shroud. I laid Alffinna, swaddled in a fine linen blanket, in a basket with bunches of flowers tucked around her. As we prepared the bodies, Vidar, Jan and Young Birger dug Caterine's grave on the large square of green in front of our home, the burial ground.

Caterine was interred to the ground immediately, buried with spinning tools, food and the few little keepsakes she owned, including a wooden crucifix hung from a leather thong and a little figure Young Birger had carved for her. Rowena and I stood with Melisende between us, next to Caterine's grave, the children huddled closely beside us. Vidar and Jan, with crude shovels in their hands, stood at the edge of the burial grounds beside a few others from the town.

Caterine, like Rowena and Melisende, had been Christian, so in respect to her, we conducted a short Christian funeral for her before we buried her. We were without a Christian priest, so Melisende led the funeral for her, in Caterine and her native Francian tongue, though we said the prayers in Latin, the Church's official language, as all Christian prayers were.

We all remembered the prayers said at mass and at funerals in our homelands before we had come to Denmark, and my three thralls had continued to pray, in hushed, secretive tones, whilst living in my hall. Christianity had been hammered into us all from birth, though the four of us had been from different villages and different countries, the Latin prayers and order of service did not differ, and unitedly we prayed to the Christian God on Caterine's behalf.

I felt like a hypocrite as I made the sign of the cross, touching my forehead, my chest and each shoulder in turn. Rowena and Melisende (and Caterine in her life) were devout Christians, but I had given up on that God long ago and worshipped the Norse pantheon instead. But Caterine had loved her God and had believed in the power of prayer, so in her honour, I prayed, whether I believed in the words I spoke or not. Part of me wanted to, part of me was desperate to speak to her Christian God. I wanted to beg him to allow Caterine through the gates of Heaven. Caterine, who had risked her life to save my son, Sander, all those years ago; Caterine who lived through hell on earth when she was stolen away and forced into slavery; Caterine who raised and loved my children as though they were her own; Caterine who was my friend – Caterine deserved Heaven.

> *"Ave Maria, gratia plena, Dominus tecum.*
> *Benedicta tu in mulieribus,*
> *Et benedictus fructus ventris tui, Iesus.*
> *Sancta Maria, Mater Dei,*
> *Ora pro nobis peccatoribus, nunc,*
> *Et in hora mortis nostrae.*
> *Amen."*

Together, Rowena, Melisende and I recited the Hail Mary and the Lord's Prayer, and quickly a crowd had formed beside Jan and Vidar. The townspeople hadn't cared to mumble their agitated questions, instead, they turned to Vidar and demanded why the Jarlkona of Aros was performing a Christian funeral. Vidar lifted his hand to silence them, and their tongues stopped wagging, but their beady eyes stared at us, I could feel their inquisitive gazes weigh upon us. We ignored them and continued Caterine's funeral, continued praying for her soul.

With a shaking voice and tear-filled eyes, Melisende spoke the final prayer of the ceremony.

> "Absolve, we beseech Thee, O Lord,
> The soul of Thy servant Caterine,
> That she who is dead to the world,
> May live unto Thee,
> And wipe away by Thy most merciful forgiveness
> What sins she may have committed

GWENDOLINE SK TERRY

In life through human frailty.
Though our Lord Jesus Christ.
Amen."

Melisende slipped her quivering hands into Rowena and mine. Hands clasped tightly, offering each other strength, our heads bowed, we stared soberly at Caterine's body, finely wrapped in an ivory shroud and laid in the grave at our feet.

"Eternal rest give unto her, oh Lord," Melisende whispered hoarsely.

"And let perpetual light shine upon her." Rowena and I replied in unison.

"May she rest in peace."

"Amen."

"May her soul, and the souls of all the faithful departed, through the mercy of God, rest in peace."

"Amen." We three said together.

After a few long moments of silence, I slowly turned to Vidar and Jan and nodded. Together they approached us with their shovels, Vidar passed one of the three tools to Young Birger, and gently the three covered Caterine's body with dirt. We stayed there for the whole burial, my two thralls, my children and I, watching Caterine's body and her few belongings disappear under a mountain of earth, the pungent scent of soil filling our nostrils and tears falling from our eyes.

"*Adéu*, Caterine." I murmured, watching her vanish beneath the dirt.

Their tunics sticking to their sweat-drenched bodies, Vidar, Young Birger and Jan stepped back, wiping their brows and panting, the burial complete. Sander delicately brought forward a crude cross he had made from branches tied together with a cord, a Christian grave marker – the first of its kind in Aros. Solemnly, he shoved it into the earth at the head of the grave, to the shock and horror of the townspeople crowded around us.

With the ceremony completed, I staggered back to the hall. I passed the horrified crowd, my ears bombarded with their demands and hounding questions, but calmly and silently, I ignored them and returned to the hall where my own dead child lay in a basket, still days away from her own funeral.

***

CATERINE HAD BEEN buried for two days by the time the ship we had been waiting for from Roskilde docked in the harbour. It was finally time to put my daughter to rest.

There was an odd sensation reeling in the pit of my stomach as I readied Alffinna. Though she was still and grey and her body had bloated from death, there was a hesitance that slowed my movement. Though her body was a body no more, it was a corpse that *needed* to be cremated, I wanted to take as much time as I could to prepare her for the afterlife. I wanted to hold on to every second I spent with her, for after today, I would never be with her again.

I lifted Alffinna from the tub and wrapped her in a small sheet, lightly dabbing the water from her body. Carefully I trimmed her tiny nails short, as was the Norse custom, lest her unpared nails be available for the construction of the *Naglfar*, the ship made from the toenails and fingernails of the dead, foretold to carry the army of *jötnar* at *Ragnarök*.

Her nails trimmed, I carefully bundled Alffinna in the sheet and held my dead child to my chest. I closed my eyes and hummed a wordless tune to her, gently bobbing back and forth on my feet, dancing with her as I cuddled her like I had done during her life.

"Aveline."

I opened my eyes and stared at the figure in the doorway – there stood Freydis, Vidar's mother. Her silken strands of snow-white locks were hidden beneath an ivory kerchief pinned tidily to her hair. Freydis was as beautiful as ever; even beneath the signs of age that time had etched upon her flesh, one could tell that Freydis had been dazzlingly gorgeous in her youth.

The glossy sheen of unshed tears glistened in Freydis's meadow green eyes, framed with deep furrows of age, and the full, pink-lipped smile that glowed from her fair face exuded sympathy and sorrow. In the main room of the hall, Alvar the First One's voice boomed as he greeted his grandchildren and relayed his condolences to his son, Vidar.

"I'm sorry, sweet girl. I truly am." Freydis whispered, embracing me gently, careful of the dead babe I held. "There are no words to be said that can soothe a mourning mother's sorrow."

Freydis was right, there weren't. She didn't even try to speak honeyed words to me. Instead, silently she aided me with Alffinna's preparations, helping me slip the silken underdresses and gown over Alffinna's stiff form after I had massaged a fragrant lavender oil over my baby's skin. I wrapped her in a clean, fine linen blanket and cradled her in my arms. All was ready.

"I am sad I never had a chance to meet this beautiful child before today." Freydis sighed, stroking the chestnut curls on Alffinna's head. "Though death is stealing her looks, I can tell she must've resembled you a great deal when she lived."

"*Já*," I choked on the knot of emotion that clogged my throat. "She looked just like her *móðir*."

"Would you like us to pray to Frigg together before we take her outside?" Frigg asked gently.

"Frigg?" I asked, confused. "Why would I pray to *her*?"

"She is the goddess of mothers and children," Freydis replied, equally confused. "She—"

"She is the protector of children," I said, anger growing inside me. "But she did not protect Alffinna from Thorn's blade—"

"Aveline," Freydis interrupted firmly, though she had not lost her sympathetic tone. "Not even Frigg could change fate and stop the death of her own son, Baldr. Sweet girl, when a baby is born, the Nornir choose the moment of its death. Nothing can change that time, not even the gods, no matter how hard they try."

I stared at Alffinna's still little face and lost myself in her beautiful innocence. I squeezed my eyes shut and begged in my heart for her amber eyes, identical to mine, to flutter open and let all of this be some wicked nightmare. But when I slowly opened my eyes, hers remained shut, and I knew I'd never gaze into them again.

"Give me her basket." I whispered and walked away from Freydis and into the main room.

"It's time, little fawn." Vidar announced gently, placing his large hand on the small of my back.

I nodded, cuddling my little child. Together, my husband, my children – who held items of Alffinna's – my mother- and father-in-law, my thralls and I exited through the hall's doors.

In front of our home, every townsperson of Aros had assembled. Einarr, Finnvarðr and a band of musicians were standing with the grandly dressed *goði*, his sons and his wife, a burning torch in the *goði*'s hand. At the sight of us, the musicians began their mournful melody. Drums were thumped with heavy hands, the cry of bone flutes pierced the air, bows were drawn long and slow over the strings of *tagelharpa*, lyres were tenderly plucked and strummed, and the deep, howling call of horns sounded, tied together by Finnvarðr's throaty song of lament. Townspeople joined him, singing with sadness, grieving Vidar, the children and my loss.

Aros mourned with us.

Slowly the *goði* and his family led the procession to the shoreline where Alffinna's pyre waited. Vidar, the children and I followed immediately behind them, Alvar the First One and Freydis behind us, Jan, Heimlaug and our thralls behind them, and so on and so forth, every member of Aros followed us through the town. Ice flooded through my veins and my skin was awash with goosebumps as we strode through the marketplace where Alffinna was killed. Still, we marched to the shoreline and surrounded the pyre.

The *goði* hallowed the site and cried out to the gods, while Freydis carefully set Alffinna's basket upon the tall, neatly organised stack of wood. My family were assembled close to the pyre with the *goði*, the townspeople surrounding us a respectful distance away. Young Birger was the first to place an item into the basket – carefully folding a fur blanket and arranging it inside the basket, so Alffinna would be comfortable as she rested there. He returned to Vidar's side, biting his lip so hard to hold back his tears, that a trickle of blood slipped down his chin, but he did not cry, he maintained his brave face and stared at the pyre fiercely.

It was time for me to lay Alffinna down in the basket and say goodbye to her forever. Delicately I laid Alffinna's body down.

"It's cold; she needs another blanket." I beckoned.

Immediately Sander brought me another fur. Though she was dead, though she no longer felt the cold chill of the late autumn air, I wanted Alffinna to be comfortable, as she was in life. I tucked it around her, only her sweet face peeping through.

In turn, Vidar, Young Birger, Sander, Æsa and Einar slipped Alffinna's belongings into the basket; clothes, small toys, a few food items she had favoured like berries, the cherry wood cup she had been given to play with and chew on from a kindly patron of the alehouse only weeks ago.

Einar began to sniffle and weep, but Freydis scooped him up quickly and held him, rubbing his back to soothe him. Young Birger and Sander stood beside Vidar, and Vidar gripped both boys by their shoulders. Æsa held her arms up to Alvar, pleading with tearful eyes for her *afi* to hold her, which he did willingly and immediately, embracing his granddaughter tightly.

I stumbled to my family, not tearing my eyes away from my baby for even a second. Vidar took my hand and Young Birger shifted closer to me, resting his head upon me. The *goði* came to us and passed the burning torch to Vidar. Vidar kissed my cheek and took the torch, leaving my side to set the pyre aflame. Young Birger and Sander held me, and I rested my shaking hands upon their backs, attempting to comfort them, though in truth they were comforting me, keeping me standing when all I wanted to do was fall to the floor and weep.

Vidar circled the pyre, lighting specific spots, until the flames began to rage, devouring the wood. The pyre successfully lit, Vidar returned the torch to the *goði*, and the musicians played another melody for us as we watched with bated breath as the fire grew, slowly reaching little Alffinna in her basket.

A knot formed in my throat as I watched the fire frame her small body. The furs, silk and fine linen I had wrapped her in caught flame, and my heart sank as her beautiful chestnut curls began to burn. The scarlet and gold tongues of flame-kissed her flesh delicately, lending her skin the brief glow of life – as though she was sleeping, not dead at all …

A short gasp shot from my lips, and suddenly Vidar's hand enclosed my wrist. I glanced at him, then at his hand and realised I was reaching out to Alffinna. His face was solemn, his cheeks were dry, but his eyes were filled with grief and understanding – he had seen the semblance of life flash over our dead daughter, too.

Vidar slid his fingers between mine and slowly, we lowered our clasped hands and let them hang between us, in silent support for one another. We turned our eyes back to our child, her flesh hissing as it burned, the sound deafening our ears.

CHAPTER FOURTEEN

Winter, 884

I CREPT THROUGH the darkness, the low orange glow of the fire my only light, but I knew where I was going; I could've found my way with no light at all. My warp-weighted loom stood on the platform to the left of the sleeping area door and hidden beneath a loose board beneath the loom was a small wooden box. Inside the box was the item I sought.

On the opposite side of the room from me, Rowena and Melisende slept on a platform, their bodies huddled under heavy furs, concealed by the dark. I heard their soft, steady breathing; they were thankfully asleep. The house had gone to bed a few hours ago, and every occupant was asleep – but me.

I slipped past the loom and crouched down low, my heart beating fast. I paused, held my breath, and strained my ears to hear any signs of movement – the rustle of the straw beds as the occupant sat up, the soft thump of furs as they were shoved aside, the crunch of feet upon the hard packed dirt floor – but not a sound was made.

I was safe.

Delicately, I shifted the rug that hid the loose board. I held the loose board with my fingertips and pried it up, carefully laying it on top of the rug. There was my box, no longer than my forearm and as wide as my hand, from the tip of my middle finger to the heel. The lid to the box was not fastened down, I simply moved it aside and pulled out the blanket safely hidden away inside it.

I held the folded blanket against my chest and sat on the platform, my back against the wall. I laid the blanket down on my lap and carefully unfolded it to reveal Alffinna's dress from the night she had died.

The fabric was stiff from Alffinna's dried blood and crunched as I smoothed it out, flecks of blood crumbling off on my hands like scarlet snowflakes. I held the little dress against my cheek and breathed in deeply. The stench of the blood had faded as it dried, now only a faint earthy scent exuded from the gown, with a vaguely metallic quality to it. The scent consumed me, immediately transporting me to memory.

I watched as Thorn spun around and slashed Caterine with his sword. Unlike reality, in my mind I replayed the scene in slow motion, watching every movement, examining every tiny action. I could count the threads of Thorn's tunic, see every strand of the fur wrapped around Alffinna.

I watched Thorn's blade slip through Caterine's flesh, like an oar through the face of water, watched the exact moment her skin snapped from the sharpness of the metal as it cut into her. I watched Thorn drag the blade down across her chest, watched the tip of the blade catch Alffinna's neck, slicing through her tender flesh. Caterine's blood rained down upon my child, but I could see Alffinna's own blood spurt from her wound, drenching the tip of Thorn's blade.

I heard every shuddering note of Caterine's scream as it ripped through the air, then my Alffinna's high-pitched wail synchronised with Caterine's for just a moment, when suddenly the sound of Caterine's agony ended and she fell to the ground, dead. I watched Caterine fall, watched her legs buckle underneath her, watched her arms begin to drop, dropping my baby. I watched Caterine's body collapse upon my shrieking child.

I watched Alffinna's face contort in agony and confusion, her eyes gazing at me with a storm of emotion raging inside them, begging me to take away the pain, blaming me for the agony ripping through her as I pressed down upon her wound and she tried to push away my hand.

I heard her cries grow weaker as life seeped out of her.

I watched the light of life grow dimmer in her amber eyes until finally, it was gone.

Over and over, I watched the scene replay in my head, I relived my daughter's death repeatedly, as I had done every night for the past two months since Alffinna had died. My eyes ached, but it had been a while since I had cried. Within the first few weeks, I had wept into her dress the whole night through, but there were no tears left in my body. I had no energy to cry, no energy to do anything.

Since Alffinna's death, I seemed to drift through life in a haze. I had lost all vigour, I had lost all emotion. I couldn't sleep, I just passed out from exhaustion wherever my body fell. I had lost thirst and hunger, only eating when my darling Young Birger or Sander would bring a bowl of broth to me, or a warm cup of tea made from boiled fruit or herbs, and I would swallow the food or tea just for them, just for the relief that would wash over their faces.

My children never laughed anymore. The hall was almost silent. Every now and again, little Einar would stand before me timidly, wanting so badly to be held but too scared to ask me. Wordlessly I would pick him up, and he would wrap his arms around me tightly, and for a moment I would be lost in the bliss and the warmth of his little body cradled in mine.

"You're so bony, *mumie*." Einar complained. "You're not soft anymore."

Then he would climb down from me; I was not comfortable to cuddle anymore. Bliss and warmth vanished, and I was left cold and even emptier than before. Every day he asked for me to hold him, and every day he would say the same thing and leave me. Every day he wanted his mother's warm, tender embrace, but he was continually disappointed for my body was wasting away.

Young Birger, Sander and Æsa tried their hardest to cheer my mood, and I would try to smile and laugh with them, but even they realised my smile was hollow. Their own grins would falter and, in their eyes, I could see the confusion and disappointment. Their laughter would disappear, and they would stumble off, heads hung low, their efforts failed.

"You're torturing yourself, little fawn."

I whipped my head up and stared at Vidar, who stepped out of the shadows across from me.

"How long have you been there?" I whispered, my chest tight from shock.

"I wake the moment you leave our bed; I cannot sleep without you beside me." Vidar smiled as he stepped towards me, his voice low. "The moment you kneel down and move the board, I'm here in the room with you."

"How long have you been watching me?" I asked as he sat beside me.

"Every night since Caterine's funeral," Vidar confessed. "I stay until the sky lightens from black to indigo, then I go back to bed and wait for you."

I didn't reply, too busy trying to process what Vidar was telling me. He had been here, in this room, watching me mourn every night, and I hadn't noticed.

"You're consumed with grief, little fawn. Of course, you didn't notice me." He said, as though he had read my mind.

"Why haven't you revealed yourself until tonight?" I asked softly.

"Tonight is different. I want you to come with me."

Before I could say a word, Vidar stood and offered me his hand, to help me to my feet.

"Come, now."

"*Nei.*"

"I'm not asking, I'm telling you. Come with me."

"Since when have you ever ordered me around like a thrall?" I growled.

"I am not *ordering you around like a thrall.* I am your husband and I am concerned for you. I want you to come and fight with me – you always feel better after swinging your sword."

"You really think swinging a sword will make me feel better?" I gaped, my jaw dropped in disbelief, fury boiling in the pit of my stomach. "I am not like you – I cannot just *feel better* after watching my daughter get murdered in front of me, Vidar Alvarsson!"

Vidar glared at me darkly, the corner of his lip twitching as he forcibly stopped his lips from twisting into a snarling scowl.

"I do not feel better after watching *my* daughter be murdered in front of me either, Aveline Birgersdóttir. But I cannot be consumed by my misery either – I have four other children, a wife and an entire town depending on me. You need to release your anger and sadness rather than let them grow inside you and poison you. *Get up*! We are going to fight!"

Wide-eyed, my breath caught in my throat, Vidar briskly folded the blanket over Alffinna's dress on my lap and placed it back in the box. Quickly, he hid the box away and replaced the board and rug, turning back to me.

"Come on."

***

WE STOOD ON the shore, our feet sliding in the sand. The winter night was bitter and freezing, chilling me to the bone; our breath streamed from our nostrils and lips in silvery plumes. The wind blew stronger here, biting into my flesh like the fangs of a ravenous beast, but I took pleasure from the aching cold. It burned my flesh like icy fire, pulling me out of the pit of despair that erupted inside me, forcing me to focus on the pain that seared my flesh.

Hardly a single star was visible due to the thick, heavy blanket of low cloud that was gradually engulfing the ink-black sky. The moon, still far from being swallowed by the clouds, glared brightly in a small fraction of the clear sky. Its beams illuminated the edge of the clouds and bounced off the icy waves rolling and lapping over the shore, lending us an eerie light to see each other by. The tide was coming in and its sloshing and crashing was loud enough to drown out the noise of our swords.

I shivered violently – we had left the hall immediately, taking only our swords with us. Dressed in my thin ivory nightdress and illuminated by the white moonlight, I must've looked like a ghost on the shore.

Vidar thrust my sword towards me, offering me the hilt. I stared at it for a moment and he shook it – *take it*, he was gesturing, *take it now*. I closed my fingers around the smooth, glossy antler hilt and breathed out deeply. Vidar, with his sword in his hand, stomped a few yards away from me, turned around and raised his sword.

"Raise your weapon, little fawn." Vidar called.

As though I had never seen such a thing in my life, I examined the sword; my eyes ran down the smooth outline of the iron blade, sharp enough to cut my flesh if I but pressed my finger upon it.

"Little fawn!" Vidar barked.

I snapped out of my thoughts and stared at my husband, the bronze of his flesh turned ashen by the night, his breath a white cloud drifting about his face, obscuring it.

"Wield your sword, little fawn!" Vidar thundered. "Attack me!"

Vidar's feet were shoulder-width apart, his leading foot was slightly forward, almost square to me. His knees were somewhat bent, and he bounced gently on the balls of his feet. In one hand Vidar brandished his sword, his other arm up as though he held an invisible shield, a stance formed out of habit.

Vidar pointed his sword at me, and just as his mouth opened ready to command me again, I lifted my weapon and, with a howling roar, I barrelled towards him, all thoughts falling away as I charged. Vidar parried my blade as I swung hard at him. Immediately, I swung again.

Over and over I swung my blade with reckless abandon; Vidar deflected every hit. Sweat poured down every inch of my flesh, and I couldn't feel the cold anymore. I panted like a damn dog and my arms were heavy, as though iron rods were strapped to them, weighing them down. The muscles in my legs seared and trembled, but still, I swung.

I heaved the sword back and practically threw it forward, my arms too weak to raise it. Vidar didn't even try to block my sloppy strike, he merely stepped out the way. I stumbled forward and stopped, staring at my feet as the sand poured over them. The hilt slipped in my sweaty fingers, but I didn't tighten my grip. Instead I opened my hand and let the weapon fall to the ground with a soft thud.

"Why do I lose everyone I love?" I cried out. "My parents, my brothers, Birger, Elda, now Alffinna and Caterine ... Why did they have to die, Vidar? Why did Thorn have to kill my baby?"

My legs buckled. I collapsed to my knees and wept.

"Little fawn!" Vidar gasped, throwing his sword aside and diving to the ground beside me.

I felt his hands rest over me, and I flinched, pulling myself away from him quickly, as though his touch was hot as fire.

"Why – why won't you let me hold you?" Vidar asked, his voice small and confused.

I gazed at him through misted eyes and saw his hands were still outstretched. Slowly Vidar drew his hands back, turning his palms to face upwards. His teeth dug into his lips, his brows knitted, he examined his hands, trying to see what was wrong with them. The hurt and bewilderment upon Vidar's handsome face broke my heart. I wanted to throw myself into his arms, but I just … I couldn't.

"You haven't let me touch you since the funeral," Vidar's voice cracked with emotion. "D-do you blame me?"

"*Nei*!" I gasped. "Not at all!"

"Then why do you flee my touch?"

I tried to speak, tried to admit to him, but the words knotted in my throat. I dropped my head and stared at the grey sands, breathing heavily.

"If I hadn't let you give Alffinna to Caterine, she would still be alive."

"Then you do blame me." Vidar spat miserably.

"*Nei*, Vidar!" I cried. "*I* should've been holding Alffinna! If she had still been in *my* arms, she wouldn't have died! I should've taken her the moment Thorn fell to our feet, but I didn't! I froze – I did nothing! I was right there, and I did nothing! I should've fought him or – or jumped in front of his blade, or–"

"You had no weapon on you, and what would jumping in front of his blade have accomplished?" Vidar argued. "Alffinna would have grown up without a *móðir*, as would our other children!"

"I don't know, Vidar!" I yelled. "Anything would have been better than watching my daughter die! I was right there, Vidar, and I did *nothing*!"

"As was I, Aveline!" Vidar hissed. "As was I! I could've held Alffinna, but I didn't, I gave her to Caterine instead, and they were both killed. They were standing next to *me*, too, Aveline! I didn't protect my daughter – I couldn't even protect my thrall, and they were both within arm's reach of me! What type of man lets his family be killed right beside him? A man is meant to protect his wife, his children, his home, his thralls, and I failed. I stood there and watched Thorn kill them – I stood and watched my baby be killed! Is it my fault, then, too, that our daughter died?"

"*Nei, nei, nei.*" I whispered. "*Nei*, Vidar, *nei.*"

"Exactly," Vidar said quietly, his voice steady. "It wasn't my fault, nor was it yours. It was Thorn's fault – *he* was the one who killed our daughter. There was nothing we could've done – and worrying over what we could've or should've done differently will not change a thing. Avenging Alffinna, killing her murderer, that is all we could do, and it's done. All we can do now is put our faith in Frigg to care for Alffinna in the afterlife."

"Killing her murderer will not bring her back from the dead and does nothing to rid me of the pain of losing my baby!" I shrieked.

"You need to stop this. Your grief is killing you, little fawn." Vidar warned, slowly crawling over the sand to get closer to me. "Your children don't recognise you – you're nothing more than skin and bone – you've such dark smudges hanging beneath your eyes, it looks like you've been beaten. You need to accept that you are not at fault for her death and – *why won't you let me near you?*"

As Vidar came closer, I gawped at him like he was a monster, and shuffled away, my heart pounding in my throat.

"Of all the gods in Asgard, Aveline, I just want to hold you!" Vidar shouted. "Please, let me!"

"*Nei*," I whispered. "If I let you hold me, you'll bring peace to me. When I'm in your arms, you take away all ill feelings and thoughts, you make me feel safe and happy, and I don't deserve that."

Vidar's jaw dropped, and his brows shot up his forehead.

"You deserve to be happy, you deserve peace." Vidar said softly.

I wanted to argue, wanted to scream he was wrong, but I couldn't. I opened my mouth, but my words came out strangled and indecipherable as sadness poured out of me until I could do nothing else but cry.

My throat constricted suddenly, choking me. In painful wheezes I gasped for air, and my body quaked violently. Snot streamed from my nostrils and my eyes were ablaze with pain from crying so hard. Vidar scooped me into his arms and pinned me tightly against him. I tried to wriggle free, tried to pull away from him, but he was so much stronger than me, and he refused to let me go. Vidar held me, his own tears slipping from his eyes and dripping onto my hair.

Exhaustion weighed down my body until I was too weak to struggle anymore. My ear pressed against Vidar's chest, I heard the rhythmic thump of his heartbeat. The longer I stayed in Vidar's arms, the quicker I calmed, the song of his heart drawing me from my hysteria to peace. What I feared, what I had been trying to avoid was happening; I found tranquillity in Vidar's arms, tranquillity I didn't believe I deserved. Slowly we sank, lying down on the sand, our bodies tangled together like we were one being.

"Why did Alffinna have to die, Vidar?" I asked mutedly after an age of silence.

"I asked the same thing when my brother, Einar, died. He had seen only sixteen winters when he passed … Einar was meant to be Jarl of Roskilde – not me. He was meant to travel the world, he was meant to have a hundred children, but he didn't. Einar died." Vidar offered me a weak, fleeting smile, sighed and pressed a kiss to my tear-dampened hair. "But that's when the Nornir decided he would die, and there was nothing we could do. We wept, we mourned, we adapted, we moved on. We never forget him though."

"How do you say that so easily? How do the Norse accept death like this?" I asked.

"We believe death and life are balanced. You mustn't fear death but understand that death is uncontrollable; nothing can bring a man to his death if his time hasn't come, and nothing can save one doomed to die." Vidar said. "Life is a cycle, and death is a great part of that. Though it hurts, it is meant to be – for everyone."

"Good Christians don't fear death either," I commented, staring at the clouds scattered across the dark night sky. "All their lives Christians are meant to be good to ready themselves for the afterlife, where hopefully they will be rewarded and gain entry into heaven."

"If a man dies honourably, we believe he'll sit at Odin's table in Valhalla." Vidar said.

"Where do babies go when they die?" I whispered. "Christians believe unbaptised babies are doomed to suffer in hell for eternity. Alffinna was unbaptised—"

"Christians are *wrong*." Vidar interrupted, his voice strong and stern, shocking me with his surety. "Alffinna will not be punished for eternity, she is a Dane! She is in Helgafjell being cared for by my ancestors."

Silence settled over us again. Meekly, Vidar tilted his head down towards me, and slowly I lifted my face to gaze at him. He tried to press his lips to mine, but I turned away. He sighed.

"I miss our daughter, I wish Alffinna hadn't died, but I can't change what has happened. I can't let my sadness destroy me, there are too many lives depending on me – and on *you*, little fawn. Young Birger, Sander, Æsa, Einar – they need you. I need you … We need to find a way to pull you out of the darkness. The agony of losing a child will never truly go away, but as hard as it is to imagine, you *will* live, little fawn. You *will* go on." Vidar said. "I want to take you to see the healer. We'll see if she has a potion or remedy that can help you."

"Okay." I replied.

We gazed into each other's eyes for a moment. Quickly, Vidar pressed a kiss to my forehead, before he leapt to his feet and offered me his hand. I took it, his long fingers clasped mine tightly, and he pulled me to my feet before we stumbled through the night to Brynja the healer's longhouse.

CHAPTER FIFTEEN

"I MUST SEE Brynja." Vidar demanded as he shoved past Svala the thrall and stormed into the healer's home.

I gingerly followed Vidar. In the centre of the longhouse, the fire roared hotly, and the soft sound of slumber drifted from the sleeping area, assumedly from the children. Only Brynja and her daughters were in the main area.

"I'm here, my Jarl, what is it?" Brynja said.

Brynja was sitting by the fire with Marta, Káta and Nefja, each with a cup clasped in their hands. They rose to their feet immediately and stared at us with wide eyes and brows raised, stunned by our abrupt arrival.

"Where are your husbands?" Vidar asked, noticing the three men's absence.

"They're out drinking, they won't be back for a while, if at all – you won't be disturbed. Please, make yourselves comfortable." Káta said, indicating to two empty wooden chairs.

Káta froze, staring at me for just a moment. Her eyes widened ever so slightly, before she turned to watch Vidar carefully lay my sword on the tabletop. I dashed over to Brynja, grabbed her hands and squeezed them tightly, my heart hammering in my chest.

"Jarlkona!" Brynja gasped as she stumbled back into her chair.

I fell to my knees before her, gazing at her through aching, misted eyes. The fire danced behind me, glowing its orange light upon Brynja, its warmth dancing upon my back. No amount of warmth and no sizeable flame could thaw the coldness inside me.

"Brynja, please help me." I begged.

My voice was so thick with grief I struggled to speak; my words seemed to be caught up in the knot of emotion lodged in my throat.

"Jarlkona, what's happened?" Brynja asked. "Are you sick, dear? I've never seen you like this – all colour has gone from your flesh; you're as pale as a spirit!"

"I need medicine from you," I said. "I need a remedy – a remedy for pain."

"What ails you, my Jarlkona?" Brynja asked, her eyes flittering over me in a quick examination. "There are different brews for different pains – tell me where hurts you and I will heal it!"

"Here." I held a shaking hand over my heart.

Tears suddenly streamed down my face. I didn't make a sound, just shuddered silently. With every tear that fell, I felt my strength vanish with it. I dropped my head in Brynja's lap, too weak to hold my head up any longer.

"Káta, boil lemon balm and mint in wine, do it now," Brynja ordered, and Káta rushed into the kitchen. The healer gently wiped the tears from my cheek with the back of her fingers. "The wine will calm you and the herbs will help soothe the pain in your chest."

Brynja tenderly ran her fingers through my wild, tousled curls. I closed my eyes, ignoring the snot that leaked from my nose and the tears that tumbled down my cheeks, soaking Brynja's skirts.

"Has she been displaying any other symptoms?" Brynja asked Vidar, still rhythmically stroking my hair.

"She cannot eat, she cannot sleep, her body trembles constantly." Vidar said from across the room, anxiety in his words. "She hardly talks anymore, and when she does her voice sounds hollow – empty. Her flesh has lost all brightness and colour, and her warmth has disappeared; her touch is cold as though she's a walking corpse."

"How long has she been stricken?"

"Since our daughter was killed."

Those five words hung in the air heavily. The world around me dissolved, replaced by the agonisingly vivid image of my baby daughter's neck sliced open, her scarlet blood gushing down Thorn's blade. Her shrieks filled my ears, louder than anything I had ever heard before, but ended abruptly. Suddenly Alffinna stopped writhing in agony, and just laid there, limp in my arms …

I did not turn to look at him, but I heard Vidar cross the room, his footsteps lightly crunching in the packed dirt floor. His shadow cast over me as he stood behind me, and I felt his gaze weigh heavily upon me.

Fleetingly I felt his fingertips graze shoulder, but his touch vanished as fast as it had come. Something held him back – was it uncertainty, hesitation? Did he fear I would flinch from him again? Slowly Vidar stepped back away from me, his shadow disappeared from me, lighting me again in the glow of the fire, it's warmth dancing on my back.

"I have never seen a sadness like this." Brynja breathed.

"Do you have a medicine or a potion to heal her?" Vidar asked.

I heard the rustle of the dried herbs as Vidar spoke – he must've been sifting through Brynja's medicinal plants, hoping to identify something that might help me.

"Jarl Vidar, I wish I did! Many mothers have requested the same thing you are asking for now. I wish I could take the Jarlkona's pain away – as I wish I could for all mourning mothers, but I *can't*. Only time can do that." Brynja said apologetically, her sympathetic gaze following Vidar has he stomped about her home.

"You create decoctions that stop women from bearing children – you have brews that rid the body of pain – salves that heal battle wounds–" Vidar growled, his patience quickly disappearing. "You *must* have a remedy to help my wife!"

"Time is the only healer for the pains of the heart," Brynja said softly. "Though it hurts, death is a part of life. You must understand that, my Jarl?"

Vidar didn't answer her, at least not vocally. Brynja's question hung in the air. Her statement echoed everything Vidar had told me earlier this evening. All Norse believed this, that death was just a cyclical part of life – what was born would die and would be reborn again, in a different life or way. They all understood this, and that helped ease their grief.

The image of my slaughtered baby was fixed in my sight, I saw nothing but her bloody lifeless body … Understanding the cycle of life did nothing to ease the grief of my daughter's death.

"But why Alffinna?" I wept, my body shuddering as my tears began to cascade from my eyes once again.

"Oh, dear lamb, though it hurts, everything that happens is meant to happen." Brynja's voice cracked as tears slipped down her cheeks in sympathy for me. "Though she tried, not even Frigg could change fate and stop the death of her son, Baldr."

"But Alffinna was just a baby." I cried, lifting my head to glare at her. "Why was she meant to die? What could possibly come from her death?"

"They are questions you must ask the gods or the Nornir themselves, Jarlkona, for I do not know." Brynja said.

"Then that is what I will do." I said with sudden realisation.

My tears halted immediately. Slowly I rose to my feet, rolling my lips together as her words echoed inside my mind. I faced Vidar, and he stared back at me, chewing on his bottom lip.

"Aveline?"

Was I mad? Was I crazed by hysteria and loss?

Brynja's answer had made sense to me – why hadn't I thought of this before? Why wallow in sorrow and beg for answers from those around me who didn't have any or just repeated the same 'unalterable, predetermined' conviction, when I could demand answers from the gods themselves?

"I've asked the gods for help in the past, and they gave me what I wanted," I said distantly. As memories whirled around my mind a thrill of realisation tore through me like lightning. "They granted me the strength and knowledge to survive my first marriage, just as I asked them ... I asked Frigg to protect our sons from Erhardt, and she did – Vidar, I raised *our* boys right beneath Erhardt's nose – in Erhardt's *home* – and they were safe! Just as I had asked Frigg!"

"Then we will pray – we will sacrifice to them." Vidar said, cautiously reaching out and enclosing his hands around my upper arms gently.

Slowly he pulled me from Brynja. I let him move me, let him control me, too consumed by the number of plans and ideas forming in my head to pull away from him.

"Vidar – you yourself have asked of the gods and received what you wanted!" I pointed out, remembering the night Vidar had promised to tell the gods I wanted a daughter – and a few months later, I had birthed our darling Alffinna.

"Little fawn, you cannot ask for the dead to return to *Miðgarðr*." Vidar murmured, pressing his forehead against mine.

"I know ... But – but perhaps the gods will take away the pain of losing Alffinna?" My voice quaked. "I have so many questions for the gods, Vidar; I'm driven mad by them!"

"Then we will ask," Vidar said, cupping my face with his hands and wiping the tears from my cheeks with his thumbs. "I will sacrifice every bird, every beast and every thrall in Aros until you get the answers you seek."

For the first time since Alffinna's death, I wrapped my arms around my husband's neck and brought him into a kiss, deep and loving. From his lips I drew strength, motivation, resolve. Sacrificing animals and thralls in a *blót* and praying was not enough though – I needed immediate answers, I didn't want to wait for symbols and signs.

I needed to *find* the gods and make my demands.

"There's another way." Nefja said quietly, but her voice trailed away as all the faces in the room whipped around to stare at her.

"Another way, for what?" Vidar asked slowly.

"To speak to the gods." Nefja answered meekly.

"Nefja." Brynja cautioned darkly.

"She's the Jarlkona, she deserves to know." Nefja argued.

"It's too dangerous!" Brynja snapped.

"But–"

"Hold your tongue!"

"Speak Nefja!" I barked, glaring fiercely at the healer and her youngest daughter. "What are you talking about?"

"Destiny, it isn't final and unalterable for *everyone*." Marta said. "Even what the Nornir carve into *Yggdrasill* can be rewritten."

I released Vidar, whipped around and stared at Marta, trying to fathom the words she was saying. She was focused on the cup in her hands. She rocked it and watched the liquid swirl inside it. A golden drop of mead spilt over the lip of the cup and dribbled down the edge, onto her finger. She brought her finger to her lip and sucked the droplet up, not saying another word.

RISE TO FALL

"There are others who can alter destiny, besides the Nornir; there are some who walk the lands of *Miðgarðr* who have the power to change fate." Káta said.

Surprised, I jumped when Káta spoke. I didn't know how long she had been standing there silently, holding the mint, lemon balm and wine brew Brynja had instructed her to make earlier, but there she was, lit by the golden glow of the fire. Unnerved by her intent stare, I slowly stepped back to Vidar, and he gripped my hips in his hands, lending me a sense of security from his touch.

"Who?" Vidar asked.

"There is a völva, rumoured to be almost as powerful as Freya. She is said to live in the wetlands near the Wadden Sea." Nefja explained, much to Brynja's chagrin.

"But the cost of her aid is too high for what she can offer you." Brynja warned quickly, scowling at her three daughters.

"What can she offer me?" I demanded, my heart racing with excitement and apprehension.

"The *völva* practices the art of *seiðr* – magic which can discern and change part of the web of destiny," Marta said. "She cannot bring your daughter back from the dead, but she can enter the nine realms as a spirit, and bring back a blessing or a prophecy–"

"Or a curse." Brynja interrupted. "Jarlkona, don't risk visiting this völva. As she can heal the sick, so she can induce sickness; as she blesses with good luck, so she can curse; as she brings forth fruitful bounty, so she can blight and barren the land. You cannot trust that her prophecies are honest and true! She is set apart from society for a reason! Please, don't risk what you have, Jarlkona!"

"The gods know they will fall when *Ragnarök* occurs, but they will still fight valiantly, though their deaths are assured." Nefja said.

"Odin, in his quest for knowledge, gouged out an eye. Then, to be deemed worthy for the runes to reveal their meaning to him, Odin hung himself from *Yggdrasill*, starved himself and pierced himself with his own spear for nine days and nine nights, sacrificing himself to himself. In pain and exhaustion, he finally beheld their secrets." Káta stated.

"It is up to you, Jarlkona, whether you wish to risk meeting with the völva for the answers you seek, but as Odin has taught, that which is worth having requires sacrifice, and will *always* be worth sacrificing for," Marta said. "You must decide whether the answers you want are worth sacrificing for. You must decide if you will leave time to heal you or use magic instead."

I took a handful of my skirts and wiped the snot and tears from my face with the fabric. With a deep breath, I tried to compose myself and calm my racing heart. I gazed at the four women who stared at me, waiting for my answer – Brynja looked concerned and fearful, Marta, Káta and Nefja, however, stared at me expectantly, all three of the women unnervingly calm.

The silence in the room was suffocating.

"How do I find her?"

"Travel to Ribe. From there, go west to the sea. By foot, it should take no longer than two hours travel, less if you travel by horse." Káta explained, thrusting the wine brew into my hands and holding it still as she spoke to me. "Travel south along the coastline and you will find the völva's home hidden among the trees and the marshes. The soil is rich and fertile and seething with life, thanks to the landvættir that thrive there."

"Her *hof* is said to be small and simple, designed so carefully that it hides in the landscape of the wetlands. Keep your eyes open, you will miss it if you don't." Nefja said.

"Though her *hof* may be small and simple, do not underestimate her, Aveline Birgersdóttir," Marta warned. "As Frigg sits in Fensalir, so the völva resides in the wetlands at the sea's edge, for her magic is strongest there."

I nodded, absorbing their words.

"Worry not, little fawn, together we should find the völva's *hof* easily." Vidar smiled, excitement washing over his face for the adventure we were about to embark on.

"*Nei!*" Brynja hissed. She pointed her knobbed finger at Vidar; her eyebrows raised so high, they were lost in the loose folds of the flesh of her brow. "You mustn't go, otherwise she will never meet the völva!"

Alarmed, Vidar and I glanced at each other.

"What do you mean?" Vidar asked shortly.

"She must go alone; only the one with questions can visit the völva," Káta said. "No man is welcome. The völva has a deal with the landvættir and dísir, there. They protect her home, keeping it safe from prying eyes, and will only show worthy *women* the way to the völva. Should a man step foot near her home, the völva will hang him and hurl his body in the bog as a sacrifice to the landvættir and dísir."

"Then I will travel with her to Ribe and wait for her there." Vidar replied, unfazed.

"The *whole* journey to the völva is to be made by Aveline, *alone.*" Marta reproached. "It is supposed to be difficult, she needs to prove herself worthy of the gods' attention and the völva's time."

Vidar scowled at Marta. He chewed his bottom lip slowly, his pale eyes burning with aggravation.

"Little fawn, it isn't safe to travel there if I can't be there to protect you—"

"I will go on my own."

"Listen to the Jarl, please Jarlkona!" Brynja begged. "The völva lives so far from here and getting to her will not be an easy task, especially on your own in this bitter, merciless season. Not only do you need to fear outlaws and hungry beasts but also the spirits and monsters and trolls that roam the land! The veil between our realms has thinned and waned—"

"I will go alone." I interrupted firmly, shaking my head at Vidar and Brynja's protests.

"Take a horse with you; a fine one, white in colour," Káta advised. "But know the horse will not return with you to Aros."

"Is there anything more I should give to the völva as payment?"

"Take money and jewels. Whatever you carry, be willing to compensate the völva with them. Her magic is not free, nor are her visions." Nefja replied.

"I am to send my wife, tormented by grief, *alone* across Jutland with a fine horse loaded with jewels and gold?" Vidar asked incredulously. "She will be attacked! Little fawn, Brynja is right, we'd do better to perform a *blót* here, in the safety of Aros – why ask a völva to tell you the future, when you could ask of Frigg the very same thing? As you said before, Frigg has helped you every time you're asked."

"Vidar …" I gazed at Vidar with bloodshot, aching eyes.

Immediately Vidar's aggravation vanished. He stared at me for a few moments, his lips drawn into a tight frown, but his furrowed brow had slackened. What anger had contorted his face had turned into concern, his eyes that had flashed with irritation now gazed upon me with compassion and worry.

"Since when were you afraid of adventure?" I whispered, smiling weakly at him. "You Norsemen travel and explore the world in ships, not knowing where you're going but prepared for anything. Why do you fear the unknown now?"

"Because I won't be by your side," Vidar answered softly. "All those years ago, we vowed never to be parted again. This is nothing like you've ever faced, and I won't be there to protect you; I don't want you hurt, little fawn."

I didn't reply. He pulled me against his chest and embraced me tightly, and I wrapped my arms around his waist. He inhaled deeply as though breathing in the bitter depression that radiated from me. His breath shook as he released it from his parted lips, and he pressed a kiss to my forehead. I slipped my arms around his neck and we stared into each other's eyes, wearing identical expressions of sadness and apprehension.

"I need to go, Vidar," I said finally. "I *must*."

Another sigh slipped from Vidar's lips. He shut his eyes briefly and pressed his forehead against mine. My face cupped in his hands, Vidar silently acquiesced.

"Jarlkona, you mustn't." Brynja pleaded. Her voice was weak, though, just as Vidar, she must have realised I'd made up my mind and was steadfast in my decision. "Of the few women stubborn enough to travel to her, not many have returned. Whether sacrificed by the völva, killed by the travel, or maimed or stolen away by the álfar who wander there, not many have survived to tell their tale. I beg of you one final time, Jarlkona, don't visit the völva, her magic is not worth the risk."

"I'm going." I said.

"Should you get hurt or worse, I will kill the völva and all the landvættir that protect her," Vidar swore, before turning to glare at Marta, Káta and Nefja each in turn. "Should my wife get hurt or worse seeking the völva *you* suggested to her, daughters of Brynja, I will kill all three of you, as well."

***

"YOU DIDN'T HAVE to threaten their lives, Vidar." I reproached quietly as Vidar and I slipped back into the night, bundled tightly in borrowed furs from Brynja.

With his threat, the three daughters of Brynja stared at Vidar. Pale-faced and wide-eyed, they pursed their lips and didn't utter another word. Quickly, Brynja, just as pallid as her daughters, had their thrall Svala fetch furs for my husband and me, a polite indication it was our time to leave.

"Why not?" Vidar replied. "They have suggested a journey to you that could risk your life—"

"And you were excited to join me on that journey—"

"Because I'd be there to protect you. You've never travelled Denmark alone before, little fawn – and for your first unaided journey to be to a völva with such a dark reputation?"

"If you came with me, who would care for the children? We couldn't leave them here without us both, and we couldn't take them with us."

"We could take the children to Roskilde – Alvar and Freydis could care for them!"

"Vidar, none of this matters anyway, you can't come. It will be even more dangerous if you do."

Vidar was silent.

I slipped my hand into his and squeezed it. He gazed at me, biting his lip, emotion swirling in his eyes.

"I don't want you to go." Vidar said.

"I must." I replied, finality in my words.

The light loaned to us by the moon had diminished. The moon was gradually being swallowed by the thick, low-lying clouds as it descended in the sky. Snow would be here soon, I could feel it in my bones. Tomorrow – the day after at latest. The journey to the völva wouldn't be easy, and the snow would make it even more difficult.

We reached the hall doors. As Vidar reached out his hand to take the handle, I stood in front of him and blocked his way. I didn't want to go home yet. I tugged on his hand and forced him to follow me. Without questioning, Vidar went along with me as I led him towards one of the storage sheds behind our home. The stiff frosted grass crunched and crackled under our feet and the metal handle was painfully cold. I released Vidar's hand, pulled open the shed door and slipped inside.

I turned to Vidar and beckoned him with just a tilt of my head, and he obeyed. As he closed the door behind himself, his eyes were locked on me. I kept a steady gaze with him and dropped the fur cloak onto the floor, heat rising on my cheeks. Vidar dropped his own fur and dived towards me, enveloping me in his embrace. I held his soft, bearded jaw with both hands and pressed my lips against his.

There was an urgency in our kiss. As though we were starving, we pressed our lips together for but a moment, before our tongues lashed against each other, tasting each other ravenously. We had kissed each other less than a handful of times in the last two months and had not laid with each other at all during that time.

I could smell the faint scent of the firepit smoke on his clothes as I pulled his tunic off him. Without care or caution, we ripped the clothes from one another, tossing them carelessly aside. Our vision stripped from us by the pitch darkness of the window-less shed, Vidar's dry, calloused hands explored every inch of my flesh, eagerly learning my body once again through touch, taste, smell and the sound of my satisfaction.

I nipped his lower lip with my teeth as I yanked off the leather thong that kept his hair tied back, running my fingers through the lengths, twining my fingers in his golden stands and, with one hand clasping the back of my neck, Vidar cupped the soft globes of my breasts in turn, weighing their fullness in his palms, squeezing them rhythmically. I gasped, enjoying the delicious twinge as he lightly pinched my nipples that were hard and overly sensitive from the freezing night air.

Vidar lifted me off my feet and I wrapped my legs around his body, clamping myself against him, feeling the hardness of him pressed against me. Vidar shoved me against the stack of wood in the centre of the shed, sending a few logs tumbling from the pile. I cried out briefly, my back scratched on the raw edges of the logs, but we didn't stop. He stumbled passed the wood and slammed me into the rough back wall of the shed.

My hands ran over the bulging muscles of his arms, over the light hairs of his chest, as I bit the soft flesh of his neck, of his shoulder, the strong, clean scent of the soap he'd bathed with the day before lingered still on his skin, mingled with the faint musk of his sweat from sword-fighting me earlier.

I cried out as Vidar pushed himself inside me, moaning as he filled me, deeper, deeper … Over and over he thrust, pleasure brewing inside me like a storm, the *thump!* of our flesh colliding and his growling moans growing louder as he loved me harder and faster. Every part of me tingled, bolts of wild satisfaction streaming through every fibre of my being, until, like an explosion, every part of me was alight, burning with euphoria.

Vidar pounded into me still, and I couldn't stop gasping, until, with a final, deep thrust, he arched his back and groaned with pleasure, his flesh hot and damp from his blissful exertion. He kept me pinned against the wall, his forehead rested on my shoulder, my arms draped over his neck, as he caught his breath. I kissed his cheek gently, and he kissed my collarbones and neck in return.

Finally, Vidar lowered me to the ground, our racing heartbeats calming, our breath slowing. We stumbled around the shed and found the furs, falling onto one and heaving the other over us as we curled together, our bodies fitting perfectly as though they were made to be together, two pieces destined to be connected.

We laid together in silence, the early light creeping through the tiny gaps and cracks between the planks of the shed walls. Almost asleep, Vidar shifted, squeezing me tightly for but a moment.

"Almost a decade and a half ago, we met in a woodshed and had our first true conversation together." Vidar's voice was low with the dreamy air of reminiscence. A sadness lingered in his words though. "It was the day I wanted to ask Birger's permission to make you my wife."

"And you didn't." I laughed softly. "Four winters passed that day until you finally did."

Vidar kissed me slowly, tenderly.

"I don't want to lose you." Vidar breathed.

"You won't – you never will." I whispered.

"You're my wife and I love you. I trust any decision you make, and I will *always* support you. But I must ask this one final time, little fawn. Must you go?"

"*Sacrificing himself to himself. In pain and exhaustion, he finally beheld their secrets* ... *Já*, Vidar, I must."

RISE TO FALL

CHAPTER SIXTEEN

"MUST YOU leave, *mumie*?" Æsa whimpered.

Æsa hung from my arm while I cradled Einar, gently rocking back and forth to soothe him. Both children pouted miserably, and their eyes glittered with tears. Young Birger and Sander were standing in front of me, shifting from side to side on their feet and rubbing their eyes and noses with their fists. Their faces were ruddy from the tears they had cried in secret earlier that morning when Vidar left the hall to ready my horse for me, so I could spend some much beloved time with our children.

"*Já*," I replied softly. "I shan't be gone long at all, only a week, possibly a little more. I promise I will come back to you, my loves."

"*Nei mumie*," Einar begged. "I'll miss you."

"And I will miss you – all of you." I gazed at my four children sadly, regretful that I should leave them but knowing I had to.

All of them seemed to have aged since Alffinna's death. Beneath their eyes, grey smudges tainted their pure golden flesh, and they frowned far more than any children of their ages should. This was Sander's seventh winter, Æsa and Einar would turn five and three, respectively, in the coming spring. Einar had stopped feeding from my breast less than a year ago – he was still so young yet bore the sadness of someone far beyond his years.

As this was Young Birger's tenth winter, by Norse custom he was a man now. He truly did seem the part, his forehead furrowed, biting down on his bottom lip, he nodded understandingly – just like Vidar.

"Drífa is ready," Vidar said from the doorway. "Come, children. Say farewell to your *móðir*."

"I love you all," I said as I rose to my feet.

I kissed them all, Einar still clinging to me. I stepped slowly to Vidar and tried to pass our youngest son to him, but Einar clutched on to me still, refusing to let go.

"Einar be a man, now." Vidar chided, slipping his hands beneath Einar's arms and pulling him away from me.

Einar tried to hold on to me but to no avail. He buried his head into Vidar's shoulder and began to wail, his cries muffled, his body quaking.

"It won't be long." I reasoned, though my voice began to tremble, too.

I slipped on my iron coloured coat, trimmed with fur, and belted it shut, while Vidar gave Einar to Rowena. Vidar picked up my sword from the table top and I grabbed my light-grey hood, also trimmed with fur, and pulled it over my head, careful not to dishevel the kerchief though it was fastened securely over my brow with a woven scarlet band. The hood covered my shoulders and ended just passed my breasts, to further insulate me and protect me from the cold.

My body was heavy from all the thick woollen clothing and furs I wore. My long chestnut curls were plaited and pinned to my head, then wrapped in a white kerchief which covered my ears. Beneath my coat, I wore a russet apron atop a tight current coloured woollen dress, and a thick ivory linen shift beneath that. A silver trilobite brooch pinned the necklines securely closed.

Cat skin gloves covered my hands; on the inside of the gloves the cat's red fur remained, fluffy and soft, to help keep my hands warm, and the outer part of the gloves were treated with beeswax and fish oil to keep them waterproof.

With a final gaze at my children, yet another kiss upon each of their cheeks, I stumbled out of the hall, a bizarre mixture of reluctance and determination bubbling inside me. I didn't want to leave my children, but I had to. I had to see the völva.

"You'll be gone longer than a week, you know?" Vidar said as we strode towards my horse.

"*Já*, I know …"

The snow the clouds had promised three days ago had fallen in abundance. It crunched as I walked through it, soaking the hems of my skirts. It was so deep it seeped over the top of my ankle-high sheepskin leather shoes, which were fastened with toggles. Luckily, I had the smarts to wear multiple pairs of woollen socks over the top of my thick grey woollen leggings – it would be awhile before I felt the freezing cold against my flesh.

Dressed so well, every inch of my skin protected from the bitter weather, I could feel the cold on nothing but my face. Still, my body trembled.

Vidar helped me mount my horse, a fine white mare called Drífa, which meant 'snow drift', ironic considering the current weather. She was about fourteen hands high, her elegant head, straight and well-proportioned with a wide brow, was set upon a short, muscular neck. Broad and low were her withers, her back was long, and her chest was deep. Everything about her body was muscular, even her strong short legs. Her thick fur was coarse, and her silvery mane and tail were long and full.

"Remember to follow the road, there are way signs lining it. If you keep to them, you won't get lost. There will be a few settlements you can lodge in – make sure to rest as often as you can." Vidar instructed. "Don't travel at night-time, please little fawn."

"You fear I might get caught in the Wild Hunt?" I smiled weakly, trying to make a joke of the situation.

"I fear bandits might attack you." Vidar said.

"I'll stay in the settlements." I promised, my heart skipping a beat.

Drífa stamped her front hooves impatiently, ready to begin our journey. Vidar had readied her for me; beneath the leather saddle was a fur blanket, to keep her warm and stop the saddle straps from digging into her. Various packs and bags and furs were strapped to her, filled with food, tools and the jewellery and riches I would need to buy the völva's time and mystical talents.

"Here, keep this with you at all times, you have my knife?" Vidar said as he gave me my sword.

I nodded and slipped my sword into its wooden scabbard which hung from my outer belt. I patted my front gently, where his utility knife and mine hung from my belt, hidden beneath my coat.

"Then you're ready." Vidar sighed sadly.

"I'm ready." I breathed.

Vidar cupped my jaw in his soft-gloved hand, and I laid my hand over his. I leaned down to him and our lips met tenderly. We kissed each other for a long time, but when we separated it hadn't felt like long enough.

"If you change your mind and want to come home, there's no shame in that," Vidar said firmly, his eyes locked with mine in an unwavering gaze. "If you don't want to visit the völva anymore, at any point, you don't have to. You can *always* come back home."

I nodded, still holding onto his hand tightly.

"I love you, little fawn," Vidar said softly. "Stay safe."

"I love you too, Vidar."

***

THICK SILVER CLOUDS weighed down the sky, but thankfully they didn't break. Drífa, determined and spirited, ambled smoothly onwards, occasionally cantering and galloping – enjoying our journey thoroughly no matter the gait. We travelled south, the lands relatively flat and open, an easy ride for the twelve-year-old horse. We rarely stopped, but when we did, it was only briefly.

By nightfall I reached a small settlement, only three longhouses and a few sheds, where maybe six or seven families resided together, squeezed inside the small, low walls of the homes. The families were hospitable and kindly, recognising who I was (and who my husband was) the moment I told them my name. They fed and stabled Drífa and gave me a warm straw bed to sleep on for the night in the main longhouse. They offered me their condolences for the death of Alffinna – news I didn't realise had spread so far – and shared their evening meal with me, boiled pork and root vegetables. Though bland, the meal was satisfying, and the mead they had brewed was light and delicious.

We spoke as we ate, and I informed them I was headed to Ribe, careful to leave out my reasons. From how Brynja had reacted to my intention to visit the völva, and from the way she kept the völva a secret from me before Nefja had revealed her, I didn't know whether the strangers would react with the same fear and caution. I was determined to reach the völva and didn't want to hear any more concern or warnings. And part of me feared any stories the strangers might share, if they had any, that might persuade me to turn back. Though my journey was going well, my heart ached for my children and Vidar, but I couldn't go back home. I had to accomplish my mission.

Exhausted, my face wind chilled and throbbing, I laid down on the dry straw bed, tucked away beneath furs and woollen blankets, and fell into an uneasy slumber, waking often. It was hard to sleep without Vidar beside me.

I woke up early the next day, eating leftovers from the night before for breakfast with the family that housed me. I readied Drífa and left quickly, eager to reach Ribe. I planned to return to Aros, return to my children, in the week I had promised them, regardless of the weather, and I was a third of the way to Ribe already.

Within two hours of leaving the settlement, the snow clouds finally burst from the weight of their burden, enveloping Drífa and me. Hard flakes hurtled down from the sky, riding on the icy wind, pelting us painfully. I couldn't see the pale clouds of my breath anymore, I couldn't even tell which way was up or down, left or right, so vast and furious was the blizzard. I clung to the reins with one shuddering hand, clutching my hood and pulling it down as low as possible to shield my face with my other. Snowflakes settled on my lashes, obscuring my vision; I could see only a section of Drífa's mane and her fuzzy, snow covered shoulders.

With nothing to do but continue our journey, we pushed on, fighting through the blizzard. Everything was swallowed by this monstrous white, no shelter was visible, no stream of smoke puttering from a home like a flag of hope and welcoming. No, there was nothing. If we stopped, we would be devoured by the snow and the cold, we had to move.

"Come on, Drífa." I urged, nudging the horse in her ribs with my heels. "We've got to go, come on."

The horse grunted and whinnied, but continued, ambling blindly. With no sight and nothing but the roar of the snowstorm, we would have to carry on by instinct alone – something Drífa possessed more so than me. I shivered violently, my grey coat and hood swathed in white. My feet and hands throbbed and burned from the cold.

After a few hours, the blizzard finally subsided, and the whipping winds calmed. Snowflakes continued to fall, drifting gently but steadily.

"Woah." I pulled the reins back and Drífa halted immediately.

There before us were the wetlands. Through the eerie blue glow of the late afternoon light I could hardly tell what was water and what was land. Shrubs and trees were dotted about and on the other side of the river I could see a forest and behind them a silver ribbon of smoke unfurled through the air. I breathed a deep sigh of relief – Drífa and I could hopefully rest for the night soon. We just had to make it through the wetlands without breaking through the ice.

I urged Drífa forward and cautiously she went, carefully avoiding the eerily black frozen pools scattered about. I could see the river – it was getting closer, but dishearteningly wider. Suddenly a crack ripped through the air. Panicked, Drífa flinched and shuffled backwards, shaking her head from side to side.

"Woah!" I cried, pulling the reins to regain control of her. "Calm down, Drífa, calm down! Woah!"

The horse stopped; her muscles tensed. She grunted and huffed, streams of breath shooting from her nostrils. She had stepped upon the edge of a frozen pool that was concealed by the snow and it had cracked beneath her hoof. I dismounted, clutching her reins still, and peered at the pool, following the curve of its edge, deciphering where the land began by the slope and shadow of the snow.

"Come on." I called, clicking my tongue and forcing Drífa to follow.

Finally, we reached the river. Like a black snake, the river slithered through the snow-shrouded lands, knots of trees and thin stretches of forest lining it on either side. The ribbon of smoke I had spied earlier rose from somewhere inside the white-blanketed branches of the forest on the opposite side of the river.

With renewed motivation and a growling stomach, I stumbled along, determined to pass over the river and reach the house to which the smoke must have belonged. The river was too wide for us to cross, and I didn't know how deep it was, so we would have to follow the water further down and hopefully find a point that the river narrowed or at the very least became shallow. I led Drífa along, staggering through the snow, glancing over my shoulder constantly to keep the smoke in sight.

I didn't know whether it was the snow that crunched or my joints as I moved, so stiff from riding for the past two days in the cold and snow. Every part of me was rigid and aching, I had to drag my legs forward, wincing with pain as I did so, my calves throbbing.

We struggled along until the river finally narrowed near a cluster of grey skeletal trees. I tied Drífa to one of the hard branches and stumbled down to the riverbank. I pulled my sword from its scabbard, crouched down as far as I dared and dipped my blade into the icy water, lower and lower until I felt the hard touch of ground. With a deep breath I forced my feet into the water, crying out at the freezing cold.

I cursed every god I could think of as I dragged my sword along the slope of the river bed, measuring how high the water was with the blade. Higher and higher the water reached until I made it to what seemed to be the centre of the river, and its deepest point, where the water reached up passed my breasts. I inched further forward but luckily the water didn't get deeper – hopefully it would stay that way. This is where Drífa and I would cross.

I lurched back through the water to the bank, my skirts heavy and sodden, and shoved my sword into its scabbard. I heaved myself up the slight slant of the riverbank to the trees where Drífa huffed and puffed.

"C-come on, lets g-go."

My teeth chattered as I untied Drífa from the tree. I pulled her along to the riverbank, one hand on her neck, the other on her reins, and stepped in, cursing the cold once more. Drífa refused to move.

"You c-can do this, c-come on D-Drífa." I urged as encouragingly as possible, clicking my tongue.

She grunted and shook her head from side to side, stamping her feet angrily on the hard, snow covered ground. I lost my temper quickly and growled and grunted and yanked the rein but the stubborn horse refused to move.

"C-come on you, you d-damn mule!" I grumbled, yanking on the rein roughly. "G-get in!"

Furious with the headstrong beast, I stumbled from the water, mounted her and kicked her flanks hard. Finally, she moved. The horse slowly stepped into the river, her muscles taut beneath me, and she whined at the cold, but thankfully she stormed through the freezing waters as fast as she could, rather than backing up the way we had come.

"Well d-done!" I cried happily, patting the horse's neck. "Good g-girl!"

Once again, we navigated through the wetlands, around the dark frozen pools, and eagerly cantered through the forest, hunting for the house hidden away there. My stomach growled fiercely from the delicious scent of rich stew that danced among the tree trunks, calling me. We followed the pungent odour of wood smoke and the delectable aroma of food and it didn't take us long to find the tiny building the scents were drifting from. During the blizzard, I hadn't been able to snack on the dried foods I'd brought with me, so hungry was an understatement.

Tucked awkwardly in the trees was a tiny shack. Made with a hodgepodge of wooden planks in such a design that implied the builder hadn't much talent at carpentry, the shack still seemed sturdy enough. There was a lean-to attached to it, filled with straw, with troughs for grain and water. I slid off Drífa, my skirts sopping wet and stiff with ice in places, and opened the gate of the lean-to. The horse trotted in willingly and helped herself to the dry hay, munching away on it happily. I shut the gate securely and knocked on the door to the shack.

A short, stout, gruff old man with a tattered woollen hat perched upon his bald head answered the door, a blunt axe slung over his shoulder. My eyebrows shot up to the top of my head at the sight of him and my words caught up in my throat.

"Travelling?" He belched.

"*J-já.*" I replied.

"Get in. Food's over the fire." He said. "Horse is stabled?"

"*J-já.*"

"Saddled still?"

"*J-já.*"

"Go have your fill and warm up. I'll sort it out."

Without another word, the little old man shoved passed me to the lean-to. Not knowing entirely whether I should trust him or follow him, my stomach gave another almighty roar, and I decided I would put my faith in him, at least until I'd eaten.

Huddled against the fire, curled around my second bowl of the gorgeous stew, the little old man hobbled into the shack, his face hidden behind my saddle, packs and blanket as he lugged them into his home. I jumped to my feet to try to aid him, but he shoved his shoulder towards me and nodded to my bowl. Meekly I returned to my spot and ate another spoonful of stew while he set down the saddle and packs by the bare straw mattress and hung the blanket over a rack to dry by the fire.

He was so old, his whole face seemed to be nothing but sagging folds of loose flesh. I could barely see his eyes from his drooping lids and fuzzy grey eyebrows. His raggedy ashen beard reached his belly button, and his clothes were tattered and filthy.

"Thank you for your hospitality." I said, my teeth finally not chattering anymore. "May I stay the night? I will compensate you."

"Alright." He grunted, ladling out a helping of his stew for himself. "You're sleeping in the corner. Be out by daybreak."

"Of course." I nodded.

The old man slurped up his stew, chomping the meat and vegetables noisily.

"My name is Aveline Birgersdóttir. I'm headed to Ribe."

A guttural reverberation hummed from his throat in reply. I tried to make polite conversation with him, but bar grunting offers of food or drink, he didn't say another word, he didn't even share his name. Soon after dinner, he gulped down a massive tankard of mead, slouched back in his rickety wooden chair and promptly fell asleep, snoring the whole night through.

Though an oddity, the old man was kind. By daybreak, he had groomed my horse, saddled her and gathered together some dried meat and stale bread for me to take for the rest of my journey. I thanked him profusely and handed him some silver.

"Be safe." He grunted and stormed back into the shack with the purse of silver clasped in his gnarled hand.

"*Þakka fyrir.*" I called after him

He didn't turn back or acknowledge me; he simply slammed his door closed.

"Well, I suppose we should carry on then," I said to Drífa as I mounted her. "Come on."

***

UNFORTUNATELY, I WAS a day behind on my journey due to the blizzard. By mid-afternoon, I reached a small settlement, maybe seven hours ride away from Ribe. From what the villagers said, I could make it to Ribe by midnight. My promise to Vidar flickered through my mind – I had assured him I'd stop at each settlement, village or town I reached along the way and would not, under any circumstance, ride during the night.

But, if I continued riding today, I would make it to Ribe in the allotted time ... I gazed up at the sky as I checked on Drífa, who was stabled with some other horses. The clouds were still heavy with snow, but there was the possibility it would hold off at least until morning time. I didn't want to break my promise to Vidar, but I was on the last leg of the journey. If I pushed Drífa to gallop a good portion of the way, we wouldn't travel *that* far into the night, we could reach Ribe before midnight, definitely. But that depended on the weather holding up. It hadn't snowed all day, but the clouds ...

"I think we can do it, don't you?" I said to the horse who grunted and shit on the ground in reply. "Excellent." I wrinkled my nose. "Let's clean up and we'll go."

RISE TO FALL

But of course, the clouds did not hold off until morning time. We had travelled for three hours by the time the snowflakes started to tumble from the sky. Briefly I contemplated turning back, but the snow was not falling *too* heavily, though it *was* falling constantly with no sign of stopping anytime soon. I shook my head. We could make it; it would take almost the same amount of time to go back to the settlement as it would to reach Ribe. Anyway, Drífa was a fine, sturdy horse – she had made it through one blizzard, she could make it through a light snowfall.

Gradually, though, the snow fell harder, and the wind grew stronger; we were unable to go faster than an amble – maybe a canter if we were lucky – due to the failing visibility. As the day fell to night, the wind whipped us, pelting us with snowflakes like they were stones. I regretted my decision intensely. There *had* to be only a few hours left until we'd see the walls of Ribe – we *had* to be close!

Drífa's ears flicked back and forth.

"Don't worry, it's just the wind." I soothed, stroking her neck

The wind's scream was unnerving, high-pitched like a wailing woman. I shuddered, Drífa's nervousness and the howl of the chill wind was daunting, but I shook my head again and breathed deeply; we were fine. I nudged Drífa's flanks with my heels and clicked to her, muttering words of encouragement and urging her to go a little faster.

"After this night, the Wild Hunt will begin …"

I could feel Drífa's powerful muscles tense, bunching up beneath me. She halted, her ears pointing forward. She raised her head, her nostrils flared, and shook her head from side to side. I clung onto her as she spun around, pulling her reins to direct her back the way I wanted to go, but she kept trying to turn around, fighting my lead. She snorted a few times, voicing her discontent. It was more than discontent though. Her muscles were so rigid, her movement was stiff – she was scared.

"And alongside the restless ghosts,

GWENDOLINE SK TERRY

And the spirits of those not yet born …"

I should've trusted her instincts, but in impatience – we were so close to Ribe! – and stupidity, I ignored her. I whipped my head around, searching through the darkness to identify what was frightening her. She tucked her tail against her hindquarters, her body trembled, fear rippling through her. I slammed my heels into her sides, urging her onwards. She took a few steps then stopped, took a few steps then stopped.

Suddenly guttural roars crashed around us like rolling thunder; Drífa screamed and bolted into the darkness. I clung to her for dear life, yelling at her to slow down, but she wouldn't – she couldn't – the roars were following us.

"Mighty Odin will lead his host of dead to our realm."

CHAPTER SEVENTEEN

BLINDED BY THE snow cascading from the sky, barrelling through the darkness, I clung to the leather reins, my legs clamped about Drífa's sides, hoping beyond hope I wouldn't fall off. She flew through the air, galloping at such a speed I could do nothing to control her – I laid low over her, peering at our blurred surroundings, praying to every god I knew to slow the damn horse down.

We whizzed by skeletal trees and evergreens shrouded in white, scrubs and leafless bushes, all coated with snow. Drífa dashed this way and that, I didn't know which direction we were heading, disorientated by her flying pace. She couldn't maintain it for long though, exhausted she slowed and panicked as she did so, snorting and huffing as she pushed herself to sprint. The deep chorus of howling wolves called close by – far too close.

The wolves baying cut through the wail of the wind. Paws pounded the ground around us, closer and closer, twigs snapped, dormant vegetation rustled, snow crunched under the beasts' sprinting feet. Drífa veered through trees, crashed through bracken, kicking up clouds of powdered snow.

As Drífa galloped into flat open land, the wolves revealed themselves. There were five. Coarse tawny fur and long powerful legs, three of them were skinny but the other two were not – the other two were huge!

With a throaty snarl, the largest wolf lunged at Drífa's hind legs, snapping at them. I kicked her sides, snapped the reins, screamed at her to run – to fly again, to flee faster!

The other huge wolf dashed to the other side of Drífa, snapping and snarling, the smaller three wolves following close behind us. Though she tried to hasten, poor Drífa couldn't. So exhausted from the days travel, she couldn't maintain this dizzying, strenuous speed much longer, and the wolves could tell. They snapped to threaten and intimidate; they weren't ready to lunge at Drífa yet – but they could sense her tiring.

And tire she did.

She slowed only a fraction, but that was enough for the starving pack. At that moment, the largest lunged at her, catching the back of her forearm with his fangs. Screeching, she stopped, reared high and launched me through the air. I slammed to the ground. She spun, trying to bolt again, but the wolf had sunk its razor-sharp fangs deep into her legs, hanging from her to drag her down. Drífa flailed, tried to fling the beast off, but she couldn't.

Drífa plummeted to the hard, frozen ground.

The three smaller wolves sprang onto her, sinking their teeth into whatever part they could. The second largest dived at Drífa's throat, biting down and spraying her blood everywhere. The wolves snarled and growled, the deafening crack of Drífa's bones ripped through the air, like branches snapping in a storm, the wet tearing of her flesh as the wolves ripped her apart, until Drífa fell silent, shrieking no more.

Darkness concealed my vision; for brief moments I fell in and out of consciousness, one moment I saw the wolves devouring my horse, the next was nothing but black. I forced myself to clamber to my feet. My whole body ached and throbbed, pain tore through my every fibre, but I had to move – I had to flee, lest the wolves turned their attention to me.

My breath came in agonising rasps, searing my lungs, my heart racing in my throat. I stumbled away, falling but scrambling to my feet as fast as I could, staggering through the snow. The more I moved, the more my body stiffened.

Soon enough, the wailing wind concealed the sickening sound of the wolves feasting upon my poor Drífa and I collapsed, too weak to go any longer. I tried to rise, tried to stand but I couldn't. The raw chill of the snow gnawed at my face, my eyes fell shut and my body trembled from the cold and the pain.

Somewhere above me, the croaky caw of ravens sounded.

Oh gods, I'm going to die!

I searched the sky, but I couldn't find the birds. Their caws were drowned out by the thunderous growls rolling about me. The wolves hadn't forgotten me. There were the three skinny ones surrounding me, their snarling chops dripping with Drífa's blood.

Their tawny fur bristled, pointed ears twitched, hackles raised, their lips curled around their blood-stained fangs. Hungry growls rumbled from their throats. All their dark, beady eyes were locked on me. And there, melded with the night and the fast-falling snow, I saw the two huge wolves creep up behind them.

The instinctive drive to survive forced me to my feet. I drew my sword and pointed it at the wolves, stumbling in circles on the spot – I couldn't have my back turned to any of them. Hysteria and panic consumed me – how could I keep my back to all of them at once? They had me surrounded! I couldn't escape them!

One lunged.

Screeching, I whipped my sword at the beast as it soared through the air, catching its belly with the tip of the blade. Its shrill cry echoed to the heavens. It collided with the ground in a puff of powdered snow, yelping as it stumbled to its feet. Blood poured from the gash I had slit through it, but it lunged again regardless.

I swung again and slashed its brow. My sword smashed into the wolf's neck with a heavy thud and the wolf's skin snapped against the blade spurting out a shower of blood. Yelping, it fell to the ground, writhing in pain before its body finally stopped.

Without time to even breathe, the two other wolves attacked.

The closest wolf lunged, snarling chops wide open, spittle and Drífa's blood spraying from its gaping maw as it roared. A huge black wolf appeared out of nowhere, soared through the air, locked its jaws around the tawny wolf's throat in mid-air, and dragged it to the ground. With one swift swing of its head, a crack like the lashing of a whip cut through the air; the black wolf had snapped its neck.

Shocked at the sudden appearance of the black wolf, I didn't realise the other tawny wolf had lunged at me until it was too late. As its sharp-clawed paws slammed into my chest, my sword flew from my grip, and I smashed down to the hard, frozen ground, its snarling chops snapping at my face. I shoved my hands to its neck, squeezing as hard as I could in a vague attempt to throttle the beast. I could feel the wolf's growls and roars rumble in its throat through my gloved hands, feel its pulse pounding against my fingertips, as I tried to keep those sharp blood-stained teeth from tearing my face open.

Within moments, another black wolf suddenly appeared and tackled the tawny wolf off me. Louder than a storm, the two black wolves fought the four tawny ones, whose attention had turned from me, an easy meal, to the real threat: the huge black wolves.

The black wolves, their fur thick and ragged, were at least double the size of the tawny ones, with bigger snarling chops and longer, sharper yellowed teeth. They were fiercer, far more terrifying, like Fenrir from the Norse tales – and they looked hungrier ...

Frozen with fire, I watched the wolves tear each other apart, flesh ripping, bones snapping, fanged jaw crashing against fanged jaw. Wrenching howls and shrill yelps, thunderous snarls and growls – I covered my ears, trying to muffle the deafening noise of the beasts as they fought to the death.

Fur was ripped from flesh, blood sprayed over me. The two black wolves killed the scrawny wolves in no time, easily fighting the larger tawny wolves as they did so. The large tawny wolves and the black wolves, one-on-one, slammed against each other, fanged jaws clashing together in shattering slams, claws tearing, snow spraying around them in icy waves.

My sword!

I scrambled to my feet, hazily searching the snow for my blade, but panic blinded me. Another spray of blood splashed over me and the noises of the fight stopped. It was over. I glanced over my shoulder as I scuffed my hands through the snow wildly, my sword still nowhere to be found. The black wolves had won, and they had set their sights on me.

I ripped open my coat and fumbled for Vidar and my utility knives. I stumbled backwards, facing the wolves while pointing the pitiful blades at them. Growls rolled in their throats as they neared me, not at all intimidated by my puny blades. The knives may have been longer than their blood-soaked canines, but between them the wolves had two sets of skin-ripping blade-like teeth.

The wolves quickly came closer, and I swiped at them, gasping and crying out frantically. With a swift leap, one of the black wolves knocked me to the ground, its huge, heavy paws pressing down on my shoulders. I tried to move my arms, tried to stab at it with the knives, but I couldn't. I was pinned.

It brought its bloody muzzle to my face, reddened saliva leaking from its jowls in long thick ropes. Its nostrils flared as it sniffed my face. Slowly it opened its great maw. I slammed my eyes shut and–

I felt its long, rough, slimy tongue drag over my cheek.

It climbed off me and left, both black wolves vanishing into the night.

I rolled onto my knees and vomited into the snow.

***

THE BLIZZARD RAGED. Wind howled in ear-piercing shrieks. I didn't know how much time had passed, but I had calmed somewhat. Instead of racing in fear, my heart now pounded from exhaustion. I hoped I'd put enough space between the wolves and me. My skin stung from the coldness, my teeth chattered so hard my jaw ached, and my lips trembled just as viciously. The flesh of my hands was tight and dry, splitting from the cold, even beneath my gloves.

Whimpering as I walked, my muscles throbbing in pain, I limped and stumbled, wet, freezing and stiff. My clothes were ripped and torn, and my coat and hood were drenched, doused in a sheet of snow. Nausea still gripped me, and every now and again I'd pause and retch in the snow. The blizzard, the darkness of the night and Drífa's panicked fleeing had disorientated me completely. I had no idea where I was going, I just knew I *had* to keep going. If I stopped, the snowstorm would devour me.

The distant caw of ravens sounded above me. I peered upwards, shielding my eyes with my gloved hand. I squinted at the birds through the thick snow and watched them fly low and disappear into a clump of trees some ways ahead of me. In trepidation and curiosity, I followed them. The ravens always appeared at a revelation or a death. I had not died at their first call so they must have something to reveal.

As I drew closer to the trees I stopped.

The strong, sweet scent of fine wine drifted to my nostrils …

What was that?

There was something ahead of me.

A silhouette emerged from the blizzard. Rooted to the spot, I heard the ravens caw once more, but I couldn't see them. As the silhouette grew closer, I realised it was a man. As he neared, the delicious aroma of the rich wine grew stronger – oddly, it seemed to be coming from his direction.

He wore a black tunic, trousers and boots, with a black bearskin cloak draped over his shoulders. He came closer and closer, stopping when he was only an arm's length away. Through the hard-falling snowflakes, I saw a soft smile play on his full, pale pink lips. He was much taller than me – as tall as Vidar, maybe. His alabaster skin was as pale as the snow falling around us and his hair was as black as the night.

"Come." He said and offered me his naked hand.

I stared at his hand, no dryness nor even a single callus to be found on his palm or the pads of his long white fingers. I had no voice to speak with and I didn't take his hand, just gawped at it. The coldness had taken such a hold of me that I couldn't reach for his hand even if I wanted to.

How could he not be affected by the cold?

Was he a man?

A spectre?

A shapeshifter or an *alfr*?

Was he … a god?

Slowly he closed his long, thin fingers around my wrist. When his skin touched mine, a burning warmth surged through my body. He turned and led me through the blizzard. Blinded by snow, I had lost sight of him, knowing he was there only by the grip of his hand on my wrist.

He led me to a shelter in the trees, smoke sputtering from the hole in the roof. Unlike the shack in the woods I had stayed in the night before, this cabin was small and well made, fashioned from fine oak planks. The door was sturdy, with elaborate hinges and a large iron ring pull handle. He opened the door and stepped inside, gently pulling me in behind him.

The heat inside the cabin was incredible, thick and welcoming, exuded from the fire that roared in a circular pit in the centre of the room. I pulled my arm free and rushed passed the stranger, falling to my knees in front of the fire, my whole body shivering violently. I ripped off my gloves and tossed them to the dirt floor, holding my hands up to the flames. My hands were scarlet from the cold and dried blood congealed on the backs of them from where the skin had split. The heat was welcomed though my hands throbbed and stung the moment the warmth touched them.

I heard the strange man close the door and walk across the room, his feet crunching on the dirt floor. Gingerly, I looked about the single-roomed shelter, stealing tentative glances at the stranger as I did so. There were a few chairs dotted about the place, a drying rack, a narrow table, a cupboard and a huge pile of furs and woollen blankets. The stranger had removed his bearskin and hung it over the back of a chair. I watched him pull a loaf of bread out of the cupboard near the narrow table.

His hair was shaved on the back and sides, and the thick ebony locks on the top of his head were combed to one side, reaching the tip of his ear. He wore a well-trimmed beard on his gaunt cheeks and square jaw, his sharp cheekbones were well defined, and his nose was long, thin and slightly hooked.

Though I had never seen a man like him before, he wasn't ugly. His angular features and incredible paleness held a certain attractiveness. His dark clothes were somewhat form-fitting, displaying his lean and muscular body. As he pulled his utility knife from his belt and sliced the bread, I admired the grace of his movement, the way his sleeves clung tightly to the swell of his strong, toned arms—

He caught me staring and chuckled.

I whipped my face to the fire, my cheeks burning as hot as the flames. In the corner of my eye, I watched him crouch beside the fire, hang a chunk of the bread from the tip of his knife and hold it up to the flames, toasting it evenly.

"You'd do better to hang your coat and let it dry." He said, tipping his head towards the drying rack.

His voice was deep and low but softly spoken, his words seemed to drift from his lips in a soothing stream, imbuing the cabin with a relaxed ambience. There was a familiarity to his tone, as though I had heard his voice before – a shadow of memory from years ago, clouded from view.

I looked from the stranger to the drying rack, took a deep breath and awkwardly rose to my feet. I didn't want to undress in front of him, not even my coat and hood, but he was right, my clothes were drenched. Within the few minutes beside the fire, the sheet of snow that had covered me had melted, dripping puddles around me.

Slowly I slipped the hood from my head, the white kerchief, soggy with sweat and snow, falling away with it. The pins must have become dislodged during the wolf attack … I pulled the kerchief from the hood and delicately laid them on the rack, slipping out the pins that remained in my hair and stabbing them into the kerchief. My plaits fell from my head, trailing down to my waist, stray strands and flyaway curls springing forth, free from the confinements of the kerchief.

Hesitantly, I removed the leather belt from my waist and slipped my arms out of my coat, my face flaming. I glimpsed the man from over my shoulder – he didn't lower his eyes when I caught him; with no shame at all, he was watching me.

Like the ocean, his eyes were the palest green – or were they blue? The colours seemed to swirl together as he gazed at me, shallow laughter lines fanning from the corners of his eyes as he smiled.

I turned away from him and concentrated on removing my wet clothes, trying to ignore him. I hung the coat on the rack, removed my limp leather shoes and the multiple pairs of soaking socks, then took a deep breath. Slowly I unpinned the turtle shell brooches and pulled the apron dress over my head, hanging it onto the rack with the rest of my clothing, pinning the turtle shell brooches into the garment so I wouldn't lose them. Regardless of how sopping wet my underdress and shift were, I would *not* be hanging them to dry. Feeling uncomfortably exposed, I cautiously sat down again, on the opposite side of the fire to the stranger.

"Here, eat this." He said, offering the bread to me.

I took it, timidly biting the slice. He watched me chew for a moment, chuckling to himself again. I stared at him as I ate and realised there was a white cloud tainting the pale aquamarine of his right eye – like foam on a wave. Briefly I lowered my view back to the flames, but when he stood and returned to the cupboard, I watched him. He pulled out a heavy, round leather flask by its long thin strap, returned to the fire and brazenly sat beside me. He opened the flask and drank deeply from it, that rich sweet scent exuding from him.

We ate in silence, my eyes never leaving him for long. After I had finished the first slice of bread, he toasted me another without even asking whether I wanted it or not. I did though, I was famished, and the bread was the best I'd ever tasted, soft and fluffy on the inside, hot and crusty on the outside. With every bite I drew comfort and confidence.

He didn't eat anything, he only took the occasional swig from the flask and after a while, he offered me some. I swallowed hard and reached to accept it, but rather than take the flask, I wrapped my fingers around his wrist in a flash of bravery.

"Who are you?" I demanded.

Surprised, the man stared at my small, skinny fingers clasped around his wrist. He grinned at me.

"Would you like the wine, or not?" He asked.

I tossed my slice of bread to the floor and took the flask. I lowered it onto my lap, refusing to let go of him with my other hand. I glared at him defiantly, my lips pursed, maintaining my facade of courage despite my racing heart.

"You may call me Anders. Anders Bursson." He said finally.

"I feel like I know you, Anders Bursson," I said. "But I don't recognise your face."

"Hmm, what a mystery." Anders smirked.

"*What* are you?" I stammered.

"A friend." Anders replied.

A scratching at the door made me leap out of my skin; I dropped his wrist and whipped around to face the door. Anders Bursson snickered as he stood up and crossed the room to open the door. I yelped as the two, huge, jet black wolves from earlier traipsed into the cabin. One carried a thick branch in its teeth, so long it hardly fit through the door.

The wolf dropped its branch, and both approached me, sniffing me. Finding me of no consequence, one wolf took my bread from the ground beside me, chomped and swallowed it quickly, before they circled the fire, sniffing the room, my clothing, the food cupboard.

Anders shut the door and sat down beside me. Following his cue, the wolves laid by the fire with us, the one wolf gnawing on its branch. Anders patted the wolf nearest me and pointed to me. With a huff, the wolf rose, tossed itself to the floor and curled itself around me. It twitched its large shining nose and blinked a few times before shutting its glossy black eyes and falling asleep.

I gawped at Anders, shocked and terrified, but all he did was laugh. The wolf's belly pressed against my back, its long legs stretched out on either side of me, those long claws like daggers permanently extended from its massive paws. It rested its head against my thigh, so close I could feel it swallow. I gawked at its huge head, its long muzzle with black lips lolled, giving me a glimpse of those long, pointed, yellow teeth that had ripped apart four wolves just an hour or two ago.

I couldn't move. This huge wild beast could rip me apart any second if it wanted to!

"*Oh!*" My whole body jolted as Anders leaned towards me and reached into my lap – but as the weight on my legs disappeared, I realised he had just taken the flask from me.

"Don't fear them," Anders said, opening the flask and sipping from it. "They mean you no harm. If they did, they would have attacked you earlier."

"You were there?" My voice was faint.

"Are you thirsty?"

Immobile, I stared at him, my mouth gaping open like a fish. My heart ricocheted in my chest, crashing against my ribs. I couldn't breathe, air was caught in the knot of shock lodged in my throat.

"Surely it's a good thing we were there?" Anders said as he brought the open end of the flask to my lips and poured a trickle of the wine into my mouth. "Otherwise you would have been killed."

I drank slowly at first. The wine was sweet, rich and bursting with the succulent flavour of berries and cherries – the most delicious wine I had ever tasted. Inelegantly and without shame, I closed my hands around the flask, took it from him, and drank deeper, glugging it as though it were ale. My eyelids fluttered shut as the enchanting flavour of the luscious, liquid gold danced upon my tongue. The wine sent warmth through my throat, my body, to the tips of my extremities. Instantly my heart slowed to its normal pace, and the moment I removed the flask from my lips I panted, gulping in air as though the wind had been knocked out of me.

Indelicately, I took another deep draught of the flask, my breath calming, my head spinning, and handed it back to him. Anders didn't make a comment about my crude behaviour, in fact, he sat there silent, grinning, his ocean-coloured eyes glittering with amusement.

"Have you been following me?" I demanded.

"*Já*, since your horse raced passed my cabin with wolves on its hooves, I thought it was the right thing to do." Anders said.

Relief washed over me. It was an adequate answer that I would accept for now though the unshakeable feeling that I knew this man still raised the fair hairs on my arms.

The next few hours we spent silently taking turns draining the flask of wine until there wasn't a drop left. Delicious warmth ran through my veins, my tense, sore muscles relaxed, and the throbbing ache of my bruised body had faded to a whisper. My head spun terribly, though, and a wave of exhaustion crashed over me, to the point I couldn't sit up any longer. My eyelids were too heavy to hold open anymore. I closed them and slumped back onto the wolf who twitched and huffed but didn't move away or bite, thank the gods.

"Perhaps it's bedtime?" Anders said.
"Perhaps." I mumbled.

I listened to Anders stand up and cross the room, heard the soft rustle of the furs being rearranged before Anders's footsteps sounded again, nearing me. Without even asking if I could stand (which I didn't know that I could), Anders scooped me up into his arms. My head lolled against his chest; I could feel his heartbeat, low and steady like a drum. Far too inebriated to be ashamed of my current state, I allowed him to carry me across the room to the straw bed that had been hidden beneath the mountain of furs.

Anders laid me down and pulled the blankets over me, tucking me in like I was a child. Enveloped in a bundle of blissful warmth, cocooned in the silky soft furs, I murmured my thanks, answered by yet another soft chuckle.

Anders sat on the floor beside the bed and, to my surprise, stroked my hair. I scrunched up my face and groaned, but he ignored me. He took one of my plaits, untied it and ran his fingers through the lengths, untangling them. He took another plait, paused and patted his leg; I heard one of his wolves cross the room and drop on the floor by the bed. Seemingly satisfied, Anders finished undoing all the plaints in my hair and tenderly stroked my wild curls instead.

It was glorious, the feeling of his fingertips gently massaging my scalp, the comforting weight of his soft hand drifting over my head, the light pull as he gently teased the knots and snags out of my locks with his fingers, the warmth that shot through my body every time his fingertips grazed my flesh ...

Images of Vidar appeared in my mind, bringing a smile to my face; his bronze face and golden hair glowing in the morning light, his icy eyes gazing down on me, that smirk turning up one corner of his lips. I loved when Vidar would play with my hair ... Dreams of my husband beckoned me, luring me into the peaceful depths of slumber.

"Are you travelling to see the völva?" Anders whispered.
"*Já.*" I mumbled.

Anders' question pulled me from the dreamworld the images of my husband were leading me to, but still so at peace from Anders' touch and on the delicious edge of sleep, it didn't shock me that Anders knew where my destination was, even though I had never told him. Was it even a surprise – who else would come to this place if they were not intent on visiting the völva?

"There's not far to travel 'til you reach her. My wolf will accompany you and keep you safe." Anders' voice was low.

Brows drawn together and lips tightened, I tried to open my eyes, but Anders ran his fingertips down my cheek and along my jaw, sending a wave of relaxation through me, immobilising me.

"Where will you be?" I breathed.

"Around." Anders whispered.

"The ravens?" I asked.

Without answering, Anders pressed his lips against mine in the most delicate of kisses.

***

IN THE HAZE between wake and slumber, for just a moment I thought I was still face down in the snow, from the coldness chilling my cheek. I kept my eyes shut, focusing on the icy fingers caressing the exposed skin of my face, the events from the night before drifting into my mind, and I wondered whether it had all been a dream.

I brought my fingers to my tingling lips, feeling Anders' light kiss still dancing upon them, and a stab of guilt pierced through me. The world around me gradually solidified; I felt the weight of the warm, soft furs laid over me, the firmness of the straw mattress beneath me, noticed the brisk wind wasn't sweeping over me in freezing wafts anymore. It had all been real.

A loud, yowling yawn sounded from beside me. Startled, I leaped up in the bed and my eyes darted around the cabin. Anders Bursson was gone. He had left one of his wolves, who was stretching on the floor by the remains of the fire, and his bearskin cloak still hung on the back of the chair. The wolf glanced at me and I sighed.

As I climbed out of bed my joints popped and cracked, and my muscles were stiff and throbbing. My body still ached from being hurled from Drífa and from the wolves' attack, though not as much as I had expected it to, a small mercy which I was thankful for. I pulled my clothes, which were rigid but dry, from the rack and dressed gingerly, my body tweaking in pain every now and again.

While I dressed, I stared at the bearskin, unable to look away, so mesmerised by the garment. I wiped the dirt from my feet with my socks before slipping them on, yanked my leather boots on over them then drifted over toward the cloak. I ran my fingers through the long black hairs, thinking of the mysterious stranger. I closed my eyes and his handsome, pale, angular face filled my mind, his blazing, ocean-coloured eyes, his ebony hair, his pale pink lips …

I opened my eyes, turned away from the cloak and, in the corner of my eye I noticed something – there on the table were my packs from Drífa, and – *thank Odin and Frigg!* – my sword! Excitedly, I grabbed it and slipped it into the scabbard. I didn't know how Anders had retrieved my things, but I was more than thankful he had. I opened the packs and checked the insides, pleasantly finding all the jewels and riches still there. Without a second thought, I removed a purse of silver and laid it on the table, a gift of thanks to Anders Bursson.

With a whistle to the wolf, I made my way outside. I opened the door to a crystalline paradise; the blizzard had ended leaving the world coated in deep glittering snow as far as the eye could see. I heard the caw of ravens above me and glanced upwards, watching the direction they flew. For once their throaty, raucous call didn't send apprehension or fear skittering down my spine – I felt confident, safe.

Gripping the straps of the packs tightly, I followed them.

CHAPTER EIGHTEEN

I TRUDGED ALONG behind the wolf, my footsteps crunching in the dense layers of snow, kicking up powdery clouds with every step. The wolf padded softly and surely, and I dutifully followed him, panting as I did so. We had walked for over an hour, and I could smell the salty scent of the sea carried on the light breeze – we were close.

The wolf led me along the edge of a vast forest where the ground sloped down to the frozen wetlands. I stopped for a moment and leaned against a tree trunk, lifting my stiff, aching feet in turn and rolling them in circles. The cold seeped through my boots and the snow had melted against my legs and dripped into my woollen socks, freezing my feet.

I could just about make out the far-off barking of seals in the distance, though I couldn't see them. I gazed out, sweeping a few stray hairs from my face, but could hardly see the vast, flat coastal wetland to the other side of us, for snow had devoured it.

Waves, tidal channels and estuaries whispered in the distance; we were far from the water, it was nothing more than a dark grey sheet sprinkled with floating ice that stretched out from the snowy land. The mudflats were frozen solid and crusted with ice and the beaches were blanketed away by whiteness, I could see only the tall prickly tufts of yellowed seagrass sticking out from the snow-covered dunes and salt marshes. On the bright side, the bitter winter weather repressed the pungent odour saltmarshes and mudflats usually exuded.

I flinched as the wolf let out a sharp yap. It glanced from me to the tree line ahead of us and emitted a short, impatient moan. I exhaled, stood up and staggered over to it.

"Come on then." I mumbled.

We walked further along the tree line before the wolf turned into it. Stumbling over the unseen roots and bracken strewn across the forest floor, hidden by the snow, I followed the wolf, pressing my gloved hands against tree trunks to keep from losing my step. We walked deeper into the forest and arrived at an opening where the saltmarshes cut through, and there amongst the trees, enveloped by huge unruly bramble thickets on both sides, was the völva's *hof*, the front door facing the marshes.

"Though her hof *may be small and simple, do not underestimate her, Aveline Birgersdóttir. As Frigg sits in Fensalir, so the völva resides in the wetlands at the sea's edge, for her magic is strongest there."*

Skeletal remains of vines, from finger-width to as thick as ropes, sprawled over the house and under the roof from the wild thickets. The *hof*'s wooden walls were old and weathered, but the carvings that framed the doorway and trimmed the roof were elegant and clear in the ageing wood. It was an unassuming little building, easy to overlook if one wasn't searching for it – in fact, had the wolf not led me directly to it, I'm not sure I would have noticed it at all.

The wolf yipped at me for a final time before approaching the house. As we neared, seagrass snaring the hem of my dresses and leggings, I noticed various *taufr* – charms and talismans; bones and sticks with runes carved into them – adorning the overhanging branches. Various animal skulls and bones were scattered around, tied to branches or eerily peeking through piles of snow at the base of trees.

Was that a human skull?

My eyes settled on one particular pile of skulls across the way from us. Empty, cavernous eye sockets leered out from the snowy heap. Smooth and shining, some of the skulls were complete, others were missing mandibles, but for the most part they were in flawless condition. Absentmindedly, I touched my cheek, feeling the hard curve of my cheekbone beneath the cold skin of my face, my eyes following the curve of the cheekbone on one of the skulls. I shuddered, goosebumps cropping up over my flesh. Human skulls ...

The wolf nipped at my ankles, forcing me towards the house. I ripped my sight from the skulls and stumbled to the door. I quailed before it, clutching the packs to my chest with both arms, seized by a wave of trepidation and doubt. The wolf sat beside me, glaring at the door; I reached out and touched the top of its head. It didn't move, it let me rest my hand upon it, and I drew courage from that small touch, bravery from the knowledge that I wasn't alone. I came here, I made this journey for answers, and that was what I was going to get.

Brynja the healer's words suddenly howled in my brain – "*Of the few women stubborn enough to travel to her, not many have returned …*".

I sucked in a deep quivering breath of the thick cold air and released it through my dry, cracked lips. I had been stubborn enough to travel to the völva, and I *would* return. I came to the völva for a reason – though fear now consumed me, I would not return to Aros without obtaining what I sought, no matter what the cost. The answers I sought *were* worth sacrificing for.

I curled my numb, trembling fingers into a fist and gingerly knocked on her door. Once … twice … three times … a long pause between each tap.

The door slowly opened and there, illuminated by the orange glow of a fire and the vast array of candle flames and fish oil lamps burning behind her, stood the völva. A tall, slender woman with rich brown hair loose and flowing about her waist, she was lavishly dressed in sapphire blues, scarlet reds and pelts of ermine, fox, minx and sable, decorated heavily in gold and silver, gems adorning all her fingers. She had seen forty winters, maybe a few more by the looks of her, but the touch of age on her flesh gave her an attractive elegance – she reminded me of Freydis.

There were two other women inside her home, sprinkling ashes on the floor and sweeping them into the dirt. One was fair, the other was dark (from the Blálands maybe?), each had long hair that fell to the middle of their backs like veils. They were both dressed in ankle-length gowns, sheer, loose and flowing about their slender bodies, not even a belt cinched at their waists. The cold draught from the open door didn't seem to bother them – they hadn't even looked at me when the völva opened the door. They continued their chores diligently, paying no mind to anything but their work.

"You have travelled far to see me." The völva said, turning her large pale brown eyes to the wolf beside me. "And I see you have had help. Where did you come across this beast, girl?"

"It belongs to a man named Anders Bursson." I replied timidly.

"*That's* the name he is going by now, is it?" She giggled – her voice was smooth like honey and her laugh trilled beautifully like a morning birdsong, yet the hairs on my arms rose in unease. "And how do you know *Anders Bursson*?"

"He – he's a friend." I stuttered, my cheeks flaming hot.

"Oh, a friend, is he?" She laughed again, surveying me through narrowed eyes as I shivered on her doorstep. "Where is your *friend* right now?"

"He's a-around." I stammered.

"I'm sure he is." She said, staring over my shoulder. "If *Anders Bursson* has aided you here, then I will help you. Come."

With that, she turned her back on me and drifted into her home. Her movement was so fluid, I couldn't tell whether she was walking or gliding – her sapphire skirts were so long they swept across the floor, concealing her feet.

I slowly crossed the threshold, my heart hammering in my chest; I could feel my palms moisten inside my gloves. The pale woman (I didn't know whether the two were thralls or apprentices) whisked passed me and shut the door tightly behind me. I heard the turn of a key and the creak of a latch and glanced over my shoulder. She drew shut the assortment of luxurious curtains that hung over the door, hiding it from view. There was no turning back now, I was locked in …

The *hof* was a single rectangular room with a low ceiling, lit by two firepits and numerous candles and fish oil lamps. Runes were etched into the wooden posts that ran down the centre of the *hof* and cutting through the floor was a path of stone slabs an *ell* wide. The building was deceiving – it had seemed so small from the outside but inside I realised how spacious and long it was.

We walked by the long rectangular firepit where the dark-skinned woman was sweeping. The browned vines that had crept through the roof had coiled around the rafters, hanging and snagging my hair as I walked beneath them. There was a table shoved up against the wall on one side of the firepit and tucked under the table was a bathtub. Along the other wall opposite the fire pit were piles of split logs, baskets, trunks and a cupboard filled with who-knows-what. A few decapitated chickens and birds hung from the rafters above the baskets, their blood draining into soapstone dishes on the floor beneath them.

Along with the vines and the birds, hanging from the rafters were bundles of plants, some in muslin bags others just tied in bunches with string, already thoroughly dried out but left to hang, regardless. The various sweet and sharp scents of the drying plants, the tangy odour of birds' blood and the ashy smell of smoke permeated the *hof*, pungent yet somehow comforting – it reminded me of Brynja's home.

Glittering trinkets sparkled in polished wooden bowls on tall stands and along the walls were more baskets and chests. There were shelves bursting with bottles and jars of mysterious looking powders and liquids. Carved faces of the gods and goddesses leered at us from around the room. Some of the statues and statuettes were made from stone but most were carved from wood. The smaller statues were positioned on top of pedestals and stands or tucked beside jars and baskets on shelves, while the others stood on the floor, large and imposing.

The völva signalled for me to sit on one of the many stools, three-legged with a half-moon shaped seat, that were scattered around the *hof*, while she drifted back to the long rectangular firepit to speak in hushed tones with her dark-skinned associate. I sat as instructed and pulled my hood from my head. I held it tight against my front, over the packs, and looked around. The stool I was sitting on was set in front of a small circular table, next to a platform where the only high-backed chair in the *hof* was situated. The chair was ornately carved like a throne, with plush looking pillows on the seat, while the stool (like all the others) was hard, bare and simple.

A few steps away from my stool was the secondary fire burning in front of the platform. Hanging over that circular firepit was a huge blackened pot, the contents bubbling and emitting a scent I'd never smelled before; it was pungent though not at all unpleasant.

Upon the platform, behind the völva's throne, was a wooden altar, the top stained with mysterious dark patches, and behind the altar was a huge four-poster bed covered with furs and silks, knotwork and runes carved into the tall bed posts. I glanced at the völva; her hand was rested on the small of the dark-skinned woman's back. For a moment I wondered whether the three women shared this bed together ...

With a small, coy smile playing on her pink lips, the völva came to me and sat on her throne, resting back in it comfortably. She lifted her head expectantly.

"M-my name is Aveline Birgersdóttir." I stammered. "I was told you are powerful, with the gift of sight – I heard you can give blessings and that you're a powerful healer and–"

"What is it you want from me, Aveline Birgersdóttir?"

I breathed in deeply and slowly released my breath through slightly pursed lips before staring the völva in the eyes.

"My youngest child was killed. I haven't been able to eat or sleep, I haven't felt happiness since her death. I can feel myself dying, but I have four more children I must live for – I need you to heal me, to take away my sadness–"

"It is quite auspicious that you should come to me on Mother's Night of all nights. A propitious coincidence, perhaps?" She said.

"It's *Jól* already?" I asked, surprised.

"*Já*, it is." The völva purred. "The Wild Hunt rides its fiercest tomorrow eve."

It was the first celebration I had missed attending with my children ...

"Tell me why I should help you on the first day of *Jól*, when no work should take place and I should be performing rituals for Frigg and the Dísir." The völva said. "What can you offer to persuade me to do what you wish on tonight of all nights?"

I laid my packs on the tabletop between us with a heavy *thunk*.

"There are silver, jewels, coins and gold in these; payment for your help."

The völva took the packs, opened them and examined the contents, her eyes widening with pleasure.

"Usually I ask for a white horse as well. Were you told that, too? I noticed you came here on foot." Her gaze flittered briefly to my filthy worn boots.

"I brought one, but it was killed by wolves on my way here." A pang of worry struck my words.

"No matter, I suppose. Luckily for you, there is more than enough in these packs for me to give what you want." The völva said.

"I want something else." I blurted.

Her narrow jaw dropped, a mixture of amusement and surprise dancing on her face. I cleared my throat.

"*Gør þú svá vel*, völva. I have questions for the gods – I was told you can travel to the spirit world and speak to the gods themselves?"

"That is true." She nodded. "You want me to make a request of them for you?"

"*Nei* – I want you to take me. I want to go to the spirit world and speak to the gods myself."

"I see. So *that's* why you brought so many riches." She stroked her finger along one of the packs.

Her silky laugh cascaded from her soft lips again, bringing an embarrassed blush to my cheeks.

"I am willing to let you *try* to enter the spirit world." The völva said.

My heart skipped a beat as hope flooded through me.

"I must ask why you want to go yourself, rather than just let me ask the gods on your behalf? I am experienced, and you know nothing. You've obviously never performed *seiðr*, and I don't think you quite understand the risks." She said, her mocking tone deflating my confidence but not enough to deter me. "Travelling to the spirit realm is exhaustive on the body and the mind. There is a lot that goes into trancework, and one does not just *go to the spirit realm* the first time they attempt – it takes years of dedication, training and practice. It is highly likely that you will fail, and you can risk your life by trying.

"The silver you have brought will pay for a large supply of poppy seeds you can chew that will calm your madness over your poor daughter's unfortunate death – I can also give you a few jugs of henbane beer that will soothe you until the spring comes and you can brew the beer yourself in your own home. With the silver, gold and jewels, I can give you all that *and* enough powdered saffron and red wine, to mix and drink every day for a four-week treatment that will help rid you of your sadness.

"These are only temporary mood-lifters, however. Only time will heal the loss of your child. Not even the gods can get rid of that pain, you realise this? They cannot change that your child has died – they cannot give her back to you, you know this?

"So, I must ask you again, do you still want to travel to the spirit realm?"

"*Já*," I replied without hesitation. "I have a demand to make of the gods, and I must make it myself."

"Have you ingested henbane before, girl?"

I shook my head.

"*Amanita muscaria?*"

I shook my head again. I had seen the *Amanita muscaria* mushrooms many times, with their red caps mottled with white spots, but I had never eaten them before. They grew bountifully in the Norse lands. *Berserkr* warriors were known to eat them before battle or before raiding a village to amplify their courage.

"These are the two most important items to help you reach the spirit realm. In large quantities they are lethal. And you, a husk of a woman – it might not take much for them to kill *you*, at all." The völva snickered. "Are you really willing to risk your life for this?"

"*That which is worth having requires sacrifice.*" Marta's voice rang in my mind as I quoted her words. "I have already risked my life coming here, I won't give up now. I could have bought poppy seeds, henbane and powdered saffron from a trader or healer, but I didn't, I came here to visit the gods. If I die trying then at least one way or another, I will be able to make my request to them."

"That is one way of looking at it, to be sure!" The völva chuckled. "No matter what, then, you will be successful. If it is worth the risk to you, then it is worth the gold and jewels to me. I warn you again, there is a high chance you will fail to reach the spirit realm. I will attempt to send you, but if you don't reach it, the payment is still mine to keep. Whether you succeed or fail, whether you live or die, the payment is *mine*. Do you understand?"

"Keep it all." I replied.

RISE TO FALL

"Where are you from, Aveline Birgersdóttir? Who is your husband? I must know so I can send word of your death should you fail."

I gulped hard.

"I live in Aros." I said. "My husband is Vidar Alvarsson, the Jarl of Aros."

The völva nodded, then stood up and walked towards the cupboard across from us. She searched among the shelves for something and after a moment or two she drifted over to the circular fire pit with a silk bag clutched in her hand. She opened the bag, poured the seeds into her palm and sprinkled them onto the fire. It hissed and crackled as the seeds dropped onto the flames.

"Thralls, come." She said.

So, they were thralls ...

The völva didn't turn to either of the women as she spoke. She stared at the flames, holding the silk bag in the air. She didn't need to say anything more – the thralls rushed to her immediately, brooms still in their hands.

"Sól, bring our guest a glass of henbane beer." The völva instructed. "Nótt, fetch a bowl of *Amanita muscaria.*"

The völva pointed at the cauldron simmering over the small circular firepit.

"*Já.*" The thralls nodded and hurried off to complete their tasks.

The völva returned to her throne, her eyes sparkling with entertainment and mystery. She fiddled about with the bag of seeds, rolling the soft fabric between her fingertips.

"Henbane is very important for trancework and magic." She explained. "The henbane beer and the smoke of the burning seeds will calm you down and open your consciousness for the trance. As your body becomes heavy and sinks, the *Amanita muscaria* will free your soul and allow it take flight to the spirit world. You will become dizzy and tired, but your sight and hearing will be enhanced."

Sól, the pale thrall, brought me a tankard of cold henbane beer, and Nótt set a bowl in front of me, plump golden chunks of the *Amanita muscaria* mushroom floating in the dark liquid. I let the mushrooms cool and brought the tankard to my lips. The smell of the beer was strong and bitter; I wrinkled my nose as I took a gulp of the stuff, choking on it as I swallowed – it tasted just as disgusting as it smelled.

"Drink it quickly." The völva ordered. "It will take a while for the henbane to take effect. You will need to drink another concoction later. Thralls ready the tub, our guest must be cleaned before she makes her journey."

The thralls nodded and hurried off to prepare my bath. While they did so, I took a deep breath, screwed up my face and drained the tankard as quickly as I could. The völva clapped as I drank and laughed heartily as I slammed the empty tankard on the table, spluttering and coughing.

"My, my," The völva said. "You are determined, aren't you?"

I twitched an eyebrow at her in reply, gasping for breath and attempting to not throw up the filthy tasting beer.

"Now, eat the *Amanita muscaria*. You must drink every drop of the liquid as well." The völva ordered.

With finger and thumb, I plucked one of the soggy pieces of mushroom from the bowl, blowing on it to cool it down. It was firm but somewhat slippery, and the gorgeous scarlet colour of the fungi caps had turned golden during the boiling process. Again, I wrinkled my nose and gingerly brought the unappealing looking mushroom to my mouth and ate it – and to my surprise, it was delicious! As I chewed, the *Amanita muscaria* burst with a sweet, nutty flavour, far more appetising than the filthy henbane beer. I took the bowl in both hands and slowly sipped it down until only the caps were left.

As I consumed the mushrooms and their liquid, I watched the völva. As I ate, she crossed the room and took a few jars from the shelves and a deep silver goblet from the cupboard. She put them on the wooden altar before fetching an amphora and took that to the altar, too. She murmured a few quiet indecipherable words, (a prayer or spell, maybe?), before pouring red wine from the amphora into the goblet. She sprinkled the different powders from the jars into the wine and mixed them together with the blade of the utility knife she'd removed from her belt.

"Thralls, come." She said, returning to her throne.

The thralls stood beside us. The völva took a few gulps from the goblet, her top lip glistening pink with residue from the wine and passed the goblet to me. My stomach was so full of the mushroom stew and henbane beer it had bloated, but I brought the goblet to my lips, regardless. The wine was rich, smelling sharply of ginger and cinnamon.

"Drink more." The völva ordered.

Not able to savour the glorious taste, I forced myself to gulp the wine down, feeling guilty as I did so. Wine was the most expensive fermented beverage one could buy – grapes were not something that could be grown in the Nordic lands, and there were very few berry wines produced here. Wine was usually (and expensively) imported from the Mediterranean and saved for events. It was a rare treat to drink wine, and when one drank it, it must be enjoyed, not guzzled as I was doing.

Satisfied, the völva told me to pass the goblet to the thralls, shocking me greatly – I had never heard of one giving wine to a thrall! I gave the goblet to Nótt, who was standing closest to me, and she drank deeply before passing it to Sól. The völva took a small swallow of the wine after the pale thrall had drank her fill then ordered me to finish what was left.

"Coriander, clove, saffron, cinnamon, ginger and cardamom mixed with red wine arouses the body and the senses." The völva explained.

"Why should my body need to be *aroused*?" I gasped.

"For what is to come."

"And what is that, exactly?" I demanded.

"You'll see." The völva smiled.

After drinking their portions, the thralls returned to filling the bathtub. My head spun as I watched them walk back and forth fetching water, sheens of sweat glistening on their brows. They had lifted some stone slabs to reveal a shallow, narrow channel of water that ran through the floor of the *hof*, just wide enough for them to dip their buckets into and catch the running water. They poured the cold, clear water into the tub and heated cooking stones in the fire pit. Once thoroughly warmed through, they used tongs to pick up and toss the hot stones into the tub to warm the water.

"First, you will be cleaned of all the filth and dirt of your journey. Not only will your body be cleansed, but through the ceremonial bath, all thoughts will be washed from your mind. Then you will come up here, to the platform, and we will make your body seethe. Your body must boil and tremble – when your body quakes it will shake your consciousness free from your body, so you can fly to the spirit world. These," the völva said, indicating to her two women as we watched them. "Are my servants of *seiðr*. They will help in the trancework. They will prepare you, and they will help you travel."

I rolled my lips together and furrowed my brow, trying to understand everything the völva was telling me. My mind spun and suddenly a stifling heat overcame me. I tossed the goblet onto the table and rubbed my eyes with the heels of my hands before tugging at the neck of my dress. My clothing felt heavy, suffocating almost. The völva's concoctions must've been taking effect, and I began to worry whether I had made the right decision.

Nótt suddenly approached me and offered me her hand.

"We're ready." She said, her eyes respectfully lowered to me.

Her soft voice was heavily accented in a foreign tone I had never heard before. I didn't know what part of the world she was from, but it was surely nowhere near the Norse lands or the kingdoms of Britain.

I stared at her hand, gazing at her long, slender fingers, the delicate lines on her palm. Slowly I took it and allowed her to lead me to the tub. My body was heavy and beads of sweat dripped down the side of my face. We stopped by the tub, and I examined her intensely as she drifted around me, carefully removing my clothing.

Nótt was phenomenally beautiful and unusual – in both the Kingdom of the East Angles and Denmark, I had never seen a woman such as her. I thought of Aaminah, Freydis's personal house thrall, a favourite of hers. Aaminah was dark-skinned and ebony-haired – she had come from a town in the desert lands, near the Caspian Sea, where most people had black hair and swarthy skin – but even Aaminah was not as dark as this woman; the völva's servant had skin as dark as night.

There was an intense exquisiteness in Nótt's unique appearance. High cheekbones protruded elegantly from her round face. Her full lips were pursed as she solemnly undressed me, her eyes still lowered respectfully to me. My outer garments removed, Nótt unfastened the brooches that held up my apron dress.

Nótt seemed to me like a mysterious goddess. Long, clean-limbed and svelte, with perfect posture; her shoulders back and head held high. Through the sheer fabric of her simple gown, I could spy her figure – her narrow waist, the swell of her wide hips, the fullness of her large breasts and the roundness of her plump buttocks. Though Nótt was thin, her body was strikingly shapely.

Soon enough I stood naked before her; she had delicately peeled away each layer of clothing from my body. The cold air kissed my flesh, but the warmth of the fire before me staved off my shivering. Nótt unpinned and unfastened the many plaits from my hair. She brought my long wild tresses over my shoulder, detangling them with her fingers.

Nótt's tightly curled locks of deep brown hair cascaded to the small of her back; every glossy curl of her long mane was flawlessly coiled, not a single strand out of place. My hair, however, once released from the plaits, was wild and untamed; a tousled and dishevelled mess that burst from my head to my buttocks in thick waves of loose spirals and fierce tangles.

She brought her hands away from my hair, seemingly satisfied with her work. As I lifted my eyes, we caught each other's gazes, and a jolt of shock shot through me. Nótt's eyes were of the palest blue! My jaw dropped; I couldn't stop staring. Like diamonds shining on black velvet, her eyes were striking. Noticing my obvious surprise, Nótt offered me the smallest of smiles before she stepped across the room.

Gaping still, I realised that someone's fingers had gently enclosed my wrist. It took effort, but I tore my eyes away from the beautiful dark servant, to find whose hand gripped me now.

The fair servant, Sól, gazed at me with eyes of onyx. So black were her eyes, I couldn't tell where the pupil ended, and the iris began. She guided me into the tub, gently touching the back of my thigh to indicate I had to step in. My feet were heavy as though tied with invisible weights; it took effort for me to lift them, but with each soft touch my body obeyed the pale servant and I stepped into the tub, narrowly avoiding the heated stones that warmed the bath water.

Green, grey and light purple flecks floated in the water; Sól had tossed a handful of various powdered herbs and dried flowers into the bath. Sufficiently infused in the hot waters, the herbs gave off a rich and beautiful scent. A thin haze of steam wafted around me, and more beads of sweat slipped down my face. Wildly lightheaded, I rested against the low wall of the tub, the heat surging through me blissfully.

I caught Sól smiling as she watched me lean back. Knelt beside the tub, she dipped a clean linen rag into the waters and whirled it around until it was soaking, dripping the droplets over my flesh almost teasingly. A vision of Vidar appeared in my mind, his handsome face smirking at me as he bathed me … I thought of Vidar running his rough, calloused hands over my body, gazing at me with those gorgeous icy eyes, and as I thought of him, a yearning, a desire, grew inside me.

"To achieve a trance state and travel to the spirit realm, you must be free of all thought – all distractions." The völva said, watching the thralls and me from her throne. "You must block out everything around you and focus on the task at hand, you must allow your spirit to shake free of your body and transcend. Only when your consciousness has been altered, when you are suspended between the worlds, will you be able to get the answers you seek.

"The rhythm of penetration causes all thoughts to disappear. As orgasm grows in the body, the mind is opened, the body begins to shake and vibrate – it trembles. It is that point between trembling and euphoria where consciousness leaves the body and one can visit the spirit world.

"*Völvur* can force their body to tremble and enter a trance state by will alone. For the novice, sexual rites are necessary to induce trembling. The wine you drank increases the arousal of the body –

it makes the body and mind more pliant and willing to participate in the rites. I'm sure you've never even thought about allowing a woman to enjoy your body like your husband does," The völva chuckled wickedly. "But wine and the right herbs will make a woman do almost anything to quench the sexual thirst the concoction gives her."

Her words ripped me from my lusting thoughts of Vidar. I sat bolt upright and gaped at her in shock – *allow a woman to enjoy my body like my husband does?*

"The hardest part of the sexual rite is to deny yourself gratification." The völva continued. "It is imperative you focus on the spirit realm – allow the pleasure to empty your mind but concentrate on your goal. You mustn't reach orgasm, otherwise the body will stop trembling, consciousness will sink back into the body, and the rite will fail."

Nótt returned, a shining ceramic jug in her hand. I stared at her as she dipped the jug into the water and poured the contents over my flesh, over and over until my body was soaking. Nótt filled the jug once more and moved behind me, setting the jug down and drawing my hair back. She trickled the water over my head, some rivulets of water dribbling down my forehead.

"It is *ergi* for a man to practice the art of *seiðr* and prophecy, only women can. Though the Allfather Odin is a notable exception." The völva briefly glanced up at the ceiling.

As Nótt lathered soap in her hands and worked it into my hair, Sól whirled the cloth in the waters beside my thigh, rang it out and lathered soap into it. She delicately took my wrist and began to scrub me clean.

With no discretion, I examined her as I had Nótt. Sól's face was round, like Nótt's, she had a full pout and high cheekbones like her, too. Sól and Nótt were also the same height – only slightly taller than me. Sól's curves were just as ample as Nótt's, she was slim and soft with wide hips and a narrow waist, just like Nótt. Their features and body shapes were almost identical; both women were beautiful, their features were perfectly sculpted, their bodies were wonderfully curved, and their skin was smooth and clear.

As there were many similarities to the women, there were many clear opposites too, Nótt's hair was tightly coiled and jet black, but Sól's hair was straight and almost white in colour, like strands of woven cloud that drifted from her head, silky and sleek. As Nótt was the darkest woman I had ever seen, so Sól was the palest. She was so pale that her skin seemed translucent; as she reached across me for my other arm, I could see the life flowing through her blue veins beneath her flesh.

Nótt rinsed the soap from my hair as Sól scrubbed my chest and shoulders, my breasts. Having completed washing my hair, Nótt left us and busied herself elsewhere in the hall. I didn't look to see where she'd gone for my attention stayed with Sól; she had risen to her feet and tipped her head up, indicating that I also stand.

Slowly I rose, water streaming down my body, flecks of the scented herbs stuck to my skin. Sól scrubbed my lower back, my tummy, my legs, my buttocks. I held my breath and closed my eyes as she delicately ran the soapy rag between my legs. She lathered me in the divine smelling soap, then rinsed the suds away with water from the jug.

Her footsteps crunched in the dirt floor; I opened my eyes and saw both the servants stood by a shelf a few feet away, examining the bottles upon them. Nótt chose three tiny bottles and an antler comb and set them on the floor beside the bed on the platform. I noticed there was a path formed of long narrow linens laid on the floor, from the platform to the tub – Nótt must've put them there while Sól was cleaning me.

Sól returned to me carrying a folded linen sheet. She took me by my elbow and helped me step out of the bath. I stood shivering beside the tub as she dried my hair and body with the sheet, before she finally wrapped the damp sheet around me. She led me to the bench, making sure I stepped only on the sheets to maintain the cleanliness of my body. Together, the two women opened the bottles and dripped the oils into their hands.

Behind me, Nótt ran her oiled fingers through my hair, combed the snarls and snags out until my curls hung smooth, glossy and sweet-smelling. She massaged my back and shoulders with her oily hands and Sól rubbed oil over my chest and ribs, each woman moving in unison, massaging my body at the same pace.

As they massaged the oils into my flesh, my knees grew weak and my body swayed. The smell of the henbane seeds burning on the fire was suffocating. My breathing laboured and my head spun, the völva's speech about sex rites whirling in my mind.

I cried out in surprise; Sól cupped her hand between my legs, massaging the oil into the silky tuft of hair there. I stumbled back and collapsed onto the edge of the bed. My body trembled, and I gripped the furs in my fists to steady myself, gasping breathlessly. I hung my head and stared at the dirt floor between my feet to steady my spinning mind, my thighs clamped firmly shut.

This was a necessary step to enter the spirit realm – like the völva had explained, my body had to *seethe*, and stimulation and arousal were the key to that. Yet I was embarrassed and ashamed; I felt as though I was betraying Vidar by allowing these women to touch me. Ashamed that a familiar, tingling warmth was growing inside me, smouldering ... Vidar was the only person in the world who had made me feel that before, and as my husband he was the only one who was *meant* to make me feel that way. But this all was necessary, it had to happen for me to accomplish what I had come here to do ...

"Let them work." The völva said as though she could read my mind. "If you want to reach the spirit realm, you must forget your anxieties, Aveline. To succeed, you must seethe. The pair will help you, so let them do their part."

Nótt appeared between my legs, kneeling on the ground in front of me. She dripped some more oil into her hands and began rubbing it into my calves. Sól climbed onto the bed beside me, cupping one of my breasts in her hand, palpating it with her slick palms. My flesh tingled wildly beneath their hands. They worked the knots from my muscles, soothed the ache from my body. Overwhelmed, I fell back, writhing beneath their touch.

"Beautiful, aren't they?" I could hear the delighted smile on the völva's lips, her tone was so joyous and proud. "Beautiful and *pure*. They stay untouched until the day they leave this place."

I peered at the völva through half-closed eyes. I watched her stroke Nótt's cheek wistfully and Nótt glowed with pleasure at her mistress's touch. They smiled at one another for a moment before the völva nodded to me and Nótt immediately began kissing my legs. Delicious waves of sensation lapped over my body as she kissed me ... I tried to focus on the völva, but my mind was spinning, and my heart beat so loudly in my ears I could hardly hear her words.

"There is a trader who brings my pairs to me. I pay him handsomely to find me them. He never fails me – he must meet my *very* specific requirements. He travels great lengths to find my girls and bring them to me. From the Norse lands, one fair beauty to symbolise day, and from the Blálands, one dark beauty to symbolise night. My trader exhausts his every connection to get me what I want. He works very hard, it's difficult to get me my pair – especially my Bláland girls."

This trader she spoke of ... there was only one man I knew of who could travel to the ends of the earth and back in search for special 'items' like the völva's pair – Herra Kaupmaðr. He *had* to be the trader she spoke of, there was no other man capable of what Herra Kaupmaðr could do. I hadn't thought anyone had travelled to the Blálands since Björn Ironside, son of Ragnar Loðbrók, had been there between the years 859 and 862, but Herra Kaupmaðr, the Lord Merchant, was capable of anything. He could go anywhere, he could take whatever he wanted, he was more than capable of travelling to the Blálands if he wanted to.

I concentrated on the völva in my best effort to ignore the thralls. She walked to the cupboard again, collecting small pots and bottles from her shelves as she went, her voice drifting dreamily. After setting down the pots on the altar, she retrieved the amphora of wine and took a mortar and a wooden *seiðstafr*, a staff or wand, from on top of the cupboard and took them to the altar, too.

With her long, slender hands, Nótt pushed her hair back behind her shoulders, her curls tickling the soft flesh of my inner thigh. She ran her wide, wet tongue between my legs, and I couldn't stop from crying out. Sól pushed me down on the bed and pinned me there. She bent her head over me and dragged her tongue over my breast, flicking her tongue over my nipple, gripping the other and palpating it gently. Another gasp fell from my lips, but it was throaty, deep and filled with pleasure.

I heard the trill of the völva's song-like laughter at my enjoyment of her pair's tending. I glared at her as she straightened out the items on the altar, watching us as she did so. She turned back to her work, opened pots and silk bags, took careful pinches of herbs and sprinkled them into her mortar. She ground them down to a fine powder with the base of her *seiðstafr*. Abruptly she put down the mortar and *seiðstafr*, took another silk bag and tossed the contents into the circular firepit – more henbane seeds, perhaps? Yes, they must've been – the flames crackled and popped and that same strong scent from before filled the air.

"Over the generations, my family have harnessed the power of *seiðr* in a remarkable way – much unlike any other völva or *spákona* you will ever meet. I am searched for by travellers from across the seas, eager for me to tell them their future or cast them a spell." The völva bragged. "How have we harnessed *seiðr*? Most other völvur, you will find, practice *seiðr* once they pass child-bearing age. In my family, we dedicate our entire lives to being völvur. Young or old, we sacrifice everything we have to the practising of *seiðr*."

The thralls paused their pleasuring of me when the völva sat on the bed, a silver goblet in her hand. She slipped a hand under my head, urging me to sit up, and brought the silver goblet to my lips, filled with the same concoction of wine as earlier I thought – it smelt the same. The völva tangled her fingers in my hair and held my head securely, tilting the wine into my mouth and forcing me to drink it.

"Oh!" I gasped as Sól closed her lips around my nipple and sucked it hungrily, spilling wine down my face.

The völva laughed and ran her finger over my chin where the wine has spilled. With a soft *smack!* of her lips she sucked the wine from her fingertip. She pushed me down onto the bed again, and Nótt buried her head between my legs.

My legs twitched from her tending, and I gripped the furs in my fists, the blazing heat growing like a forest fire. Suddenly Nótt disappeared and a vision of Vidar appeared in her place. I knew it wasn't him – it was an illusion caused by the brews the völva had given me – and yet, he seemed so real! As though it were him between my legs, leading me to ecstasy ... I knew the völva and her pair wouldn't allow me to reach orgasm, but illusion or not, the sight of Vidar took away my guilt, and I calmed. My body sank into the bed, and my mind began to empty ...

"*Seiðr* can be very effective as a group practice, so my family utilise servants to aid us ... Many generations ago, a völva of my kin found the use of young, virgin women to be incredibly beneficial, ironically, in the sexual rites – as you can attest!" The völva cackled. "As the decades went by, my ancestors perfected the use of these virgin women – *the pairs*. As the Nornir were three, so the völva and her pair are three. My family have always preferred our pairs to be opposites, gorgeous contrasts of one another – one light, one dark; the day and the night – from opposite ends of the world, but that is purely an aesthetic that we admire. Regardless of the colour of their flesh, they must be of exceptional beauty, most importantly, their purity *must* be maintained.

"Some believe virgins are magical beings, chaste and more in-tune with the gods. My family found that the virgins' need to satisfy – not *be* satisfied – helps them sooth the nerves from the body. Their beauty entices the worries from the mind and compel it to empty, thus aiding the trance to occur."

The völva rose from the bed and made her way to the altar. I couldn't concentrate on her anymore, lost in the euphoria shooting through me from Nótt's mouth between my legs, and the sweet taste of Sól's tongue dancing with mine. My whole body began to tremble as euphoria prepared to crash over me completely, but Nótt pulled away, ripping me from not just ecstasy, but tearing away the illusion of Vidar as well. Nótt crawled up onto the bed and kissed me, and I could smell and taste my own scent and flavour on her tongue, on her lips.

The völva returned to her powdered herbs and mixed them with a glossy white salve, the consistency of oil and fat mixed together.

"My trader did well with this pair – better than any of his forefathers, and I doubt that any future generation will outdo him.

Their opposing eyes – the light skin with black eyes, the black skin with light eyes – I have never seen a more beautiful pair!" She said.

The servants beamed lovingly at their mistress. They didn't say a word – but for their purrs and breathy giggles and the one or two brief words they had said to the völva, they hadn't said a direct word to me at all. Not that I could say anything, myself – when they had cleansed my body of the filth of my journey, they had washed away my ability to speak.

The völva took a handful of the salve and slathered it over the almost phallus-shaped handle of her *seiðstafr*, covering it with a smooth layer of the mixture. She approached the bed, *seiðstafr* in hand, the white salve on its handle glittering in the firelight, and immediately Nótt and Sól climbed off the bed and stood at the end of it. Quietly, the pair began to sing in soft, repetitive drones, their tones only slightly different in pitch.

"Think of the spirit realm, Aveline Birgersdóttir." The völva said softly. "Think *only* of the spirit realm. Breathe deeply – long slow breaths. You mustn't pay attention to the pleasure coursing through your body – instead, feel the motion of the *seiðstafr* as it moves back and forth inside you, listen to the rhythm of the chant, follow it and allow it to lead you out of your body."

The völva joined her pair in the chant, deep and eerie, no discernable words, just sound. The pair opened my legs to let the völva to stand between them. The völva rested her hand on my abdomen and pressed the rounded handle between my legs, rubbing the cold salve over me.

My legs shuddered, but the pair held them wide open, and the völva slowly pressed the greasy end of her *seiðstafr* into me, the intense coldness of the salve freezing my insides. I gasped and cried out, but my body was suddenly too heavy to move. The heavily scented smoke of the burning henbane seeds filled my nostrils and my mouth, almost suffocating me. My eyes fell shut; I was unable to keep them open any longer.

Slowly the völva filled me with her *seiðstafr*, moving it back and forth slowly. The freezing coldness of the salve dissipated, warming to my body temperature quickly, tingling invigoratingly.

With each thrust of the *seiðstafr* that delectable euphoria rose inside me again.

The three women's chant increased in volume though the rhythm remained steady, mesmerising. The völva increased the pace of her thrusting. My body began to quiver, it shuddered, it trembled violently, I felt as though I was rising from the bed. A soft groan rolled in my throat, I gripped the furs of the bed, my body tensing as the fire inside me grew.

"Think of Odin!" The völva exclaimed. "Let his ecstasy flow through you! Let it take you to the spirit realm!"

Set on the edge of euphoria, suddenly, I flew.

RISE TO FALL

CHAPTER NINETEEN

MY BODY TURNED to shadow. I rose into the air, drifting delicately like tendrils of smoke from a candle flame, free from the confines of my physical body. I contorted and twisted, then dissipated into the atmosphere. The völva and her pair had vanished, though their chanting remained, just whispers in the distance.

Reality became ephemeral, bending, twisting, fading until all substance dissolved. The walls and floor became supple, they flexed and moved, before losing their solidity and becoming vapour, then disappeared completely. No more did I lie on the soft, fur covered bed. No more was I trapped inside the ancient wooden walls, its ceiling and rafters hidden beneath coils of browned ivy, vines and the prickly lengths of scrambling brambles. No, instead I found myself flying through the silver winter sky, the bitter biting chill absent from my flesh, for I didn't have flesh anymore. I was a ghost, a spirit, a breeze drifting higher and higher, away from the world.

The absence of body, the sensation of floating, it was dangerously enticing. If this is what death felt like, the separation of spirit from body, drifting upwards in absolute peace with a complete lack of care and no feeling to speak of, I could certainly see the appeal. My mind was empty of thought, I was consumed by a total calm. Though the völva and her pair had not allowed me total gratification with their pleasuring of me, I didn't feel the overwhelming longing and incompleteness as I had when Nótt had halted tending of me when I wavered on the cusp of orgasm.

No, I wasn't whole, and that realisation was somehow wonderful.

As I drifted ever upwards, I found myself rising above the clouds to a place I'd never known before. It was grey, in between the shadow of dark and the brightness of light. Ahead of me was a deep blackness, which I was drawn to – there was a comfort beckoning me towards it. I gazed over my shoulder and saw behind me a blinding white that sent chills down my spine and an ache in my heart. A solidity formed beneath my feet, some sort of flooring or ground I could feel but couldn't see. Whatever it was, it was hard and unyielding, and I ran upon it, dashing towards the black abyss, putting as much space as possible between myself and the frightening light.

As I neared the darkness, the scent of rich wine drifted to my nostrils. A vision of Anders Bursson flashed before my eyes and I ran faster, drawn to that familiar, alluring smell. The memory of his kiss suddenly tingled upon my lips, blazing as though our lips had only just parted. I wanted to find him, his arms open wide, inviting me into his embrace …

But he wasn't there.

There was nothing.

I slowed and stopped at the edge of the darkness. For a few moments all was still, the völva and her pair's chant barely audible. I could feel my heart racing in my chest and my cold breath falling from my lips in pants. For an age I stood staring at the blackness, rooted to the spot.

Suddenly the shadows receded, like black silk pulled away by some invisible being, revealing a massive, towering throne carved of oak with a great figure sat upon it. Dragon heads roared silently from each corner of the terribly high back, and the snarling heads of wolves howled soundlessly from the throne's arms. The figure's long fingers curled around the wolves' heads, his mighty hands gripping the chair's arms firmly. I gazed up the massive, muscled arms, spying his wrists, covered in a light down of fair hair, beneath the long sleeves of his indigo tunic. Black leather boots covered his large feet, dark blue trousers clung to his thick legs, and only a fraction of the indigo tunic upon his torso was visible, the face of the being, his shoulders and half of his body upper body was completely shrouded in shadow.

"Who are you?" I asked before I realised I'd even opened my mouth to speak.

"You know who I am, Danethrall." The deep, booming voice replied, his words echoing around me.

I flinched; *he knew me*. My first husband, Jarl Erhardt Ketilsson, the previous Jarl of Aros, had been the last person to call me 'Danethrall' – no one had dared call me that name since Vidar killed Erhardt and slaughtered half of Aros to rescue me, all those years ago ... But this great being dared – he knew that name. I swallowed hard, suddenly afraid.

"A-are you the Allfather?" I asked.

"I am known by many names ... *Alföðr, Hávi, Fjölnir, Sigföðr, Biflindi, Valföðr, Grímnir, Bölverkr, Yggr* ... These are but some, there are yet many more."

The shadows still concealed his face. Was it him? The ruler of the Æsir? The god of wisdom and poetry and battle and the gallows?

"Why did you come here?" He demanded.

"Surely you already know?" I clapped a hand to my mouth, shocked by my own forwardness but the mysterious being sitting before me didn't seem to mind – in fact, he chuckled.

"Of course, I know all." He said, amusement alight in his words. "I want to hear you speak, Danethrall. You must ask your questions before I share the answers, for I will not tell you what you do not ask to know."

I took a deep breath and a step forward.

"My daughter, Alffinna Vidarsdóttir–" I paused, a knot forming at the very mentioning of her name. I cleared my throat and continued to speak, but my words shuddered as I forced them out. "–She was murdered. She had not yet seen her first winter – far too young an age to die. I want you to give her back to me."

The being exploded with laughter. I slapped my hands over my ears, the sound of his mirth so deafeningly loud. It wasn't an unpleasant laughter, it was musical and delightful, but so great in volume that even the air seemed to tremble from the intensity.

"Brazen woman! Are you foolish or daring?" He exclaimed. "I cannot give your dead child back to you. There is no more anyone can do; your daughter is dead."

"If you are the Allfather, then you can! Please–"

"Don't beg, Danethrall." He scolded.

"Stop calling me that." I shouted, balling my shaking hands into fists. "My name isn't Danethrall, it's A—"

"Aveline." He said in unison with me.

I fell silent, scowling at him, my heart racing in my chest, unshed tears burning my eyes.

"I know who you are, I know your pain." He said softly. "If your children's times have come, no matter how much it hurts, not even the gods can save them. They will die at the time chosen for them by the Nornir. Not even my dear Frigg could change the fate of Baldr, the most beloved of all the gods – nor could anything bring Baldr back from Hel ... If I cannot bring *him* back from death, what makes you think I can change the fate of your children? Your children who are inconsequential in the great scheme of the universe."

"They aren't inconsequential in *my* universe." I snarled.

"Of course not, but that changes nothing." He said matter-of-factly. "They will die when they are meant to. I cannot change that, I cannot bring them back."

My heart wrenched, and fury blazed inside me.

"Then tell me when my children are doomed to die." I growled through gritted teeth. "If you cannot give me back my daughter, then tell me when my other children are destined to pass!"

"You think you'll find peace in that knowledge?"

I stared hard at him, refusing to let my tears to fall. Though I couldn't see his face, I knew he was staring back at me – I could feel his gaze resting heavily upon me, cropping goosebumps over my flesh. He chuckled, like the deep thrum of a lyre.

"You'll be driven mad. You might find that your children will live well into old age ... But you might find they won't. What would you do if you knew they were to die in just a year, and no matter what you tried *nothing* would stop them from dying on that specific moment? Do you really want to know?"

"So, this was all for nought – coming to the spirit realm? I left my children for *nothing*?" I spat. "What use are you, One-Eyed god? You have denied my every request!"

He sat forward in his throne, and the shadow that veiled him vanished. His beard was so long it reached his middle, it was plaited loosely and was white as the sun's rays. One of his eyes was the palest blue, like ice – like Vidar's eyes! It blazed as he gazed at me, whereas his other eyelid hung flat and hollow, seemingly sewn shut to his lower eyelid. He surveyed me with his single eye for what seemed like an age before tossing himself back in his throne. The only shadow that returned to him was a small dark circle over the permanently closed eyelid hung shut over his empty socket.

"Of course, this journey was for nothing." The great being said. "You've known this all along. This was a selfish escape for you. You abandoned your husband and children – who are as broken and devastated as you over Alffinna's death – you abandoned them, so you could run away. You could've bought remedies from your healer, but instead you wasted jewels and riches and a fine horse so you could escape Aros. You wanted to run away from *everything* there, didn't you? You wanted to die on this journey – but that was not your fate, was it? For here you stand before me, alive."

I stared at him in horror, my heart pounding painfully in my chest, my ears ringing with his words.

"But why are you so desperate to die, Danethrall?" He asked, tilting his head to the side as he gazed at me lazily. "You've lost only one child out of your five, most other women aren't as lucky. In fact, you are quite a lucky woman, aren't you?

"Did you ever wonder, little Danethrall, why you're so lucky? Why you were seemingly beloved by so many in such high places? Why, there is nothing unique about you, is there? What great things have you done in your life? Look at you – but for your pretty eyes, you're plain. You're inconsequential in the grand scheme of things, just like your children.

"How did a poor little Christian girl from the Kingdom of the East Angles become a rich jarlkona in the land of the Danes, I wonder?" He laughed loudly again.

His laughter was deep and warm. Had this been any other conversation, any other moment in time, his laughter would fill me with joy – his was the type of laughter that exuded cheer, like the sound of happiness itself, infectious and delightfully so.

But it wasn't any other moment in time and his laughter pierced me, jeeringly.

"You're right." I growled. "I *was* a poor little Christian girl from the Kingdom of the East Angles, so why should my life be decided by the Nornir of the Norse? Surely it should be the Christian God who chooses my fate?"

"Then why did you come to me, instead of him?"

I couldn't answer him. Every word that had fallen from his lips spun in my head in a tumultuous maelstrom, roaring and crashing about my mind. I hadn't even thought of praying to the Christian God, not even briefly, in all the despair and pain Alffinna's death had wrought, I hadn't once considered turning to my previous religious saviour. Not even once.

"When you were a child, you didn't dream of a marvellous future, did you? You expected to marry some boy in your village, birth his children, raise animals, work on your farm …" He waved his hand as he spoke, as though batting away these *boring* life expectancies he was listing, all the while his amused grin grew on his face and his single eye blazed. "But look at you now. Your husband rules Aros – a town growing bigger and wealthier with each passing day – and he holds many settlements under his power.

"When Alvar the First One dies, your husband will take control of Roskilde *and* he'll inherit all of the settlements Alvar rules. He will become one of the richest jarls in Denmark – why, he could even become a king! And he chose *you*, Danethrall, to be his wife, a decision you have more than benefited from. You never expected all this, did you, Danethrall? All the riches, the finery – you never could've dreamed of being so wealthy as to wantonly waste jewels and money on ridiculous selfish decisions like this, could you? What a difference your life is to what it could have been!

"Do you know who decided to give you such a fate? Do you? *The Nornir* – the same Nornir who decided your baby daughter must die."

"I would trade all my riches for Alffinna to be alive again!" I hissed.

"Would you?" He asked, sounding surprised. "Surely, this life you lead is a good one, is it not? You want for nothing. You live in finery and splendour – most would willingly give their firstborn son for the life you lead."

"No amount of riches is worth giving up the life of a child!" I shouted, my words reverberating through the air.

"What if your five children were all alive and starving?" The being asked, not flinching in the slightest. "What if you were offered food and riches to sacrifice one and save the others, what would you choose? Would you allow all five to suffer, poor and hungry until they all eventually died, or would you give up just one of them and end all of their pain?"

A strangled gasp sputtered from my lips as tears burst from my eyes and streamed down my face. Visions of Young Birger, Sander, Æsa, Einar and my poor dead Alffinna whirled in my mind. Frantically, I rubbed my eyes with my shaking fists, trying to get rid of the images.

"It is a good thing you don't have to make that decision," The being said softly. "The Nornir made it for you."

"But my children *weren't* starving!" I yelled. "Tell me – why would the Nornir grant these *imaginary* parents their fifth child if the Nornir planned on killing it? If the child wasn't born in the first place, this decision to kill it would not need to be made!"

"The Nornir decide the time of a man's death, not whether the man has sex or not." He laughed. "That is man's decision. Just as it is man's decision to make the best of what he can with the life given him. Sure, some things are predestined for him, but if he has courage, if he shows worthiness, he may change the course of his fate for the better. Should a man just sit and accept the hand dealt to him in nihilistic apathy? Or should he fight for what he wants? Nothing can kill a man if his time has not come, and nothing can save one doomed to die. To die in flight is the worst death of all.

"When you were married to Erhardt Ketilsson, you didn't just *accept* that life forced upon you, did you? Did you try to run away, or did you fight?" The being paused, a smile growing on his lips. "You suffered – you were beaten, you were raped – but you fought through it. Through cunning and wiles, you manipulated Erhardt and saved yourself from him – you fought to protect the lives of your sons! You fought, Danethrall. In your own way, you fought. Through patience, intelligence and suffering you survived that marriage. You didn't apathetically accept your fate – you fought it and lived!

"When a baby is born, the Nornir choose the moment of its death." He said. "No man can live passed the moment chosen for him by them. Most else in life isn't predetermined, but nothing can change that time."

"But – but that implies that other things *can* be changed? I can alter some things in my destiny?" I gasped, my tears halting; I stared at him with shock and hope.

"Of course! Have you learned nothing in all the years of living among the Danes? All beings who are subject to destiny have some degree of power over their own destiny, and the destiny of others. Alffinna, though her death is heart-wrenching for you, influenced your destiny – she brought you here, to the spirit realm, did she not? If she had lived, would you have sought the völva? Would you have come to make demands of *me*?

"Fate, destiny, whatever you want to call it, is a constantly evolving tapestry weaved by the Nornir, and one must suffer for destiny to earn the ability to change it. If you prove yourself worthy, they may alter the direction you will go, but ultimately there *are* decisions staunchly in place for you, and your life will end at the precise time decided by the Nornir at your birth.

"As the Nornir weave the world's fates, they may change the pattern by crossing threads or by cutting others. Every person you meet in your life, you were destined to meet, for they will influence your life as you will on theirs.

"You were destined to come here, Aveline. You were destined to be a Dane, a jarlkona, a wife, a mother. When Birger Bloody Sword travelled to Britain, your thread crossed his. He thought he was destined to be alone after the death of his wife and children, but you altered his fate and became his daughter. Just as you thought you were doomed to die by the blade of a Dane, he gave you salvation and a new life instead."

"But I lost my parents, my brothers, my family and friends–"

"That is another lesson you surely must've learned after so many years with the Danes. *That which is worth having is worth sacrificing for.* You lost your Anglo-Saxon family, but you gained a Norse father, a Norse family, a Norse husband and Norse children." He pointed out. "Orientate yourself to what you're looking at, Danethrall. You see, the losses of your Anglo-Saxon life, your parents and your brothers, all of whom were meant to die in their homeland. Do you remember the other captive woman – the one who held you as you sailed to Roskilde?"

Mildritha ...

"The moment she held you in her arms, she affected your life. She protected you, she was a constant link to your past, and when she died, that link was severed. When she died, that final piece of your past life disappeared, and you were able to accept and immerse yourself into your new life! In simplistic terms, Danethrall, your parents', your brothers' and Mildritha's lives, those that were so significant to you in Britain, were sacrificed for the new life you gained in Denmark."

"But I didn't ask for this life!" I argued.

"It was your fate."

"Why was I forced to pay those precious lives for a fate I never asked for?" I yelled.

"An eye for an eye, Danethrall." He laughed, pointing to the shadowed, empty socket in his face. "I hung from *Yggdrasill* for nine days and nights, pierced by my own spear, *and* I sacrificed my eye, to get what I wanted. You must always sacrifice something in return for something great."

"You sacrificed yourself and your eye *willingly*! I did not!"

"Would you prefer to be dead? A second chance at life – escaping death – *that* is something great and deserves a great sacrifice! These lives paid for that, for you, for this life you live now, whether you chose it or not. Why are you so ungrateful?"

"How am I meant to live with the guilt?" I cried out frantically. I stumbled backwards and fell to my knees, his words ringing in my ears dizzyingly. "With the burden of those deaths resting on my shoulders?"

"You honour them. You live the greatest life you can in respect to them. Nine deaths paid for you to *live* as Aveline Birgersdóttir, not to *die* as Aveline Eadricesdohter."

My heart stopped.

My breath caught painfully in my throat.

I had been known as Aveline Birgersdóttir for so long, I hadn't heard the names of my family – the name of my father – since I was a child ... It sounded so strange – like a distant memory, I recognised that name and yet it didn't seem to be mine. But here it was, my first name, the name of my birth father, spoken from the mouth of a god.

Aveline Eadricesdohter ...

"What of the years that separated you from Vidar Alvarsson? The years you were wed to Jarl Erhardt? You never gave up hope that Vidar would return. You did not know what your fate was to be, whether you'd see him again or not – but you continued fighting. You suffered, you fought. You *earned* your marriage to Vidar, and it was much more precious to you when you received it, was it not? You earned your marriage and your husband earned his jarldom. That which is worth having is worth sacrificing for, and that which you must sacrifice for is worth having absolutely.

"When you face fatal situations like war or the cruel hand of man, you must be bold and fight with all your might, for there is nothing to fear; in battle, you will either fall or you will come away alive, it is as simple as that.

"You should be grateful for the life you have now, Danethrall. Willingly or not, those nine lives *were* sacrificed, and you should be thankful they granted you this second life. You should be grateful for every struggle, every tear, every heartache. You should be thankful for what the Nornir have given you, tragedy or not.

"Stand to your feet, Aveline Birgersdóttir!" He suddenly yelled, like the snarling of a wolf. "By weeping on the floor, you disrespect those who were sacrificed so you might live this second life! You kneel to no one – *not even a god!*"

My tears stopped flowing immediately. I quickly blinked away the mist from my eyes and glared at him fiercely. Without ripping my bloodshot, aching eyes from him, I slowly rose to my feet, my hands clenched into fists as my sides.

"You came to me through blizzard and snowstorm. You ingested possibly fatal potions from a witch so you might enter the spirit realm and make demands from a god! You wanted to die on this journey, but when the wolves attacked you, you fought them! Their blood drenches your blade; you fought, and you killed to come here!" The being exclaimed, holding out his hand.

My sword, my nameless sword my husband had spared no expense in making for me, materialised in the god's hand, blood fresh upon it and dribbling down the blade. He tossed the sword to my feet, and I swooped down and picked it up, feeling the smooth hilt, cold against my palms. For just a moment I shut my eyes, and I felt the splash of the wolf's blood hot across my flesh. I opened my eyes and glared at the god on the throne, holding my sword out, the tip of the double-edged blade pointing at him.

"I gave up part of my world vision for internal vision." The god said. "Part of me had to die so another part could gain wisdom and understanding. As we advance through life, we lose some small parts of us for new wisdom to take their place. Face what you're seeing, woman. You have lost a child – a tragic part of life you had previously avoided, unlike most other women. The death of your daughter has shown you an agony more painful than anything you'll ever know. You can choose to let that pain destroy you, or you can draw wisdom from it.

"You can accept, as hard as it is, that death is a natural part of the cycle of life, and you can draw strength from the knowledge that nothing will ever hurt you as much as this has. *Or* you can kill yourself now and end the pain. Which do you choose?"

My voice was suddenly lodged in my throat like a rock. Visions of Vidar and our four living children materialised before me, solid and clear as though they were truly there in front of me – as though I could reach out and touch them, grab them and hold them against me. I couldn't kill myself; I couldn't leave my family when they mourned such a loss. The death of Alffinna had affected them as harshly as it had affected me, but I had been too selfish in my sorrow to think of anyone else … Of all the things I wanted at that very moment, it was not death I yearned for – I longed to embrace my beloved children, to kiss them and apologise to them and cry with them.

"Tell me, Danethrall, why do you weep and mourn the life of the Anglo-Saxon Aveline? Her family, her home? You're not Aveline Eadricesdohter, are you?" He leaned forward in his chair and surveyed me. "Your husband doesn't know Aveline Eadricesdohter, does he? Do your children? Of course not. Aveline Eadricesdohter was nothing more than a whining little Anglo-Saxon child. Aveline Eadricesdohter would not have travelled so far to make demands of a god; she would have wept and stared up into the sky, snivelling and weeping to her Christian deity.

"Aveline Eadricesdohter wasn't a mother – but Aveline Birgersdóttir is.

"Aveline Eadricesdohter was not brazen – but Aveline Birgersdóttir is.

"Aveline Eadricesdohter wept and cried, begging her god to rescue her – but Aveline Birgersdóttir stormed to her god with her head high, demanding a deal.

"I don't hand blessings out easily, Danethrall; one must earn what they want from me. I will make no promise just to coddle a weeping babe, but I'll strike a deal with a strong, bold, fierce woman. Which one are you, Danethrall?"

"I am Aveline Birgersdóttir," I growled, taking a step closer to him. "And I demand you protect my living children, Allfather! Do as I request!"

"I cannot change the day they are destined to die, but I can grant blessings upon them through their lives. And, as the völva can prophesy, so can I; I will give you a prophecy of what is yet to come – but what will you give me in return?" He asked, leaning forward in his throne.

"What can a mortal woman give a god?" I spat.

"Nine lives."

I gaped at him, eyes as round as coins.

"Nine lives granted your second life. Nine more lives will grant your children my blessings. Your children will battle, they will fight, they will charge into war and come out victorious. When your sons *do* die, they will be honourable deaths. They will be fathers – they may even be grandfathers. Your daughter will be a wife, a mother, a grandmother. Your children will die long after your flesh has rotted beneath the earth." His pale blue eye twinkled brightly.

"Who do I sacrifice? How do I give you these lives?"

"Your word is enough. All you must do is agree."

"You know when my children are destined to die, don't you?" I realised. "That is why this vow is so easy for you to make! You *know* they won't die as children!"

He is face was still, betraying no emotion or hint. He refused to answer, not even with a nod or shake of his head.

"I will not tell you the age at which they die," The god said firmly. "Nor will I tell you the names of those you will lose, but of your second life, you have lost five loved ones already."

"Five?" I breathed.

Immediately I thought of every death, every loss, since I had come to Roskilde, each face spinning before my eyes.

"Birger, Estrith," we said in unison – though his voice was strong and mine was faded. "Caterine, Alffinna …"

"And Freydis." He announced.

"Freydis isn't dead!" I exclaimed.

"She will be by the time you return to Aros." He said. "This is the prophecy I promised you. Now, you may leave, Aveline Birgersdóttir. I have made my vow to you."

"And who are you, great Norse god? Are you truly the Allfather or are you the *trickster*?" I demanded, remaining staunchly in place, scowling at him.

"I am the one you came here to see." He said.

"Tell me now! Are you Odin or are you Loki? Is this a true promise by the mightiest of gods, or a cruel trick played on me by the mischievous one?"

He rose from his throne and stepped out of the shadow, descending the staircase that kept him lofted above me. He stopped before me, huge, mighty and intimidating, but I stood tall, my head raised and shoulders back, meeting his one-eyed gaze with a steely scowl of my own. Slowly he reached out one of his large hands and delicately cupped my jaw. He lowered his head closer to my face, his singular startling blue eye staring at me.

"I am … a friend."

RISE TO FALL

CHAPTER TWENTY

AS THOUGH I had been stabbed in my sleep, I woke up recoiling in pain and scrunched up in the bed gripping my aching stomach. I felt vomit rise in my throat – I flung myself over the edge of the bed and heaved onto the dirt floor. Blinded with agony from the pain that threatened to rip my head in two, I flopped back onto the bed, choking air down my raw, burning throat, spittle and dribbles of sick oozing down my chin. My body was on fire, sweat poured from my brow in slick, salty streams, every piece of me hurt.

"Did you find what you were looking for?" I heard the völva ask softly from across the room.

Before I could answer, darkness swallowed me.

***

MY EYES SNAPPED open. I didn't know how long had passed, but my head still pounded, and nausea bubbled in my stomach. For a few moments I laid still in the bed, allowing myself to come through to consciousness completely. My body throbbed, and my mind spun, but sense and sensation slowly returned. My stomach was sore, but it didn't ache as dreadfully as it had the first time I had woken – how long ago had that been? Hours – *days*?

I could feel the weight of the linen sheet and fur resting on me, heavy but comforting and soft against my naked flesh. Gradually I sat up in the bed, groggy and nauseous, my stiff body cracking and rigid muscles popping as I moved. I buried my face in my hands, rubbing my stinging eyes with the heels of my hands, breathing deeply, trying to clear the mists from my blurry vision, my mind whirring yet again.

Able to see somewhat more clearly, I wearily glanced about the room. As my mind registered the *hof*, it seemed different ...

Somehow it was so very different to how it had been before the trance. Most of the candles and fish oil lamps had been extinguished, as had the fire that had previously glowed in the small circular firepit, and the pot that had boiled the *Amanita muscaria* had been cleaned and was balanced upside down on a rafter to dry. The stench of the burnt henbane seeds had faded considerably, barely noticeable on the pungent scent of wood smoke that filled the *hof*. In the corner of my eye, I caught sight of the *seiðstafr*, the only item upon the tidied alter. No salve glistened on its phallus-shaped end, it was clean.

Not just the physical differences had changed, but the whole atmosphere of the *hof* had. The *hof*'s eerie and mystical air had vanished along with the candle light. This place was no longer the sacred entrance to the spirit realm, but a home – a home which I was trespassing. Though anger bubbled alongside the sickness in my stomach, the overwhelming knowledge I didn't belong here overwhelmed me. I needed to leave, I needed to go to *my* home.

I spotted the völva's thralls across the room, curled together on the floor in a pile of furs, and I found the völva silently sat beside the large rectangular fire, a silver goblet in her hand. And there, folded neatly at the foot of the bed, were my clothes, my turtle shell brooches rested on top of the tidy pile.

I snatched up my belongings and gathered them against my chest, my eyes darting between the pair and the völva, in case they noticed I had woken. I slipped from the bed, stumbling somewhat, and hastily pulled on my leggings, shift and woollen dress. The völva and her pair didn't move, didn't stir, didn't make even a single sound of acknowledgement to my abrupt dressing, or the cusses I swore under my breath as I accidentally stabbed myself with the pins of the brooches while I fumbled to fix them to the front of the apron. No, the pair continued to sleep, and the völva continued to stare into the flames.

I found my socks, boots, coat and hood hanging over a chair beside the large rectangular fire, across from the völva. Swallowing hard, I bravely strode over to the fire, staring at my clothing. The völva cleared her throat, but I didn't dare look at her. I knew she was awake; I could feel her gaze rest heavy on me. I yanked on my socks and boots, fastened the toggles with fumbling fingers, then pulled my coat on.

"Don't you want the thralls to bathe you before you leave?" The völva teased, her smooth, liquid laugh dripping from her lips.

With hot cheeks, I ignored her. Though my skin was encased in a sheet of dried sweat and the foul taste of bile filled my mouth, I refused to stay in the *hof* for longer than I had to. I pulled my hood over my mass of tangled curls and lunged towards the door of the *hof*. I ripped the curtains open and pulled the handle, thankfully the door was unlocked.

"Don't forget your medicine." The völva yawned. "The herbs are in the packs."

I glanced at her briefly and she tipped her head to the wall across from me. I saw my sword leaning against the wall, next to a large jug of henbane beer, a tall amphora of wine, my packs and belt. I stormed across the room, snatched up my belt and hurriedly buckled it around my middle. I slipped my sword into the wooden scabbard, grabbed my packs and left.

***

THE SKY WAS jet black but for the ivory stars and the moon, silver and skinny like the blade of a newly forged sickle. I stumbled through the thick blanket of snow, wishing that Anders' wolf was still travelling alongside me. I didn't know where, but the wolf had gone – the völva hadn't let it inside her *hof*, nor did the wolf try to enter. I assumed the animal had returned to Anders after the *hof* door had been closed.

I still didn't know how much time had passed – how long I had been in the spirit world? How long had I laid feverish in the völva's bed? Regardless, I journeyed on, trying to remember the way the wolf had taken me, but cautious not to venture too far into the trees and the clumps of woods and forests, lest another hungry pack of wolves caught scent of me. My body ached, my calves throbbed, and I could feel vomit slowly creeping up my throat from my aching belly.

As I stomped and stumbled through the crisp, crunching snow, my thoughts flittered from the pain in my body, the sickness in my stomach and the freezing cold of the bitter night air, to my conversation with the Allfather ...

My conversation with the Allfather ...

But for the völva herself, who else could say they had spoken with the Allfather? Not through symbols or signs or sacrifices, but truly, face-to-face spoken with him. There was a pride, a pleasure that surged through me – I must've been one of the few people in the world who had addressed a deity, an exciting realisation to be sure!

Then doubt settled inside me ... Had I truly spoken with the Allfather? Had that *truly* happened? Or had that been just a trick of the mind created by the völva's brews?

I paused in the night, surrounded by nothing but barren trees and snow, the trickle of estuaries, tidal channels and waves whispering in the distance. I closed my eyes and focussed. I thought of the Allfather, of the mysterious place above the sky, made of shadow and light, of the mighty throne on which the god had sat. I thought of every word that had fallen from his lips, every word that had tumbled from mine, I thought of his hand cupping my jaw as he told me who he was ...

"... *A friend.*"

Slowly I brought my hand to my face and touched the place the Allfather had held. My skin tingled beneath my fingertips as though his hand still rested there. Surely, I couldn't have imagined meeting him – his touch had been so real! Or at least, it had *felt* real. His hands had been smooth and soft, he had held my jaw so gently, and a warmth exuded from it, not imperceptible as in a dream – real warmth, *true* body heat, a solid touch from a real, living being.

My mind drifted to the völva's brews again; the *Amanita muscaria*, the henbane seeds, the henbane beer ... Could they have tricked my mind to make an illusion seem as genuine and tangible as reality? She obviously possessed the knowledge of powerful magic; if she could create brews that made fantasy seem like reality, then the possibility she could, and did, send my spirit to the spirit realm was feasible, surely?

"*Coriander, clove, saffron, cinnamon, ginger and cardamom mixed with red wine arouses the body and the senses.*"

Yes, there was another brew she had me ingest ...

For a moment, the touch of her pair, of her two thralls – so beautiful and similar, yet so different as well – danced over my body, caressing and groping, squeezing and stroking ... That brew had indeed been powerful, it had worked. It had been easy to agree to partake in the völva's sex rite, but it had been hard to *actually* participate. I had never been pleasured by a woman before, though the act was not unheard of in the Norse lands it was still not common and was something I'd never done before.

I had betrayed Vidar. When I married him, I promised my body to him – no other would enjoy me, only him. Yet I let not one, but all *three* women pleasure me ...

My body had to tremble to allow my spirit to 'shake free' of the confines of my body and transcend to the spirit realm, I understood this. Allowing the women to enjoy my body was an entirely necessary part of the ritual. Being penetrated by the *seiðstafr* to the edge of orgasm had been another essential part of the ritual, and yet ... Had he known I would let another enjoy me sexually, would Vidar have supported me to go on this journey? Had I known there were sexual rites involved, would *I* have chosen to go?

Suddenly, my legs became weak, and I collapsed onto my hands and knees and retched into the snow. Nausea had been building inside me since I had left the *hof*, but recalling my willing infidelity, my unfaithfulness and the possible repercussions of my actions ... I couldn't hold back the vomit, shocked to the core by my actions, and so deeply ashamed of myself.

I spat the filthy remains of vomit out of my mouth, stiffly rose to my feet, and brushed the snow from the front of my coat and skirts before I continued walking, my head spinning again. Vidar would stand by me, surely? He always had in the past. Would he view this as a transgression, or would he see it as necessary? I didn't actively go out to lay with these women, I went out in search of answers from the völva ...

But then, what about Anders? More than likely, Vidar would understand the rite to travel to the spirit realm, but what of my kiss with Anders? There was nothing necessary to him, to his kiss ... I took a deep breath and turned my gaze to the dark skies above me.

As there were no wolves beside me neither were there any ravens soaring above me. I was thoroughly alone. With no guide to speak of, I needed to focus on where I was going: Ribe. I tried to remember the directions Káta had given me ... To get to the völva, I should've travelled west to the sea, about two hours walk, then south along the coastline until I found the völva's *hof*. Therefore, sense dictated that I had to go north from the völva's *hof*, then two hours east to reach Ribe – and that was exactly what I would do.

It took at least double the expected amount of time to trudge through the frozen night, but finally, the moon lower in the sky, I arrived. As I stood before the walls of Ribe, marvelling at the trade centre, my mind still spun from the völva's magic. Ribbons of grey smoke drifted from smokeholes, distinct against the charcoal backdrop of the sky, and the streets were empty. There were still a few hours until the day would begin for the townspeople here, I would need to find the alehouse and rest there until the day began.

I was still dizzy, my flesh stung from the cold, my dry, cracked lips were swollen, my legs ached, and nausea consumed me. I paused for a moment longer before stepping into the trading town. It was then that I collapsed. I didn't feel the pain of hitting the frozen, snow covered ground, didn't feel the bitter coldness consume my flesh and burn me as though it were fire – the world turned to black halfway through my fall.

***

THE IVORY CLOUDS of my breath danced in the frozen air, swirling and twisting in the silver light that streamed through the smokehole. Though the sky was white with cold, though the air was chilled like ice, I could feel fiery heat radiating from my flesh and sweat spilling from my brow. I watched a bead of sweat drip down the bridge of my nose, slipping onto my cheek and tumbling down my face like a tear. With consciousness came awareness; as though I had been set afire, my body smouldered, and my throat ached. Air seared my lungs as I inhaled and exhaled each shallow, rasping breath.

There was movement somewhere across from me. Slowly I turned my head, searching for the cause.

"Awake, are you? The gods must favour you. Not many come out of a sickness like that alive. Frøstein," she called, glancing over her shoulder at someone across the dim room from us. "She's awake."

"Who—" I croaked, but I couldn't finish, my throat hurt too much to speak.

Noticing me wince and grasp my throat, the woman disappeared out of sight. A few moments later, the dark, gaunt face of a man — presumably Frøstein — was gazing down on me, a sympathetic frown on his lips. After a while of awkward silence (but for my rasping breath), the woman returned, a steaming cup in her hand.

"Marshmallow root tea with honey." The woman explained warmly. "Drink it, it will soothe your throat."

The woman passed the cup to Frøstein, so she could help me sit up in the straw bed. Hesitant to accept a brew from a stranger but too weak to resist, the woman took the cup from Frøstein and brought it to my lips. For a few moments I breathed in the steam, the warm vapour drifting up my nostrils and into my sinuses, soothing my aching face immediately. Impressed by the prompt relief of inhaling the steam, I parted my lips and let her trickle the tea into my mouth. The bitter, earthy flavour of the tea was mostly concealed by the sweetness of the honey mixed with it, and I managed to swallow the liquid without my stomach turning.

The ravenous cry of a baby pierced the air. The woman stood up and gave the tea to Frøstein, before rushing to the child, her hand briefly touching her breast as she hurried to tend to the babe. I knew that touch; I had fed each of my children at my breast and their cries would initiate a sharp sting inside them, my body desperate to respond to their hunger. I glanced down at my own breasts, empty of the nourishment that had filled them to feed my beloved Alffinna only a few months ago ...

The baby screamed for its mother, its shrill cries setting off a maternal alarm inside me, ordering me to tend to the child, but soon enough the cries faded as the child noisily fed from its mother. A jolt of jealously shocked through my heart – how I wished I had my baby ...

Before I could lose myself in my thoughts, Frøstein tentatively offered the marshmallow root tea to me. Though my arms were heavy, I took the cup from him and brought it to my mouth, delicately trickling the tea through my dry, stinging lips.

"Eirný has cared for you well." He commented, tipping his head in the direction of the woman. "We didn't expect you to live."

"Am I in Ribe?" I croaked.

He nodded.

"You've been here for three days." Frøstein replied. "I must've found you soon after you'd collapsed; your breathing was shallow and lips blue, but there was still life in you."

"The völva–" I whispered but halted when he raised a soot blackened hand to me.

"You're not the first to fall before the gates of Ribe, after visiting that witch." He said, rising to his feet.

"When Frøstein brought you here, you were dreadfully sick. You slept all the time – we had to watch you every moment of the day and night, for you would vomit in your slumber." Eirný explained, appearing in the room as Frøstein disappeared without another word.

I couldn't see the baby, bundled so heavily in furs, but I heard its desperate suckling and the occasional grunt. My racing heart calmed at the sound of the contented child.

"The second day you didn't vomit as much, but you continued to sleep, sometimes your eyes would open, and you would speak a little – fever dreams. In the middle of last night, we thought you had succumbed to your sickness – you stopped talking and groaning and shaking – but thankfully it was your fever that had broken, you weren't tormented by the dreams anymore." Eirný said, leaning and placing her hand on my brow. "You're warm but not fevered – you're getting well."

"*Þakka fyrir.*" I rasped, heartened by the sincere smile that lit up her face.

"*Þat var ekki.*" She beamed. "I'm just glad you're healing – as Frøstein said, we were nervous you wouldn't make it."

Frøstein returned with a bowl of broth, I assumed from the scent. I gulped the rest of the marshmallow root and honey tea before accepting the bowl.

"You must slow down. You haven't eaten in days; your stomach is still delicate." Eirný cautioned.

I smiled at her weakly, appreciative of her motherly concern for me. Beyond the lines of stress that were deepening in her flesh, she must've been a similar age to me. When the baby had fallen asleep into a satisfied, milk-induced slumber, she placed it down in its crib and slowly fed me the broth. Halfway through it, she had Frøstein bring some bread to me. She dipped it into the broth until it was soggy and dripping then brought it to my lips. Slowly and carefully I ate it – or rather, I sucked the broth-sodden slush, pausing if my stomach began to lurch. Thankfully, over the course of an hour or two I managed to consume the broth, the bread and a second cup of marshmallow root and honey.

As I ate, the husband and wife didn't ask questions or pry into my visit to the völva, much to my relief. Simply, they fed me until I was well enough to feed myself, ever patient and kind to me. From every warm, soothing mouthful, I felt my strength return to me, felt energy grow inside me. My head didn't ache any more, and my vision had cleared. Though I felt rough, I was much better than I had been. Privately, I decided that I would return home today.

Half the day had passed. Eirný, forever at my side, chatted as she looked after me and her baby son. Frøstein, a black smith, had left for work soon after I had consumed my meal. Determined, I had left the bed and ambled around her small home. The more I moved, the better I felt, and the more resolve I had to leave and return to *my* home.

As the day went by, Eirný and I spoke a lot about children. I longed to hold my own – it felt like a lifetime had passed since I had seen them. Eirný and Frøstein had lost three of their four children to various illnesses and sicknesses over the past six years.

"*You've lost only one child out of your five, most other women aren't as lucky.*"

"And how many children do you have?" Eirný asked, grinning at me as I pulled silly faces at her little boy, much to his delight.

"Five ... *Nei*, four – I, I *have* four." I said, my heart jolting with realisation. "I lost my youngest child only a few months ago. That's why I came here."

Eirný nodded knowingly.

"It's a pain greater than anything else in the world." She said sympathetically. "It never truly goes away, but, over time, you learn to live, you recover."

"*Já.*" I murmured, watching her baby grab my finger and bring it to his toothless mouth to gnaw on.

"Aveline, how are you feeling?" Frøstein asked as he entered his small home.

"*Allt vel, þakka.*" I replied, relieved by the interruption.

"Well enough to walk?" Frøstein said.

"*Já.*" I replied.

"There's a man at the hall," Frøstein said. "He's looking for you."

"Who is he?" I asked urgently.

Frøstein shrugged his shoulders.

"The jarl has requested you come to the hall the moment you are awake and well enough to walk." Frøstein said.

"What does the man look like?" I asked, my heart hammering in my chest.

"I didn't get a good look; I was sent back to check on you as quickly as I could." Frøstein replied. "He was tall, blue eyes – maybe green – with a big, black, bearskin cloak."

Could it be – was Anders Bursson searching for me?

I pulled my finger away from the baby, and staggered around their home in a daze, trying to find my belongings. Already dressed and wearing my boots, I pulled on my coat and buckled my belt around me, my sword safely sheathed. It was heavier than I had remembered it to be ...

RISE TO FALL

I bid farewell to Eirný and thanked her for all she had done for me. I had no money or jewels I could give her in thanks; instead I shuffled through my pack and pulled out a small muslin bag of saffron and gave it to her – they could sell it for a good sum.

Frøstein carried my packs while I carried my hood, and together we made our way through the icy, labyrinthine streets of Ribe to reach the Jarl's hall in its centre. Frøstein opened the doors, and I scurried in, glancing around in search of Anders. Frøstein led me to the Jarl of Ribe, who sat on his throne on the other side of the huge hall.

"I am Aveline Birgersdóttir, Jarlkona of Aros." I announced. "I was told there is a man here, searching for me?"

"*Já*, I am." A familiar voice said across the room from me.

Bathed in shadow, the tall, hulking figure of a man stepped into view, a thick black bearskin cloak wrapped around him.

"Vidar!" I cried out.

Every thought fled my mind, shocked and ecstatic, I dropped everything and rushed towards my husband. Vidar ran to me and we collided together, flinging our arms around each other. He lifted me into the air, and our lips crashed together urgently, passionately, so relieved to be reunited. For the first time since Alffinna's death, I was happy.

"What are you doing here?" I gasped between kisses.

"Káta said you were to make the journey *to* the völva alone. She said nothing about the journey back to Aros." Vidar grinned. "Four days after you left, I assumed you must've reached the völva, and I decided to come here and accompany you on your way home."

"*Oh*, Vidar!" I laughed, kissing him through giggles.

"Very good! Excellent!" The Jarl of Ribe said, admiring our reunion. "I'm glad you have found each other. I invite you both to stay for the night, perhaps we can celebrate this wonderful occasion?"

Vidar lowered me to the ground, but our arms remained wrapped about each other. We glanced from each other and to the jarl, ridiculous grins on our blushing faces.

"Well, little fawn?" Vidar asked.

Vidar's icy blue eyes gazed into mine, twinkling with mischief, the corners of his brilliant eyes creased from his beaming smile. I kissed him once more, quickly and longingly, before turning to the jarl.

"I appreciate your kind offer," I said sincerely. "But I must return home as soon as possible. It has been far too long since I last held my children in my arms."

"The roads are dangerous at night; the Great Hunt still rides." The jarl cautioned.

"My children are worth the risk." I replied firmly.

With a fingertip on my jaw, Vidar turned my face to look at him and pressed a sweet, deep kiss to my lips.

***

VIDAR PROCURED TWO fine brown horses from the gracious Jarl of Ribe. Saddled, my packs strapped to my mare, Vidar and I were ready to begin our journey home. We bid farewell to Frøstein, whom Vidar gifted a silver arm band to thank him and his wife for saving me and healing me back to health. Vidar vowed to Frøstein that we were indebted to him and his family for what they had done for me; if they ever needed something, they were always welcome in our hall.

"Tell me what has happened in my absence." I said soon after we left Ribe. "How are the children?"

"The children miss you dearly; they were very supportive of me coming here to get you. I left Jan in charge at the hall; he's watching the children."

"You realise we will not have a hall to return to then?" I quipped.

"I'm sure Jötunnson can handle the children." Vidar smirked.

"I'm sure the children will be incredibly dependable and mature in our absence; it's Jan I'm not so sure about."

Vidar laughed.

"You're right – maybe it was a questionable decision on my part." Vidar grinned. "Here's hoping Aros survived. As for what's happened, life has much been the same. You're very missed; the townspeople are confused by your absence – I didn't share the details – but I've assured them you'll be home soon."

"I'm surprised to hear that, I thought they'd be weary or distrusting of me after they saw me participating in a Christian funeral." I commented, remembering the remarks made by the townspeople at Caterine's funeral.

"You were loyal to your friend and conducted a Christian funeral in honour of her. They don't distrust you for acting in respect for your friend." Vidar said firmly, though privately I was rather sceptical of this. "Speaking of funerals ..."

"What?" I gasped.

Vidar was silent. I watched him chew his bottom lip and stare fixedly ahead. My stomach knotted up inside me as I remembered the prophecy the Allfather had told me.

"Vidar?" I pressed. "Is it – is it Freydis? Did she die?"

"*Já*," Vidar said, turning to stare at me incredulously, his brows knitted. "How did you know?"

"The Allfather told me." I replied, my voice hollow and distant.

"*The Allfather?*"

I didn't say anything else, this confirmed it – I *had* gone to the spirit realm! I *had* spoken with the Allfather! And his prophecy had come true, Freydis was dead. Vidar did not push me to reveal anything else to him; we spent most of the day's ride in silence.

We had left Ribe at noon, and by evening time we reached the small settlement seven hours or so outside of Ribe I'd rested at on the beginning of my journey. When the settlement came into view Vidar, lightening the mood of our travel, challenged me to a race. Laughing, we raced each other on our horses. When we reached the settlement, we found lodging for the night, ate a good meal with the family we were staying with and, when all the members of the house were asleep, Vidar and I curled together on a pile of furs on a bench close to the fire.

The family's thrall was asleep on the floor of the kitchen, while the family were together in the sleeping area; Vidar and I were alone in the main room. By the light of the fire, Vidar watched me remove all but my shift while he laid on the platform in just his tunic and trousers. Blushing at his eager smile, I crawled onto the bench beside him, and he engulfed me in his arms.

Under the cover of the night, tangled together, Vidar rested his forehead against mine. His warm breath danced on my face, sweet from the mead he had drank earlier. I inched my lips closer to his until the soft fair hairs of his beard tickled my face. With his rough, calloused hands, Vidar gently brushed my hair back, cupped the back of my head and pulled me into a kiss.

Unable to hold back our hunger for each other, our kiss grew more urgent, and our hands raced over each other's bodies. I tugged at the waist of his trousers. Vidar pulled my skirts over my hips, yanked down his trousers, and laid between my legs. He kissed me softly as he entered me, and together we satisfied our longing for each other, our need to be together, to be one with each other.

I *needed* Vidar inside me. More than just an animalistic desire to copulate, I needed him to love me physically and cleanse me of the all that had happened on my journey. His kiss was forgiveness, his love was my safety.

Panting, the seed of his pleasure spilling from inside me, Vidar flopped onto the bed. He slipped his arm beneath my head and drew me against him, his tunic damp with sweat. I was dizzy with the satisfaction I'd drawn from him, absolute calm overcome me. My eyes fluttered shut and gradually my breathing calmed. On the verge of sleep, Vidar shifted in the bed and whispered my name.

"*Já?*" I mumbled.

"Will you tell me what happened?" Vidar asked.

My heart jolted.

"*Já* ... But not tonight."

Vidar rolled onto his side and encased me in his arms again, kissing the top of my head.

"*Þakka fyrir*, little fawn."

***

WE WERE ONLY a few hours away from Aros when I finally decided to tell Vidar what happened. It had taken us four full and thankfully uneventful days to travel from Ribe to Aros, due in part to a sudden snowfall halfway through our journey. It had taken me four days to reach the völva's *hof*, and through our conversations I calculated that I must have been asleep or in the trance at the *hof* for at least three days. I had also been in Ribe for three days, unconscious for two of them, and on the third Vidar and I rode home. In total, it had been thirteen days since I left Aros, thirteen days since I last saw my children.

It was late afternoon, Vidar and I rode side-by-side over relatively flat, lightly wooded and snow covered land, talking nonchalantly with each other, when the cawing of ravens struck through the sky. Without even looking, I knew they were Anders' ravens.

"Vidar, can we – can we break for a little while?" I asked timidly.

"*Já*, we can." Vidar replied faintly, his attention locked on the two black birds soaring high above us.

We tied the horses to a tree and Vidar spread his bearskin cloak over the ground, so we could sit and not get wet or freeze from the snow. Vidar pulled out a leather flask of mead and some cheese and bread wrapped in muslin from one of his packs and sat down beside me.

"Where did you get the bearskin?" I asked, staring at the ebony fur beneath us.

"Alvar gave it to me when he and Freydis came for Alffinna's funeral." Vidar said, taking a deep swig of the mead. "Would you like some?"

Vidar offered the flask to me. Silently I accepted it and drank a little, the ravens crying out above me. All of a sudden, the words poured out of me; I told Vidar everything, of the settlements I had stayed in, of the odd man and his shack in the woods, of the wolves' attack, of Anders and his kiss ... Before Vidar had a chance to comment, I continued, not daring to lift my gaze from the bearskin cloak to his eyes.

I told Vidar of the wolf that led me to the völva, and I told him of the völva, of the *hof*, of the pair of thralls. I told him about the brews, the *Amanita muscaria* stew, the sex rite. I told him of the *seiðstafr*, I told him how I flew. I told him about the spirit realm, the Allfather, the conversation I had with him, the prophecy and the promise.

Everything that had happened since I had left on my journey cascaded from my lips in infinite detail. There was not one thing I had left out. I told Vidar everything, and I apologised. I apologised for leaving him, I apologised for abandoning our family in a time of need. I apologised for wasting so much of our riches on the journey, and not returning with even half of the items I had purchased from the völva, I apologised for the rite.

"Stop apologising, little fawn." Vidar said.

I looked at him. Vidar's stare was fixed on the bearskin; he was pinching clumps of the ebony fur with his dry fingertips and twisting the hairs, occasionally plucking some out. His calm expression confused me; of everything I had told him, I had expected some sort of reaction, anger – sadness? Something, but instead, he was calm, still. I watched Vidar chew on his bottom lip, his nostrils flaring slightly as he breathed in deeply.

Then Vidar looked at me. His ice coloured eyes, rimmed with cerulean, pure and so beautiful, stared at me. His pale pink lips curved into his usual smirk, and he laughed softly at the disbelief on my face.

"You've been through a lot." Vidar said gently. "Did you find what you were looking for?"

"*Já.*" I nodded. "I did."

"Then you wasted nothing." Vidar said. "You didn't *abandon* us, you left on a quest and succeeded at what you set out to do. If that makes you a stronger, wiser woman, then it was worth it – not just for you, but for the children and me as well. And your children don't begrudge you, they love you and miss you, and want you home. As do I, little fawn."

Tears cascaded down my face. Vidar grabbed me and pulled me into his lap, holding me tightly against him.

"Anders Bursson – *he kissed me*!" I wept, my voice thick with guilt. "I was falling asleep, and he kissed me, a-and I didn't stop him, Vidar! I didn't stop him!"

Vidar didn't say anything. He didn't stop rocking or squeezing me, he didn't stop comforting me. Enclosed in his arms, his heart beat thumping rhythmically in his chest, steady and calm, the musky scent of his body from the days of travel drifted up my nostrils, soothing me.

I had kissed another man! I had betrayed my husband – I didn't deserve to be comforted! I tried to break free from him, tried to pull away, but Vidar was so much stronger than me, and he held me against him, his head rested on mine. Quickly I gave up on my attempts to escape his grasp. Instead, I gripped him tightly and cried, the cold air chilling the tear tracks on my cheeks, stinging my face.

"I-I'm so sorry." I whispered.

"*Ssh.*" Vidar said softly. "I don't begrudge you – and I cannot begrudge the man who saved your life."

"The man, Anders Bursson …" I murmured. "He – he had two wolves and the ravens, they appeared just before him and flew near wherever he was. Do you – do you think … Maybe he was – *was* he the–"

"*Já*, maybe." Vidar interrupted. "Which is why I *cannot* begrudge the one who saved your life."

***

WE ARRIVED HOME in the dead of night. Aros was wrapped in darkness and the moon was high up in the sky. Vidar woke two field thralls and charged them with unsaddling and stabling the two horses while he and I slinked into the hall. The fires were low, the house was warm, and the thralls were curled up on the floor of the kitchen, oblivious to our entrance.

We found Jan half-naked and snoring away on a bench in the main room. Vidar and I smiled as we crept passed him on our way to the sleeping area. I paused in the doorway and gazed at my children; they were already asleep, cuddled together in a heap, their straw mattresses pushed together to form one large bed. Young Birger and Sander cocooned little Æsa and Einar between them protectively, their backs turned to the world, their arms wrapped around their siblings.

My lips curved into a half-hearted smile. Their embrace warmed my heart, but a pang of shame rang through me for leaving them for so long. Until my visit to the völva, I had never spent even a day away from them, and when I decided to leave for weeks on end, it had been amidst the darkest moment of their lives.

Selfishly, I had abandoned them to find answers for my pain, leaving them to wallow in their own. I was not there to dry their tears at the loss of their sister. I had not been the column of strength for them to turn to with their distress. I left them in the darkness when they needed me to shine light.

A tear slipped down my cheek.

They hadn't been able to depend on me, their mother, and had turned to one another instead. Though I was proud of Young Birger and Sander, holding their siblings in this protective embrace, I realised what I had done. I had failed them as a mother – the weight of what I had laden upon them with was too heavy for children of their ages to bear. I had burdened them, my eleven- and eight-year-old sons, with a responsibility I had been too weak to endure.

Never again.

No matter what happened, I would not fail my children again. Nothing would replace Alffinna in my heart, but I couldn't hold on to my sadness, I had to live for my four remaining children; I had to fight for them.

CHAPTER TWENTY-ONE

Spring, 885

"I DEMAND RETRIBUTION!" Magnus Geirsson roared as he stormed into the hall, a thrall scurrying close behind him.

Vidar and I were sitting together beside the fire talking between ourselves as we watched Einar, laying belly down in the centre of the floor, play with a few of his wooden horses. Æsa and Sander were playing with some *Hnefatafl* figures at the table near us while Young Birger was carving a doll from a small chunk of oak beside the fire pit.

At Geirsson's brusque entrance, Einar, Æsa and I jumped, so surprised by his loud and sudden appearance. I rushed to Einar, scooped him up into my arms and glared at Geirsson as I returned to my seat beside my husband.

"Why do you come into my home yelling as though I am a thrall here to serve you?" Vidar asked evenly, still slouched casually in his chair. "Surely you have some respect for your jarl and his family?"

"I apologise, Jarl, I mean no disrespect." Geirsson said, his voice lower but still simmering with fury. "I am overwhelmed with anger – I *must* speak with you at once!"

"Oh?" Vidar replied sarcastically. His lips were drawn in a hard line, his ice-blue eyes gleamed with irritation. "Do tell me, what brings you bursting into my hall like this?"

"Her!" Geirsson barked.

Geirsson stood before Vidar, who still hadn't risen from his chair to welcome him. Geirsson cleared his throat, but his thrall continued to quiver behind him. Vidar surveyed the Dane dramatically, tilting his head left and right and looking him up and down. Geirsson, realising his thrall was still hiding behind his bulky figure, spun around irritably, grabbed her by the arm and shoved her in front of him.

"Your thrall?" Vidar said calmly.

"She is with child!" Geirsson exclaimed.

"Congratulations." Vidar said, sitting up and resting his hand on my knee. "Surely expecting a child is not something to be angry about?"

"The child is not mine!" Geirsson bellowed.

"Before we go any further," Vidar said, finally standing up. "If you speak to me like that again, I will throw you out of my hall. If you wish to speak to me, I suggest you calm yourself and speak in an appropriate tone."

"My apologies, Jarl Vidar." Geirsson cleared his throat again. "*The child is not mine.* My thrall was raped – ruined! Her maidenhead was intact, but a *hrafnasueltir* took it from her, and now she carries his child! I demand retribution."

"Can your thrall name her attacker?" Vidar asked.

"*Já.*" Magnus grinned.

"Then he will be fined according to his deed. When the child is born, you can do with it as you wish." Vidar replied. "Who is the father?"

"Jan Jarlufson." Magnus said.

Vidar's eyebrows shot to the top of his head.

"Jötunnson?"

"*Já,* Jarl Vidar. *Him.*"

I rose to my feet and approached Young Birger. I offered Einar to him and immediately my oldest son put down his knife and wood and took his younger brother from me. Slowly I approached the trembling thrall, who kept her wide-eyed, terrified gaze diverted from me.

"Fríðr?" I murmured, touching her roughly chopped hair.

Her once beautiful long ebony tresses had been hacked away, the longest lock reached no further than her jawline. Her face was ruddy from tears, and the grey smudges beneath her eyes showed she hadn't slept for several nights.

When I had met Fríðr, she wore clothes well above her station. Her clothing hadn't been particularly grand, but it had been finer than a thrall would usually wear. Now she stood in the common thrall garb, a rough flax tunic with a thin iron collar latched around her neck. I delicately touched the horrible collar and tutted sympathetically; she hadn't worn it for long for there were no grazes or blisters from the metal rubbing against her skin, but there would be eventually.

Fríðr didn't meet my eyes. She didn't say a word. She stared at the floor, wringing her fingers, shaking. Slowly I took her hands in mine and squeezed them gently.

"What do you want to do with the child?" I asked.

"I bought herbs from the healer woman, but they didn't expel the child – it still moves inside her belly." Geirsson spat.

"Your baby will be born in only a few months." I said, gently touching Fríðr's belly and ignoring Geirsson.

Fríðr peeked at me from beneath her thick black lashes.

"Would you like to keep the child? Or would you rather ..." My voice trailed away.

I followed Fríðr's eyes as she glanced at Geirsson.

"Jarlkona, with all due respect, why are you asking *her* these questions? I own her therefore I own her child." Agnarsson stated.

"When I first met your thrall, her hair was long and flowing, you dressed her in a freewoman's clothes and there was no collar around her neck." I met Agnarsson's steely gaze with my own. "You once respected your thrall. If the healer's herbs had worked, would you have cut her hair? Would you dress her in finery or rags?"

Geirsson said nothing.

"You may have lost your respect for her, Magnus, but she still deserves to be heard. As you said yourself, she didn't give her maidenhead away, it was stolen from her."

"Rowena," Vidar said, spotting our thralls hovering nervously in the kitchen doorway. "Get Jan Jötunnson, I want him here at once. Melisende, fetch five meads." Vidar sat back in his chair and glared at Geirsson. "When Jötunnson arrives, we will settle this matter."

***

JAN SWAGGERED INTO the hall behind Rowena, greeting us cheerily. Melisende shooed the children off into the kitchen, but

I spotted Einar peeking his face around the corner, eager to see Jan. Melisende popped up behind him and whisked him back into the kitchen, scolding him quietly in François.

Fríðr cowered behind her owner, staring at the floor. Geirsson sat at our table, angrily awaiting Jan's arrival. Upon sight of him, I watched Geirsson's hand curl into a fist on the table top. Vidar stood immediately, pointing to a chair across from him, signalling Jan to sit in it.

"*Góðan morgin.*" Jan smiled. "What can I do for you all?"

"You whore's son!" Geirsson roared before Jan had even sat down. "You ruined my prized thrall!"

"*Hvat segir þú?*" Jan asked, staring at Geirsson.

Geirsson grabbed Fríðr and forced her forward, roughly brushing the hair from her face. She glanced at Jan wide-eyed, clutching her protruding bump protectively. A note of recollection flashed across Jan's face.

"Ah." Jan said.

Fríðr looked away from him, tears streaming down her face. Jan took a step towards her, but she quickly scarpered behind Geirsson.

"You recognise the thrall?" Vidar asked slowly.

"*Já*, I do." Jan said levelly.

"Magnus Geirsson is accusing you of raping her." Vidar continued.

"*Já*, I took her." Jan admitted.

"You must be punished for what you did!" Geirsson exclaimed.

"He will be." Vidar sighed, taking a deep draught from his cup. "Fríðr is just a thrall, so Jan Jötunnson Jarlufson will not be outlawed. He will, however, pay a fine for the damage to your property."

"I have damaged nothing of his." Jan protested.

"The thrall is carrying your child." Vidar stated; Jan shut up quickly. "You will pay Magnus two-and-a-half marks of silver for raping his thrall."

Jan nodded slowly, and Geirsson grinned at the hefty sum of the fine. A female thrall was never worth more than two marks, most male thralls were sold for only 12 *aurer* or one and a half marks.

"And what of the baby?" Jan asked carefully.

"It is my property." Geirsson spat.

"It is *my* child," Jan replied heatedly. "I want it. I will buy the child from you – I'll pay you two marks of silver for it now."

"Ha!" Geirsson laughed. "Two marks of silver for a thrall's bastard that isn't even born yet? Are you being funny, Jarlufson?"

"Not at all." Jan replied. "I want the baby. Two marks of silver for the child on top of the two-and-a-half marks for the fine."

"I'm not selling the child." Geirsson said.

"What do you need it for?" Jan demanded, finally losing his cool demeanour. "I'm offering you more than a decent sum for it!"

"I want the baby, so you don't have it!" Geirsson snapped. "I was to sell Fríðr for *five* marks of silver – so long as she retained her maidenhead! And you took that from her – you took that silver from me!"

"Then five marks! I'll give you five marks for the child!" Jan argued.

"*Nei*!" Geirsson spat.

"Fríðr–" Jan exclaimed, turning to the thrall.

She flinched when Jan said her name and shuddered as he stared at her.

"Marry me and we'll raise the child together." Jan pleaded. "You will be a free woman – you won't be a thrall anymore!"

I gaped at the scene before me, shocked at Jan's desperation. Jan had never offered to marry any of his bastard's mothers in the past. When retribution was demanded of him, Jan had paid his fines and saw his children intermittently at best. Those bastards were dead now, though, and his only living child had vanished with his wife.

"Never!" Fríðr gasped, tears streaming down her cheeks. "I'd rather be a thrall than your wife! You raped me, now you're trying to take my baby from me, before it's even born! And what of the Jarl's thrall who was killed because of you? *Nei*, I refuse to marry you! You're cursed!"

A visible pang of pain and shock rang through Jan.

"Please, Fríðr – I won't keep the child away from you, I just want to make it free – not a thrall." Jan begged, but he was answered by her shaking head.

"Her answer doesn't matter anyway, Jarlufson." Geirsson said. "A thrall's child belongs to their mother's owner, remember? Fríðr is mine, and any child born from her is mine. I won't sell the child, and Fríðr won't marry you. Accept it and pay your fine!"

"I cannot lose this child!" Jan cried out, hammering his fist on the table. "At least let me see the child. I'll – Fríðr," Jan turned to the thrall, his sapphire eyes boring into her wide, pale blues. "I'll give you two-and-a-half marks to apologise for raping you. What I did was wrong, I shouldn't have taken you against your will – *I'm sorry!* But, please let me see my child, please! I'll – I'll give you two *aurer* a month until the child is married!"

"What?" Geirsson barked.

"Jötunnson?" Vidar said slowly.

"*Já!* I'll pay you two *aurer* a month until the child is an adult and marries a Dane. If the child is never freed and remains a thrall for the rest of his life, I will pay one *eyrir* a month until the child or I die – whichever happens first. I *will* do all this, Fríðr, I vow it – I swear to all the gods in Asgard, and on all the nine realms, I will! Just let me see my child."

"*Nei*," Geirsson said. "I don't want her bastard interfering with her work, nor do I want it raised alongside my children. If you will give *me* half the monthly stipend you have promised Fríðr, I'll allow you to collect the bastard before breakfast and return it after evening meal has finished, then Fríðr will have no more duties for the rest of the night and can care for it. You get your child. What say you, Jan Jarlufson?"

"Agreed. But she–" Jan pointed at Fríðr. "Has to vow, under penalty of death, that she will never take the child away from me. And if you or your family harm my child, Geirsson, I will kill you."

The fair downy hairs of my arms stood on end as I watched Jan and Geirsson glare at one another.

"Agreed." Geirsson finally replied.

The men threw out their right hands and clasped each other's arms briefly – their agreement was officially confirmed now, and Vidar and I were witnesses.

"Now, the payment you owe me." Geirsson said.

Jan took his coin pouch from his belt and dug through it and tossed the two and half marks of silver to him. He turned to Fríðr and held out his purse.

"Your silver." Jan said, shaking the bag.

Fríðr glanced between Geirsson and Jan, her hands pressed against the sides of her stomach. Geirsson nodded to her, and she swiped the purse. She held it against her breast, eyes wide with shock at the sum in her hand and the agreement made.

"I will make the first payment when the child is born. Send a thrall to me when Fríðr begins birthing the child." Jan said.

"Fine." Geirsson grunted. He turned to Vidar and me, bowing his head slightly. "*Þakka fyrir*, Jarl Vidar."

Geirsson nodded to Vidar and me, then he and Fríðr left.

"Jötunnson," Vidar sighed, flopping into his chair and rubbing his temples with his fingertips. "What are you going to do with a *child?*"

***

VIDAR'S HEARTBEAT THUMPED steadily in his chest. We had been lying in bed for a while, silently holding each other. I didn't know if Vidar was asleep yet or not, but we were both silent. The children were already sleeping, the soft noises of their slumber humming quietly in the darkness. Through the smokehole I could see the moon high in the sky, half covered in cloud.

Fríðr's attack had haunted me since *Vetrnætr*. Her screams had rung in my ears for days, but I had been unable to tell Vidar what I had seen – what Jan had done to her. I knew he wouldn't have reacted as outraged as I had. Raping a thrall wasn't a huge issue with the Danes – they considered thralls no more important than livestock. Slavery was a trade, nothing more, and a profitable trade at that. Thralls were nothing more than property ...

But I had walked in Fríðr's shoes; she was human to me. I knew what it was like to be terrified, to be taken so viciously and unwillingly, to be so helpless and alone. I hated Jan for doing what he did to her and now her voice wasn't being heard regarding the child in her belly.

Did she want the child? Could she love the child?

Fríðr refused Jan's proposal, preferring to be a thrall than his wife. And why wouldn't she? The life of a thrall was hard, but better than being married to her attacker. I had been married to mine, and I was relieved when Vidar had come to me, drenched in my first husband's blood, and told me he had killed him. My horrid marriage finally over ...

I had been lucky that Erhardt Ketilsson had not got me with child during our marriage. I had feared it – I had thought about that possibility endlessly, terrified that it should happen. Though the child would have been mine, it would have had his blood running through its veins. It would have been a constant reminder of Erhardt and everything he had done to me. I wondered whether I could have loved a child I'd conceived with Erhardt, and I truly didn't know that I could.

Could Fríðr? Could she look at that child and love it as a mother should love her child? Or would she see nothing but Jan, remember nothing but the night he had forced himself on her? Remember the pain of him taking her, remember her screams echoing into the night? I had been too late to save her ...

Geirsson had tried to rid Fríðr of the child with herbal medicines. Had Fríðr taken the healer's herbs willingly, or had Geirsson forced her to ingest the concoction? It hadn't worked either way. But what if Fríðr had *wanted* to expose the child? Now she was forced to keep the child because of Jan's monetary proposition and Geirsson's greed. Now the reminder of her rape would stay with her for the rest of her life.

Hopefully she could love the baby and accept it. Hopefully ...

"I had an idea this had happened just after *Vetrnætr* when Jan had left, and you were mad with him." Vidar murmured. "Why wouldn't you tell me?"

"I didn't think you'd care." I replied shortly. "You said it yourself, and so did Jan, so does every Dane here – there's nothing wrong with raping a thrall and that's all she is ... She's just a thrall."

"Jötunnson was a fool for what he did," Vidar said. "And I was a fool for saying that. I'm sorry, little fawn. You don't approve of raping thralls, and nor do I."

"What do you think of all this?" I shifted closer to him.

"I think Jötunnson is a madman for offering to pay such a sum of money to Geirsson and his thrall." Vidar said with a quiet chuckle. "But I understand his need to care for his child. The sum guarantees the safety of the child which is all that matters to him as a father."

Vidar's hand crept under the blankets and danced tenderly over my stomach. When I had been married off as peace-pledge to Erhardt Ketilsson, I had been pregnant with Vidar's child. Only Vidar and I had known of my pregnancy when I was married off. Thinking the baby was his, Erhardt had treated Young Birger well after he was born. Trapped in that marriage, Vidar was unable to claim our son as his. I had done everything I could to keep Erhardt from spilling his seed inside me after Young Birger's birth, but on the few times Erhardt had taken me after I had the birth, we had thankfully not conceived a child.

I was given to Erhardt to bring peace to Roskilde and Aros and end the feud between the two towns. Vidar had been away from Roskilde at the time and had been unable to stop me from being married off – Vidar would've killed every one of Erhardt's men had he been there ... By the time Vidar returned to Roskilde, I had long since been married and moved to Aros. On Vidar's return, Erhardt travelled to Aros and presented his daughter, Ursula, as a peace-pledge bride, and Vidar was forced to marry her, to guarantee my safety – Erhardt threatened to kill me if he didn't.

Vidar and Ursula had travelled from Roskilde to Aros, to celebrate the birth of Young Birger, who Erhardt believed to be his first and only male heir. During their stay in Aros, Vidar and I had managed to be together in secret, meeting in the shadows or under the cover of night. Vidar had vowed we would conceive a child together during his stay, and a year after the birth of our son, he would kill Erhardt.

Vidar's prophecy had come true – I gave birth to Sander nine months later. Sander was so obviously Vidar's, he was bronze skinned, blond and had ice-blue eyes like Vidar. Erhardt had been dark, with mud brown eyes and dark brown hair. My eyes were amber, my skin was pale, and I had chestnut hair. Sander was Vidar's, and a year after his birth, Vidar slew Erhardt as promised.

I had been consumed with worry for the safety of my children – what if their true paternity was found out? I detested being Erhardt's wife, I hated everything he did to me, and I loathed that my sons had called him '*faðir*'. But for their safety, I kept up the facade for so long.

Vidar had experienced the same fears and anxieties, but I hadn't stopped to consider what else he must have felt – so far away from his children, with nothing he could do to save them but wait and plan … I had physically been there to protect my sons, Vidar hadn't.

"I think Jötunnson finds trouble no matter which way he turns." Vidar said, biting his lip. "I have never met a man worthier of Valhalla than Jötunnson, but the gods seem to enjoy playing with him."

"Playing with him, or torturing him?"

"They are one and the same for poor Jötunnson, are they not?"

CHAPTER TWENTY-TWO

Late Spring, 885

VIDAR WAS JITTERY. As we walked down the dirt streets towards the bay he seemed to bounce on his feet, hurrying us along frequently. Young Birger and Sander strode along beside us, trying their best to match their father's quick pace, snickering between themselves; Vidar's excitement was infectious. He carried our five-year-old Æsa upon his back, prancing about like a horse every now and again, much to her amusement. I scurried along with Einar on my hip, thankful for the coolness of the day for perspiration was forming on my brow. A grand ship had pulled into the bay, displaying the red, black and white eagle-wing war banner of Roskilde.

It had been two weeks since we had seen Alvar last, and he had made no mention of coming to Aros. As ever, I feared the worse, but Vidar didn't. There was a feeling inside him, something he could sense right down to his bones, that Alvar's arrival here mean something good.

What if it wasn't Alvar who had come here? I thought.

"You're as clear as glass, little fawn." Vidar chuckled as we made our way towards the bay. "Alvar isn't dead; he wouldn't allow himself to die anywhere but a battlefield."

"He didn't intend to outlive Freydis – in fact, he didn't intend to live to such an old age at all." I pointed out grimly.

"My *faðir* isn't dead, I know it." Vidar said firmly. "Wait and see."

Soon after our return from Ribe, we had travelled to Roskilde for Freydis's funeral. Poor Alvar had been in quite a state over her death – Freydis had been the love of his life; he had enjoyed various women before her, but from the moment he had lain eyes upon her when he was just a young man, he had not even gazed upon another woman since.

Freydis's death had cast a large, dark cloud over Alvar. Worried, we stayed in Roskilde for a full four weeks after the funeral, to comfort him, before we reluctantly returned to Aros, much by Alvar's request as well as our duty to our town. Although he adored having his grandchildren around him and appreciated the company Vidar and I offered, Alvar accused us of coddling him. Not wanting to affront him, we returned to Aros.

We took comfort knowing we left him in the trustworthy, capable care of Aaminah, who had taken great care of Alvar and Freydis over the years, and loyally continued to do so. Though she was a thrall, Aaminah had been a dear friend to Freydis, and both Vidar's parents had valued her more than any other thrall.

We didn't want Alvar to be insulted by our worry for him, but we visited him much more frequently than we had before. Every two months we would sail to Roskilde to visit him for a few days, perhaps a week. By Alvar's request, at the end of winter, we had left Young Birger and Sander in Roskilde with him for two months. Alvar was grimly planning on his own eventual demise and wanted to teach Young Birger and Sander all he could, in preparation for when they would become jarls.

"With my knowledge and your *faðir*'s knowledge, you will be the greatest jarls there ever were!" Alvar had exclaimed happily to his eldest grandsons.

It had been incredibly difficult for me to allow Young Birger and Sander to be gone from home – from me – for so long, but Vidar had been steadfast in allowing it. He sympathised, he understood my apprehension and anxiety, but the boys *had* to go.

"The Allfather promised you blessings upon the children, correct?" Vidar had asked.

I nodded silently.

"Then there is nothing to fear." Vidar smiled.

I knew Vidar was right, but I still worried. No matter the age of her child, a mother will always worry. The two months that Young Birger and Sander were absent were abnormally quiet, but luckily, they went by quickly. I immersed myself in Æsa and Einar's education. Æsa was already competent in the runes, but by the end of the two months Einar was too, and Æsa had improved significantly. I had also decided, in my fervour, that the children would become fluent in Ænglisc and hardly spoke to them in Norse at all, even when I recited the tales of the Norse gods, I did it in Ænglisc. Even Vidar, whom I had taught Ænglisc over the many years we'd been together, spoke to the children in my native tongue rather than his when we were inside our hall.

When Vidar wasn't attending town business or working in the shipyard, he assisted me with the children's lessons, and would take Einar off with him so I could focus on Æsa's spinning, weaving and sewing. The most important lesson I taught them was trapping and fighting, and Vidar was *always* present for those lessons. Einar was still too young to learn to shoot a bow or fight; usually we waited until our children had seen four winters before we took them out with a bow, but I chose to teach him anyway – what would it matter if he learned a year earlier?

Einar enjoyed shooting a bow a lot more than I had expected. He almost poked his own eye out while messing around with an arrow, but for the most part he was careful (especially after *that* incident), attentive and obedient. Æsa, ever the young huntress, was phenomenal. Proudly I admired her, her perfect stance, her thin fingers wrapped around the bow, rolling her lips together as she aimed. Æsa had a very good hit ratio considering she was only five, and on one of our outings she even shot down a fat goose flying above us, which we happily ate for dinner that night.

Finally, the day came for us to collect our sons from Roskilde. When we arrived, Alvar had sung their praises with every breath in his being. Young Birger, eleven years of age, was already fit to be jarl, in Alvar's opinion. Young Birger was wise beyond his years, logical, level-headed and such a talented craftsman – Young Birger, Alvar had bragged, would build great ships and, with his unsurpassable tactical thinking, lead Roskilde to victory in them.

Sander, an intelligent young man of eight, would be a good jarl, but he was a seafarer at heart. Sander was restless and bold; he was an animated, lively soul whose curiosity and taste for adventure would take him to all ends of the earth, Alvar had exclaimed. Sander's inquisitiveness and lack of fear would lead him, and the armies and fleets under his control, to riches beyond imagining, and glory above all.

Suffice to say, Vidar and I agreed with Alvar's opinions.

The bay was in sight; Young Birger and Sander dashed ahead towards the shore where men were disembarking. Æsa squirmed from her perch on Vidar's shoulders, wanting to follow the boys. Vidar set her on the ground and immediately she ran after Young Birger and Sander.

"Little fawn–" Vidar began, but I interrupted him.

"Go." I laughed.

Vidar pressed a brief, enthusiastic kiss onto my lips and ruffled three-year-old Einar's mop of curly golden hair, before sprinting after our children. I laughed as I watched the father and children, privately impressed that Vidar had caught up with them so quickly when the three children had such a head start. As Vidar passed Æsa, he scooped her up under his arm and bolted passed Young Birger and Sander, who laughed and cursed at him indignantly for overtaking them.

I heard Vidar's laugh echo up from the shore as Alvar the First One strode off the ship, his long saffron hair blustering about in the wind, his furs drawn about him. Alvar the First One was a very hard man to miss; he was towering, broad and huge, like a bear. In fact, when Sander had first met Alvar, he had accused him of being a 'golden bear', a very apt name for him indeed – Alvar was a hulk of a man who dyed his long hair and bushy beard yellow. Alvar had seen sixty-two winters, a very old age; not many lived to see their grandchildren. Though he was old, Alvar had maintained the fierceness of his youth; he strode off the ship with his shoulders back and head high, and from the distance at which I stood, I could see the crowds almost quaking at the sight of the mighty Jarl of Roskilde.

"Aveline! It's wonderful to see you again, dear daughter-in-law." Alvar exclaimed, embracing me when I had reached him. "And how are you, little Einar?"

"*Gōd, pancung and þū?*" Einar beamed at his grandfather.

I gaped at Einar with a mixture of surprise and pride at the clarity and fluency of his reply. Vidar, however, burst out laughing while Alvar just stared at me gormlessly.

"I'm sorry, I've been teaching him the Anglo-Saxon tongue." I blushed. "That means 'good, thank you, and you?'."

"Ah. He's doing well," Alvar smiled, turning to Einar. "You sound just like an Anglo-Saxon!"

I didn't know whether that was positive or not, but Einar brimmed with pride at his grandfather's comment.

"Þakka, afi." Einar beamed. "I can teach you too, if you'd like."

Alvar boomed with laughter and ruffled Einar's golden hair.

"I fear I am too old to learn new languages, but I appreciate your offer, *sonarson*." Alvar grinned, his teeth shining from beneath the long wiry hairs of his beard and moustache, which were so bushy they concealed his lips almost completely. He turned to Vidar, "Take me to your hall, we must drink and eat and talk. I have great news to share with you – *and* a marvellous offer."

"Offer?" Vidar asked brightly, his lips curved into a smile and his icy eyes alight with curiosity.

Alvar nodded and winked to his son. Vidar turned to Alvar's crew, throwing his arms out wide.

"Mead at my hall!" Vidar beamed. "All are welcome!"

***

QUICKLY THE HALL was filled to bursting with Alvar's crew and Aros's townspeople. Field thralls brought in trestle tables, stools and benches, casks of mead, ale and beer from the storage sheds while Melisende and Rowena, under Heimlaug Daðadóttir's self-appointed management, dashed around the kitchen, sweat dripping from them, preparing enough food to serve our guests.

Heimlaug had brought her own thralls who she put to work serving plates of cheese and bread, platters of dried and salted fish, fowl and meat, and dishes of dried fruit and berries to satisfy the growing hunger of our guests. A large polished bowl of wild greens Einar, Æsa and I had been lucky to find while foraging the day before was set at the high table where Alvar, Vidar, our children and I were sitting.

Many of the townspeople had brought their own thralls to serve them and serve them they did; all the thralls were perspiring heavily, their cheeks red, scurrying back and forth to bring their masters and mistresses their food and drinks. Our guests enjoyed a bevvy of drinks, jugs of icy water and buttermilk, as well as the alcoholic beverages.

"Are you waiting to be fed before you tell me your news?" Vidar asked Alvar cheekily. "Tell me, *faðir*, what is this offer you have?"

"Impatient, aren't you?" Alvar chuckled, turning his sights from Vidar to the hot bowl of stew Rowena set in front of him.

"*Já*, I am. You've got your meal now, so tell me, what is your news, what is your offer?"

"Sigfred is assembling a great army to attack the kingdoms of Francia; they set sail in the middle of summer. Sinric and a Norwegian named Rollo the Walker have agreed to join Sigfred's army, and I plan to join it as well. I am here to offer you the chance to join us." Alvar the First One announced.

Alvar the First One had fought alongside Sinric and Sigfred two decades ago in the Great Army during their attack on the Anglo-Saxon kingdoms under the leadership of the sons of Ragnar. Alvar and his men, Sigfred and Sinric and theirs, had left Britain around the same time, a year or so after Guthrum, a Dane, had come to terms with the Anglo-Saxon King Alfred. Alvar and his troops had returned home to Roskilde, whereas Sigfred and Sinric took their men across the sea to sack the cities along the Frisian coast, before spending a few years raiding east Francia.

Vidar's eyebrows slowly climbed up his brow as Alvar spoke. Alvar's proposition was enticing to say the least; the Norse – the Danes in particular – had raided the kingdoms of Francia time and time again, bribed with loot and massive amounts of silver to leave each time. I could tell Vidar was thinking the same thing as he chewed his bottom lip, excitement blazing in his icy eyes.

"How large is the army?" Vidar asked.

"At least seven thousand men – including yours, should you choose to join us." Alvar grinned.

"Seven *thousand* men?" Vidar marvelled.

"Seven *thousand*."

Alvar smirked at his son, whose jaw had dropped in astonishment at the army's numbers. Around the hall, the townspeople repeated Vidar's words, just as stunned as their jarl.

"What say you, little fawn?" Vidar turned to me.

"Me?" I asked stupidly, baffled by his question.

"Are there any other 'little fawn's' here?" Vidar smirked. "Of course, *you*. What say you? Shall we join the army?"

"Why would you ask me that?" I replied. "Of course, we shall!"

The hall erupted with cheer, the walls shaking from the sheer intensity of their applause.

"My wife has spoken." Vidar beamed, standing to address his townspeople. "We have less than half a season to prepare. I believe that will be ample time for us to assemble our forces! In midsummer we will join the great army and attack Francia!"

***

DRESSED IN FINERY from head to toe, I rode my beautiful dapple-grey mare, Dimma, beside Vidar as we finally returned home after a long two weeks of touring the settlements surrounding Aros. All the settlements who owed fealty to Vidar – and the ones who had newly pledged their allegiance to him on our expedition – had agreed to join Aros and attack the Franks.

As well as reaching out to settlements, over the past few weeks Vidar and I had joined Alvar in Roskilde for meetings with Sinric, who had come to Denmark to recruit more men on Sigfred and Rollo's behalf. During their meetings, Sinric relayed Sigfred and Rollo's tentative plan to attack the kingdoms of Francia.

The kingdoms of the Franks were rife with internal issues making it an easy prey for predators like the Norse. The plan consisted of sailing from Denmark, along the coast of east Francia, attacking whatever village we stumbled upon to the river Seine. The army would then row down the Seine, plundering along the way, to the Paris basin where Sigfred would take a small division of men and demand a tribute of *danegeld* from the Franks. All the while, the army of seven thousand would be waiting. Whether the Danes received the *danegeld* or not, we would push through Paris to the wealthy countryside past it, which we would loot and raid for more spoils.

With only four weeks left until we were due to set sail, Aros was alive with activity and excitement; the time everyone was waiting for was drawing ever closer. Ships were mended and prepared, rations were gathered, weapons were readied. This was the largest raid in recent years, and the riches we expected to seize would be immense.

Vidar and I had raided the coasts of the Kingdoms of Francia a few times since we had become Jarl and Jarlkona of Aros, but we had never been to Paris before – though Sinric and Alvar had, and they told us in excited detail of its riches. Not only was Paris full of silver and gold, but along the way to the Frankish island city, there were apparently many monasteries, packed with the usual fantastical Christian artefacts and treasures, like golden chalices and pyx, ecclesiastical silver, jewels and most importantly, money – the tithes the monks collected amassed quite the fortune. Unprotected and far from aid, the monasteries were sitting ducks for the Norse raiders' attacks.

A shadow of guilt cast over me.

Having never actually *raided* anywhere myself, though I had attended a few raids with Vidar over the years, I was nervous. During those few raids, I had stayed at camp or on the ship, waiting with the other women for our men to return with their spoils. I had never stolen or plundered, and I had killed only a handful of people in my time living with the Danes.

When Erhardt Ketilsson of Aros had waged a surprise attack on Roskilde, I had killed eight warriors defending Freydis from the invaders. I had killed only one person outside of battle; I had stabbed to death an Anglo-Saxon thrall. She had been one of Alvar and Freydis's thralls. The thrall, Hilda, and I first met when I was fifteen; she hated me immediately, branding me a traitor to our Anglo-Saxon people for befriending the Danes. Years later, when I was married to Erhardt and he and I had visited his daughter (and Vidar) in Roskilde for *Midsumarblót*, she had caught Vidar and

I in bed together. She threatened to tell Erhardt, knowing he would kill us and our children ... I had no other choice but to kill her.

I had never actually killed an innocent person in cold blood before (in my eyes, Hilda was not innocent) and undoubtedly many innocent people would be slain in Francia – unarmed, unsuspecting, innocent people would be killed because of the Norsemen's greed and lust for battle. Rather than being an innocent victim of the Norsemen's attack as I had been twenty years ago, this time I would be one of the vicious, bloodthirsty monsters attacking the innocent ...

A pang of realisation hit me; the Danes had attacked the Kingdom of the East Angles in the autumn of 865. Exactly twenty years later, in the autumn of 885, *I* would be the Dane attacking the Kingdom of the Franks.

***

Summer, 885

I STOOD OUTSIDE the hall and watched the townspeople. The streets were packed full of men decked in what armour they had and fully armed with whatever weapons they could find. Not many could afford a sword, most men carried spears, sax knives, bows and arrows, axes and sharpened farming tools.

Some wives were accompanying their husbands to make camp for their men on the Frankish shores, and so they bustled along towards the ships, their thralls carrying trunks full of useful belongings like blankets, food and medicines. Even crates of chickens and ducks were carried down to the shore. I saw new faces hurrying along, too, men from the settlements Vidar and I had visited.

Pride brewed inside me at the sight of all these people. They were going to war, prepared and proud. Though a lot might not make it, there were no tears – in fact, I heard laughter and songs being sung as they traipsed to the shore, sweating in the early morning sun. What touched me most, however, was the fact these people were willingly going to battle at Vidar's behest. These men supported and trusted my husband enough to risk their lives, and they did so without a shadow of a doubt. Vidar promised a fine battle, riches and reverence, and every man and woman walking to the water's edge *knew* Vidar would fulfil his promise.

I was proud of the townspeople, and I was proud of my husband. Vidar Alvarsson, leader, jarl, warrior. He would head his army and lead them to glory. Whatever guilt I had, whatever misgivings, they were not strong enough to overwhelm the love I had for my husband, and the support I would give him in whatever decision he made.

"Aveline, how are you?" Jan asked as he approached the hall.

A head taller or more than the crowd, Jan pushed through the people with ease.

"Jan, come in." I smiled, standing aside to let him in the hall.

Rowena immediately went to fetch drinks for us, her eyes wide and gaping at Jan. Curious at her reaction to Vidar and my dear friend, I turned to Jan and examined him. Then I realised his alabaster face was ashen, and his eyes were swollen and bloodshot with deep black bags hanging beneath them.

"What happened to you – are you okay?" I gasped.

"Never better." Jan lied, though he lied convincingly, for the smile on his face was deceivingly warm and sincere. "Where is your darling husband?"

"Readying the ships with Young Birger." I replied staring at the large wet patches drying upon the front of his charcoal grey tunic. "Jan, *what happened?*"

I touched his tunic, the liquid transferring from his clothing onto my finger; it was red – *blood*. Jan looked down briefly, pulling his tunic out to examine the splotches.

"Ah, *that*. Fríðr gave birth earlier."

"Jan! How dare you not tell me that immediately!" I exclaimed, throwing my arms around him.

Jan laughed, embracing me tightly for a moment.

"Congratulations! That's wonderful!" I beamed up at him. "Is it a boy or a girl?

"A girl." Jan replied. "I named her Jóra."

"Jóra Jansdóttir, how beautiful." I swooned. "When do I get to meet little Jóra?"

"Unfortunately, you don't." Jan's smile faltered. "She was born dead."

"Oh Jan!" My heart sunk in my chest; this was the sixth child Jan had lost. "How is Fríðr? Is Geirsson kind to her, considering?" My voice trailed off.

"He doesn't need to be – she's dead, too. She died during the birth." Jan explained with a deep sigh. "Geirsson *is* surprisingly being kind, though; he is burying Fríðr with Jóra in Aros and has promised to mark the grave, so I can find it upon my return from Francia."

"I'm so sorry, Jan." I breathed.

I opened my arms to him, and he pulled me against him, squeezing me tightly.

"I am, too." Jan whispered. "I – I think sometimes ... Maybe it's a good thing that Thórvar and Thóra and left. Maybe Thórvar is better off without me in his life ... If he stayed with me would he be dead now? I don't know ..."

"Jan!" I gasped.

Jan cleared his throat and gazed down at me.

"On the bright side, I don't have to pay Geirsson any money now." Jan quipped, a lopsided smile on his face.

"Jan–"

"It's alright, Aveline. It's fine." Jan said firmly, shaking his head and closing his eyes.

I squeezed him tighter, clutching him against me with all my might. Jan had endured so much loss when it came to his beloved offspring, Jóra would make the fourth bastard child of his, and the fifth of his six children to die ...

"Come on, then." Jan said, releasing me. "As much as I'd loved to stand here and cuddle you, Aveline, we have an army to join."

CHAPTER TWENTY-THREE

WEST FRANCIA
Summer, 885

TWO HUNDRED WARSHIPS carrying seven thousand or more warriors, with wives, children and thralls as passengers, moved down the valley of the river Seine. It was a powerful sight to behold, the beautiful, long and light warships of various builds, the *snekkja*, *bússa*, *skeið* and the fierce dragon- and serpent-headed *drekkar* – all these great, beautiful, long and light warships gliding across the water, oars fracturing the clear, glossy face of the river, propelling the magnificent ships onwards.

Vidar and I headed our fleet from our dragon ship Storm-Serpent; Alvar's fleet rowed in front of us, and behind us was Sinric's. A spectre fear shivered through me at the sight of these ships, harkening to my life two decades ago, when even a handful of Norse ships struck terror through entire villages.

There had been more than a handful of ships that had attacked the Kingdom of the East Angles twenty years ago ... I remembered when I was nine years old and Birger Bloody Sword carried me to the shore after the Danes had murdered my family and burned down my village. Upon the waters were the plethora of ships belonging to the Great Army, (or the 'Great Heathen Army' as the Anglo-Saxons called them). The Danes sailed in so great a number never seen before until today that is; the fleet we sailed with today definitely rivalled the Great Army in size. Back then, the moment I laid my eyes upon Great Army's ships I had given up all hope, but now ... Now, on every fraction of the water around me sailed a Danish or Norwegian ship and it exhilarated me; I was *part* of this army.

We met with Sigfred and Rollo's troops in Louvain, where they had fought and raided before our arrival. We were amazed to find Sigfred's troops armed with siege weapons – ballistae and battering rams. Young Birger had been especially astounded by the masterfully crafted weaponry. We had been told that the Norwegian, Rollo the Walker was so large and muscled that even a horse could not carry him, and when we met him, we found the rumour to be true. Rollo the Walker was gigantic, bigger even than Jan, and Jan was neck-achingly tall.

Together, our numbers bolstered, we sailed south along the Seine valley to a town named Rouen, the battering rams and ballistae carried in two longships near the rear of the fleet. The wise townspeople of Rouen knew better than to fight the Danes, and so they surrendered immediately, still aching from the wounds of past assaults by the Norsemen. Rouen had been assailed many a time over the years, Rollo and Sigfred being two of the warriors who had attacked in the past, and proudly gloated their successes over the town. With hardly any effort, the Danes seized and ransacked Rouen.

Quickly, the scores of Norsemen and women worked together to create a fortified camp on the opposite side of the river from Rouen. Every man, woman and child worked on digging up the earth to create a huge mound encircling the camp. Any child who had seen eight winters or more were expected to help whether by running errands or assisting with heavy labour. Surprisingly, the children did not complain, they were proud to help the men, proud to do their part in preparing for the battle against the Franks.

Young Birger and Sander shadowed Vidar. Young Birger's woodworking skills had been put to good use, he worked alongside the men building the wooden fortifications that protected the camp, while Sander would dash about fetching tools or nails when the builders ran out.

After days of endless work, the defences were completed. We now focussed on sharpening weapons, readying chainmail and leather and hide armour, and planning our next move.

During the downtime, Sander, Einar and Æsa ran about with a band of other children who had come to Francia with their parents. The excitement of the dawning battle had infected the children; they ran about with wooden sticks fighting one another, laughing and squealing while they played.

Young Birger pestered Sigfred and his men, trying to find out who had built the great weaponry. He had been successful and had spent many nights around the fire hounding the engineers for every detail about the war machines, finding every detail he could about different types of siege weapons. Luckily the engineers were not troubled by Young Birger's constant barrage of questions; they happily imparted their knowledge, telling him of all the other siege weapons they'd seen and built in the past, like mangonels and belfries – machines too big and bulky to haul up the Seine. It's not as though they would be needed anyway, Paris was expected to be a quick victory, the city was renowned for paying tribute to the Danes in return for safety.

"Then why do you have ballistae and battering rams?" Young Birger asked.

"One look at these weapons and the Frank's will give us all the gold we want and let us pass, and after that we can raid along the rest of the Seine to our hearts content." The engineer grinned. "And if the Franks of Paris *do* decide to fight us, we will use these weapons against them, and we will win."

One morning, after much anticipation, our scouts spotted an army of Franks not far from us, heading in our direction. To our surprise, the Frankish troops had stopped, and it didn't take long for rumour to circulate around the camp that the Franks were waiting for reinforcements.

"They're probably waiting for nightfall." Alvar chuckled.

"A night attack, how clever." Rollo mocked, grinning with Alvar.

The day passed, and the Franks didn't attack. We watched their numbers grow. The Norsemen's anticipation had faded somewhat and transformed into impatience; a few of the warriors wanted to leap out of the encampment and charge at them, but thankfully they stuck to the plan. When the moon was high, and most of the fires were extinguished, everybody laid down on the ground feigning sleep and waited for the Franks to attack. Some of the children, fatigued from anticipation and excitement, fell asleep, but all the adults stayed awake, ready and waiting.

The children, thralls and women, who were armed, slept in the centre of the camp, protectively surrounded by the men. I laid down and cuddled up with Æsa and Einar; Sander was already asleep on the other side of the two children, snoring away. I rested my arm on Einar and Æsa held my hand. Young Birger was lying down beside Sander, a sax rested on his chest. We caught each other's eyes and smiled. He rolled onto his chest and reached out to take my hand, squeezing it for a moment.

"I'll protect you." Young Birger whispered.

I beamed, emotion rising inside me. Young Birger had only seen eleven winters, and the true battle had not yet begun, but already he was a man.

It wasn't until dawn that the creeping footsteps of the Frankish soldiers sounded, crunching on the grass, their armour creaking as they scaled the mound. Through narrowed eyes I saw the nearby Danes' fingers twitching close to their weapons, tiny insignificant movements that hadn't been noticed by the Franks.

The Franks were far from the women and children in our position surrounded by the men, and the men would not allow the Frankish forces much closer. My heart pounded. More Franks crept into the camp, inching closer and closer.

Seemingly at once, the Danes leapt to their feet, stunning the Franks for moments – just long enough for the Danes to pounce on them, thrusting their knives, spears, axes, swords and saxes into their foes.

It was a quick slaughter – the Danes didn't suffer many casualties. Some of our warriors climbed to the top of the mound and shot arrows at the Frankish troops that encircled our camp. Vidar rushed to me, splattered with blood and dirt.

"The battle begins!" Vidar grinned, his eyes flashing with bloodlust.

He planted a quick kiss upon my lips and began to dash away, but I caught his wrist and pulled him back.

"Am I not fighting with you?" I demanded, my other hand curled around my sword's hilt.

"Not today, little fawn." Vidar replied hurriedly, wincing a little at the darkness of my scowl. "Next battle you will be at my side, I swear it."

Angrily, I remained at the camp while the Danes and Rollo the Walker's Norwegians charged over the mound and attacked the remaining Franks. Young Birger had gone missing in the fray, but I found out through Sander that Vidar had taken Young Birger with him and his men to fight the Franks. Insulted that Vidar took our eleven-year-old son to battle rather than me, I had greeted Vidar with coldness when he returned to camp later than night, sweaty and covered in blood and filth. Regardless of my animosity towards him, I cleaned his wounds and his clothes and fed him well that night.

The Danes did not plunder and raid the neighbouring villages while the Frankish army were about; their focus rested on defeating the army confronting them first. Whilst in Rouen for those few weeks, I remained in the camp while my husband and eldest son fought side-by-side against the army of Franks. Usually boys would not be allowed to join battles until they were at least twelve years of age, but – as ever – Young Birger was the exception. He was close to twelve, anyway, Vidar had reasoned, and with his skill and his eagerness to learn, when given the opportunity to fight, we should let him.

When Ragnold, the duke who led the Frankish army, was slain, the Franks withdrew, and the Danes began plundering again.

"I'm tired of washing your clothes and cooking your food." I fumed, tossing a bowl of heated stew in front of Vidar – leftover food from the night before. "I came here to fight, Vidar, not pick up after you."

Vidar grabbed my hand and brought it to his lips. My scowl relaxed somewhat, and I felt the iciness inside me melt but tried to keep up my furious facade. Vidar could tell I'd softened towards him though, damn him, and he chuckled a little louder. He turned my arm and ran a trail of kisses up the soft, tender skin of my inner forearm.

"Alright, little fawn. You'll get your chance to fight – today, in fact." Vidar smiled. "We sail on to Burgundy, get your bow and *Úlfsblóð* ready."

"*Úlfsblóð*?" I asked, furrowing my brow.

"Your sword." Vidar said, his voice alight with excitement. "The blood of the wolf was the first thing your blade tasted – I thought it'd be an apt name for it, unless you've already named it something else?"

"*Nei, nei* I haven't." I beamed. "*Úlfsblóð* is perfect."

Confident in their pending success, Sinric and his men remained in Rouen, planning to raid the surrounding area, a few days after which they would meet us in Paris. There was a long road that led directly from Rouen to the Frankish town Pontoise near the Oise river, and Pontoise was just a short travel from Paris. Sinric and his men would ride down that road to join us.

None of the other leaders were bothered by Sinric's proposal to raid for a few more days; Paris was renowned for paying tribute to the Danes and letting them by for the city's own safety. We planned on taking our time rowing up the Seine, raiding whatever villages we found along the way. Sigfred, Rollo, Alvar and Vidar thought it best to leave a large contingency of men in Rouen, to secure the town and guard the mouth of the Seine, should the Franks receive reinforcements.

Between the five leaders, we had begun with roughly seven thousand men altogether. With Sinric going raiding rather than heading directly to Paris with us, we had maybe six thousand men remaining. Deducting the men left in Rouen, there were still over four thousand warriors sailing upstream to Paris in just over a hundred boats; an army large enough to terrify the Franks.

We planned to sail upstream, following the Seine the whole way passed Paris and moor in Burgundy, where the battle would truly begin. We planned to stop at Paris, where Sigfred would enter the city with a team of warriors and demand the Franks to pay tribute to the Danes and give our army safe passage through to Burgundy, otherwise we would raze Paris to the ground.

"Hard offer to refuse, that." I said dryly, gazing around me at sea of warriors itching for battle.

"I'm sure the Franks will see it the same way." Sigfred laughed.

Strategy agreed upon, morning meal eaten, and ships filled, our army sailed up the Seine. Alvar and Sigfred's ships led at the front of the great fleet, Vidar and Rollo the Walker's ships following, together we rowed up the river. In the distance at the confluence of the river Seine and the river Eure, we spotted two wood and stone forts on either bank with a long bridge stretched over the river between them.

The three military leaders at the front of the fleet shared distant glances with each other. The air grew thick with anticipation, my heart raced, beating hard in my ears.

"Shields up. Prepare yourselves." Vidar ordered.

The warriors on the front ships lifted their shields above their heads, forming top cover and walls around them, the ships behind followed suit, all spying the bridge as it came into view. The women and children shuffled together around the centre mast, hidden beneath shields so protectively I could hardly see them in the darkness, the shields blocking the light of the sun.

Sander, Æsa and Einar were in the throng of women and children huddled by the mast with Ebbe's wife Borghildr Hrafnkelsdóttir and Domnall's wife, Guðrin, who had both come to Francia with their husbands. Ebbe and Borghildr had brought their brood of ebony-haired children, and Domnall and Guðrin had brought their only child, their son Yngvi.

Borghildr was tall and broad with hair as black as night, muscled and had a permanent line between her brows from the stern expression she frequently wore. Nevertheless, she was a beautiful woman, with fair skin and rosy cheeks, dark brown eyes and a wide, bright smile. Ebbe was a fair amount shorter than his wife, plump, with sun-browned skin and wispy mousey brown hair. They looked humorously mismatched, and though Ebbe's constant unfaithfulness enraged his wife to violence, they loved one another dearly – somehow their relationship worked and neither had any intention of divorcing the other. They had four children together, three sons and one daughter, who were all mirror images of their mother but for the plump cheeks and light brown eyes they had inherited from their father.

Domnall and Guðrin were both tall and ghostly pale, but where Domnall was hulking with muscle, Guðrin was lean. She had wide hips and large breasts, the epitome of a Danish woman; I wondered if the Valkyrie were based on her – strong, blonde and beautiful. Guðrin had long sleek golden locks, always kept tightly braided to her head and tucked beneath a kerchief, whereas Domnall had red hair which he kept shaven on the back and sides of his head and long on top, and a large, bushy beard. Their tall, slender eleven-year-old son had inherited his father's fiery hair and his mother's heart-shaped face, in due time he would gain muscle like his parents.

I found my children's faces through the dark and smiled at them. When our eyes met, Sander – grinning from ear to ear – tried dashing over to me, but Borghildr swooped down and trapped him in her vice-like grip. He would stay with her and be safe.

"Are you ready, little fawn?" Vidar grinned.

I lifted my bow and nodded in reply. I glanced at Young Birger, who was also armed with his bow. He nodded, his face more solemn than I had ever seen – he was nervous.

"Are you ready, my love?" I whispered to my son, my voice so quiet only he and Vidar could hear me.

Young Birger nodded, his grip tight on his bow, an arrow ready in his other hand. Closer and closer, we neared the bridge, peeking through the narrow gap of Vidar's slightly lowered shield. We stared at the bridge, waiting for the Franks to appear.

But they didn't.

Our ships sailed beneath the bridge, and no attack came. In fact, not a single Frank had been spotted on the bridge. A few bands of Danes and Norwegians had disembarked from their ships and climbed up the river bank, stealing across the bright, dew swept grass towards the fortifications.

"Where are they?" I murmured to myself, watching the Danes enter the fort on the north side of the river.

Black smoke billowed from the forts and soon enough long tongues of flame flashed, devouring the fortifications. The Norsemen who had stormed the forts paused on the grassy banks, admiring their work, before rushing back to their ships.

Thankfully the bridge didn't catch fire until after all the ships had made it through. Smoke curled in the sky in great black plumes, dancing with the orange and gold flames. Charred and smouldering pieces of the bridge collapsed, splashing into the water. Cheers erupted from the crews on the ship, and Vidar's face was glowing with delight. The Franks hadn't garrisoned the forts – this was a good sign.

"If things carry on like this, we should reach Paris in no time!" Vidar beamed. "If they're too scared to battle, they'll give us our silver and let us on to Burgundy without any trouble."

Blinded by his excitement, Vidar didn't notice the scepticism on my face. I didn't say a word, though, I allowed him his happiness. Privately there was a sinking feeling in the pit of my stomach, I was dubious. Sure, Rouen had been quick to seize, and the Frankish army's lack of resolve to fight had been palpable, from what Vidar and the other warriors had said – the moment the duke was killed, the troops withdrew, leaving quicker than they had arrived – *but* could it truly be this easy? I glanced at the fleet.

Our army was made up of an intimidating number of men, all much larger and more muscled than the Franks, and slathered in terrifying black war paint. Their bloodlust and eagerness for battle radiated from them, scorching like fire, burning to the bone. Maybe it could be this easy. Maybe …

We rowed up the Seine for hours, pausing every now and again to raid small villages along the way, before we finally met with Frankish soldiers. They had created a huge blockade across the stretch of the river in front of us with their ships.

I heard the Frank's horns echo across the water, and we watched them ready their bows. There was a rattling *clack!* as the Frankish soldiers nocked their arrows in unison. With a boom of wood upon wood, the Norsemen raised their shields above their heads or held them out to the sides, overlapping like thick scales, to allow not even a single arrow through – or at least, we hoped not, anyway.

Another Frankish call.

With a loud *swoosh*, like a sudden gust of wind, the Franks fired their arrows. The volley of arrows howled as they sliced through the sky before landing upon our shields with thunderous cracks and thuds. Splashes sounded as arrows and a few of our warriors fell into the Seine, pierced by the arrows, but luckily not many of our men were hit.

RISE TO FALL

Immediately, Alvar the First One's horn sounded, then Sigfred's. Hallmundr brought our ship's horn to his lips and blew hard, the deep roar of the horns echoing across the waters. Behind us we could hear Sinric and Rollo's horns sound. The shield walls and roof maintained, we readied our bows in a deafening rustle. I brought my bow up, an arrow knocked and ready to fire at any given second. Young Birger was at my side, doing the same. My stomach was twisted into knots and Young Birger was deathly pale.

"Remember, *consistent stance*." I whispered.

We grinned at each other. Adrenaline surged through my body; I wanted to laugh hysterically, so excited and anxious, but I stifled the urge. Young Birger also stifled his own anxious need to laugh – he bit into his bottom lip so hard blood trickled down his chin, though he didn't seem to notice.

Another blast of the horns sounded.

"Heil Odin!" Jan roared, lowering his shield and hurling a spear across the waters, impaling a Frank.

With this, the rest of the shield roof opened for just a moment – long enough for us to release a volley of arrows upon the Franks. Every arrow fired, the shield roof closed again, and a quarter of our crew dropped to the benches and grabbed the oars. A long howl of the horns sounded, urging our men to drive the oars deep into the waters. Light and narrow, our warships were perfectly crafted and equipped for sailing over sea and through shallow rivers. They soared across the water towards the Franks; our ships much faster than theirs.

The shield roof opened, and we unleashed another wave of arrows upon the Franks. Alvar the First One's fleet had reached the Franks before anyone else's, (no one was surprised – he was known as *the First One* for a reason). Alvar's crewmen lowered their shield wall, and we watched Alvar's hulking figure leap from his ship onto one of the Frank's, an almighty roar bellowing from his throat. The Frankish vessel rocked violently as Alvar landed, and he cleaved a Frank in the neck with his axe, bringing it down and splitting the Frank's shoulder apart. With pure brute strength,

Alvar ripped his weapon free, the Frank's blood spraying, and swooped around to smash another in the face.

Alvar the First One's men followed their jarl in suit, leaping from their longships roaring like wild beasts and landing onto the Frankish vessels, slaughtering the Frankish soldiers. The Frankish ships in the rear began to retreat, but Sigfred and Vidar's longships managed to circle around the majority of the Frank's fleet, trapping them. The Frankish soldiers screamed and shrieked as the Norsemen crawled all over their ships, like a vicious infestation, hacking and slashing and ripping apart all their enemies, leaving bodies strewn in their wake.

"Spears!" Vidar commanded his crewmen, his eyes fixed on the Frankish ship closest to us. "Young Birger, stay on the ship. Grab my spear and protect the women and children. Little fawn," Vidar glanced at me with a smile on his lips. "Will you fight by my side?"

"*Já* – of course!" I gasped.

I tossed my bow down, lifted my shield and drew out my sword, *Úlfsblóð*. We closed in on the Frankish ship, much to their horror.

"Gangplanks ready!" Vidar bellowed.

The Franks were so close now, I could see their hands trembling and beads of sweat drip down their faces. *Oh god, they're so scared!* Their fear struck my heart, but I shook my head, trying to ignore it. Adrenaline was rushing through me; I felt my own body tremble. I gazed at Vidar, who was staring at the Franks hungrily. As though he could feel my gaze, he turned to me and smiled warmly – the bloodlust in his eyes muted temporarily.

"It's okay to be scared, little fawn, but you can't turn back now. You can do this, I know it." Vidar said. "I love you little fawn, I'm glad you're by my side."

My heart felt as though it had stopped beating, my chest was tight, and I wanted to vomit. I glanced at Young Birger, whose golden skin was now pasty and pale. In his icy eyes though, I saw a glimmer of excitement – just like Vidar.

"*Nú!*" Vidar thundered.

Immediately our crew slammed the two gangplanks down onto the Frankish ship. The Frank's tried to push them down but to no avail, the moment the gangplanks had so much as touched the

Frankish ships, our warriors bounded on to them. Vidar leapt onto the gangplank closest us and dashed down it towards the Franks. As though I was attached to him by an invisible rope, I jumped onto the gangplank and dashed across after him, my skirts billowing behind me.

Most Franks stared at me in horror, shocked to see a woman bearing down on them, sword raised, and I took advantage of their hesitation. Hot red blood slapped across my face, my body, my flesh, as enemy after enemy, I killed them.

**

"I'M PROUD OF you, little fawn." Vidar said as we collapsed onto our ship, panting.

Young Birger was splattered in blood, and so was Sander – he had excitedly proclaimed he'd escaped Borghildr's clutches, found a spear and joined his brother in slaying the Frankish enemies. It horrified me to hear how proud both of my boys were of their kills and yet I was proud of them, too.

"Thanks." I wheezed, trying to catch my breath.

"*Mumie*, you're dirty." Einar exclaimed, wrinkling his nose at me. "You need a wash."

"*Já*," I puffed. "Quite."

The entire slaughter of the Franks had flashed by in a whirlwind of blood and breathlessness. The moment I had stepped on the gangplank, all thoughts had fled my mind. All I could focus on was killing the Franks lest they kill us. Primal survival instinct had overwhelmed my guilt; a mixture of fear and adrenaline spurred me on to kill several men. I didn't keep count as I murdered them, and I was glad I hadn't – my body was calming, and my guilt was returning, and I didn't want to think of the men whose lives I had stolen.

Suddenly, I jumped up from the bench, leaned over the edge of the longship and vomited into the Seine.

"*Mumie?*" Æsa asked. "Are you okay?"

"*Já*, my love. I'm okay." I rasped between retches.

"I threw up my first time, too, *mumie*, it's okay." Young Birger comforted, rubbing my back with his blood covered hand.

My eleven-year-old son should not be reassuring me like this. I thought, but I said nothing, for another wave of nausea crashed over me and I vomited again.

It took us a long time to make it up the winding, twisting Seine. The Franks had set up various blockades along the snaking length of the river, but we crushed each one of them, with minimal casualties on our side. We stopped and made camp now and then, or paused our journey to loot nearby villages, but by the time autumn arrived, foliage blazing gold, copper, bronze and scarlet, like treasure spattered in blood, our army finally arrived at the island city of Paris.

RISE TO FALL

CHAPTER TWENTY-FOUR

PARIS, WEST FRANCIA
Autumn, 885

"THEY REFUSED TO pay tribute." Sigfred announced.

The army had rowed up the Seine to Paris the day before and at morning's light Sigfred had entered the island city of Paris and approached the bishop, a Frank named Gauzelin, to demand tribute from them and safe passage through Paris to reach the countryside beyond the city.

As Sigfred had announced, our *request* had been denied. Sigfred didn't seem particularly upset at the Bishop's refusal to pay, however, or his refusal to allow us passed Paris, and neither did Alvar, Rollo or Vidar. The Danes and the Norwegians knew the Franks had the silver they craved and a little thing like fighting for it didn't dampen their spirits at all.

The Franks had been well known for paying off their enemies with ransoms and tributes of silver for decades. Beginning almost a decade before King Ragnar Loðbrók's attack exactly forty years ago, the Franks had formed a habit of frequently giving in to the Norsemen and paying them great ransoms of *danegeld*, thousands of Frankish *livres*, for the Norse to leave and guarantee the safety of the Frankish people.

King Ragnar had been paid seven thousand pounds of silver. A few years after Ragnar's attack, Danish king Harald Klak's son, Godfred, had attacked Paris and captured the abbot and the abbot's brother and ransomed the two captives for over six hundred and eighty pounds of gold and three thousand, two hundred and fifty pounds of silver. Over the course of a year, a Norseman named Volund had received two tributes amounting to a massive nine thousand pounds of silver from the Frankish emperor Charles, and another army of Danes had ransomed four thousand pounds of silver, as well as a supply of wine from the Franks.

"So, what would you like to do?" Vidar asked, one eyebrow cocked and smirking mischievously.

"At dawn tomorrow, we attack." Sigfred grinned.

That night I couldn't sleep. We had laid furs down on the grass and curled up on them with yet more furs on top of us to stave off the bitter chill of the autumn night. There was still some time before dawn would break, but I still hadn't managed to fall asleep. I laid on my side, Vidar wrapped around me, his breath warm and steady on the back of my neck, while Einar was asleep in my arms beside me. Æsa was sleeping in the middle, with Sander and Young Birger beside her. It took me quite some effort, but I untangled myself from my family and slip away without stirring them.

I crept through the night, passed all the sleeping warriors, some curled around their families as Vidar and I had been, other men sleeping alone. Every warrior slept beside his weapon and his shield. At the outer edge of the camp, there were warriors on watch. They nodded respectfully or politely greeted me but didn't question me; I was apparently not the only one roaming sleeplessly that night.

I wandered for a while. There was a campfire glowing close to me, the meagre flames offering hardly any heat. I paused beside it and gazed at the great city of Paris across the river. It was nothing more than a dark, imposing silhouette set against the dim, navy blue twilight, but there was a certain undeniable beauty to it. The great city perched on a narrow island, and the moon and stars reflections glittered upon the calm, dark waters surrounding it. I could make out the massive stone walls and the towers that protected the city; the walls had made it difficult for our ships to land on them, so we had made camp on the northern bank across from the city instead.

"Jarlkona Aveline."

"*Gott kveld*, Sigfred. Or rather, should I say, '*góða nótt*'?" I said.

"Or perhaps even '*góðan morgin*'?" Sigfred chuckled.

"Why don't we just settle for *heil*?" I smiled.

"*Já*, much easier." Sigfred said. "*Heil* Jarlkona."

"What are you doing up?" I asked. "Surely you should be resting, dawn is almost here."

"I could say the same to you." Sigfred said. "Your husband informed me you plan to fight with us."

"I do." I said, bristling at his comment. "You don't have any objections, I hope, Sigfred?"

"Of course not, Jarlkona." Sigfred replied, calming me immediately. "I think it's honourable that you want to support our campaign. Are you sure you wouldn't prefer to stay in the camp with your children?"

"I'm sure." I said firmly. "I didn't come here to wait for my husband, I came here to fight beside him."

Sigfred smiled at me, then turned and eyed the great city of Paris.

"I don't think it will be a hard battle. We have far more men than them, from what I saw when I spoke to their bishop." Sigfred said.

"Including the army that attacked us in Rouen?"

"*Já*, including them. We outnumber them vastly." Sigfred beamed happily.

"Regardless of numbers, do you really think it will be easy?" I asked. "I mean, look at their walls."

"I never said *easy*, I just don't think it will be too difficult." Sigfred winked. "The biggest issue we face are the two low-lying foot bridges that lead from the island to the land – they are so low, our ships can't pass them. When I first came here, years ago, neither bridge had towers, but now both bridges have two guarding each of them."

"And bringing down the towers will make it easier to bring down the bridges and cut off Paris from the mainland and we'll be able to travel passed it." I said, reciting the plan Sigfred, Vidar, Alvar and Rollo had devised the day before. "But are you sure you shouldn't burn down the wooden one, first?"

"The Franks will have garrisoned the wooden bridge heavily with men, expecting us to attack there first. The northern tower may be made of stone, but the Franks haven't completed its construction; it's their weak point." Sigfred explained.

Sigfred examined the city shrewdly as he spoke, the light of the moon and stars sparkling just as brightly in his azure eyes as they did on the river surrounding Paris. Sigfred pointed to the stone bridge across from us.

"If the Franks hold the bridges, *we* will be cut off – vulnerable to any army that might come to the Franks aid. You see that tower? That's the one we'll be attacking. It may be made of stone, but as it's unfinished, it shouldn't be hard for us to destroy. If we destroy the northern tower, if we destroy the bridge, the Franks *will* give us what we want: tribute and passage."

Bolstered by his determination, I beamed at the Dane. Sigfred returned my grin with his own.

"If only they'd agreed to pull down the bridges like you asked, eh?" I commented.

"It would have been easier for them." Sigfred laughed. "I promised them if they let us through, we would leave Paris alone, but their bishop Gauzelin refused. He said he'd been entrusted by emperor Charles to protect the city, and he wouldn't betray that trust." Sigfred snorted. "Stupid man, honourable for keeping his word, but stupid nonetheless."

"And would you have kept yours?" I smirked.

"Maybe, maybe not." Sigfred winked. "Never mind, I like a good battle. As does your father-in-law – Alvar has insisted he and his army lead the attack on Paris."

"Of course, he did." I said proudly. "He is *the First One* for a reason."

"He's a grand warrior, Alvar." Sigfred said earnestly. "A man of his age and still fighting strong! He slaughtered many of the Franks at the blockades and suffered hardly any wounds. One would think he's invincible."

"My son Sander calls him a 'golden bear'." I mused for a moment. "I agree with you, Alvar is a powerful man."

"And you, Jarlkona? What of your strength?" Sigfred said, catching me by surprise. "You've come here to fight, but battling is exhausting – on the mind just as much as the body. You may even die – are you willing to risk your life for this?"

Taken aback by his questions, my eyes popped open wide and I was silent for a moment, my lips pursed and pulled down in a small frown at the corners. I turned my back to the city of Paris and looked across the camp to find my family still lying asleep together, a smudge in the dark but I knew it was them. I felt my expression soften as my gaze rested on them.

"If my husband deems this a worthy enough cause to risk his life, then so do I." I said.

"You don't fear death?" Sigfred pressed, his voice low and my flesh prickling with goosebumps from the weight of his stare.

"*Nei*, I don't." I said, and I truly didn't. "A friend once told me when you face war, you must be bold and fight with all your might, for there is nothing to fear; in battle, you will either fall or you will come away alive. Nothing can kill a man if his time has not come, and nothing can save one doomed to die. To die in flight is the worst death of all – and I don't intend to flee or be an onlooker. I want to be honourable and bold, which is why I choose to fight beside my husband. For as long as he is on the battlefield, then I will be, too – whether he is dead or alive."

"And if Vidar does die?" Sigfred asked, his question stabbing me like a knife to the heart.

"Then I will die fighting alongside him."

***

STREAKS OF GOLD crept across the sky, and great splashes of warm orange spilled over the deep blue of the faded night as the sun gradually ascended from the horizon. We had split into two groups, Sigfred's men, plus half of Alvar and Vidar's troops were on land, the rest of their men were with Rollo's on the water. The ships were hardly noticeable, cutting silently through the waters, veiled by the cold, silvery mists rising from the river. The vapour of the autumn fog clung to the great stone walls of Paris, the ships, the stiff, crunchy grass of the banks and our entire camp, dewdrops sparkling like diamonds in its wake.

Though cold, it was a beautiful morning, one I would have loved to have enjoyed with a hot honey tea in my hands, but that was not the case. At first morning light, I travelled with the army, *Úlfsblóð* and a quiver of arrows on my hip, my shield slung over my back and my bow in hand, to the incomplete tower on the north bank of Paris. Sander, Einar and Æsa were with Borghildr and the rest of the women and children at the camp.

We stole across the bank, the morning mist dampening our clothes, our boots sparkling with dew. Alvar and his men were up at the front pushing the battering rams, while Vidar and his men were behind them, pushing the ballistae. The wooden contraptions rumbled as they rolled over the bumpy ground, and the long damp grass slapped against the wheels and the wooden frames.

The two battering rams were massive, fat oak trunks that had been stripped of their branches and fitted with metal heads and metal bands. These trunks were suspended from ropes or chains housed inside wattle woven panelled sheds with wheels. Suspended from ropes, the men would swing the trunks to make them slam the enemy's wall, gates or door, and the roof of the sheds would offer protection to those using the ram and rolling the whole thing on wheels would tire the men less than carrying it.

The ballistae, also made of oak wood in honour of the god of war, Odin, were almost like giant crossbows that would shoot large arrows and darts, powered by twisted skeins of human hair and animal sinew, from what the engineer had told Young Birger (and Young Birger had excitedly explained to Vidar and me). The bolts were huge, long wooden posts with fierce spike tips, and two metal fletchings at the end where the feathers on an arrow would be. The ballistae were each mounted on a wheeled platform, making it easier to push along, though the engines were still bulky, heavy and cumbersome, slowing us down a lot. Regardless, I had no doubt of the effectiveness of these weapons. The ballistae might not bring down a wall, but apparently their accuracy was incredible, and they could impale more than a few people at a time.

Sigfred claimed he had seen these weapons along his travels in the Anglo-Saxon kingdoms, Frisia and Francia. According to the engineers, the ballista was based on a weapon made many centuries ago in *Grikkland*, and the battering ram was just as ancient. They were incredible war machines, and Sigfred was as excited as Young Birger to use them.

The men, perspiring despite the biting chill of the autumn morning, heaved the battering rams and ballistae across the dewy bank. We reached the northern tower, tall and strong, the morning moisture glittering upon the glorious grey stone. The top section was unfinished, but it connected to the bridge and was in more than usable condition.

"Load the ballistae." Sigfred ordered.

Two men to each ballista, they simultaneously attached the ropes to the winches and cranked them back, the wood creaking from the tension, then hooked the rope onto the release bolt and removed the winches. The ballistae were ready to fire.

"Ready?" Alvar bellowed to his men, beaming from beneath his bushy golden facial hair. "*Nú!*"

All at once the men began jogging, quickly breaking into a full run. With a deafening *boom!* the metal heads of the rams collided with the huge gate of the tower. Immediately, the men swung the trunk back then, on Alvar's command, they slammed it against the door again, another *boom!* echoing about us.

It didn't take long for the Frankish bishop Odo and his men to hear us. Frankish soldiers decked out in chainmail and helmets, crossbows and bows in their hands, blades at their hips, burst over the bridge, appearing at the parapets and battlements.

"For Odin!" Jan roared, hurling a spear high at the wall.

Jan's aim was true, the spear pierced a Frank's chest, and he tumbled down.

"*Nú!*" Sigfred roared.

Immediately, the bolts were placed upon the barrels of the ballistae. The ballistae turned with ease as their users took aim – a process so quick I was surprised to see the bolts soar through the air so suddenly. It took only a quick pull of the trigger and the squeak of wood as the rope snapped forward and sent the bolts cutting through the air. One of the bolts soared high over the walls, crashing down upon a building or some sort of structure, for there was a mighty din of glass shattering, wood splintering and screams howling from behind the walls.

The other bolt soared and impaled a Frank square in the chest, ignoring his chainmail armour as though it was nothing. The man tumbled from the battlements to the ground, instantly dead.

Alvar and his men, encouraged by the successful beginning of the battle, pounded on the tower with more enthusiasm than before. Chorused with the booms of rams pounding on the gate, the men roared as they struck the doors with all their might, the wood groaning and splintering from the metal heads of the rams, but still they stood. Those of Alvar's men who were not operating the battering rams pounded on their shields, roaring out to intimidate the Franks and excite our warriors.

The call of horns rose with the fog upon the river. There was a loud *swoosh* and hundreds of arrows hurtled up at the bridge, filling the sky like a huge black cloud. A few arrows passed through the window slits, but many became lodged in the wood of the bridge.

Then the Franks retaliated.

The Frankish orders echoed from their high positions atop the wall. The creak of bowstrings and crossbows being drawn – the familiar sound of Norse horns blaring – the swoosh of arrows soaring down – the *slam!* of arrows piercing wooden shields – the *clang!* of arrows ricocheting off metal helmets – the cry of men impaled by the enemy's arrows and bolts – the splash of bodies tumbling into the water.

"*Nú!*" Vidar thundered.

Our men swung their leather slings before releasing a barrage of stones and rocks at the top of the tower where Frankish soldiers were readying their crossbows to fire upon us. Some Franks dodged behind the stone walls, other were smashed in the face or neck by the stones. Frankish bolts shot down upon us, smashing into the woven wattle sheds protecting the battering rams, others flying at the stone-throwers.

Young Birger and I, and a team of other archers, were crouched behind the mound of the bank, our bows ready. Carefully aiming at the window slits in the tower, we released our arrows, some arrows piercing Franks, others bouncing off the stone walls and tumbling to the ground.

"The rams aren't doing anything." Young Birger hissed. "They haven't got through the gate yet!"

"Give it time." I replied, ducked behind the berm while nocking another arrow, the thrill of battle filling me with excitement and nausea. "Now fire!"

***

NIGHT FELL UPON us as we staggered back to camp, our numbers far less than they had been that morning. Bodies aching and bleeding, muscles stiff and screaming, we stumbled over the banks and collapsed at the camp. We hadn't taken down the tower. We had lost a lot of men, carrying their bodies to camp with us. This battle was going to be more difficult than Sigfred had first thought.

"It's just the first day." Vidar said when I quietly confessed my fears to him that night, curled together by the fire. "We'll bring it down, don't fret."

At dawn once again, we crept along the bank of the Seine, toward the northern tower. We had our siege engines, our archers, our swords and stones and spears, we had axes and pickaxes. Battering rams situated at the doors of the tower, our two ballistae and archers aimed at the high walls of Paris across the river from us, archers on the banks aimed at the bridge. Upon the waters were Sigfred and Alvar's men this time. They planned to leap upon the narrow bank of the island and dig beneath the wall while yet more archers covered them from on the longships.

There was a bizarre smell filling the air, thick and filthy, bitter and pungent. I couldn't think of what it was, but black smoke drifted upwards from various points on the walls and the towers.

The Franks didn't wait for us to begin pounding the walls with our battering rams; almost as soon as we reached the northern tower, arrows and bolts showered down upon us – including a massive ballista bolt!

The bolt shot through the air and skewered seven Danes at once! The crack of their bones filled the air as the bolt ran them through. The men shrieked, a blood-curdling scream ripped from my throat and I fell to my knees and vomited. Our men – men from Aros! –

impaled one on top of the other on this great pike, groaning and wailing with pain, their blood seeping ...

There was nothing we could do. Shields lifted, we stormed towards the tower, rage boiling inside each one of us – and fear. The cries from our men as they slowly died filled our ears. Waves of fear crashed through my body. I screamed with the men as they roared, beating their shields as they charged at the tower and attempted to climb it. Battering rams smashed against the doors, stones hurtled through the air, arrows soared.

Arrow after arrow I fired at the Franks. With Young Birger beside me, we shot at the enemies, arms aching but fury motivating us as we watched our friends and comrades fall. We ducked behind our shields, wedged into the berm to give us cover, as the Franks fired from above at us and when our arrows ran out, we hurled stones.

As day grew bright, from the battlements of the wall I could see the great cauldrons that issued the smoke. My eyes travelled down to the banks below where Alvar and his men were digging. My heart raced in my chest. I spotted Alvar, his saffron yellow hair and hulking figure unmistakable even from the distance.

"Vidar – Vidar! They need to get out of there!" I screamed, pointing at the wall. "Sound the horns!"

Vidar released his arrow, which pierced the neck of a Frank and sent him tumbling from the tower, one hand clenched around the arrow. Vidar hurriedly examined the wall and spotted the cauldrons; his icy eyes shot open wide and his jaw dropped. Before he could say even a single word, it was too late. The Franks tipped the cauldrons, stinking thick black viscous liquid cascading out onto our men; boiling hot wax and pitch.

The howling roars and shrieks of agony erupting from the banks was deafening. The stench of wax and pitch was more pungent as it poured from the cauldrons, but the reek of melting human flesh was even stronger. I dropped to my knees as I watched Alvar's saffron yellow hair turn black, his deep wrenching shriek of pain ripping through the air. Clinging to his melting scalp, locks of his hair falling away with the pitch that dripped down him, Alvar stumbled and collapsed into the Seine with a huge splash.

RISE TO FALL

Alvar the First One was dead.

Vidar roared.

Sound disappeared. My vision became blurry and my heart suddenly stopped beating. I couldn't blink nor tear my eyes away from Alvar's body, floating face down in the Seine. His was not the only body to fall, boiled and burning from the pitch and tar, flesh falling away. The bodies of the men of Roskilde – of *our* men – the men Vidar had known all his life – piled up in the water. Some men ran from the walls of Paris, scalps falling away beneath fingers, faces melted, skin burned black and scarlet. The screams faded as our men quickly died.

"*Faðir! Faðir, nei!*" Young Birger yelled.

My heart thundered in my chest and a high-pitched ring whined in my ears. In a daze I glanced around, searching for my husband and son. I spotted them, Vidar, his sword and shield drawn, was charging towards the Seine, Young Birger on his heels. *Oh, Frigg, no!* I threw down my bow and arrow and ran to them, shoving my way through the warriors recklessly, narrowly missing an arrow that hurtled towards me from the wall.

"*Faðir, nei!*" Young Birger shouted again, catching up with Vidar and grabbing his arm. "*Nei!*"

Vidar, blinded with rage, shook his arm so violently he sent Young Birger flying to the ground. He glared from our son to the walls and roared, storming towards the river. With his shield raised over his head, arrows showered down on him, miraculously missing him and piercing only his shield. Vidar stormed into the river, wading waist deep before Young Birger managed to jump to his feet and catch up with him again. Young Birger grabbed Vidar's arm, yelling at him to stop, and tried to drag him back up the bank.

"*Nei, faðir!*" Young Birger begged. "Come on, come on!"

Above the din of dying men, the clatter of stones upon shields, the thud of bodies hitting the ground and splashing into the river, of blade clashing against blade and the fierce gust of arrows darkening the sky, horns sounded. Jan suddenly appeared on the shore and dived into the water towards Vidar and Young Birger.

"Go, Birger, go!" Jan bellowed as he neared them.

I hurled myself down the bank, screaming my son's name. Reluctant and panicked, Young Birger glanced between me and Vidar. He stumbled backwards, not ripping his gaze from his father and Jan. Jan grabbed Vidar's shoulder, who raised his sword ready to cleave him, but Jan grabbed his wrist in time. There they stood, glaring at one another, Vidar's face red and contorted with rage.

"We're retreating!" Jan yelled. "We must go!"

"*Nei*!" Vidar bellowed.

"*Ja*!" Jan shouted. "Come, we must leave! We must get Birger and Aveline to safety!"

Vidar's face was frozen, his brow furrowed and eyes wide, his lips curled in a vicious snarl. He turned to Young Birger and me, watched me pull our eldest son from the water, arrows hurtling past us, screaming out and begging Vidar to retreat with us. There was a flash in Vidar's icy eyes and his expression softened to one of shock. He pulled his arm from Jan and waded through the water towards us, his shield raised once more, dashing to us as fast as he could. Reunited at the bank, we ran together, Young Birger and I shielded from behind by Vidar and Jan, sprinting to safety.

The Franks fired bolt after bolt from their ballistae, but somehow, we came out unscathed. We had been lucky, but many of our men had not.

CHAPTER TWENTY-FIVE

WE STAGGERED BACK to camp, aching, ashamed and angry. It was barely noon and already we had lost a lot of the men of Roskilde. Many of us had ran, leaving the siege engines behind, until we were a safe distance from Paris and were able to board the ships. Several of Roskilde's ships had been abandoned, bobbing empty on the Seine, the burned corpses of the seafarers that had filled them only hours ago floating in the river surrounding them.

"*Mumie*, are you alright?" Æsa gasped as I tossed *Úlfsblóð* down and collapsed on the ground beside her.

"I'm tired," I replied, touching her arms that she'd wrapped around my neck.

Einar laid down on me, hugging me tightly, and Sander just stood and gazed at us briefly, turning his sight to the men crawling from the ships, all wearing the same dismal expression and covered in mud, sweat and blood.

"Where's *afi*?" Sander asked, a note of panic in his quiet voice.

"He's dead.," Young Birger replied.

I turned to my eldest son and caught his body shuddering involuntarily, all colour drained from his face, but no tears filling his eyes. Young Birger sounded as though he meant to carry on, but he stopped, unable to continue, unable to share with his younger siblings the grisly death their grandfather met.

"*Mumie*?" Æsa whispered, staring at me desperately.

"*Afi* is dead." I nodded slowly. "He – he's dead, my love."

Einar repeated my words, *afi is dead*, over and over, his voice growing quieter the more he repeated them. Sander breathed in quick, shallow gulps of air, his face growing red and eyes puffy as he tried to hold back his tears, rubbing his eyes fiercely with his fists when a tear trickled.

"When are Sinric and his men to return?" Vidar demanded.

Vidar was a short distance away with Sigfred. Women surrounded the pair, trying to understand why we were back so soon.

"Today, or the 'morrow." Sigfred replied, holding a filthy rag to his shoulder where an arrow or blade had caught him.

"We need his warriors! We must return to Paris at once! We can't let our men die in vain!" Vidar snapped.

The herd of women around them rallied with Vidar – of the group of women, many had lost their husbands. Their faces were ruddy with tears and contorted in anger. They mimicked Vidar, yelling at Sigfred for the warriors to leave camp at once and attack Paris.

"Paris must burn!" Vidar snarled.

"And it will!" Sigfred hissed. "We will recuperate, then attack again."

"You have an hour, Sigfred." Vidar said darkly. "In an hour I will be leading my men – the men of Aros *and* Roskilde – to Paris."

***

VIDAR DIDN'T EAT, he hardly even spoke. He paced around the camp, scowling, watching his men force down spoonsful of stew and tankards of mead, waiting for them to be done so we could fight again. The children didn't dare approach their father, and I didn't either. Alvar had died in battle, he would be in Valhalla, but though he had died honourably, Vidar would claim vengeance for the agonising death the Franks had made Alvar the First One suffer.

Bellies filled and bodies somewhat rested, the army was ready, rage and need for vengeance boiling in the pits of their stomachs and etched on their faces. Silently, in the cold midday sun, we rowed towards Paris yet again, determined for victory. In the distance we saw Franks on the river bank looting bodies, killing those that still breathed. A low growl rolled from Vidar's throat as he watched them, his hand curled around the hilt of his sword.

The Franks on the land were wearing matching blue tunics hemmed in gold fabric and brown boots on their feet and some wore yellow cloaks about their shoulders, but none of them were wearing any chain- or scale-mail body armour – they must've been low soldiers, though a few had armguards, and all had helms on their heads and lances in their hands.

A sudden cloud of arrows hailed down before us in the water, a warning from the Franks for us to leave. On the banks, the Franks panicked, abandoning the corpses of our men in favour of drawing their weapons. Scores of Frankish soldiers stormed down the bridge, the gates of the tower opened, releasing the horde onto the banks. The ramparts were filled with Frankish archers, and there, dressed in his holy robes and scale-mail with bow and axe, a crucifix in one hand, was the Bishop Gauzelin, prepared to battle us, too.

Horns sounded, our shields went up, we rowed determined down the Seine, ignoring the arrows that pounded upon our shields. Behind us, horns bellowed, warriors leapt from the boats into the water, splashing like waves in a storm. They climbed up the banks and tore towards the Franks, roaring, pounding their shields with their weapons. With Young Birger beside me, we followed suit, we jumped into the waters and waded to the land, scrambling up the muddy banks to meet our enemy.

Chaos erupted around us, swords clanged, spears and stones hurtled through the air, arrows soared. Young Birger stayed behind with a team of archers, firing at the men on top of the tower, while I dashed ahead with Vidar, both our swords drawn and shields in hand. We needed to reach our ballistae and rams and steal them back from the Franks.

I stormed towards the war machines, lost in the fray, men falling beside me – both Franks and Norsemen – others clashed in fierce battle. Everything seemed amplified, sight, sound, smell – I could feel the gust of air as men drew back their swords or thrust forth their spears. The dull tear of flesh as iron slashed or pierced it, the squelch of body organs ripped by spearheads or tumbling from stomachs slashed open by blades.

The metallic stench of blood, the foul reek of shit and sweat and death permeated everything, the bitter, filthy odours weighed heavy in the air to the point I could taste them. I couldn't hear my heart racing in my chest over the noise surrounding me, though I could feel its frantic hammering against my ribs, like it was trying to smash them to pieces. My hands shuddered, but I held my shield and sword in a vice grip – they were my survival.

"Shit!" I cried out, stumbling to a halt.

Before me, a Frankish soldier whipped around, his lance pointed at me. His sallow face was contorted in shock, his hands trembled and made his lance shudder, but still the sharp tip was aimed at me. Rather than thrusting the lance at me, however, his eyes widened as he eyed me, noticing my breasts and skirts no doubt.

"*Une femme?*" He spluttered. "*Une femme en bataille?*"

"*Oïl, une femme!*" I hissed, understanding him from the François Caterine and Melisende had taught me over the years.

My chest tightened, and I gasped for air. Oh gods, his eyes – they were hazel, flashes of green dancing in an almost golden brown – his pale face was narrow, his milky white hands trembled ... I knew I had to kill this man, but he wasn't a faceless enemy anymore. He was a man – a man who possibly had a family, children, maybe even a farm to tend. He was a human like me, and that stopped me from raising *Úlfsblóð* and taking his life. I never had the chance to see the men I had killed on the ships or the morning and day previous – I had hurtled through them, swinging and stabbing wildly, but here I stood now, face-to-face with a man I had to kill.

A body thudded down to the ground nearby us, and I saw Vidar in my peripheral, glancing at me as he fought a Frank. I needed to kill the man in front of me, lest I distract Vidar and risk his life ... Taking my chance while I still could, with my shield raised in front of me, I swung *Úlfsblóð* and slammed it against the wooden post of the Frank's lance. My sword didn't break it, but the lance went flying from his hands and landed a little way from us.

"*Putain!*" He gasped, glaring at me in disbelief.

"*Oïl, je suis un putain, le putain norrois qui va t'envoyer á ta mort!*" I snarled.

Suddenly a massive bolt shot by us, impaling two Danes upon it, narrowly missing the Frank they had been fighting. My enemy and I both stared at the Franks who were loading another bolt onto the Danish ballista. Another opportunity – the Frank was distracted. Sickness shot up my throat and my stomach ached, like it was clenched in some invisible fist. Every fibre of my being screamed at me not to murder an innocent man, but I had to. I had to reach the ballistae and the battering rams – the Franks would not hesitate to kill me or my husband or even my son, so I couldn't hesitate in killing them.

I swung my sword struck the Frank in the cusp where his neck and shoulder met. Frozen in shock at the barbarian woman attacking him – the barbarian woman who could speak his language – he didn't even try to fight me. He just stood there, quivering, his mouth hung open, his brow furrowed. He met his death without a fight, he met his death with shock. My blade buried in his shoulder, he stared at the blood spurting from his wound, then turned to me, the surprise on his face twisting to anger but it was too late. The light vanished from his beautiful green and gold eyes and he fell to the ground, dead.

At the same moment, Vidar appeared, standing above the corpse of the man I'd just slain.

"Little fawn?" Vidar asked, his voice filled with concern and hurry.

I stared at the body for a moment, my blade dripping with his blood. He was far from my first kill – I had slain so many men since we set sail in the summer – but this ... I felt like a murderer, not a warrior. He was unarmed, he was scared, he made no move to kill me.

"Little fawn?"

"I'm okay," I replied, shuddering. "Where's Young Birger?"

"He's safe, he's with the archers – Finnvarðr is with him."

I nodded, catching my breath for just a moment, before Vidar and I ran towards the Franks guarding the ballistae. Rather than run directly towards them, there was a fray of Danes battling to the right of the ballistae. Both teams of Frankish operators swivelled the weapons around and took aim at the mass of Danes, who were easily conquering the Franks in the fight.

Domnall, huge red-haired and fierce, appeared beside us, and so did Jan, both men reeking of blood and filth, both men bleeding and bruised, both men bursting with the thrill of battle.

"You have a plan, Jarl?" Domnall asked, panting for breath but a grin upon his face.

"Two men are on each ballista." I interrupted. "We sneak up now, while they're distracted – Jan, Domnall, you take the ones who are loading, Vidar and I will get the ones aiming. Ready?"

The three men briefly glanced at each other and nodded their heads. We sheathed our swords and pulled out our saxes, shields still held in our other hands. Together we ran, Jan and I towards the closest ballista, Domnall and Vidar to the other. The Franks thankfully remained distracted, focussed on aiming the ballistae. When we were only a few paces from them, Jan and I dropped our shields to the ground. Jan pounced on the back of one Frank and sliced his neck with his sax, whereas I – not tall enough to slit the Frank's throat – crept behind him and stabbed him low in the side over and over.

"*Mon Deu!*" The Frank howled, kicking me to the ground and staring at the blood pouring from him, before he fell to his knees.

We had the ballistae!

"Ready, Jarlkona?" Jan grinned, helping me to my feet.

"Aim at the wall!" I exclaimed.

As we turned the ballista, we saw Vidar and Domnall, who had slain their two Franks, turn their ballista to the wall as well. Vidar and I aimed at the Franks above the gate.

"Tell me when, little fawn!" Vidar shouted to me.

"*Nú!*" I roared.

Simultaneously we pulled the triggers and sent the bolts soaring over the Seine, impaling Franks and sending them flying out of sight. Over and over, we loaded the ballistae until there were no more bolts left, slaying any Frank who tried to stop us or steal the ballistae from us. The Danes had managed to reclaim the battering rams and the thundering boom of the rams slamming into the doors resounded, and suddenly horns ripped through the air.

We looked up from the ballistae and saw them – it was Sinric and his men! They'd finally returned! Upon their horses they galloped through the battlefield, slaying Franks from up high, stabbing them with spears, cutting them down with their swords.

"There's a breach!" We heard Sigfred bellow near us.

And there was! One of the rams had managed to smash a hole in the gate of the tower!

"Jan, take the ballista!" I exclaimed, grabbing my shield and dashing to the gate.

Vidar did the same, leaving Jan and Domnall to operate the ballistae. I pulled *Úlfsblóð* from its sheath as I ran, joining the horde of Norsemen storming the gate. There was a band of Franks trying to block our entry from the tower, and at the top of the tower Frankish archers fired down on us desperately attempting to protect their comrades below. We crashed into them, bodies pressed against bodies – squashed in the swell of Norsemen shoving against the door, I could hardly breathe, the stench of death and sweat suffocating me, my aching body crushed by my fellow Norsemen as we pushed.

The crunching of bones and ear-piercing shrieks filled the air as we trampled the Franks to death. Some Norsemen managed to force their way passed the band of Franks and ran up the narrow stairways to battle the Franks on the higher levels, the rest of us left to fight the band defending the breached gate.

Vidar and I, with Einarr and Lars and a few of Rollo's Norwegians and Sinric's Danes, held our shields over our heads and crouched as low to the ground as we could, to protect ourselves from the archers firing down from above us on the tower.

"Watch out!" I yelled, dragging Vidar backwards as the Franks poured yet more boiling wax and pitch from the top of the wall.

They missed us – oh thank the gods, we were unscathed! One of Rollo's men was splashed by the pitch. Howling, he ripped his tunic from his body and threw it to the floor, a black splatter burning the flesh of his chest. Pitch dribbled down the gate, the black liquid puddling before us.

"Fire!" I barked. "We need fire – burn the gates!"

The Norsemen created a wall around me with their shields while I hurriedly fumbled through a pouch hanging from my belt. I pulled out a charcloth, my flint and steel fire-striker; I gave Vidar my charcloth and hastily tried to strike sparks onto it. Thankfully it didn't take much time, soon enough the charcloth was smouldering. Vidar brought it to his lips and blew on it, briskly nurturing the flames until they grew tall and devoured the charcloth. He dropped the charcloth onto the puddle of pitch and we immediately dashed away from the gate; with a great *whoosh!* the pitch burst into flames.

One of the Danes threw the Norwegian's tunic onto the fire, then we grabbed the corpses of the dead Franks around us, using them as shields as we ran toward the gate, and tossed them onto the pitch, building the fire as large as possible. The flames grew tall, licking the hot wax and pitch on the door, consuming the fabric of the dead soldiers' clothing, and soon enough, their flesh. Jet black smoke issued up from the burning corpses and pitch, filling the sky like storm clouds. We gazed upwards, but couldn't see the Franks anymore, they were completely concealed by the billowing ebony smoke.

Enveloped by the smoke, we coughed and spluttered, stumbling away from it blindly, crouched behind our shields. My throat and nostrils were raw, the taste of pitch and burning flesh filling my mouth. Suddenly sharp bursts from a distant horn sounded.

"The Franks have reinforcements!" Vidar snarled.

Forced to abandon the growing fire, we ran from the gates, a few of Sinric and Rollo's men pierced by arrows, some dying and some only injured. As we ran, we saw a huge group of Franks riding on horseback, led by a man dressed head to toe in shining silver armour. They were coming up behind the archers – behind Young Birger!

We skidded down the narrow staircase, crashing into friend and foe alike. I ignored every ounce of pain surging through my body, desperate to reach my son. We were so far away, the Franks were on horseback, they were so much faster!

Vidar was ahead of me – he snatched a spear sticking out of a corpse and threw it with all his might at a Frank on a horse near us. Impaled, the Frank fell to the ground, and the horse reared up on his hind legs, braying loudly. Lunging at it, Vidar grabbed the reins and swung onto the horse, controlling the beast in moments. Kicking the horse in the flanks with his heels, he charged off toward the Franks – towards Young Birger.

"Jarlkona!" A voice called out.

I whipped around and saw Sinric riding towards me on his brown stallion. He brought the horse to an abrupt halt beside me and reached out a hand. I tossed my shield to the ground, grabbed his hand, and he pulled me onto the horse. My arms wrapped around Sinric's waist, we rode after Vidar.

My heart in my throat, pulse pounding deafeningly in my ears, I watched Vidar hack and slash at the Franks as he rode past them, trampling some with his stolen horse. Closer and closer to Young Birger, I watched him push his horse, ramming his heels into the beast to urge it onwards. There on the ground I could see Finnvarðr – was he alive or dead?! – and there, beside him, Young Birger was pulling a spear from a Frank's corpse.

Another Frank was riding up behind Young Birger. Young Birger saw him; though he tried, Young Birger just couldn't pull the spear free. The Frank's sword was unsheathed, his eyes were trained on Young Birger, he rode with a purpose, to cut down my son.

"Get down, Birger!" I shrieked, tears streaming from my eyes. "Run! Move! Leave the spear!"

The Frank was looming closer to Young Birger. My son heard me though. He glanced from me to the enemy behind him, but rather than abandon the spear and run to safety, he continued his attempt to yank the spear from the corpse.

"Birger!" I shrieked, my voice cracking as I screamed.

The Frank was upon him. Just in time, Young Birger managed to free the spear and threw himself to the ground, rolling away and narrowly missing being trampled by the horse. The Frank forced the horse to slow and turn towards Young Birger again, and at the moment the horse turned, Young Birger dashed towards them and thrust the spear into the horse's chest. The horse bucked, sending the Frank flying to the ground. Young Birger grabbed a sax from one of the bodies and pounced upon the Frank, dazed from the fall. Before the Frank could lift his sword to defend himself, Young Birger stabbed him in the face, roaring.

The horse's braying screams ripped through the air. Covered with blood, Young Birger stood, wavering on his feet. I squealed with happiness as Young Birger's victory and was relieved when Vidar reached our son. He stretched out his hand and pulled Young Birger onto the horse behind him and galloped towards us. There were more Frankish soldiers coming – their horsemen far outnumbering our own.

Reaching us, Vidar slipped off the horse and Young Birger scooted forward, taking the reins. With so many horses, the din of battle had grown deafening. Bodies were building up and our horses were agitated by the stench of blood and smoke, braying and huffing, stomping the ground with their ears pinned back, flinching at the clangs and booms and thuds and screams.

"Aveline, go back to camp!" Vidar shouted as he helped me off the back of Sinric's horse. "Wait for me there – the sun will set soon, I'll be back when night falls!"

I pressed a brisk kiss against his lips.

"Don't die, Vidar Alvarsson – Odin doesn't need you yet!" I ordered.

"Wouldn't dream of it." Vidar smirked – his icy blue eyes glittering brightly through the filth and blood splattered on his face. "I love you, little fawn."

"I love you, too."

Vidar helped me onto the back of Young Birger's horse, before he hopped onto the back of Sinric's.

"The luck of the gods with you!" Sinric bade us before urging his horse towards the looming enemy.

***

VIDAR THANKFULLY RETURNED to camp that night, as he had promised, well after darkness had fallen. We had slain many men, but the Franks had won the day, driving the Norsemen away from the tower with their reinforcements led by the man in shining silver armour. Immediately, the women saw to the men, feeding them and tending to their wounds. Finnvarðr was in bad shape. Vidar had brought him back, lain across the horse, unconscious but breathing, though his rasping breaths were shallow and weak. As I cleaned Finnvarðr's wounds with cold, fresh river water and covered them with honey and bandages, Vidar filled me in on the rest of the day's battle.

Sinric and Vidar had charged towards the oncoming Franks, Sinric's other riders following them towards the Frankish cavalry. During the battle, Vidar had managed to drag a Frank off his horse and take the horse for himself. He had chased after the man in silver armour and fought him on horseback. Vidar had managed a great swing at him, slashing his arm and knocking him off his horse, but the Frankish cavalry had overwhelmed the Norsemen. Not knowing whether the Frankish leader was dead or alive, Vidar had been forced to abandon him, fighting back the Franks that had swarmed to rescue their leader.

In the end, the Norsemen had to flee the battlefield. Even with our numbers bolstered by the arrival of Sinric and his men, we had lost hundreds of warriors, and many more of our longships had been abandoned on the Seine.

The following day, we had risen at daybreak to continue, just as we had the previous two days, and that night we had returned to camp, defeated and lessened in number once again. Not only did the Frank's army increase with reinforcements troops, the Frankish citizens had sallied from Paris behind two Frankish bearers with saffron banners, fighting us with farming tools and weapons, and during the night, the Franks had yet again made hasty repairs to the battered northern tower.

Miserable from a third day of defeat, we packed up the camp and drew off, our initial storm of the tower failed, our attempts to siege Paris failed. Through the cover of night, we stumbled across the right bank to an abbey we found, the abbey of St Germain l'Auxerrois we later discovered, which was not far from the bridgehead of the Grand Pont. We slaughtered most of the monks that had remained in the abbey, but kept some captive, locked away in cells in the abbey, along with wounded Frankish soldiers we had dragged back to camp, holding them prisoner should we find a use for them later. Over the following weeks we turned the abbey into a fortified camp, using earth, wood and stone, preparing to stay there for winter.

The days grew colder, mimicking the bitterness the Norsemen felt towards the Franks.

"We need more war machines." Young Birger said, early one morning, huddled with his younger siblings by a fire in the abbey.

A wooden crucifix was burning atop the fire, the flames licking the effigy of Christ, burning him black and consuming the wooden cross.

"What do you suggest, Birger?" Vidar asked.

Since seeing his eldest son on the battlefield, Vidar had stopped referring to him as 'Young' Birger. Named after my adoptive Danish father, Birger Bloody Sword, he had received the moniker, 'Young', for being the younger of two Birgers, though he had never actually met my adoptive father, who had died fighting alongside the Great Heathen Army in the Anglo-Saxon kingdoms whilst I was pregnant with my eldest son.

Young Birger had demonstrated immense skill, bravery and intelligence on the battlefield, especially considering his age – at eleven years old, Young Birger had *proved* himself to be a man during the last three days. Vidar, so proud of his eldest son, refused to treat him like a child any longer – even by referring to him as 'Young' Birger. He was Birger Vidarsson, man, warrior and future jarl.

"When I spoke to the engineers who built the ballistae and rams, he told me of other siege engines they had seen on their travels." Young Birger said. "They spoke of these catapults called mangonels. The engineer said they're not very accurate to fire, but they're incredibly powerful."

"Did he say how to design them?" Vidar asked interestedly.

"*Já*, I think I could make one." Young Birger smiled, jumping to his feet. "In fact, I've been working on figuring it out – hold on a moment."

Young Birger dashed away towards the abbey excitedly.

"He's not going to appear with a mangonel, is he?" I laughed.

"I'd be interested to know how he hid it from us." Vidar chuckled.

A few moments passed, and Young Birger appeared again, a large box in his hands and a massive grin on his face. The children's faces lit up when they saw the box, intrigued to know its contents. Jan, Ebbe and Borghildr, Hallmundr, Domnall and Guðrin, Lars, Einarr and Finnvarðr, who was still healing from the wounds he'd received during the last battle, were sitting with us at the fire and all peeked at the box as eagerly as the children.

"Here," Young Birger beamed, presenting Vidar with the box. "While we were in Rouen, I was trying to understand how they were constructed from what the engineers told me, and I think I know – I think we could make them!"

Vidar lifted the lid of the box and immediately Young Birger pulled out the catapult he had described to us – and it *was* incredible! The model was small, half an ell or so in length, but it still looked like an effective weapon. Vidar set the box onto the ground, took the mangonel, and examined it.

"Would you like to see it work?" Young Birger asked.

Our group cried out a rousing exclaim of "*Já*". His cheeks rosy with pleasure, biting down on his bottom lip, Young Birger set the lid back on the box and delicately placed the little mangonel on top of it. He shuffled around the floor for a moment, finding a stone to go in the sling. Successful, and a bigger crowd – Sigfred, Rollo and Sinric included – surrounding us, Young Birger placed the stone he'd found on to the box top.

"The mangonel has a long wooden arm with a bucket." Young Birger explained, pointing to the wooden spoon he had used in the creation of his miniature catapult. "The bucket holds the thing you want to throw – rocks, stones, whatever you want – and there is a rope attached to the end. You pull the arm back, tug on this rope and it releases the arm which hits this block here to stop it from spinning all the way and sends the item in the bucket soaring."

Young Birger did as he explained, pulled back the arm, loaded the bucket, tugged on the string and sent the stone soaring. The stone shot across the way and into the fire.

"There's one more thing I'd like to show you." Young Birger said.

He gave the mangonel to Jan, who again looked it over and passed it around. Young Birger removed the lid of the box and pulled out two small towers. He held them against his chest as he put the lid back on his box, then set the two towers on the box.

"These," Young Birger announced. "Are siege towers or belfries. They don't shoot anything, *but* they can help you storm the walls. It's a tall structure with wooden walls to protect from archers, and a series of ladders inside so you can climb to the top. When the belfry is positioned where you want it, you can drop the gangplank and cross it to breach the walls." Young Birger said.

"Amazing." Sigfred smiled, carefully picking up the belfry without wheels and examining it. "We may win this battle yet!"

CHAPTER TWENTY-SIX

SHADOWS DANCED ON the stone walls, cast by the orange glow of the many fires burning in iron braziers about the room. Sleeping bodies littered the abbey. Many of us had chosen to sleep in the nave of the church rather than in the abbey dormitory; though draughty and cold, the smoke from the fires flittered up the lofty ceilings, offering us clearer air to breathe. Others had chosen to stay in the dormitory, the luxury of a bed was worth staying in the cold, dingy room no matter how musty and hard the mattress.

I was thankful for the night, the leering face of the great Christ effigy looming over the high altar was hidden in the darkness. It was one of the few effigies left in the monastery – most had been pulled down and used as firewood. Earlier that day, as we hacked apart the wooden pews to burn on the braziers and dragged straw bales into the church to act as beds, I could feel the Christ's judgement weighing heavily on me. For now, he was concealed, and I could ignore him until the morning daylight crawled in through the arching stained-glass windows.

Vidar and I were sitting on the floor by a fire in the nave. Vidar leaned against our straw mattress, and I sat between his legs, nestled in his embrace. We didn't speak, we just held each other, the heat of the fire dancing over us. Circled around the braziers, tucked away beneath furs, were our children. The straw bales rustled beneath them as they stirred in their sleep. My eyes drifted over each child in turn until they finally rested on Young Birger. On the stone floor beside his bed were his siege engine miniatures.

"Do you think we can do it?" I murmured.

"Do what?" Vidar asked softly.

"Build the weapons."

"*Já*," Vidar yawned. "I think so."

"The engineers are dead." I glanced up at him.

"I have no doubt in my mind that Birger will do just as good a job as them." Vidar said, his confidence igniting a spark of hope inside me. "His miniatures are exact – he said he built them under the guidance of the engineers when we were camped in Rouen. As long as we follow Birger's instructions exactly, we *will* be able to build them. Hopefully they'll give us a chance to turn this battle around …"

Vidar's voice drifted off.

"I'm proud of him." I whispered.

"I am, too." Vidar smiled. "I'm proud of them all."

"As am I."

Eventually we dressed into our nightclothes, Vidar wearing nothing but a pair of breeks despite the biting cold of the night, and settled into our straw bale bed, the rough, dry yellow stalks covered with woollen blankets. Vidar pulled his black bearskin over the top of us and I snuggled close to him. He laid on his back, his head rested against my chest. I stroked his bare shoulders, gently running my fingers over the few scabs, grazes and bruises marring his bronze flesh.

"Perhaps," I said, tucking stray hairs behind his ear. "One day I'll throw these seeds and brews away and we can see if the gods will bless us with another fantastic child."

"I would like that very much." Vidar grinned up at me, his eyes sparkling. "We'll have to wait until this damned battle is over, though."

I made a soft noise of agreement, returning his smile with my own. Delicately, Vidar touched my jaw with his fingertips, and I lowered my lips to meet his. Our bodies tangled together, we fell asleep.

Unfortunately, daybreak came sooner than I'd hoped. The morning was cold and damp, clouds hung low in the chilled air. Winter would be here soon. Already the trees were bare, and the dried leaves rustled in the wind, whipping around the square courtyard and collecting against the walls of the cloister.

Women set about heating the leftover stew from the night before for breakfast. Other women were baking bread out of the rye, wheat and barley flour, salt and water that we'd taken from the abbey stores. Some women had even started culling chickens and plucking their feathers to eat for this evening.

Most of the livestock we'd brought with us, a few goats and chickens, were penned in the abbey garden, protected on all four sides by the cloister. We kept the chickens mainly for their eggs and the goats for their milk, but we planned on exploring the village in search of more animals – men could not survive on eggs, milk and bread alone. We had plenty of our rations left, various flours, oats, dried meat and salted fish, as well as all the root vegetables in the abbey stores, but there was nothing like taking a bite out of a gloriously roasted pig or a rich beef stew.

In the nave, Vidar was gathering his men. Armed with tools – various sized axes, hacksaws and handsaws – there would be no battle today, rather the men would collect wood and begin building a palisade around the abbey.

Now Alvar the First One was dead, the warriors of Roskilde regarded Vidar as their leader. Though Alvar's men could choose to promote a different man to the position, they backed Vidar loyally. Ruling Roskilde was Vidar's birthright, and no one objected to it, trusting in the Jarl of Aros.

"When Alvar the First One dies, your husband will take control of Roskilde and he'll inherit all of the settlements Alvar rules. He will become one of the richest jarls in Denmark – why, he could even become a king!"

The Allfather's words flittered through my mind. I turned away from the men and stared at the foreign countryside outside the stained-glass windows. The winter haze drifted up from the stiff, dull grass, the vibrancy of its colour muted by the cold season. It seemed the Allfather had given me more than just one prophecy in the spirit realm.

I sighed deeply. It was bizarre to realise Alvar the First One was gone, to know we'd return to Roskilde and give the news of his death and have nothing but memories of him ... Alvar was with Freydis now, something he'd wanted all his life, especially since her death a year ago. Though he'd managed to stifle his sadness, I couldn't help but wonder if Alvar had come to Paris with the intention of dying and returning to her arms.

Einar's squeal of delight startled me from my thoughts. I glanced over at Vidar, who was tickling Einar's stomach while his men assembled, making the boy hoot and squirm – much to the amusement of the warriors surrounding them. A smile crept over my face and I caught Vidar's eyes briefly; he was smirking and with every giggle from Einar, the smile grew on Vidar's face.

Vidar missed Alvar terribly as all sons do when they lose their father, but grief would not destroy Vidar Alvarsson. Alffinna's death had cut Vidar deeply, he had wept, he had mourned, but he managed to stay strong for our children and carried me out of my darkness rather than falling into his own. Freydis's death had come so soon after Alffinna's, but Vidar focussed on his father, making sure Alvar's grief didn't drown him. Now his father was dead, and Vidar's attention shifted to avenging Alvar, and the warriors of Roskilde were as hellbent on vengeance as Vidar. Vidar had willingly accepted the jarldom of Roskilde, but he had done so sombrely and subdued.

Though Vidar was a much more powerful man than he was before, now he ruled two large towns and so many settlements, he stood to become so wealthy he could become a king, just as the Allfather had prophesied, but Vidar made no comment on that. Indeed, he'd gained that all from his father's death, a solemn gain and one Vidar understandably didn't want to celebrate. He would perform his duty, though, he would be the best jarl he could to both Roskilde and Aros.

"Come then," Vidar said to the crowd of men in front of him, still holding Einar in his arms. "Let's build this palisade."

The men were separated into groups, the men who were well enough, at least. Those who were severely injured were left at the abbey infirmary for the women to tend to. Blacksmiths set about assembling a few makeshift smithies to mend broken weapons and armour. Hunters were sent into the forests and fields to hunt boar and deer, set traps for rabbits and fix nets in the river to catch fish. Vidar led the largest team of men to the forests to gather wood, while Rollo headed a team to build a stone wall around the abbey with what rubble and brick they could find, and Sinric and Sigfred had the best shipbuilders and craftsmen mending our fleet of ships.

Torn between the ships and the forest, ultimately Young Birger went with Vidar to make sure the right trees were chosen and cut properly for his siege weapons. Vidar had taken Sander with him – Sander could strip bark from the tree trunks and collect tinder for the brazier fires.

Rather than spin wool to make sails or pluck feathers from chickens, I left Einar and Æsa with Guðrin in the courtyard milking the sheep and headed to the abbey infirmary.

The monks had an impressive array of medicines. They had cupboards bursting with pots of honey and folded strips of linen bandages, salves and balms, herbs I knew and mysterious ones I'd never seen before. There were even jars filled with live leeches in filthy water for bloodletting.

There were a handful of other women already tending to the sick and injured when I arrived in the infirmary. Sheets had been pulled over the men who had passed away from their wounds during the night. I stopped at the first bed, lifted the sheet to see the dead man's face, and prayed to the Allfather silently on the warrior's behalf. I didn't recognise the warrior – he must've been one of Rollo, Sigfred or Sinric's men – but I prayed for him, regardless.

"Here," I said, beckoning the nearest thrall to me. "Find me two strong men and tell them the Jarlkona needs them in the infirmary. They need to carry our dead outside so we can ready them for burial."

The thrall nodded and scurried off. I breathed out deeply and pulled the sheet back over the dead man's face. I couldn't help but think of all the dead men scattered over the banks of Paris and those whose corpses had undoubtedly sunk to the bottom of the Seine by now. They would not get the burial they deserved ... Alvar would not get the cremation nor the ship burial that such a mighty jarl deserved.

I moved on to the next dead man's bed and lifted the sheet.

"Oh, Kolfinnr," I sighed.

I had known Kolfinnr the Quick during my time in Roskilde. I prayed to the Allfather for Kolfinnr and pulled the sheet over his head again. The bed immediately beside Kolfinnr's held yet another dead man. I pulled back the sheet and my heart sank – it was Kolsveinn, Kolfinnr's younger brother.

Kolsveinn and Kolfinnr the Quick were the only two sons of Kolbrandr, a warrior and farmer from Roskilde. They three were hailed as the stealthiest men in Roskilde; Alvar had used them frequently for spying on the enemy. I swept the hair from Kolsveinn's face. He was three years younger than me and had two daughters. Kolfinnr was a year younger than me, with two sons and a daughter. Just like that, their wives were now widows and all five children had lost their fathers.

"Is Kolbrandr dead, too?" I whispered, stroking Kolsveinn's hair. "Let's ready you for Valhalla. I'll tell your children how honourably you fought – you, too, Kolfinnr. Everyone will know how gloriously the sons of Kolbrandr fought and died."

"Jarlkona?"

"I need you both to carry the dead men outside and begin digging a grave." I said, surveying the two tall, muscled young men the thrall had fetched. "While you carry them out, I'll gather the things for burial."

"*Já*, Jarlkona."

"Do either of you know this man?" I nodded to the first body I had prayed over.

"I think he's a Norwegian."

"Ask Rollo to identify him and find out if he has any belongings here with him."

"Of course, Jarlkona."

I watched the men take one of the stretchers, two posts with animal skins affixed to them, leaning against the wall and carry it to the first dead man's bed. They put the stretcher on the ground beside the bed and carefully laid the dead warrior on it. Before they carried the body away, one of the men retrieved the dead man's sword from underneath his bed and rested it on the body.

I would've preferred to burn the dead men on pyres, but we couldn't spare the amount of wood it would take to build so many, and we respected our fallen too much to have them share pyres.

No, each man would be buried in his own grave with his weapon and whatever belongings he'd brought to Francia.

I prayed to the Allfather for Kolsveinn, and for his father, Kolbrandr, too. I hadn't seen Kolbrandr since the second day of fighting the Franks on the banks of Paris. I moved on to the final two dead men whom I learned to be two more of Rollo's Norwegians.

While the two Danes came in and collected the bodies, I tended to the injured, redressing wounds in clean bandages and feeding broth to those too hurt to eat solid food. When the Danes came for the last body, I followed them outside to ready the five dead men for burial.

There was a lot of superstition involved in the Norse burial process. We wrapped our dead warriors' heads in strips of cloth, covering their eyes so that they wouldn't be able to see lest they reanimated after death, becoming *draugr* – again-walkers. We trimmed their nails, so that *jötnar* wouldn't steal the unpared nails and use them to build their ship, *Naglfar*, that would carry the *jötnar* at *Ragnarök*. We dressed them in clean clothes and tied their boots together, to hinder them in case they became *draugr*. Finally, we buried them with their weapons, combs, tools – whatever belongings they'd brought to Francia – for them to use in the afterlife.

By evening time, I had readied the bodies with the help of two other women. Their bodies had been placed into the graves dug for them, and their belongings had been carefully set on the bodies. The hunters and Vidar and his men had returned from the forests. Everyone assembled around the graves, and I led the funeral for the fallen men, sacrificing a goat for each man.

At least two men died from their wounds every day that we camped in the abbey of St. Germain l'Auxerrois for the first two weeks, and every night I conducted their funerals. Though I readied their bodies much quicker as the days crept by, the heaviness of their deaths never lightened.

***

Winter, 886

YULE HAD PASSED only two weeks ago. We had been staying at the abbey of St Germain l'Auxerrois for almost six weeks, protected by the palisade and stone wall we had erected around it. It had been a cold winter, flurries of snow had spluttered from the sky, but none of it had settled for more than a week or two. The sky had grown darker, and the air had grown bitter, much like the warriors' morale. Though all the men excitedly built the war machines, they were restless when night fell, longing to attack the Franks, longing to succeed this time.

Sigfred stomped around the camp most days, gruff and irritable when he wasn't building, furious that the attack on the Franks was not going to plan. As he had told me the first day of battle, he hadn't thought the battle would be easy, but he hadn't expected it to be difficult, either. The three days of battle, the three days of constant defeat, had proven him wrong – we had been in the Kingdom of Francia since summer and had been camping outside the walls of Paris for almost two months. By now he had hoped we'd have returned to our homelands with countless treasures. Instead we had a pittance, some prizes Sinric and his men had seized during their sacking and looting of the abbeys around Rouen, but nothing on the scale Sigfred had imagined.

While the men were busy building the siege engines, hard and laborious work, the women and young children ventured out in search of food. There was a village on the bank opposite Paris that the dwellers had abandoned for the safety of the city. We stole what food, clothing and treasures we could find, we took farming equipment and the few weapons we came across, like forgotten quivers of arrows or a worn axe or two. We took livestock from their enclosures, chickens, sheep, goats and cows, and stabled them inside the abbey. The forests and fields were filled with boar and deer, which we hunted happily, foraging for what modicum of greens we could find.

The men had built one belfry and two mangonels, but they intended to build at least two more belfries and another mangonel by the time winter was over. Since the engineers who built the ballistae and battering rams had died during the three days of battle with the Franks, Young Birger headed the assembly of the structures based on the miniatures he had made. Excited to see his siege engines coming to creation, he gifted his small examples of the machinery to his younger siblings, who were delighted to play with such fantastic toys.

Though this winter marked the twelfth year of his life, Young Birger thrived as leader of the construction and put his carpentry skills to good use; he made sure he was involved in the production of all seven machines at various points, from selecting the right trees to stripping the branches and bark from the trunks, from chopping the wood down to the correct size to cutting, hammering and nailing the pieces together. He orchestrated meetings with the other builders, explaining his design in fine detail, which the men paid careful heed to, absorbing the information Young Birger gave them.

It was amazing to see so many seasoned warriors and builders listening and following the directions of my twelve-year-old son; when I watched him instructing or building, I was filled with pride. It was easy to imagine the man he would be in a decade, the great jarl he would be; he already exhibited so much promise. Sander, Æsa and Einar were impressed by him, too. Sander, so in awe of his older brother, did whatever he could to help Young Birger, from aiding in the stripping of the bark and branches and collecting the pieces and taking them to the abbey to dry for kindling, to dashing about delivering nails from the blacksmiths to the builders.

It had been yet another long, cold day. A new wave of snow had fallen, souring the moods of all those in camp even more so. We sat about the nave eating soup made of onions, cabbage and barley groats with thin slices of pork and bread, at crude tables the craftsmen had hammered together, their efforts focussed on mending the ships rather than building fine furniture.

"Bring me more pork." Sigfred barked at a passing thrall.

"T-there isn't any, sir." The thrall stammered.

"What do you mean *there isn't any*?" Sigfred demanded.

"All the pork is g-gone, sir." The thrall said. "There's no more."

Sigfred threw his bread to the table and rubbed his face in his hands. He released a deep breath and cracked his fingers, a vein throbbing on his brow.

"Bring me some beef from yesterday's meal, then." Sigfred said, managing a level voice despite his obvious frustration.

"I'm s-sorry, sir, I can't, that's gone, too." The thrall cowered behind the tray of mead she was clutching.

"What meat is left?"

"I-I can bring you some dried pork? Or salted herring?"

"I don't want it dried, I want it fresh!" Sigfred roared, standing up so ferociously, he sent his stool flying back. "Get me boiled pork or beef or mutton, now!"

The thrall cowered under Sigfred's seething glower, her tiny body trembling. I went to stand, but Vidar placed his hand on my lap as he felt my body move.

"Here, take mine, you're obviously hungrier than me." Vidar said.

Vidar tossed his slice of pork across the table at Sigfred like he was a dog. The nave fell silent. The colour had drained from the thrall's face. My heart raced in my chest; *what was Vidar doing?*

"Perhaps you'd like what's left of my soup instead?" Vidar continued.

He slung his bowl across the table. It toppled over the edge and clattered on the floor, the contents spraying over the stone slabs and Sigfred's shoes. Sigfred's face turned a hideous shade of purple-red and he clenched his hands into fists at his sides.

"Why are you throwing food at me, Alvarsson?" Sigfred snarled.

"You're doing nothing but barking and bitching like a dog, I thought I may as well treat you like one." Vidar growled, glaring at the Dane.

"What did you say?" Sigfred hissed.

"You're bitching about the food, about the weather, about the battle, about the Franks, about waiting." Vidar grumbled. "If you were a dog, I'd have slit your throat for yapping so much. Eat your meat and be quiet, Sigfred."

Sigfred snatched his sword, which had been leaning against the table by Sigfred's stool as he ate.

RISE TO FALL

"Draw your sword, Alvarsson. No one insults me and gets away with it." Sigfred snarled, grasping his sword hilt so tightly his knuckles had turned white.

"I don't need a sword to fight you." Vidar smirked darkly. "I could beat you with my bare hands – but please, if you need a blade feel free to use it."

Sigfred tossed his sword to the ground, scowling at Vidar. The moment the sword clanged against the stone slabs, Vidar leaped over the table, sending plates and cups and food flying. He collided with Sigfred, knocking him to the ground. The men tussled, rolling across the floor, slamming against stools and table legs. Men leaped to their feet, staring in shock at their two leaders brawling, but none dared to intervene – Vidar and Sigfred had to work their differences out themselves.

Vidar landed a few punches on Sigfred's face, before Sigfred threw Vidar off him with an almighty roar. Separated, the two men scrambled to their feet and lunged at each other, throwing punches. Vidar slammed his knee into Sigfred's stomach, and Sigfred doubled over in pain, the wind knocked out of him. Vidar grabbed a fistful of the front of Sigfred's tunic and brought Sigfred up to face him, Vidar's other arm arched back ready to hit Sigfred again. Before Vidar had a chance, Sigfred grabbed Vidar's shoulders and headbutted him in the nose.

"Argh!" Vidar bellowed, stumbling back and falling onto the table, blood streaming from his nostrils.

Sigfred grabbed a stool from the ground and held it over his head as he strode towards Vidar. Sigfred brought the stool down onto Vidar, but Vidar kicked the stool out of his hands just in time. He jumped to his feet and slammed his fists into Sigfred's head. Sigfred ducked and managed a few blows to Vidar's ribs, sending Vidar tumbling to the ground. Sigfred jumped on top of Vidar and brought his fists down on him, but Vidar caught his forearms and held him back. With an almighty roll, Vidar flipped Sigfred to the floor and the two men struggled against each other, trying to free their fists to beat each other again.

"That's enough!" I roared, glaring at Rollo and Domnall, the two men closest to me. "Separate them!"

Immediately they dived at Vidar and Sigfred, dodging blows and punches. Domnall grabbed Vidar by the shoulders and dragged him off. As Sigfred jumped to his feet, Rollo caught him and pulled him away from Vidar, putting as much distance between them as possible.

I was horrified to see Vidar and Sigfred fighting each other – but anger brewed inside me too. I was furious to see them wasting their time fighting over something so stupid. Morale was low and tempers were high, but as two of the four leaders of this great army, they shouldn't squabble like children, rather they should set an example to their men.

I glowered at the two of them. Vidar spat out a glob of bloodied saliva onto the floor and wiped his blood-drenched lips with the sleeve of his tunic, his eyes locked on Sigfred. A smirk twisted Vidar's lips.

"Are you happy now? You're not bored anymore?" Vidar sneered.

Sigfred tried to lunge passed Rollo. Though Sigfred was impressively strong, Rollo was far bigger and far stronger, and held Sigfred back with just one hand on his shoulder.

"Stop it!" I hissed at Vidar. "Go cool off!"

Vidar stared at me, as though he had just realised I was there. I glared vehemently at him, at the innocent surprise on his face. He passed another disgusted look at Sigfred, spat on the floor again and shrugged his shoulders and stalked away from us. Sigfred shirked himself out of Rollo's hold and staggered to a stop a few paces away from me.

"That's it – do as your woman tells you." Sigfred taunted. "Who is the bitch now, Alvarsson?"

Vidar whipped around but before he could even take a step, I slapped Sigfred across the face. My hand throbbed, but I ignored it. Sigfred stumbled back, clapping his hand to his cheek, astonished that I had struck him.

"Hold your tongue, Sigfred." I snarled.

Vidar's laughter rang behind me, and Sigfred's bloodied face grew redder.

RISE TO FALL

"Come walk with me." Rollo murmured to Sigfred, putting his arm around his shoulders and directing him away. "Don't do anything stupid."

As Rollo led Sigfred away, I turned my back on them and stormed towards Vidar.

"Come." I muttered.

***

VIDAR TOOK A lamp from the sill of one of the plain arched windows that gazed out on the moonlit courtyard. We stepped through the dark stone corridors of the abbey by the tiny dim orb of lamp light. I rubbed my stinging hand as we walked, still furious at Vidar and Sigfred's ridiculous display. Voices from the nave travelled to us, dulled and muffled, with the occasional peel of laughter. I hadn't heard laughter like that for some time now. Everyone was cold and exhausted, though the siege weapons had offered some hope, no one had forgotten our terrible defeat at the hands of the Franks.

I opened the door to the cloister and stepped out into the cold night air. A thin layer of snow covered the barren vegetable beds, and fresh flakes sprinkled down from the sky. The livestock we usually kept in the courtyard had been herded into the abbey and stabled in one of the rooms to keep warm during the long winter nights.

"The look on Sigfred's face when you slapped him." Vidar chuckled as he dusted snow from a bench for us to sit on.

"Stop." I groaned. "I'm mad with you for making me join in with your stupid fight. Did you *have* to throw food at Sigfred?"

"*Já*, I did." Vidar said, sitting down.

I scowled at him, irritated by his innocent expression.

"You sound like Sander." I said, rolling my eyes.

"And you sound like my *móðir*, not my wife." Vidar retorted. "Why are you so cross, anyway? The men got a show, they were amused, perhaps this will cheer them up for a few days."

"That's what all this was?" I gaped. "You made yourself look like a fool to amuse the men?"

"Usually that's the best way to amuse people."

"You're bleeding, your tunic is ripped, your face is bruised, all during a fight over damned pork!"

"Nothing is broken, and my men are laughing." Vidar said with a shrug. "It seems worth it to me."

"I do hope Sigfred feels the same way, considering how much you embarrassed him." I threw myself on the bench beside him.

"I'm sure he will. Besides, he insulted me just as much as I insulted him. We settled it with the fight, now it's over. Tomorrow it'll just be a tale to laugh over." Vidar assured me with an irritating certainty in his voice.

"How do you do this?" I snapped, slapping Vidar's hand away as he tried to rest it on my thigh. "How are you so sure of yourself? How are you so positive?"

"It takes me some time to be sure of myself. I have to weigh everything over in my mind before I'm sure of any decision I've made." Vidar said, retracting his hand from me and folding his arms behind his head instead. "And I'm not positive *all* the time. I am positive that you're beautiful, though."

Vidar tilted his head at me and smiled sweetly at me.

"I'm positive that you're annoying." I groaned.

There was a clatter as a far door to the cloister opened. The muffled sound of music and laughter drifted out to us. Jan staggered through the door and, noticing us, waved cheerily. He walked a few paces, turned his back on us, lowered his trousers and commenced pissing on the cloister wall.

"Jarl, Jarlkona." Jan called out over his shoulder. "Lovely evening, isn't it?"

"Indeed, it is, Jötunnson." Vidar snickered.

I rolled my eyes and let out an exasperated sigh.

"You're coming to join us?" Jan asked, pulling his trousers up.

"*Já*, give us a moment though?" Vidar grinned.

"There may not be much fresh meat, but there's plenty of mead!" Jan said.

"We'll be there in a while."

With that, Jan returned inside.

"It seems our performance did the trick." Vidar winked at me.

"Urgh!" I groaned, though I was relieved things had smoothed over quickly, and Sigfred's men and Vidar's wouldn't be turning on each other in support of their squabbling leaders.

"Come on, let me show you something." Vidar said, grabbing my hand.

I snatched up the oil lamp and let Vidar lead me inside. Through the shadowed corridors, our footsteps echoing on the stone slabbed floor, Vidar took me to the opposite end of the abbey, where we were unable to hear the noise from the nave. Vidar opened a door and stood aside for me to pass by.

It was the abbey library. There were shelves upon shelves of scrolls, some empty where the Danes and Norsemen had taken the papers to burn on the fires. There was an ornate cabinet with glass doors filled with little jars of liquid – ink for writing – and pots filled with gorgeous quills of various sizes. Desks filled the floor space in front of the only window of the room.

"Why have you brought me here?" I asked, glancing at some of the colourful papers left half-finished by the monks before we'd come here and slaughtered them.

"I come here sometimes, to think." Vidar replied. "It's quiet here. No one bothers with this room – there's nothing valuable in it, there's no food or mead; the men ransacked it for all its worth when we first arrived here. It's the perfect place for me to think."

"I've never seen you come here." I commented.

"I come here during the day, when the men pause to eat, or I slip out of bed at night-time for an hour or so."

"What do you do here? Just sit and think?"

Wordlessly, Vidar took the oil lamp from me and vanished off to the other side of the room. Within a few moments he had a fire roaring in an iron brazier. Vidar pulled two stools up to the brazier and I drifted to him and sat down, watching him, puzzled. He didn't sit with me, instead he disappeared behind the shelves. There was rustling and scraping as Vidar moved things around. He returned to me with a pile of papers in his hands.

"*Já* I do ..." Vidar said, handing me the papers.

I looked through the papers and found some crude painting. On looked like the Hnefi, the king, from Hnefatafl, but it had yellow hair. Another looked like a woman, perhaps? She also had yellow hair. The final painting looked as though it was meant to be a child wrapped up in blankets, with curly dark hair springing from her head. The final paper didn't have any pictures, instead it was filled with runes, runes that spelled out hundreds of names.

"I'm not always sure of myself, and I'm certainly not positive all the time. I question myself often, wondering whether I've made the right decision …" Vidar murmured.

"Vidar?" I whispered; a lump formed in my throat.

"Alvar," Vidar explained, pointing to the Hnefi picture. "Freydis, Alffinna. The names are every warrior from Roskilde and Aros that have died during this damned siege …"

I wanted to speak but emotion overcame me, the knot in my throat wouldn't let my words passed, no matter how hard I tried to swallow it down.

Gently Vidar took the papers from me and gazed through them, biting his bottom lip. He was a sight to behold, his golden moustache and beard were stained red with blood from where Sigfred had headbutted him in the nose, but his icy eyes glistened with sorrow, his brow furrowed and his frown deepening as he stared at his pictures.

"All men strive to reach Valhalla, and every name on this list has reached it." Vidar murmured. "At least I hope they have …"

"Vidar?"

He didn't look at me. Like we were carved from stone, we were both frozen in spot, Vidar gazing at the papers in his hands, and me staring at him.

"After this battle is over, I will return to Aros, I will go to Roskilde, and visit every widow, every mother, every child, and inform them that their husband, son or father is dead. I will hold them as they weep, then we will celebrate their lives, we will celebrate their sitting at Odin's table … And yet, I can't help but wonder … Are they?"

"Are they what?" I gasped.

"Are they in Valhalla? Every name on this list have died in a hopeless battle – there is no glory for the living, so is there for the dead?"

RISE TO FALL

Vidar's words shook me to my core. How could he question such a thing? The men died valiantly, diligently fighting against the Franks. Did our constant failure to defeat the Franks affect the fallen warriors' chances to go to Valhalla? I thought Vikings need only die bravely in battle for Odin to take them to his hall?

"I'm afraid of the deaths that will come ... I'm afraid that I am leading men to die in needless battles, and I'm afraid I'm leading the survivors into dishonour. We cannot return home as failures! I rallied my men, I led them on this venture!" Vidar shook the papers in his hands furiously, turning to glare at me. "Were their deaths worth it? Was Alvar's death worth it?"

Vidar slammed the papers onto the nearest desk, and paced the room, rubbing his face in his hands.

"We are thousands of warriors! There are but a few hundred of the damned Franks, and yet they beat us at every turn!" Vidar barked. Suddenly he whipped around, pointing at me. "You said the Allfather gave you his blessings!"

"He gave *our children* his blessings." I said carefully. "They have the rest of their lives beyond this battle to earn glory and victory."

"But these men don't deserve Odin's favour?" Vidar scowled up at the ceiling, as though glaring into Asgard itself. "Those who survive this war will be shamed! They will be dishonoured! They will return home with nothing!"

"You don't know that, yet, Vidar!" I exclaimed, rushing to him and taking his hands in mine. "We have yet to use the siege weapons! What if the odds are rising against us, so that our eventual glory will be that much more immense? The Franks are stronger and more impressive than we thought, which means every slain warrior deserves entry to Valhalla!

"Anyway, my love, even if we do not take Paris, that wasn't our intention anyway, was it? So, we haven't failed, really, have we? When we return to Aros, we will still have the loot from the abbeys and towns from along the Seine, so we will not be empty-handed. And we will raided other abbeys and monasteries along the way back home! But this battle with Paris has only just begun, don't count it as a loss before it has yet to end."

Vidar chuckled softly at my desperate attempts to cheer him up. He pulled me against him, and I squeezed him with all my might. We sank to the floor, our embrace never faltering.

"It feels like the gods are toying with me." Vidar sighed. "First they took Alffinna … Then they nearly took you. They took Freydis and now Alvar. Will they take my victory too?"

"A great man once told me, that death and life are balanced. You mustn't fear death but understand that death is uncontrollable; nothing can bring a man to his death if his time hasn't come, and nothing can save one doomed to die. Life is a cycle, and death is a great part of that. Though it hurts, it is meant to be – for everyone." I said.

"The Allfather told you that?" Vidar asked.

"*Nei*, you did." I grinned tearily up at him. "I understand your heartache Vidar; you know I do. And I know that just because you understand that death is a part of life's cycle, it doesn't stop the hurt. But you must orientate yourself to what you're looking at, my love. Are the gods really toying with you?

"With Alvar's death, you have become jarl of Roskilde *and* all the settlements under Alvar's rule, as well as Aros and your own settlements! You're now one of the richest jarls in Denmark, you could even be a king!

"Though Freydis and Alvar's deaths are devastating, they've influenced your destiny, and that of our sons, too. You've become an even greater man than before.

"The Nornir chose this glorious life for you. And look at the glorious life they laid out for Alvar – they let Alvar live such a long life, he fought and won the love of Freydis, he was a great leader and jarl, they let him grow old and meet his grandchildren and teach his eldest grandsons how to be great jarls. And Alvar died in battle, he died fighting honourably and he resides in Valhalla now, at Odin's side, I'm sure of it.

"Now they've given you this damned battle with Paris to deal with – and you will rise in the face of this adversity because you are Vidar Alvarsson, and you are bold and strong and the most powerful, determined, and bravest man I know."

Vidar pressed a kiss to my brow and pulled me tighter into his embrace.

"You've become very knowledgeable since your visit to the spirit realm." Vidar commented.

"I learned a lot from the Allfather, but I also have a wonderful husband who weathers every storm with me, who stands beside me through thick and thin. I don't know what I did to deserve you, Vidar Alvarsson, but I'm glad you're mine."

"I'm glad you're mine, little fawn." Vidar beamed.

"It's hard to find a moment of peace on the battlefield," I said. "But here, maybe, I can sit with you, sometime? In silence … Maybe I can sit and think and mourn with you?"

"I'd like that, little fawn." Vidar replied, kissing me. "I'd like that a lot … I think, perhaps, we'll mourn tonight?"

"Okay," I nodded.

"I'd like to mourn for … Sigfred's pride."

"Vidar!"

"You're still mad, little fawn?"

CHAPTER TWENTY-SEVEN

"RUN!" VIDAR ROARED.

Overhead, huge stones flew, hurled by some sort of massive catapult from inside the walls of Paris. I shielded my eyes from the sun with my hand, sweat pouring from my brow, and stared at the massive projectiles sailing across the sky. The thick ropes of the catapult sling whipped through the air before falling out of sight, doubtless to be loaded again by the Franks. The blocks of stone cast massive shadows over us as they hurtled above. With howling screams and a deafening *crash!* the stones plummeted to the ground, smashing our last ballista and the men operating it, plus the unlucky few close enough to be impaled by the wreckage.

"Keep digging, we have to get the belfries across!" Vidar thundered.

We had been fighting the Franks in a renewed attack for two days now. It was growing dark and we would have to return to camp by nightfall. The Franks had destroyed both of our ballistae, killed countless warriors and we couldn't get our belfries close enough to storm the tower let alone get them across the river. We faced yet another day of dismal failure.

Norsemen dug the earth with shovels, heaving the dirt by hand or on their shields and tossing it into the river, while others dashed about grabbing branches and bracken, rubble and stone, the bodies of the dead, anything they could find to throw into the moat. Some Danes had even ridden back to the camp, brought our prisoners and slaughtered them, tossing their corpses into the water.

We had to fill the moat around Paris to roll the belfries as close as possible, so we could storm the ramparts. The Franks rained arrows down on us, and the air was thick with the stench of pitch, billowing clouds of black rising up from the cauldrons bubbling on the battlements.

Our army of Norsemen had separated into three groups, two groups on the water, one large group on land. Vidar and Sigfred headed the land faction with the siege engines, or what was left of them. We tried to focus our attacks on the tower, whereas the two groups on the water, commanded by Rollo and Sinric, focused their attacks on the bridge and the walls.

Upon the banks, Sigfred and Vidar's men fought Frankish soldiers, trying to protect the Danes digging and filling the moat. Rollo and Sinric's men fired arrows and hurled stones and spears at the Frankish soldiers on the bridge from their longships on the waters. Bodies splashed into the river, both of Franks and Norsemen, their blood turning the Seine red.

There was a crash as stones smashed into the gates of the tower, exploding on impact and spraying those nearby with dust and rock fragments. We may not have had our ballistae anymore, but we still had our mangonels. The mangonels were not powerful enough to bring down walls, but they were strong enough to kill those we targeted with the stone and rock and whatever we could load it with.

A low rumble thundered behind us, quickly increasing in volume. I glanced over my shoulder and saw one of our belfries being led onto the battlefield by the two oxen we had seized and stored in the abbey with our other livestock. The dark brown, long-horned oxen wore a yoke about their necks that was attached to the belfry by ropes. Sigfred and another Norseman steered the oxen forward by whipping the beasts with long thin rods. The oxen were obviously mad with panic as they dragged the huge structure down the bank. The belfry rocked unnervingly as the oxen stopped and started, the beasts attempting to veer back the way they came but were struck with the rods when they tried.

The deafening noise of the rolling belfry grew louder and louder as it neared the tower. From the ditch I was sprawled in, I shot an arrow at the tower, hitting a Frank who collapsed over the edge and fell into the Seine. I glanced at the belfry – Sigfred had cut the oxen free and they ran back up the bank, trampling any and all in their path. Hopefully we'd be able to find them again ...

As the panicked oxen fled, scores of men loaded into the belfry. Within moments the gangplank at the top platform had been dropped open. Now on eye level with the Franks on the tower, our archers and spear- and stone-throwers had far better aim and dodged behind the cover of the belfry walls after firing. A few of the men surrounding me, including Vidar, sprinted to the nearest belfry and entered it, disappearing from my sight. I stayed on the bank, to protect those digging and filling the moat. I reached to my hip and pulled an arrow from my quiver–

"*Oof!*" I gasped.

All air was knocked out of me, my vision vanished for a moment, a sharp pain seared through my chest. Head spinning, I realised I was suddenly on the ground, a Dane on top of me, wrestling with a Frank. I groaned and wheezed, unable to breathe for the sheer weight of the men on top of me. The Dane couldn't hear me, I didn't think he even realised I was beneath him.

The Frank, his dagger raised, had disarmed the Dane and was straddled over him, attempting to stab him. The Dane gripped the Frank's wrist, struggling to keep the dagger away from his chest, his other hand squeezed the Frank's neck. The Frank's face was red, splattered in mud and blood, his eyes bulging. Blood rushed to my face as I struggled to breathe – the Dane was so much bigger than me, he was crushing me!

I felt the Dane lift his leg and kick the Frank, sending him flying from us, dropping his dagger and holding his belly, recoiling in pain. Hot tears cascaded down my cheeks as the Dane's heel smashed into my shin. Far too consumed by bloodlust and fury, he still hadn't noticed me. He rolled off me – *thank the gods!* – and staggered to the Frank. The Dane stood over the Frank and hammered his fists down onto the Frank's head. Terrible cracks filled the air as the Dane shattered the Frank's skull, blood gushing over the dirt and covering the Dane's fists.

I swallowed deep rasping gulps of air, coughing and spluttering, gasping for breath, my lungs and body aching. Like a hot iron rod pressed against my flesh, my shin burned and throbbed with pain.

RISE TO FALL

It took every ounce of strength in my body to struggle to my feet, but I collapsed again, my injured leg unable to bear my weight. I dared not look down at my shin, a wave of nausea washing over me. I swallowed hard, still panting for breath, trying to stand up again.

"Jarlkona!"

It was Finnvarðr. He appeared beside me and wrapped one arm around my waist, lifting me to my feet, his other hand holding his sword. Finnvarðr's pale face was marred with bruises, old and new and scarlet scars and scratches, some bleeding others congealed into crusted scabs.

"You need to get back to camp, Jarlkona!" Finnvarðr yelled over the deafening noise of the surrounding battle.

"I'm fine!" I lied, gripping onto his filthy tunic. "I've far fewer wounds than you!"

Finnvarðr laughed, and we grinned at each other briefly when something grabbed hold of my skirts and yanked me to the ground. I cried out in shock and landed on a corpse. I whipped around and saw Finnvarðr locked in battle with a Frank. Their swords clashed together and Finnvarðr, considerably taller than the Frank, shoved the Frank and made him stumble backwards.

"Jarlkona, run!" Finnvarðr exclaimed.

I tried to stand up, but my injured leg shook violently, searing bolts of pain shooting through me. My leg gave way, and I fell down again, cussing and seething with anger and pain. The Frank had leapt up and charged towards Finnvarðr, his sword raised. Finnvarðr was ready for him. He parried the Frank's attack with his blade, arced his sword and brought it down upon the Frank. The Frank tried to deflect Finnvarðr's blade with his own, but there was too much power behind Finnvarðr's attack. Finnvarðr smashed the sword out of the Frank's head, slicing through the Frank's shoulder. The Frank roared with pain and dropped to the ground writhing.

Finnvarðr sheathed his sword and dashed to me, he wrapped his arm around my waist again, and I clung on to him.

"Don't worry, Jarlkona, I'll help you." Finnvarðr said, hauling me to my feet. "You have to get out of here."

He took my weight against him and hobbled along with me, desperately trying to get me to safety. Around us, Frankish arrows sprayed, hitting multiple Danes as they dug, their bodies tumbling into the moat they were trying to fill. Finnvarðr and I hobbled away from the edge of the Seine as fast as we could, stumbling over corpses, shoving passed our own men, and throwing ourselves to the ground when arrows came tearing past us, far too close for comfort.

Another barrage of arrows landed close by. Finnvarðr cried out in anguish, dropping me as his body jerked suddenly. I stared at him and saw an arrow sticking high up into his back, his pallid face even greyer than before. He reached over his shoulder with a trembling hand and tried to grab the arrow to yank it out–

"Finnvarðr!" I screamed, pointing behind him.

"What–" Finnvarðr started as he turned to see what I was pointing at.

A spear careened through the air and shot through his mouth, sending his body flying to the ground and impaling it to the ground. I shrieked, gawping at poor Finnvarðr. His eyes were bulged open, his body twitched as life fled him, before finally he fell still, pinned to the earth by that spear.

"Little fawn!"

"Finnvarðr was helping me, then – then–" I cried, gawping in horror at his corpse.

Vidar, bloodied and so filthy I could hardly see his skin beneath the dirt, ran over to me. He saw Finnvarðr's body, cursed the Franks and pulled the spear from his mouth, the spear head squelching and ripping the insides of poor Finnvarðr's skull. Vidar knelt beside Finnvarðr's and closed our dead friend's eyelids. He whispered something I couldn't hear to Finnvarðr, then pressed a quick kiss to his forehead.

"We're retreating." Vidar said, crouching beside me. "Birger is with Jan, they've already left – I came to find you."

I nodded briskly and tried to stand but collapsed yet again. I swore loudly, furious that I couldn't walk. I hadn't dared lay eyes on my wound, but Vidar did – I watched his eyes widen in shock at the sight of it.

"Your leg—"

"I can't walk, Finnvarðr was helping me—"

Vidar scooped me up quickly and ran up the bank with me in his arms, carrying me to safety.

***

I SHRIEKED AS Borghildr set my leg, the bones crunching loudly. Searing white light flashed before my eyes. Vidar held me down by my shoulders and two women pinned my legs down while another stood behind Borghildr with stints and strips of linen in hand. I felt the shards of my broken bones scratch against each other as Borghildr twisted my leg into place, the scraping noise loud in my ears. My body was so hot I thought I was on fire. Hurriedly, Borghildr's assistant positioned the two long, thin wooden stints on either side of my broken shin and wrapped the linen tightly around them, binding the stints – and my broken bones – in place. Once the centre of the stints was wrapped, Borghildr let go of my injured leg and wrapped the rest of the strips around the stints.

I wept and groaned, and Vidar kissed my forehead, whispering soothing words. I squeezed the table top I was lying on so tightly, I could feel splinters from the aged wood dig beneath my nails, but I paid no heed nor lessened my grip. I twisted my head away from Vidar, not caring for any of the kind words or soothing sounds. I wanted him, Borghildr and the two women to let go of me. By the time the stints were bound in place, I was exhausted and stopped flailing. Borghildr approached me with a large tankard filled to the brim with consecrated wine we'd stolen from the monastery.

"You won't battle tomorrow. It's not the worse shin break I've seen, but it will take at least three months to heal completely." Borghildr said firmly. "You can't walk, you'll be useless. You *need* to rest; if you strain your leg anymore, you'll lose it."

Vidar carefully sat me up on the table. He slipped his arms beneath mine while Borghildr and the two women lifted my legs carefully. Gently they carried me to a pallet covered in furs and set me down on it. Vidar immediately sat on the floor beside the bed, the tankard from Borghildr in his hands, and medicated me through the evening with the wine.

At some point I had fallen asleep, plied with the dry, bitter tasting wine, my head spinning, and my body numb. Rest had been welcomed. When I woke, darkness had fully covered the earth, I could hardly even see stars in the sky outside the windows of the abbey. Oil lamps glowed softly, scattered about the room. The flames were so low, they hardly cast a light on the injured men around, some snoring, other moaning quietly from their pain and tossing in their beds.

Though we had looted what treasures we had found in the abbey and turned a few rooms into stalls for animals, we had the large dormitories alone, all pallets beds in place. The pallets in the individual cells had been reserved for the leaders of the siege, Vidar, Rollo, Sinric and Sigfred, and the ones in the dormitory were for the injured. There were so many injured warriors that the four leaders gave up their pallets in favour of straw bales or even just furs on the ground so the injured would have a bed to sleep in.

Vidar had situated some straws bales around my bed for him and our children to sleep on, all of us close, all of us together. The children laid half on their straw beds, half on my pallet, their hands or feet gently touching some part of me, reassuring me they were there and drawing comfort from my touch. I gazed at them, barely visible in the darkness, but I could hear their breathing and I could feel their touch and that calmed me.

Vidar was also lying half in his bed and half on mine, his head rested on the pillow. I could feel his breath dancing on my skin, rhythmic, soft. I turned and placed a wine-dampened kiss on his brow and a soft noise rolled from his throat, acknowledging me.

"Are you okay, little fawn?" Vidar whispered.

He hadn't been sleeping – his voice was not addled by tiredness, it was clear and alert, low so he wouldn't wake the children or any of the injured men surrounding us.

"Don't die tomorrow, Vidar Alvarsson." I whispered. "Odin doesn't need you yet."

RISE TO FALL

Overcome suddenly with emotion, my voice trembled as I spoke, and a knot formed in my throat. I didn't know how quietly I had spoken, for my mind was still spinning from the wine Vidar and Borghildr had plied me with earlier. I inhaled a deep, shuddering breath, tears slipping from my eyes onto Vidar's face.

"Wouldn't dream of it." Vidar chuckled quietly, kissing my tear-dampened cheeks.

And he didn't.

The next night, Vidar and his men staggered back to camp, the number of warriors greatly lessened, yet again. The Norsemen had brought more bad news. They had surrounded the tower, using the ditches we'd dug for protection, and had managed to push all three belfries onto the banks, one against the gates, the other close to the tower but not quite close enough, and the final one close to the walls. Unfortunately, the Franks had sailed out and had captured two of the belfries. A few warriors had managed to enter Paris itself, but they were killed quickly. Rumour had it that even the count of Paris himself had fought on the ramparts, but he had survived the battle. Finally, the Danes and Norwegians had filled three longships with straw and oil and set them aflame, floating the crewless ships down the river in hopes of burning the bridge down – but unfortunately the fire had licked at the stone, nothing more, and the longships had burned out.

Yet another day of failure.

A few days later, however, we received great news; the river Seine had flooded and split the bridge between the city and the left bank down the middle! The debris and bodies we had been filling the river with for the belfries had crashed against the other bridge and destroyed it, leaving the northeast tower defenceless. Morale renewed, our army set out and attacked the tower at daybreak the following morning. They found a small troop of Franks guarding the isolated tower when they arrived, who the Danes and Norwegians killed mercilessly, before slaughtering the men garrisoned in the tower as well, and setting the tower on fire, the other Franks watching helplessly from the ramparts and battlements.

Sinric and Rollo sailed their men, and a good portion of the warriors from Roskilde and even Sigfred's men, up the Seine to raid and pillage the cities beyond. The rest of the warriors remained with Vidar and Sigfred outside of Paris. We moved from the abbey of St Germain l'Auxerrois to an abbey across the river, the abbey of St Germain De Pres, and made camp there instead.

Shortly after our move and after most our army had sailed on to raid, Paris had received aid in the form of Henry of Franconia, the duke of Saxony and his soldiers – a piece of information one of the Norsemen had gleaned from one of the duke's soldiers, before he had killed him. Duke Henry and his men had been easy to defeat – they had marched throughout the winter and were obviously exhausted from it, they had fought for only a short while before retreating.

Over two months passed, waiting for Paris to give in to us. Rollo, Sinric and the others had returned, their ships filled with treasures. Sigfred's spirits were lower more than I'd seen during the long battle; he was short tempered and furious, kicking whatever item in his path, killing or torturing any Frankish soldier we had taken prisoner. The cold winter had turned into a wet, bitter spring and we were getting nowhere with this siege.

"That's it – I'm done." Sigfred growled, tossing his bowl and spoon to the ground.

It was morning time. We were sat around the fire eating morning meal – a paltry stew made of mostly water, a few root vegetables and some of the remaining salted meat from our stores. I glanced at Vidar, who continued to chew a bite of flat bread, his icy eyes watching Sigfred innocently and without reaction.

"I'm sick of waiting around in this bloody abbey, I'm sick of trudging around in the dirt and getting nowhere!" Sigfred grumbled.

"If we hold out longer, we will get the silver we want." Rollo the Walker commented calmly.

Rollo held the bowl in just one of his massive paws, his long fingers curled around it, almost hiding it from view. It was almost comical to see his giant, hulking form perched on the rickety seat, his knees almost up to his chest, the spoon so tiny clutched between his long, thick fingers. The atmosphere in camp was anything but amusing, however. Sigfred was not the only warrior who was tired of the siege.

"I'm with Sigfred, I've had enough, too." Sinric said. "Look at the loot we've seized from just a few weeks raiding passed Paris! There are so much more to be had if we stopped wasting our time here."

"I'm leaving." Sigfred announced, maintaining his unbroken stare with Vidar. "I will demand tribute from the Franks again, then I'm taking my men up the Seine to raid."

"My men and I will go with you." Sinric said, to which Sigfred grinned and nodded.

Sigfred gazed at us all victoriously, emboldened by Sinric's support. He paced around for a few moments, before throwing himself onto a stool, leaned over his knees and stared at Vidar. Vidar quietly returned Sigfred's gaze, taking another bite of his bread.

"Do what you like." Rollo yawned. "I'll see this siege to the end."

"You're quiet, Jarl." Sigfred said to Vidar finally.

Vidar tipped his head side to side in return, tossing the last chunk of his flat bread into his mouth before leaning back in the chair, his arms raised behind his head. Nonchalantly he continued to chew, making no effort to hurry and reply to Sigfred. The leaders were all staring at him, now, and the crowd that surrounded us had gone quiet.

"The Jarlkona is still injured, she won't be able to walk for another week or so, and the men of Roskilde have suffered the most losses." Sigfred said. "Are you staying, Jarl? Or do you wish to raid with Sinric and me? Give your men a chance to seize real plunder and glory rather than waste away here for nothing."

Vidar swallowed the food in his mouth and brushed the crumbs from his lips with the back of his hand. He smiled at all the leaders staring at him. Vidar's smile seemed sincere, his eyes sparkled and wrinkled in the corners, there was a serene happiness that glowed from his face.

"Actually." Vidar said, his smile widening on his face. "I plan on letting my men decide."

Vidar turned to the warriors surrounding them.

"Tell the men, women and children of Roskilde and Aros – the injured and the healthy – to meet me in the church. I'd like to offer them a choice." Vidar smiled.

Soon enough, all the warriors, women and children of Roskilde and Aros, plus Rollo, Sinric and Sigfred and a lot of their men, were crammed inside the church of the St. Germain De Pres abbey. As everyone filed in, a filthy rancid stench filled the church. Though we had tried to clean ourselves once a week as was habit back home, some had not been able to immerse themselves in a proper bath for months. The reek of body odour, sickness and shit was overwhelming. Lying on a stretcher made of wooden posts and animal skins that Vidar and another Dane would carry me around on, I shifted my fur over my face a little higher, covering my mouth and nose in an attempt to block the stink.

Vidar and I, and the three other leaders were on the altar beneath a huge effigy of Jesus – the Christ figure was made of silver and the crucifix was bronze. The Norsemen had not yet ripped *all* the valuables from the abbey, but in time the figure looming above us would be torn down and hacked apart for the valuable metal it was made from.

"My people!" Vidar called out, his voice echoing. He held his arms wide – eerily similar to the crucified Christ above him. "We have fought long and hard. We have lost so much and gained so little in return. For this reason, I would like to offer you some choices. Sigfred and Sinric have decided to take their men raiding further up the Seine. There are towns there, rich with silver, untouched as of yet. I offer you the chance to sail with them.

"Rollo the Walker has decided to remain and finish the siege, hoping to take Paris. The spies we have in the city have given word to us that there is a disease spreading throughout Paris – if we wait a bit longer, Paris will be weakened and should be easier to take. I offer you the chance to see this siege through alongside Rollo and his men and reap the riches of your patience.

"I want to offer you a third option." Sigfred, Rollo and Sinric stared at Vidar, eyes wide – as did I. He had not mentioned another option to us. "I want to offer you *home*. We have been gone from

RISE TO FALL

our homes since the summer of last year, some brought their families here, but most of you did not. I want to offer you the chance to take the plunder you have home – and allow you the chance to take more along the way back."

Silence settled over the mass of Danes and Norwegians in the church for but a few moments, before mumbling and muttering erupted as men and women talked between themselves, weighing the positives and negatives of their options.

"All those who wish to remain with Rollo, say *já*." Vidar said.

More men than I had expected called out '*Já*', but considering the amount standing before us, there still weren't many who had chosen to stay. Vidar nodded, carefully finding each face and studying them.

"All those who wish to sail with Sigfred and Sinric, say *já*."

More men called out to go with Sinric and Sigfred than had called out to stay with Rollo, but again the number was few.

"All those who wish to go home, say *já*."

"*Já!*" The church rumbled from the thunderous volume of the men's call.

Vidar couldn't help but laugh. He grinned at each the men before him, shaking his head gently.

"I have one more offer."

The church fell to silence. My heart lurched in my chest – I had no idea what he was about to offer. Vidar turned to me and winked, his icy eyes sparkling with mischief.

"I plan to sail to the Kingdom of the East Angles before I go home. All those who wish to join me, say *já*."

CHAPTER TWENTY-EIGHT

WISBECE, THE KINGDOM OF GUTHRUM
Late Spring, 886

RAIN HAMMERED DOWN on us and our longship, Storm-Serpent, lurched violently on the vicious waves of the channel between Francia and Britain. I could barely see the Anglo-Saxon Kingdom of Sussex, though the Danes said we were close. I shuddered from cold and terror, gripping my children tightly while chanting soothing words to them, but my trembling voice was lost in the roar of the wind and the waves. I held Sander, Æsa and Einar, but my gaze never left Young Birger, who rowed beside Jan across the longship to me. I was consumed with fear that my eldest son might get thrown clear off the ship by one of the monstrous waves that tossed Storm-Serpent about.

It had been smooth rowing down the winding Seine, but the moment we entered the channel, we entered a storm; the bitter wind picked up ferociously, ruffling the calm waters into choppy, angry waves that quickly grew taller and more chaotic. Rain drummed upon the wooden ship and upon our shivering bodies, accompanied by the howling wind and bellowing waters crashing against Storm-Serpent in a terrifying melody. Huddled beneath furs, I quailed by the mast with the few other women and children, my children and I clinging to each other.

The rowers suffered the wrath of the weather, the spray and the breeze were icy cold, reddening their skin and faces. Young Birger's bronze flesh was whipped scarlet by the winds and gleamed with sweat and sea spray, yet through the mists and the rain, I saw the smile beaming on his face.

Sander was also excited, he had jabbered nonstop about the Kingdom of the East Angles and pestered me with questions on the journey down the Seine. Sander hadn't been able to talk to me since entering the channel – the rainstorm and waters were too loud for him to be heard over – but he remained enthusiastic, nonetheless. His arm linked with mine, Sander fidgeted beside me, his head turning this way and that. Sander had been like this on the way to Francia, too; ever eager to dive into the unknown. The frenzied waves of the channel and the ferocity of the rainstorm didn't seem to dampen his spirits or bother him at all – I was sure our arms linked together was more for my comfort than for his.

Æsa and Einar were not as elated as their older brothers at all, refusing to even admire the beauty of the cliffs despite the end of the rainstorm and the calming of the waters. Their heads buried against my chest, hidden beneath my furs, keeping them warm and comforting them in their misery; their tears soaked through my clothing as they wept against me.

Ebbe and Borghildr had decided to sail back to Aros with most of our forces, devastating Æsa; she had enjoyed playing with Borgunna and was miserable that she wouldn't see her for a while. Einar didn't care who was or wasn't on the ship, however; he was sick to his stomach of being on the channel – *literally*.

The angry waves lapped hungrily upon the ship, pitching it to-and-fro violently. The beams and rigging shrieked, the planks groaned loudly, rain pounded down, and the bow was rising and falling with terrifying altitude and intensity. Poor Einar had spent a good portion of the voyage vomiting onto the planked floor of the ship, rattled entirely by Storm-Serpent's violent lurching.

When we reached the narrowest point of the channel, finally, the rain lightened, gradually coming to a complete stop, and as we left the channel, the violent waves subsided, thank the gods. As we passed them, we snatched glimpses of the striking ivory cliffs of the Kingdom of Kent to portside, blindingly bright and gleaming magnificently through the grey, dreary weather.

Ours was the only ship sailing to Britain, most of our people had decided to return to Roskilde or Aros, though a few of our warriors had stayed with Rollo or raid with Sinric and Sigfred. Storm-Serpent was fully manned with a crew of sixty men, and carried perhaps twenty passengers consisting of women, thralls and children, including myself and Vidar and my four children.

Though our numbers were small, we didn't sail to raid, we didn't sail to fight, we sailed to explore. Numbers didn't matter.

We had stayed in Paris for two more weeks after the meeting in the church, to ready ourselves for our journey to Britain, and to make sure I was able to walk. I hobbled about with minimal pain; Borghildr had been right, it wasn't the worse shin break (though it had seemed like it to me at the time), but it had taken a full three months before I was able to rest my body weight on the leg without wincing or collapsing. I would be able to walk onto my ship and hobble around Britain, and that was all that mattered.

We had managed to come out of the channel unscathed, thank the gods. Francia was completely out of sight now, disappeared somewhere to our rear. Einar dared to peek out from the furs and glanced around briefly, his wide amber eyes bloodshot from crying. A soft groan rumbled from his throat and he hid his face beneath the furs again.

"I don't think he's going to be a seafarer when he's older." Vidar commented sympathetically, sitting beside me closely and wiping his brow with his sleeve.

The wind was blowing favourably, so the oars were raised, and we depended on the billowing sail for a while instead, giving the rowers a chance to rest for a while. Æsa immediately crawled into Vidar's lap and he wrapped his arms around her, whilst Sander scuttled off to sit and talk with Young Birger and Jan.

"We're almost there, my love." Vidar cooed to Æsa, kissing her blonde head. "Not much longer now."

"I want to go home, I miss Borgunna." Æsa whined.

"We will go back, and you'll see her again, just be patient." Vidar said. "This is your chance to see your *móðir*'s homeland."

Æsa wrinkled her nose and pouted, still firmly disappointed she wouldn't see he friend for an undetermined time yet. She buried her face into Vidar's chest, clamping her eyes shut and sticking her bottom lip further out. I giggled at Æsa and rubbed her back, leaning against Vidar, little Einar still clinging to me beneath the furs. I kissed Vidar's shoulder and gazed up at him. His icy eyes twinkled, and his smirk broke into a grin.

"Are you excited, little fawn?" He asked.

RISE TO FALL

"*Já.*" I said. "Mostly nervous."

"We should be there in a few hours. Do you think you'll remember the way to your village?"

"I doubt it." I replied.

"Do you remember anything about your village?"

"A little ... It's called Wisbece, it's surrounded by marshland, but there's a river that runs through from the North Sea. It's small; when I lived there, there was maybe ten houses there, total. I don't know how many there are now – if any." I gave a nervous laugh and Vidar chewed his bottom lip. "We couldn't grow much because of the marshes, but we grew what we could, fished a lot, and focussed mainly on raising sheep ... I loved those sheep." I added nostalgically.

"Do you miss *our* sheep?" Vidar asked softly.

I couldn't help but laugh at him.

"Of course, I miss them." I grinned.

"I can't promise that Wisbece will still be there when we arrive, little fawn, but we will try to find it." Vidar said. "A lot has changed in the last twenty years – it has been the Kingdom of *Guthrum* for almost a decade now."

"I know." I said, closing my eyes. "It's alright."

It seemed odd referring to my village by its actual name, Wisbece. None of the few Danes I'd spoken to about my Anglo-Saxon home had ever heard of it, so I simply always referred to it as 'my village'. I never thought I'd see Wisbece again, indeed I had doubts I would even see it now, for the last time I had been there, the few homes in the village were being set alight by the Danes.

"Little fawn, look, there it is!" Vidar cried out.

Vidar pointed at a murky swath of land across from us, hardly distinguishable from the dark waves and the grey sky. Bolts of excitement surged through me, lifting the hairs on my arms. Of course, I didn't know what the Kingdom of the East Angles looked like from the sea, I could've been gazing at the Iberian Kingdoms for all I knew, but Vidar knew where we were going, he knew which way we had been, he knew the layout of the land in his mind's eye.

Immediately a wave of eager chatter flooded the ship; the men enthusiastically sharing tales of Britain with each other. Every man on the ship had been to the land of the Anglo-Saxons at least once in their lifetime, most had been at least a handful of times for short raids or participating in long wars.

As they chattered, the men returned to their seats and picked up their oars, ready to row when needed. We kept Britain in our line of sight while we sailed the North Sea, following the edge of the Anglo-Saxon kingdoms. We'd be rowing around the curving outer edge of the East Angles before entering the Gewæsc, a rectangular bay and estuary in the northeast corner of the Kingdom of the East Angles, where the East Angles met the Kingdom of Mercia. There, we would find and travel the River Nene in the eastern part of the Fens, which belonged to the Kingdom of the East Angles – the rest of the fens belonged to Mercia. Not far down the Nene, we would reach Wisbece – or what was left of it, anyway. The Fens was a marshland mostly around the coast of the Gewæsc. Wisbece sat on a strip of solid, liveable land surrounded by the swamp, alluvium and marshland of the Fens.

Blotches of sunlight blared out through small holes in the clouds, bouncing off the waters surrounding us. Gradually the sun cracked through the clouds completely, offering us a paltry warmth, but lifting our spirits, nonetheless. Einar fell asleep, exhausted and weakened by his sickness. I scooped him into my arms and kissed his damp little head. I listened to the conversations buzzing around me, anticipation and anxiety growing inside me.

From the various discussions buzzing around me, I managed to gather a great deal of information on my old homelands, but it made my heart ache more. It had been twenty years since I had lived there, and it really wasn't the place I remembered at all ... A deep sigh fell from my lips, goosebumps scattered over my arms.

A great deal of change had occurred; I had feared Wisbece wouldn't be there when I arrived on the land of Britain, and now I knew the Kingdom of the East Angles wasn't there either. I would not be stepping foot in the East Angles, for it was now known as the Kingdom of Guthrum after the Danish King who had signed a treaty with King Alfred of Wessex and taken ownership of the kingdom.

In the year 865, the Great Army, led by the sons of Ragnar Loðbrók, attacked the Kingdom of the East Angles. It was during that year and that attack that my family had been murdered and Birger Bloody Sword had taken me to Roskilde, a town that would become my first home in Denmark. Jarl Guthrum and Jarl Alvar the First One and the warriors of Roskilde had sailed with the Great Army, but where Alvar plundered and returned to Roskilde when his ships were filled, Guthrum, like the sons of Ragnar, remained in England. Alvar might not have been inclined to settle in Britain, but the others were. Two years after the Danes attacked, they captured Northumbria and took the city of Eoferwic. They placed Ecgberht of Northumbria on the throne – their puppet king.

In the year 869, Ivar the Boneless, one of the sons of Ragnar, led another attack on the Kingdom of the East Angles. The Danes killed King Edmund of the East Angles, thus conquering my homeland. For two years, the Danes and the Anglo-Saxons fought and battled, but then King Æthelred of Wessex died in the spring of 871 and his sickly brother, Alfred, took the throne. There was peace for a time – apparently King Alfred's army was weak, and the Anglo-Saxon king was forced to pay tribute to the Danes for some time.

Within ten years since the Great Army arrived in the Kingdom of the East Angles in the autumn of 865, the Danes had conquered not only the Kingdom of the East Angles, but Northumbria and Mercia as well. Guthrum had his sights set on Wessex and attacked them, winning initially, before brokering peace with the King of Wessex. A year later, Guthrum broke the peace and battled Alfred, winning various skirmishes, but eventually Guthrum was captured by the Anglo-Saxons. Alfred made a peace treaty with Guthrum, and Guthrum left Wessex, but again the peace did not last long.

On the Christian feast day of Epiphany, at the beginning of 878, Guthrum made a surprise attack on Alfred and his court. Five months later, King Alfred defeated Guthrum, besieging the Danes for two weeks before they finally agreed to negotiate yet another peace treaty. Guthrum received baptism, with Alfred as his godfather. With that, there was a boundary set separating the Anglo-Saxon lands with that of the Danish ruled lands. He removed his army from the borders facing Alfred's territory and moved to the Kingdom of the East Angles, settling it as the Kingdom of Guthrum, where he was still living to this day.

"Are you alright, little fawn?" Vidar asked, rousing me from my thoughts.

"*Já.*" I said, though my reply came out as more of a question than an answer.

"You're pale, are you feeling sick, too?"

"*Nei.* To be honest, I don't know what I'm feeling."

And I didn't. My chest ached from how fast and hard my heart pounded as we entered the Gewæsc. My anxiety had peaked, but I couldn't quite put my finger on what was ailing me. I shifted Einar higher up my lap and tucked my furs around him a little closer.

"What's going through your mind?" Vidar asked softly, shifting closer to me. "Thought or memory?"

"Both." I smiled at him weakly. "I'm remembering my life here before, but I'm thinking about all that's changed since then."

"The change worries you?" Vidar pressed.

"I suppose. I'm – I'm worried I won't find my home – Wisbece. But then I realise … It hasn't been my home for a very long time."

"I can't say I'm sad to hear that, little fawn." Vidar said.

I stared at him, confused.

"I've worried you might want to stay in the East Angles now you've returned – maybe you'll regret marrying a heathen and divorce me for a good Anglo-Saxon Christian." A light blush glowed on Vidar's bronze cheeks.

"Why would you think that?" I asked incredulously, a faint smirk curling one corner of my lips.

"You're returning *home* Aveline. Maybe you won't want to leave this time?" Vidar said, his icy eyes sparkling with innocence and sincerity. Vidar's handsome face was still and serious. "You've never referred to Aros as your home." He added quietly.

"My love," I sighed, kissing his arm and gazing up at him. "Like I said before, Wisbece hasn't been my home for so long; I'm worried I won't find it, but I already *know* it's not there. Wisbece isn't home, Aros isn't – Roskilde isn't, even. My home isn't defined by a place, Vidar – it's defined by *you*. You and the children – our family is my home. I could never regret you, and I certainly would never divorce you. I'm not going to revert to Christianity, or leave you for a Christian, I promise. I won't leave you for anyone."

"Then why are you worried?" Vidar asked, a smile finally spilling over his face.

"I don't know." I paused for a moment's contemplation. "I suppose I'm nervous to return here because I *know* it's not home anymore, and I'm not who I used to be … I'm a Dane now, *I'm a heathen*," I chuckled. "But I'm happy right now, I know who I am, what I am, and I'm happy. The life I lived here ended such a long time ago … I suppose I'm nervous that, by coming here, am I waking the ghosts of the past, when I should just let them lie?"

"If you're happy with whom and what you are, then there's no need to fear those ghosts if they do rear their heads. We've been through so much, little fawn, but we've come through it, we weathered those storms *together*. We'll fight and survive whatever else the Nornir decide to throw at us, ghosts and all – just like we have in the past." Vidar grinned. "My biggest fear is losing you; if I don't have to fear that, then what's the worst that could happen?"

"Don't tempt the Nornir." I warned, though the smile on my face grew stronger.

"They can do their worst, I will always be with you little fawn. Always."

The fierce surety and confidence in Vidar's voice filled me with a blistering warmth; he was right. Vidar bent his head down, cupping my jaw with one hand and bringing my lips to his in a beautiful, passionate kiss. Unfortunately, it was cut short by Æsa, who squealed and pushed our faces apart with her little hands. Vidar and I laughed, both of us rosy cheeked, and apologised to our daughter.

The rowers began to shift, arranging their oars to row once more. Vidar slipped Æsa off his lap and returned to his seat, excitedly telling us we were about to row around the curve of the East Angles and enter the Gewæsc. Once there, it would only be three or so hours before we'd reach Wisbece – or what was left of it.

***

"WHERE ARE WE?" I gasped, stepping off Storm-Serpent and gazing in awe at the village.

"This is Wisbece, Jarlkona." One of our men replied. "We're an hour ride from Grantanbrycg at a full gallop."

"This is *not* Wisbece."

"It is Jarlkona, I assure you." The confused Dane replied.

"Little fawn?" Vidar smirked.

Just as Vidar had said, the Kingdom of the East Angles was so different to how I remembered – in the fleeting recollections I still had of it, that is. The village laid out before my eyes was *huge*! Wisbece had comprised only ten households when I lived there – now there had to be at least twenty-five households! There was still no church, but Wisbece had greatly expanded, nonetheless.

I dashed up the shore, Einar bouncing in my arms, and hailed the first passer-by I found.

"Is this Wisbece?" I asked in Old Norse.

The stranger glared at me.

"Wisbece! Is this Wisbece?" I demanded impatiently, but in Ænglisc this time. "Where am I?"

"This is Wisbece." The stranger said, gawking at me as though I had three heads.

I stared at him, wide-eyed with surprise, and mouthed the word 'Wisbece' repeatedly. I turned around in circles, scrutinising the village – was this really Wisbece? How did it survive the Danes? How did it flourish? The stranger sighed loudly and pointedly before he stomped away, muttering something about *mad foreigners* as he left.

"What's wrong *mumie*?" Einar asked, biting his lip, his forehead puckered.

"Nothing's wrong, my darling." I said. "We're here – this is my homeland; this is Wisbece."

CHAPTER TWENTY-NINE

IT WAS BIZARRE. Wisbece had changed extraordinarily; I wandered around slowly, my mouth hung open, gawping at the houses, the absolute multitude of homes. Of course, Wisbece was still just a village. Roskilde and Aros were both far greater in size than Wisbece, but they were great towns not measly fishing villages. We could muster a thousand fighting men from each, whereas Wisbece had maybe one hundred and fifty *possibly* two hundred inhabitants – women, children, elderly and the odd thrall here or there included. It still wasn't a rich village, but it was a growing village; perhaps in a hundred years it would be a bustling town?

"Little fawn," Vidar called, jogging over to me. "There are a few Danish households here. We've requested food and shelter, but this town isn't big enough to house all of us for the night. Some of the men will ride on and find shelter elsewhere. Jan, Einarr, Lars and a few others will stay here with us."

I nodded and looked passed him to the little crowd waiting behind him. Jan, a few of our men and Vidar and my three older children were standing with two men and a woman I didn't recognise. By the woman's clothes and the rings on the men's arms and hammers hanging from their necks, I assumed they were some of the Danish settlers Vidar was referring to.

I turned back to my husband, trying to focus on him but my whole body tingled with shock, my mind drifted wildly; Danes had come to settle in Wisbece? Never in my life would I have imagined Danes settling in Wisbece. Never would I have imagined Wisbece to be flourishing and growing as largely as it had, and now it was home not just to a few poor Anglo-Saxon farmers and fishermen, but to Danes as well …

"Will you come with me to arrange everything?"

"*Nei* – I want to explore the town a little. Do you mind?"

Vidar looked at me in shock, his brows had shot up his forehead and his icy blue eyes were wide and staring.

"*Nei, nei,*" He said, surprise ringing in his voice. He cleared his throat and continued in a somewhat calmer tone. "Of course, you can, little fawn, I don't mind. Stay close though, would you? This may be Wisbece and there may be Danes here, but we don't know how the locals will react to a strange Danish woman wandering on her own."

"*Mumie* isn't on her own, I'm with her!" Einar laughed brightly.

"Be a good boy and look after your *mumie*." Vidar grinned, ruffling our youngest child's hair.

"I have *Úlfsblóð* should I need it." I said as warmly as I could, resting my hand on the pommel. "I'm sure I won't though."

"Just in case, little fawn." Vidar said, pressing a kiss to my brow. "You *are* a Dane, and a newcomer at that."

"I am indeed." I winked.

Hesitantly, Vidar returned to the group. I waved to them, took Einar's hand in mine and together, my youngest son and I turned and walked away from them.

"*Mumie*, wait!" I turned and saw Æsa running towards me. "I want to come too!"

"Come along then, my love." I grinned.

With my son and daughter's hands clasped in both of mine, we wandered Wisbece. Though I had only fleeting memories of my village, this place seemed far noisier and busier than it had been all those years ago. I strained my memory, reached to the corners of my mind, trying to recognise and remember more details about my Wisbece of the past and compare it to the Wisbece of the present. There was nothing to compare though. I recognised none of the faces, I recognised none of the home, I recognised nothing. I suppose I had been right in my fears; I was worried I wouldn't find it, but I knew it wasn't here, and it truly wasn't. The Wisbece I knew was gone.

Even the layout of the village had changed. The number of houses had disorientated me to where I had thought my own house had once stood; no matter how far the children and I walked, no matter how many pens and houses we wove past, I could not remember where my house had been. Of course, though there was a small glimmer of hope that I might find the wreckage of my old home, I knew we weren't going to come across it. Realistically, the wreckage would have been sifted through, anything that could have been retrieved and reused would have been, and the rest of the wreckage would have been burned as firewood. Someone would have built upon the land where my home had stood, and whatever trace there had been of my family's home would be gone.

It saddened me, but I couldn't say I was surprised if they had. That was exactly what Vidar had done to Erhardt Ketilsson's hall when Vidar had taken the jarldom of Aros; he had burned Erhardt's hall to the ground, rid the town of any hint that Erhardt's home had existed, and built upon it, destroying all evidence it had ever stood there.

My mind began playing cruel tricks on me. I would spot a landmark, like a particular cluster of trees or a certain angle the river could be spotted, and think I'd found the spot my house hand once stood, but no. In all truth I was searching for something I'd never find. I had told Vidar I feared waking ghosts that I should let lie, and yet I found myself delving through Wisbece in search those very ghosts, hunting them down and begging to awaken them.

"Are we done yet? I'm hungry." Einar moaned, tugging on my hand.

We'd been wandering for an hour, around and around the pens, the pastures, the houses, the barns, along the river and over the shores. Presently we were standing near a few farm houses on the outskirts of Wisbece, far from the Gewæsc.

"*Já*, we can go back." I said reluctantly.

"We haven't found your old house yet, though." Æsa said.

"I know," I said, a pang in my heart but I tried to keep my tone light and matter-of-fact. "I don't think we will though, they've probably built on top of it by now, it has been twenty years."

"Look! A lamb!" Einar suddenly exclaimed, pointing.

Æsa and I whipped our heads around and sure enough, there was a lamb ambling about in front of us. It was young, perhaps only a few weeks old, and bleating for its mother. It gazed at us momentarily before turning and bleating again – it wasn't afraid of us, obviously it had been handled a lot by its owners.

"Let's find the lamb's home before we go back, okay?"

Excited, the two children dashed over to the lamb. Shocked by the children's sudden movement, it pranced backwards, bleating like mad. I scolded the children and made them stop. Luckily the lamb stopped running off, and I managed, with a few large strides, to catch up with the little thing. I scooped it up and held it tightly against my chest, *ssh*-ing it soothingly.

"Who does it belong to?" Æsa asked, scratching under its chin.

"I don't know, let's go look."

But we didn't need to look; around the corner of a house appeared a man and a boy about Æsa's age, perhaps a year or two older, and both of their faces lit up at the sight of the lamb.

"Beth!" The little boy exclaimed. "You found her!"

"No talking now, unless it's in Ænglisc." I warned the children. I grinned at the boy who was dashing over to me. "Is this little lamb yours?" I asked in Ænglisc.

"She is, her name is Beth." The boy beamed, holding his hands out to me.

Carefully I gave him the lamb, and he snuggled it close to him, sprinkling the little animal's face with kisses.

"*Ic þē pancie.*" The man said, standing behind his son with his hands rested on his shoulders. "The lamb got out this morning, we've had trouble catching her."

"*Georne.* We haven't had her long, she just appeared a few moments ago." I smiled.

The man blushed and the wrinkles around his dark eyes deepened as he grinned warmly at me.

"We raise the lamb in the house, it's my boy's pet. The mother died birthing her and none of the other ewes would take it. Rather than eating it, my Turstan wanted to keep the damn thing." The man chuckled. "Usually the lamb's safe in the house or it's in the pen out back, but the gate was left open–" He cuffed his son gently upside the back of his head, indicating it was his son who had left them open. "And the lamb just walked out."

RISE TO FALL

"Well I'm glad she's back where she belongs." I beamed at the young red-cheeked boy. "Your lamb – Beth – she's lovely. You're a kind young man, Turstan."

Turstan didn't pay much attention to me, however. He murmured thanks, but his eyes were locked on Æsa, who stood in front of him stroking the top of the lamb's head. The scarlet on the boy's cheeks had darkened, even the tops of his ears were red.

"I like Beth very much." Æsa said, stroking the top of the lamb's head, her cheeks burning ferociously too. "She's very sweet."

"She's the sweetest lamb I've ever met." Turstan said eagerly. "Do you want to hold her?"

"I'd like that." Æsa nodded.

Turstan carefully gave her the lamb, who bleated a little, and gazed at Æsa proudly as she cuddled the little animal. The man and I passed a knowing glance between each other at both children's bright blushes.

"Can I hold it too?" Einar asked eagerly.

"No, you're too young." Æsa said quickly. "Here, stroke him instead."

"Forgive my forwardness, but your eyes are beautiful." The man said.

"Oh, well, that's very kind of you to say." I stammered, taken aback by his comment.

"Have you ever lived in Wisbece before? Many years ago, there was a family that lived here, and all of them had eyes as striking as yours. The Danes killed them, though, and I've not seen eyes like yours since." He said.

"Actually, yes. I was born and raised here." I said, my heart racing in my chest.

"What's your name?" He asked equally excited as me.

"Aveline – Aveline ... Eadricesdohter."

"*Eadricesdohter?*" The man repeated, his eyes wide in astonishment. "The only daughter of Eadric and Cynewise?"

"Yes, that's me!" I cried out. "I had seven brothers–"

"Kenrick, Sigbert, Dunstan, Sibbald, Beric, Bryni and Oswin."

"Yes!" I exclaimed happily. "That's my family!"

"I'm Guthlac – Guthlac Teowulfing." The man grinned. "I was friends with Bryni and Beric – I used to live two farms down from yours."

I stared at him, examining every inch of him. I didn't recognise him, but then I had a hard time remembering faces from my past; I could only picture my parents and brothers' faces when I thought as hard as I could, and even them the images of them I conjured in my mind were blurred by time. I definitely couldn't remember Guthlac Teowulfing.

When they weren't working with our father, my brothers did go out and play with others boy in the village. I had played with them, but not as often as I had liked to. I had played a lot with Oswin – he was only two years my senior, closest in age to me than all my other brothers. My brother's Bryni and Beric were three and five years older than me respectively and spent most of their time playing with the other boys in the village. I couldn't remember what any of their friends looked like …

"I thought the Danes had killed you." Guthlac marvelled. "But here you are!"

"Here I am." I smiled. "I'm actually trying to find where my house once stood – I want to show my children where I grew up."

"I can help you." Guthlac said. "I know where your house was, but … but Aveline, I'm really sorry, there isn't anything left."

"That's alright, I didn't expect there to be." I replied softly. "I'd still like to show my children."

Guthlac nodded understandingly and led the way. It wasn't too far from where we were. Guthlac had lived only a short distance from my home, he explained. As we spoke, I found Guthlac remembered an astonishing amount of how Wisbece had been twenty years ago. I supposed that was because he never truly left Wisbece. Guthlac still lived in his childhood home, the Danes had burned it, but only the roof and one wall had been damaged, he had managed to rebuild it for the most part. My childhood home had not been as lucky.

I stared at the barn before me, large, strong horses ambling around it, chewing tufts of grass. This is where my house had once stood. There was nothing left, just faded memories. Æsa, Einar and Turstan stood at the fence stroking a friendly pregnant and mare. Guthlac and I stood a few paces away, watching the children chatter, ripping grass from the ground and offering it to the plump mare from their open palms.

"This last thing I remember is my mother screaming …" I mumbled. "She told me to run, and I did … I saw Kenrick killed, I saw Sigbert's daughter, Estrun, dead … I didn't see the Danes set fire to my home, but I saw other houses burning so I assumed they would burn mine, too. It's odd … Even though I knew my house was gone, actually *seeing* it's gone … I'm *still* shocked, even though I expected it."

I sighed and kicked at the ground with my foot. Overcome with regret and sadness, my breath shuddered. I swallowed hard, trying to push down the knot that had formed in my throat.

"I understand." Guthlac said. "The Danes did some damned awful things back then – they still do, sometimes."

"What's it like living under the Danes rule?" I asked.

"Honestly? They're not so bad." Guthlac said.

"What?" I gawped at him, my eyes wide and brow furrowed.

"The heathen bastards have done some terrible things, to be sure. They killed my parents, my siblings, they killed almost everyone I knew, but not all of them are bad. There's some Anglo-Saxons here that are just as bad as the bastards who attacked us back then." Guthlac said.

"I never expected to hear an Anglo-Saxon say something nice about the Danes." I smiled. "I'm surprised you haven't been strung up for being a Danish sympathiser."

"Luckily the Danes would protect me – I hope at least." Guthlac smirked. "A few years ago, I probably would have let an Anglo-Saxon skin a Dane alive for all I cared, I still harboured anger against them for what they did twenty years ago, but, when an *Anglo-Saxon* man tried to rape my daughter when she was twelve, it was a Dane who saved her. A while after he saved my daughter, I found him being beaten by Anglo-Saxon on the shore … I couldn't let the man who'd saved my daughter get beaten to death, so I beat that bastards who were attacking him. After that, the Dane and I became steadfast friends and two years later, my daughter married his son and moved to Denmark with him. The Dane ended up being a jarl over there, apparently. He looked after me, he appreciated what I did for him and I believe he and his son are taking great care of my daughter. I owe my riches to the man, it's thanks to him I have all this land and all the horses, this beautiful barn." Guthlac shrugged his shoulders, turning his gaze back on the horses and barn in front of us.

"Want to know something?" I asked him, nudging him with my elbow.

"What?" Guthlac smiled, looking at me from the corner of his eye.

"I like some of the Danes, too." I whispered, and we laughed together for a moment.

"What happened to you Aveline? Where have you been all these years?" Guthlac sighed.

"A Dane took me to Denmark. He adopted me and raised me as his daughter." I explained simply. "I met a wonderful Dane and married him. We have four beautiful children together and I'm a jarlkona now."

"It's mad what life throws at you, isn't it?"

"It is." I chuckled.

"Is this your first time back, then?"

"First time in twenty years." I nodded.

Suddenly Guthlac's face dropped and all the colour drained away.

"Have you – have you been anywhere else?" He asked.

"No, we came directly to Wisbece." I replied, a little unnerved by his sudden behaviour change.

"Have you spoken to Beric?"

"What do you mean? Beric's dead."

"No, he's not!" Guthlac exclaimed. "Beric's alive!"

CHAPTER THIRTY

"AVELINE! THERE YOU are." Vidar called in the Norse tongue as he strode over to me.

"*Faðir!*" Einar exclaimed happily, running over to Vidar, who scooped him up into his arms and held him tightly.

"Who is this?" Vidar asked, surveying Guthlac shrewdly.

"My name is Guthlac Teowulfing." Guthlac replied in Norse. "I'm a fisherman and I raise horses here in Wisbece. I'm an old family friend of Aveline's."

"You speak decent Norse for an Anglo-Saxon." Vidar said in Ænglisc. "I am Jarl Vidar Alvarsson of Aros and Roskilde. I'm Aveline's husband."

"Nice to meet you, Jarl Vidar." Guthlac said, nodding respectfully to Vidar and reverting to his native tongue. "You speak pretty good Ænglisc for a Dane."

"Usually it's the Danes who learn the local language." Vidar smiled. "I'm pleasantly surprised to hear an Anglo-Saxon speaking Norse."

"I had to learn Norse; I'd like to go to Denmark and see my grandson one day. His name is Halfdan Ólafson, grandson of Jarl Helgi Johansson of Viborg." Guthlac said.

"Your grandson stands to inherit a great town when he's a man," Vidar said. "I've been to Viborg a few times myself and enjoyed it there every time. Jarl Helgi Johansson is a good man–"

"Wait, stop!" I snapped, finally finding my voice. "Enough about Viborg, what about Beric? What do you mean *Beric's alive*? He died twenty years ago!"

"No, Aveline, he didn't, he survived – I was with him the day the Danes attacked; Dunstan helped us get away." Guthlac said.

I glanced wide-eyed between Guthlac and Vidar, who was staring at me in confusion. My heart raced in my chest, my palms were wet, and my knees shook. I tried to process what I was hearing, but it was as though Guthlac was speaking a foreign language – his words resounded in my mind, but I couldn't make sense of it.

"*Nine deaths paid for you to* live *as Aveline Birgersdóttir, not to* die *as Aveline Eadricesdohter.*"

When I had spoken to the Allfather in the spirit realm, he had told me that nine deaths had been sacrificed for my second life as a Dane. *Nine* deaths! The Allfather told me my parents' lives had been sacrificed, Mildritha's life had been sacrificed, my brothers' lives had been sacrificed, but he had not specified how many brothers had died. How had I not realised this before? *Nine* deaths paid for me to live as Aveline Birgersdóttir, not ten! Had all my brothers been killed by the Danes, then it would have been ten deaths! Beric was alive ... *Beric was alive!*

"What's going on?" Vidar asked.

"Aveline's brother Beric is alive." Guthlac explained to Vidar before looking back at me.

I trembled with shock. Vidar placed his hand on my shoulder and squeezed me firmly, silently offering me reassurance and stability despite my rudeness towards him. He beamed down at me but all I could do was stare back at him, thoughts racing through my mind. *Beric was alive ...*

"Come to my home, let's sit down and talk about this." Guthlac offered.

Vidar quickly agreed before I could argue, calling Æsa over. Guthlac did the same, beckoning his son to his side, before leading us to his home across the way. Guthlac's home was large, larger than most of the other houses in Wisbece, but not nearly as grand as a hall. It, like most Anglo-Saxon homes, was built from a pit dug in the ground and had low wooden walls, a huge, sloping, neatly thatched roof, and a wide, short doorway.

Vidar stooped low to step down through the doorway after Guthlac, who was much shorter than him. Guthlac's son, Æsa and Einar scurried in afterwards. Inside the rounded single room, we found Guthlac's wife tending to the fire, and their older daughter sitting next to her, spinning wool. They stared at us wide-eyed and frowning somewhat as we entered but warmed when they spotted Einar and Æsa.

"Welcome to our home." Guthlac said. "This is my wife Somerhild, and our daughter Saewynn."

"Nice to meet you, my name is Vidar, this is my wife Aveline, and my son and daughter, Einar and Æsa." Vidar said in Ænglisc, nodding respectfully to Somerhild.

"You're Danes?" Somerhild asked.

"We are."

"You're thirsty, hungry?"

"Yes, we are." Vidar smiled.

"Saewyn, fetch the mead."

It took all the power I had to not to shout at Vidar and Guthlac. I didn't want introductions to Guthlac's family, I didn't want all the niceties of food and mead. For the last twenty years I had lived under the knowledge that all of my Anglo-Saxon family was dead – hearing one of my brothers was alive … My world was upside down. I needed answers, I needed to know where Beric was, I needed to find him. But I waited, trying to calm myself down while Vidar and Guthlac observed all of the stages of politeness and hospitality, my body trembling and my mind spinning.

"Aveline." Vidar said, nudging me.

I snapped out of my daze and looked up. Saewyn, ten years old from the looks of her, stood in front of me smiling meekly and offering me a tankard of sweet mead. I took it, mustering as warm a smile as I could, but from Saewyn's expression I think I must've failed, for her smile faltered and her dark brown eyes grew wider. She scurried off to her mother's side the moment the mead was in my hands, eyeing me nervously.

"Your daughter speaks fine Ænglisc for a Dane." Somerhild commented. "Your son is so young, but he knows a lot of the language already too."

"Aveline has been teaching them all since they were born." Vidar smiled. "Their accents are heavy, but their words are clear enough."

"Aveline is Beric's younger sister." Guthlac explained, touching his wife's arm, and she nodded slowly, her mouth forming a small 'o'.

"Tell me about Beric." My voice shuddered with emotion. I cleared my throat, speaking somewhat more steadily. "Tell me everything, Guthlac. What happened?"

Guthlac sighed, taking a few deep gulps of his ale. He was sitting on a chair across the fire from Vidar and I, his wife and daughter sitting beside him. On the other side of the room near straw beds, Æsa, Einar and Turstan were sitting on the rush-strewn floor playing with Turstan's collection of wooden toys.

"When the Danes attacked, Wisbece was in chaos, as you remember, I'm sure." Guthlac said to me softly. "Everyone was screaming, everyone was running. No one had any real weapons, but I saw men and boys seizing up farming tools and rushing towards the Danes as they came off their ships. I glimpsed the Danes with their swords and axes, I saw the old forks and scythe my older brothers and father had grabbed to fight with, and my stomach sank; I knew the Danes would defeat us. As did my mother, I believe … She grabbed me and thrust me out of the house, she told me to run towards the forest, to run as far as I could, to go to Grantanbrycg. There we would find men to help us, men with real fighting weapons … Lots of people ran for the safety of the forest, that's where we came across Bryni and Oswin and Beric."

"They'd been working with *fæder*." I whispered, snippets of the day's events trickling through my mind as Guthlac spoke. "I spent the day spinning with *modor*."

"Sibbald was already dead by that time, they said. He'd fought the Danes with your *fæder*." Guthlac said.

"*Fæder* was dead by then, too?" I asked, my eyes burning with emotion.

"I don't know. They said when they saw Sibbald get killed, they ran and didn't look back – they couldn't."

I nodded understandingly, swallowing hard to get rid of the lump in my throat, but to no avail.

RISE TO FALL

"We ran as fast as we could, but a group of Danes caught up with us. Dunstan and a few others from the village saw them chasing after the women and children and followed them. My mother tried to defend Bryni and Oswin – they were just too slow, the Danes cut them down so quickly ..." Guthlac cleared his throat, his voice thick with emotion. "Soon enough, it was just Beric and me left. Dunstan fought as hard as he could and kept the Danes occupied so Beric and I could flee ... We turned back only once, and watched Dunstan get stabbed through by a Dane, everyone else littering the forest floor, bleeding, dead ... Beric and I ran all the way to Grantanbrycg like my mother had told us to.

"We were so young, so scared ... We just ran and ran. Our feet were bleeding and had swollen twice the size, our shoes were in tatters. We didn't know anyone in Grantanbrycg, but we told everyone who would listen about the Danes attack. Somerhild's family took us in immediately, they protected us. I slept for a full day and my legs were stiff and ached for a week after we arrived in Grantanbrycg." Guthlac said, rubbing his eyes with the heels of his hands. "A few others managed to escape Wisbece as well, some adults, some children. When the Danes had left Wisbece and travelled further in land to Thetford, we went back in search of survivors, to bury the dead, salvage belongings from our ruined homes and the like, you know?

"When we got there, most of the villagers were lying in the dirt, dead, being picked at and devoured by seagulls and ravens and dogs. Between the lot of us who had escaped, we managed to identify almost all of the dead. We found your brothers, your parents, Kenrick's three sons and wife, Sigbert's wife and daughter. Most of the villagers had been killed, only a few women and children were missing ... Like you."

Guthlac's gaze rested heavily on me.

"What did you and Beric do next?" I managed to utter, a few fat tears rolling down my cheeks.

"We buried the dead then went back to Grantanbrycg. Beric and I had both seen fourteen summers, we found jobs and worked as much as we could. I worked hard to rebuild my home in Wisbece. Six years went by, I was living in Wisbece full-time at that point, trying to make some sort of life for myself. I married Somerhild, we had our eldest daughter Elfilda … Beric went to Lundenne to join one of King Alfred's *fyrds*." Guthlac shrugged. "I haven't seen him since Elfilda was wed two years ago. He visits Somerhild's family in Grantanbrycg every so often, he shares his stories, gives gifts, then he goes off wherever the *fyrd* takes him, he fights the Danes and the Norsemen. He married a woman in Lundenne and had a child or two, but I've never met them. Beric is a full-time soldier, he doesn't seem to set aside time for much else."

"What do you mean? What about farming or other work?" I asked. "How does he take care of his family?"

"There's always Danes to fight and someone who will pay you to fight them." Guthlac said, passing an apologetic smile to Vidar, who chuckled in response.

"Where is he now?" I asked.

"In the East Angles to be sure. There were a lot of riots here last year, an army of Danes broke the peace established between them and King Alfred. He sent an army to quell the fighting. Beric was with them, they passed through Grantanbrycg and he was able to stop by at Somerhild's parents farm briefly, but that was it." Guthlac explained.

"Is there a chance he'd be in Grantanbrycg now?" I asked hopefully.

"No." Guthlac shook his head. "Guthrum, the Dane who rules the East Angles now, lives in Grantanbrycg and surprisingly he and his Danes had nothing to do with the uprising. Last I heard, Bryni was going to Gipeswic. There's a large community of Danes there, there were a lot of riots and fighting there. I don't know if he's still there, but he might be."

"Vidar." I turned to my husband, my eyes blazing with resolve.

"Tomorrow, little fawn." Vidar answered. "Let the men rest, let the children rest. We will set off at daybreak tomorrow."

***

I COULDN'T SLEEP that night. Tossing and turning on the old straw bed the Danish family had provided Vidar, our children and me, I couldn't sleep. We had spent some time with Guthlac and his family before taking them to the Danish house to meet Young Birger and Sander. Æsa and Einar were not fond of getting back into Storm-Serpent so soon after setting foot on land, but all of our crew had happily agreed to set sail once more in the morning. Gipeswic was a huge town about half a day's voyage from Wisbece; there would be alehouses for our people to sleep in, there would be things for all to do and see. Wisbece had grown, but it was still a simple village, Gipeswic was a town on the scale of Ribe, large and bustling.

We had been in Wisbece for just a day, and already I had been shocked to the core multiple times. Of all of the surprises, one realisation I had was that, though the Danes were still attempting to conquer the entirety of Britain, there was no shudder of fear that shook the Wisbece villagers at the arrival of our fearsome *dreki* ship. Even with the recent violence over the past year, the villagers did not flee, they did not throw themselves to their knees and beg protection from God, they did not lock their doors and quail in fear until the Danes had passed through. No. The townspeople eyed us severely but continued their daily life. We had not drawn weapons; we had come in a single ship. Danes owned these lands now, and the Anglo-Saxons could do nothing.

I sighed deeply.

So much had changed. Twenty years was a long time, and the world was so different now …

The noise of a rooster crowing somewhere outside filtered into the house. The pale morning light crept in from the smokehole above the firepit in the centre of Guthlac and Somerhild's house, slowly eating away at the darkness and shadow. We would be getting up soon and loading the ship. By the late afternoon, we would make it to Gipeswic, where I might find my brother – my brother I'd thought dead for the last two decades. Would he recognise me? Would I recognise him?

I thought of Beric, tried to remember what he had looked like. He had been taller than me – but all of my brothers had been – he had been skinny, incredibly skinny. I remembered he had pale skin like me, the amber eyes and dark chestnut hair we had inherited from our mother. Our father had had dark brown eyes and mud coloured hair, but he had been pale too ... I had our mother's heart-shaped face, but I believe Beric had our father's long one. Yes, and Beric had a long thin nose like our father, too!

Beric was five years older than me – he was fourteen when the Danes attacked. He'd be turning thirty-five this coming winter, whereas I would turn thirty in the autumn. I tried to imagine what Beric would look like now, with twenty years of age added to the faded memory of his former twelve-year-old self, but I managed to conjure only a slightly different image of my father. Would there be lines of age etched over Beric's face?

"What's the matter, little fawn?" Vidar whispered, shifting closer to be in the bed, the straw mattress rustling beneath us.

"Am I wrinkled?" I asked, touching the skin beside my eyes with my fingertips.

"You're as youthful as the day I married you." Vidar said, taking my hand and kissing it softly. "You've no lines on your face – only one or two around your eyes when you grin or laugh. But they only appear you're truly happy. I can always tell a fake smile from a real one, because when you pretend to be happy the lines don't appear, but when you're happy, *truly happy*, without any cares in the world happy, your smile touches your eyes."

"You pay a lot of attention to me, don't you?" I beamed, rolling onto my side to face him, wrapping a leg over him.

"Of course, I do. I haven't been able to think of anything but you since the day we met in the woodshed." Vidar winked.

The grey spring morning light did nothing to diminish the beauty of Vidar's eyes. Gleaming cerulean and silver, they sparkled as he gazed at me so lovingly. I leaned forward and kissed him, his lips warm and soft. We embraced each other as completely as we could, our bodies tangled together beneath the fur blankets, pressed together tightly, kissing each other over and over.

"I love you." I whispered.

"I love you, too, little fawn." Vidar murmured between kisses.

***

RISE TO FALL

GIPESWIC, THE KINGDOM OF GUTHRUM

MUCH TO ÆSA and Einar's chagrin (and a few other children's as well), we boarded Storm-Serpent straight after the morning meal. As our crew and passengers boarded Storm-Serpent, I stood on the bank with Æsa, bidding farewell to Guthlac, Somerhild, Turstan and Saewyn. From the corner of my eye, I watched Æsa say goodbye to Turstan, hugging him before planting a quick kiss on the seven-year-old boy's cheek. I giggled, watching his pale cheeks turn crimson, before Æsa dashed onto the ship where Vidar was already with our sons, her cheeks scarlet.

"Good luck finding Beric." Guthlac said as we embraced. "If he comes through here, I'll be sure to send him your way. We'll be travelling to Grantanbrycg later, I'll leave a message with Somerhild's parents to tell Beric if and when they see him."

"*Ic þancie þē*, Guthlac. I appreciate it." I said earnestly. "It was lovely meeting you and your family. Before we voyage back to Aros, we will stop in and see you."

"I'd like that." Guthlac beamed. "When you next go to Viborg, stop in and see my daughter and grandson for me, would you? Kiss them for me and give them our love."

"I will." I promised.

It took us half a day to reach Gipeswic, thankfully the seas were calm, and the wind blew briskly in the direction we headed – we had garnered the blessings of Njörðr and Ægir it seemed. Einar didn't vomit as much as he had before, thankfully, perhaps he was getting used to the sway of the ship? We sailed on the North Sea, around the outer edge of the East Angles (or rather the *Kingdom of Guthrum*. It was surprisingly hard for me to refer to my old homelands by its new name), before rowing up the River Orwell and mooring on the dock of Gipeswic quay.

"Stay with *faðir* and me, okay?" I said sternly to the children before we disembarked from Storm-Serpent – particularly to Sander. "If you disappear here, we will never be able to find you again."

"Perhaps we should tie a rope around Sander's middle?" Vidar suggested quietly in my ear.

We were both watching Sander, who wasn't paying attention to us at all. He was gazing longingly at the massive town, the temptation to explore splashed plainly across his face. I giggled and grinned at my husband. I couldn't blame Sander too much, I was just as eager to explore Gipeswic.

"Where would you like to go first?" Jan asked cheerfully, clapping a hand on Vidar's back and grinning as he surveyed the huge town before us.

"First we find an inn, preferably near the marketplace." Vidar said. "We'll buy rooms for the next few nights and we'll stable the horses. We'll stay in Gipeswic for two weeks, then we'll set off back for Aros."

We rowed the ship into the harbour beside a dock where we met the dockmaster. We paid him handsomely to moor Storm-Serpent safely in Gipeswic for the next fourteen days – far too handsomely in my opinion, but we were forced to pay the substantial fee whether we liked it or not, and he was not open to haggling whatsoever. The harbour was buzzing with activity, fishermen and their boats filled rowed in and out of the harbour, alongside massive merchant ships, where men were ceaselessly unloading their packed ships or packing them away with their new merchandise to take to other towns and countries.

Our gangplank lowered onto the dock, Vidar and Jan disembarked, each holding a sack in their hands. As our crew and passengers got off, the elegant Storm-Serpent jolting with every footstep, Vidar and Jan handed a small purse of silver to each adult, much to their surprise and pleasure – money to pay for food and shelter during the stay. Vidar was a generous Jarl who shared his riches happily – garnering him a vast number of loyal followers and retainers. In two weeks, we would all meet in the marketplace and return home to Aros.

Gipeswic was massive, equal to, if not possibly larger than Ribe. Ramparts surrounded and protected it and the streets were laid out in a grid pattern, positioned around the marketplace where a chapel was situated. In the centre of the town, large, rectangular timber buildings lined the street edge, with small yards where people were crafting – bone- and antler-working, weaving, metalsmithing, we even saw some people potting, spotting the kiln they used to cook their wares.

At least a thousand people filled the town, maybe even more. The buildings were tall and crammed together tightly in their uniformed rows. Most of the buildings were sunken-featured like Guthlac's house, and a lot in the centre of the town were even two-storied. Some of the streets and skinny alleys between shops reeked of piss or animal shit. There were many alehouses and inns in the town, but we would have to find out which ones were safe for Danes; in large towns where inns and alehouses were plentiful, most held some sort of political sway. We as Danes would not want to find ourselves entering a vehemently anti-Dane establishment for our own safety.

In the marketplace the delectable scent of cooked fish and food from the market stands and shops filled the streets, overpowering the obscene smells drifting from the alleyways. The marketplace was heaving with people, with shops offering absolutely everything you could imagine, including a massive platform selling slaves dressed in tattered rags with iron collars around their necks.

"Stay close." I reminded Sander, gripping the back of his tunic.

It didn't take long for us to find a suitable inn, beside which was an alehouse that seemed to serve Danes and Norsemen exclusively. Ironically, both buildings were opposite the Christian chapel.

The inn had two levels, the ground level resembling a Jarl's hall. There was a large rectangular fireplace with a low-burning fire in the centre of the room, with benches and tables scattered about, a lot of three-legged stools and a few high-backed chairs here and there. Rushes were strewn across the dirt floor. On one end of the rectangular room was a kitchen area, shelves lining the walls filled with vegetables, wooden cups and tankards, barrels presumably filled with mead, salted meats or oats for simple meals.

On the other end of the room was a huge set of stairs that led to the upper level. The ceiling was high but there was no smokehole, causing the entire inn to be smoky, dry and stiflingly warm, even with a low fire. Vidar paid the tall, skinny Danish innkeeper a few ounces of silver to purchase our rooms. The innkeeper ordered two thralls to carry our trunks upstairs, and we followed close behind.

Upstairs the floor was made up of worn, scrubbed wooden planks, which were unnervingly pliant beneath our feet. The stairs opened up to a narrow hallway with archways along each side that led to a few open rooms filled with beds with trunks at the foot of each occupied bed, much like the dormitories we'd seen in monasteries. At the very end, the hallway opened up into a skinny rectangular strip with three doors belonging to private rooms. Vidar had paid for all three rooms, offering us privacy during our stay.

Sander, Einar, Æsa, Vidar and I would share one room, Young Birger, Domnall, his wife Guðrin and their son Yngvi would share another and the third room would be used by Jan, Einarr, Lars and Hallmundr. Each room had four straw beds squashed together inside with just enough room for four beds and a skinny path between each bed to the door. Privately I wondered how well Jan and Hallmundr would do sharing such proximity with one another – for the most part, they were good friends, but they bickered when together for too long.

Guðrin and I took the children downstairs and left the men to unpack, already it was sweltering in those cramped little rooms, the rooms were poorly ventilated, and the air was so thick with smoke, sweat and the odour of the previous occupants of the room, I already couldn't stand it in there. I smiled privately to myself, I suppose Vidar had spoiled me with our huge, spacious hall … I found myself missing Aros, missing Denmark. Vidar was right, I hadn't referred to Aros as home before, but now I had been away for a year, I found my heart yearning for it.

I would find Beric.

I would meet my brother again.

Then I would go home – home to Aros

"Ready to explore?" Vidar asked, perspiration dotting his brow.

"*Já*," I said, looking at him quizzically. "What happened to you?"

"I rearranged the room a little. We now have a large bed on one side of the room for you and me to share, and the two singles on the other side of the room for the children." Vidar grinned. "I'm not sleeping in a bed without you in it, and now we have space to do … Other things together, too."

I rolled my eyes and laughed at him.

"Come on then, let's explore." I beamed.

***

WE HAD BEEN in Gipeswic for a week already, and still there was no sign or word of Beric. Vidar, Jan, Domnall, Hallmundr, Lars and Einarr, with Yngvi, Young Birger and Sander on their heels, frequented the alehouses and spoke to Danes, Norsemen and Anglo-Saxons alike. They questioned merchants in the marketplace, quizzed fishermen on the docks, but none could tell them any information about an Anglo-Saxon soldier named Beric Eadricing. Guðrin and I took Æsa and Einar through the farms beyond Gipeswic town, knocking on door after door and begging for information from all those who would listen to us. I was beginning to lose hope already.

"If I have to share a room with you for one more night, so help me, Odin–" Hallmundr thundered.

"You'll do what?" Jan scoffed.

"I'll beat your pretty face in!" Hallmundr roared, slamming his mead on the tabletop.

"Jealous, are you?" Jan smirked.

"What's going on with you two now?" Vidar asked wearily, slipping into the chair next to me and resting his hand on my lap, squeezing my thigh for a moment.

"Jötunnson keeps bringing his whores into the room, making noise throughout the night!" Hallmundr fumed.

"We've offered for you to join in." Jan said, winking at me.

I hid my smile behind my hand, staring at the tabletop and trying my hardest not to laugh.

"I wouldn't share a woman with you for a thousand pounds of silver!" Hallmundr spat.

"More for me, then." Jan grinned. "Anyway, I'm surprised you can hear us considering how loud you snore – Lars can attest to that, can't you?" Jan pointed at Lars. "He's sleeping in the hall with the other bastards thanks to your noise! You're like a bear grunting and farting away all night long."

Hallmundr rose so quickly from his chair, he sent it flying across the alehouse. Immediately Jan laughed, infuriating Hallmundr further.

"That's enough you two, you're worse than my children." Vidar chided.

"*Já*, calm yourself, Hall! Remember when you told me bedding a woman would relieve my frustration and calm me down? Maybe you should heed your own advice – it worked for me."

"You're the most insolent, irritating–"

"Alright children, time for bed." I said, standing up and herding my children together.

With a collective gasp of disappointment, my four children rose from their chairs. They had been excitedly watching Hallmundr and Jan argue, deciding between themselves which man might strike the other first.

"I'll come with you." Guðrin said, rolling her eyes at Hallmundr and Jan.

Together, Guðrin and I, with our five collective children in tow, left the alehouse, the crashing sound of furniture colliding with the wall sounding the moment we reached the inn door.

"Who did it? Who started the fight?" Sander gasped, spinning around and lunging towards the alehouse.

Unfortunately for him, I caught him around the middle before he could get anywhere.

"We will find out tomorrow. Come on – bed! We have a long day tomorrow."

"I don't want to go to bed! And I don't want to run around this town anymore. We're not going to find your brother; we're wasting our time!" Sander grumbled.

I released him. He stumbled forward and glared at me angrily.

"Go to bed." I said, my voice dangerously low.

Sander's eye widened, but he maintained his stubborn glare, shoved the inn door open and stomped away. Young Birger glanced between Sander and I, scooped up Einar and took him and Æsa into the inn, Yngvi leaving with him.

"Aveline," Guðrin said sympathetically. "He didn't mean to hurt you, he's just—"

"He's right." I whispered. "If Beric was here, we would have found him by now ... Sander's right."

Guðrin took my hands and squeezed them. She opened her mouth to say something, but I interrupted her; I didn't want to talk about any of this at that moment.

"Could you put the children to bed? I need to go for a walk, clear my head." I swallowed hard and pulled my hands from hers.

"*Já*, I'll get them to sleep." Guðrin nodded. "Take your time, Jarlkona."

I whispered my thanks to her, and she offered me another sympathetic smile before hurrying into the inn after the children. I breathed in the cool night air, listening to the cheers, laughter and the crash of furniture erupting from the alehouse next door; it seemed Jan and Hallmundr had not yet settled their differences. I shook my head and began walking towards the harbour; I needed quiet, away from the idiots fighting in the alehouse. Jan and Hallmundr's was a foolish argument fuelled by one too many meads; they would beat each other bloody and insult one another all night, then wake up aching and laughing together in the morning. They were entertainment for all those in the alehouse, there would be betting on who would win the fight, drinks would be poured in abundance, and all the while Vidar would stay there until either the fight ended or if Hallmundr and Jan took it too far and force Vidar to intervene.

This was a usual thing for Danish men. Danes loved to fight. When they weren't attacking the Franks or the Anglo-Saxons or whoever else, they were attacking each other. A show of skill and brawn, and an amusing way to pass the time, which is why Sander wanted to stay.

He'd said those things to me in anger, he hadn't meant them. And yet ... He was right. We only had seven days left before we planned to leave, seven days until we would gather together with the rest of our people in the marketplace and board Storm-Serpent and voyage back to Aros.

I wasn't ready, I didn't want to go back, knowing Beric was in the East Angles and I hadn't seen him. I didn't want to spend another twenty years away from Britain, especially knowing now he was still alive – he was still out there ... Just to meet Beric, just to speak with him and tell him I'm alive, to introduce him to my children and perhaps meet his ... That's what I wanted.

My children would have an uncle, an aunt, they would have cousins! They didn't have that in Denmark, their blood family comprised Alvar and Freydis when they were alive, Vidar and me and their siblings. Vidar had had a brother named Einar, but he had died years ago, when he and Vidar were just children, long before I arrived in Denmark. Einar Alvarsson had been a boy, not old enough to wed or have children, and Alvar and Freydis hadn't had another child after Vidar.

I wondered how quiet their hall must have been with just Alvar, Freydis, Einar and Vidar living in it? Even then, when Vidar saw his eighth winter, he had been fostered to Jan's parents, before Jan was born, as was customary for a Jarl's family to do for families with only one or no children in Denmark. That great hall had homed just three people for many years. So big, so empty, so quiet.

My home had been noisy ... It had been loud and cramped with my parents, four of my brothers and I stuffed inside the little, one-roomed home, but we were happy for the most part. I didn't remember ever living with my older three brothers, they all had their own homes and wives and children. My eldest brother Kenrick's three sons were all just a few years younger than me, so I played with them often, in their home and in mine. I never felt alone in the Kingdom of the East Angles.

I sighed again and stopped beside a few crates abandoned in the harbour by some merchant. I gazed out at the waters and found Storm-Serpent through the darkness, drydocked on the edge of the river, the rippling reflections of the silver moon and stars dancing on the water beside it.

My eyes followed the smooth curve of the prow, an elegant neck for her fearsome and intricately carved serpent-head. But the serpent-head wasn't there at that moment, we had removed it and hidden it away on the ship when we had neared Gipeswic, so as not to be mistaken for raiders. When we had removed her serpent-head, we had taken away the fierceness from her, but she had not lost her beauty. Shrouded in shadow and bobbing on the waters as though she rested upon the chest of a sleeping beast, gently rising and falling in a soothing rhythm, Storm-Serpent was graceful and magnificent.

I understood why Sander was angry, why he was sick of searching through Gipeswic for a man he'd never met. Though my children didn't have cousins or uncles in Aros, they still had each other, they still had family, they still had noise, they had plenty of friends, and they had the whole town of Aros who looked out for them – they even had the people of Roskilde looking out for them when we visited Alvar.

Now Alvar was gone and Roskilde was Vidar's. I hadn't stopped to think about it, but we'd be travelling back and forth to Roskilde a lot more frequently now Vidar was Jarl of both towns. In seven years, Young Birger would be old enough to take charge of Roskilde, just as Alvar and Vidar intended, just as they had trained him, and one day Aros would belong to Sander.

The children had so much in Denmark. So, did I. While Denmark was my home, while I appreciated my life there, while I wouldn't want anything to change, I couldn't shake the overwhelming yearning to see Beric, to find him, and I knew I wouldn't be able to focus on anything else until I'd found him.

I'd been uneasy with coming back to Wisbece, in case I would wake the ghosts of the past, when it was better to let them lie ... And that was exactly what I'd done. Maybe it would have been better to carry on living under the idea that Beric was dead. It had taken me so long to come to terms with my family's deaths, knowing Beric was alive somewhere out there, far out of my reach ... It tormented me. Chances were I'd probably never find him. I should've let the ghosts of the past rest.

"*Gōdne ǣfen.*"

"Oh! *Gōdne ǣfen.*" I exclaimed, clapping my hand to my heart.

"I didn't mean to scare you, *sārig.*" The man said, rubbing the back of his head and smiling apologetically at me.

"It's alright." I said, though my heart was still racing in my chest. "L-lovely night for a walk, isn't it?" I added awkwardly.

"It is indeed." The man agreed. "Although, it's not safe at night for a woman to be walking unaccompanied at night – this town is rife with those Scandinavian heathens."

"I'm sure I'll be fine." I smiled as warmly as I could.

"You're not from Gipeswic, are you?" The man asked.

"No, I'm just visiting with my husband and children." I said.

"Your husband allowed you to walk alone in the night, in a foreign town to boot?" He gasped disapprovingly.

"I assure you, I'm perfectly safe." I said firmly. "I came out to clear my head and I've not been bothered by a single *heathen*."

"*So far.*" The man said, raising his thick eyebrows. "You can't trust them. Even the ones who claim they are Christian – they're liars and violent monsters, the lot of them. Indeed, on my way here I heard yet another brawl in one of their alehouses! And the heathens were cheering the violence! They're beasts, they're dogs!"

"*Nevertheless*, I'm fine." I said glaring at him. "My family and I have been here for a week and we've had no problems with them."

He stared at me for a moment, his mouth opened slightly, as though he was ready to argue further with me. Instead, he shrugged his shoulders and sighed, ceding to my stubbornness. He turned and looked over the inky waters stretched out before us, his gaze resting on the ships.

"Beautiful ship, isn't it?" I commented, admiring Storm-Serpent.

"It's a Danish ship." He said flatly.

"It's still beautiful, is it not?"

"I can't admire anything made by a filthy Dane." He said, scowling at the ship.

"It's a ship." I rolled my eyes. "Can you not just admire the craftmanship, regardless of who made it?"

"Many years ago," He mumbled, his eyes locked on Storm-Serpent. "When I was not yet a man, the Danes attacked England. My family was killed before my eyes and I was taken to their land as a slave."

I stared at him and frowned.

"I managed to escape." He continued. "I stole a fishing boat and rowed away from the Danish lands, but the boat was unsuited for voyages. The sea swept me away and wrecked my boat on the shores of Francia. I worked hard there until I had earned enough money to buy passage back to Britain.

"Living with the Danes ... I've seen the monstrous things they are capable of in battle *and* in their daily lives. They are vicious creatures, no different to dogs or wolves. When they're not attacking or raiding other countries, they're ripping themselves apart. If you had seen what I have, you wouldn't be out here alone in the dark – you would fear them and pray to God to smite them down and rid our country of them."

I rolled my lips together and crossed my arms over my chest.

"You have my sympathies for what you suffered." I said slowly. "I didn't realise you'd had a such a horrendous personal experience with them – I simply thought the ship was pretty."

He sighed.

"I apologise – of course you didn't know." He rubbed his smooth jaw with his hand, his mouth twisted into an embarrassed frown.

"I understand. The Danes killed my family, too, when I was a child." I said softly. His eyes widened but before he could say anything, I continued. "It is late though; I'm going to return to the inn."

"May I escort you back? I wouldn't forgive myself if I let a young woman walk alone in the night."

"Of course, yes." I smiled. *"Ic pancie þē."*

"My name is Theodric." He said as we turned our backs on the harbour.

"Nice to meet you." I smiled. "My name is Aveline."

We ambled up towards the marketplace. While we chatted as we walked, I studied the stranger, Theodric. He was tall and thin, his thick brown hair was parted neatly down the middle and cut to collar-length. Theodric's face was cleanly shaven, and his cheekbones protruded sharply. Lines of time were etched deeply around his tired light brown eyes and his wide mouth, and as we neared the firelight of the marketplace, I spotted silvery scars here and there on his face. To hazard a guess, I assumed he must have been at least Vidar's age, possibly a year or two younger.

"So, are you from Gipeswic?" I asked.

"No, I'm from Wiltun." He said. "Thankfully the heathens haven't clawed their way into Wessex yet."

"What are you doing in Gipeswic? You don't sound as though you like it here much."

"I'm stationed here with King Alfred's *fyrd*." Theodric explained. "Since the Danish uprising last year, King Alfred thought it wise to station *fyrds* around all the large, Dane infested towns, to keep an eye on them."

"Oh yes, very wise." I said hurriedly. "You're in a *fyrd*, you said? By any chance do you know a man name Beric?"

"Beric?" He repeated, pondering carefully for a moment.

"Beric Eadricing." I said. "He's my brother; he's a soldier, too. I haven't seen him for a few years and … I just want to make sure he's alright."

"What does he look like?"

"He has a long, pale face and a long, thin nose – he has chestnut coloured hair like mine, and amber eyes like mine, too." I explained hopefully.

We paused in the marketplace, the glow of the fish oil lamps burning outside of the inn and alehouse doors lighting us in their orange glow. Theodric examined me, scrutinising my face, his brows knitted, frowning slightly. I stood still and hopeful; this stranger presented a real chance of me finally finding my brother.

"Now I see you in the light, you seem very familiar to me." Theodric said, tilting his head as he continued to study me. "Maybe I have seen your brother, but I don't recognise his name, unfortunately."

"He's from Wisbece originally, but he moved to Grantacester when he was fourteen. He has a wife and family in Lundenne." I offered the stranger as much information as I could to help jog his memory. "I was told by a close friend of his that he was in Gipeswic … I haven't seen him in so long."

"Are you staying in Gipeswic for much longer?"

"Only a week more."

"I will do everything in my power to find your brother." Theodric vowed. "Which inn are you staying in? I'll bring you news as soon as I am able."

"That one." I said, pointing at the inn.

"That's a Danish inn!" Theodric exclaimed.

"I have a private room." I said.

"Take my advice, with your husband or not, the Danes *will* attack you – they're dogs! I urge you, please find a *safer* place to stay."

"I appreciate your concern, I really do." I said firmly, attempting to stay calm. "But I have paid to stay here, and I will remain here until I leave Gipeswic."

Theodric surveyed me for a moment before he released a deep sigh and ceded.

"Very well. I shall ask around and see if I can find your brother, and I'll arrange for a heavier watch around this area for the next week, for your protection." He said.

"That's kind of you." I smiled. "I look forward to hearing from you."

"Is there a message you'd like me to relay to Beric, should I find him?" Theodric asked.

"Tell him I am alive and well, and that I'm looking for him."

CHAPTER THIRTY-ONE

IT WAS THE thirteenth day of our stay in Gipeswic. Tomorrow we would pack up our things, load onto Storm-Serpent and set sail. I hadn't heard from Theodric at all over the last six days. Every morning I would dash down the stairs and ask the innkeeper if there was a message left for me, and each day the innkeeper would shake his head and express his sympathies. There was a heavier presence of soldiers parading about the marketplace, just as Theodric had promised, but I hadn't seen him again since.

"He must be searching for your brother." Guðrin offered positively one morning, seeing the look of devastation on my face. "Perhaps Beric's not in Gipeswic anymore and it's taking longer to find him?"

"Perhaps." I replied glumly. "Or perhaps he hasn't found him at all?"

"Why don't we ask around ourselves?" Vidar offered, squeezing my hand. "Will you watch the children, Guðrin?"

"Of course." She smiled.

As we ate our morning meal, we planned out our final day in Gipeswic. Jan was going to peruse the alehouses with Lars and Einarr for a final time, (and bid farewell to one of the alehouse owner's daughter whom Jan had become rather friendly with over the past week), while Domnall and Hallmundr were going to ready Storm-Serpent – get her onto the water and load her – and would take Yngvi, Young Birger and Sander with them. Guðrin intended to stay in the inn for the morning with Einarr and Æsa and pack up all our belongings, after which she planned on visiting the marketplace and purchase the supplies we needed for our voyage home. Vidar and I planned to interrogate every *fyrd* soldier we met for information on Beric or, at the very least, Theodric. By noon, we would all meet at the alehouse for a light afternoon meal and discuss what further should be done, for at first morning light we would voyage back to Aros.

Vidar and I had been marching the streets of Gipeswic for an hour, attempting to converse with the *fyrd* soldiers we came across, but no matter how sweetly, politely or respectfully we approached them, they would eye Vidar and I sourly and order us to move on, or they would just walk away, their hands clenched tighter around their spears and their noses wrinkled in disgust.

"Excuse me, please, sir." I said, scurrying after a soldier ahead of me, dressed in a red tunic with a gold wyvern embroidered on both the back and front – he was a soldier of Wessex.

Wessex's standard was a golden wyvern on a field of red. The Kingdom of the East Angles standard was three golden crowns on a field of blue. Mercia was represented by a blue field with a gold 'X' across it – the flag of Saint Alban, the first saint of Britain, and Northumbria's flag was simply four gold and four red stripes alternating vertically. Sussex's standard consisted of six golden martlets upon a field of blue, and Kent was represented by a red field with a white horse rearing in the centre. The final kingdom of the heptarchy of Britain, Essex, was represented by a red standard upon which three seaxes were lying horizontally across.

Now, most members of King Alfred's *fyrd* were poor farmers who were not equipped with weapons let alone uniforms. Only the wealthy thegns and noblemen had swords and lances and gorgeously fashioned uniforms, but the few full-time soldiers in the *fyrd*, those who dedicated their lives to fighting for King Alfred rather than spending six months of the year in service and the other six months tending farm or labouring elsewhere, were afforded the handsome uniforms as well.

I could not tell which men Vidar and I had attempted to speak to were thegns or full-time soldiers, for they refused to speak with us, other than barking at us to be gone. Regardless, they were members of the *fyrd* and they were the only men who could tell me Beric or Theodric's whereabouts.

"Sir! Excuse me!" I cried out, louder this time.

Finally, the soldier stopped in his tracks and turned to me.

"May I help you?" The soldier said politely as he turned to face me.

"Please, if you would." I beamed. He was the first of the *fyrd* men we'd approached who had actually stopped and spoken to us. "I'm looking for my brother – he's called Beric Eadricing. He's a full-time soldier in King Alfred's *fyrd*, from Wisbece originally, but I heard he's stationed here for now. Please, have you seen him?"

The Anglo-Saxon soldier ran his hand through his collar-length brown hair and thought for a moment. Hope rose inside me, my heartbeat quickened, and I held my breath, my hands clasped together against my chest as though I were praying.

"I've not heard of a Beric Eadricing, I'm afraid." He said, offering me an apologetic smile. "He looks like you – same eyes, same hair?"

"Yes, he has an oval face, though." I replied.

"I'll ask around and see if anyone has heard of him." The soldier said warmly. "I'm sure he won't be hard to find – I've never seen anyone with such striking eyes as yours. If he has them too, I'm sure we'll track him down quickly."

"I appreciate that." I said. "I haven't seen him for many years, I miss him. Please, tell him his sister, Aveline, is looking for him."

"I will." He promised. "May I help you with anything else?"

"Oh! Do you know a man named Theodric? He's a bit taller than me, dark hair, swarthy. He's in the *fyrd* as well."

"I wish I could help you, I really do." He said. "I don't know a man by that name or description either."

"Oh." I sighed deeply. "Well, thank you for your troubles, anyway."

"I wish I could've been more help." The soldier said sincerely. "Good day to you."

"And you." I nodded, watching sadly as the soldier turned and walked away. "At least he spoke to me, I suppose." I commented, turning around to face Vidar.

Except, Vidar wasn't there. I glanced around, alarmed, hastily examining the crowds bustling around me for Vidar.

"I'm here, little fawn." Vidar said from behind me, causing me to leap out of my skin.

"Where in Hel's hall were you hiding?" I exclaimed, whipping around and glaring at him.

"In the crowd." Vidar smirked. "I was testing a theory."

"A theory?" I repeated blankly.

"*Já.*" Vidar nodded. "The soldiers despise the Danes. Every time we approached, they'd take one look at me and tell me to leave. I thought I'd see if they'd talk to you if you were alone – and, by Odin's eye, they did."

Vidar grinned victoriously at me.

I scowled at him.

"It would have been nice if you'd told me of your plan." I said stiffly.

"I didn't think of it until you hailed him." Vidar said, tilting his head back in the soldier's direction. "It seems we're getting nowhere because of me."

I rolled my lips together and studied my husband. It was the end of spring, the sun shone golden in the sky, bathing us in its delicious warmth, and because of this delightful weather we'd no need to wear cloaks – Vidar was dressed in a sky-blue, short-sleeved tunic, hemmed with a thick band of silver silk, the blue-black Norse tattoos etched into his arms clearly visible. His beard was thick and neatly trimmed and his golden blond hair was tied back with a leather thong, the sides and back of his head shaven to the scalp, presenting the tattoos on his head for all to see, as well. He wore a few silver chains around his neck, and silver arm bands decorated his wrists. Black, straight-legged trousers covered Vidar's legs, and he wore his shining black leather boots and a black leather belt around his waist, hung from which were a few pouches, his utility knife and his sword in its sheath.

Yes, Vidar was obviously a Dane, and a rich one at that, vastly different to the Anglo-Saxons in fashion and appearance. The Anglo-Saxons were smaller in height, Vidar was tall and strapping. The Anglo-Saxons were cleanly shaven, with their hair no longer than their collar, Vidar's was gorgeously long and thick, flowing loose from the leather thong, a few of stray tendrils dancing on the gentle breeze when it blew every now and again.

By the gods, Vidar was so handsome ...

I rested my hands on his chest, smiling up at him. He grinned down on me, gripped my hips and drew me against him, wrapping his arms about me and kissing me softly.

"I hate to admit it, but I think you're right." I said. "Perhaps I should search alone?"

"*Nei*, I'll come with you, but when you approach a soldier, I'll get out of sight." Vidar smiled. "We'll do this together."

***

VIDAR AND I had been traipsing around Gipeswic for hours with no luck whatsoever. Though I was able to converse with the soldiers when Vidar was hidden away in the crowd, none knew Beric or Theodric. Was Beric really stationed in Gipeswic? Surely at least one of the soldiers should know him if he was? And what of Theodric – surely someone would recognise his name and description as well, if he was stationed here?

It was almost noon, we had perhaps half an hour before we were due to meet with Guðrin and the others. We would have to give up the search soon … My heart sunk deep in my chest and my eyes grew hot with tears. I didn't want to give up, not when I was so close, and yet the more we searched, the further away I felt.

Vidar and I were walking along the shore of the river, our hands entwined. The noise of the marketplace hustle and bustle was replaced by the gentle whisper of the river and the grass of the bank crunching softly beneath our boots. We hadn't spoken for a while, we just ambled along the edge of the river, lost in our own thoughts.

"Can we stay?" I asked abruptly. "Just for a few days longer?"

"Stay?" Vidar said, his golden brows knitted together. "Little fawn, we've been away from home for almost a *year*. We need to go back – I need to make my presence known in Roskilde, as well, now that my *faðir* is …" His voice trailed off.

"I know, I don't want to stay for *much* longer." I pressed. "Just a few more days – I'm sure Theodric will be back soon with news on Beric. I just need to wait a few more days … Please?"

RISE TO FALL

A deep sigh cascaded from Vidar's lips. He stopped and chewed on his bottom lip silently, his hand tightening around mine.

"Little fawn," Vidar said softly. "If Theodric had news, he would have returned by now and reached out to you."

"What are you saying?" I whispered.

"I'm sorry, my heart, we can't stay any longer." Vidar said sympathetically. "I like Gipeswic, I really do, but there's so much we have to do in Denmark – we rule two towns now, we–"

"Vidar, please?" I interrupted; my eyes glossed so heavily with tears that my vision was hazy. "This hasn't anything to do with whether Gipeswic is a nice city or not, it's to do with finding my brother. *Please*, I beg of you! Let us stay for just a few more days!"

"We can't, little fawn, I'm sorry." He whispered.

I gazed at him pleadingly, a knot formed in my throat, my eyes burning with sadness, but he shook his head slowly; we couldn't stay any longer ... My bottom lip quivered, and a tear slipped down my cheek. Vidar sighed at the sight of it, his icy eyes following the tear as it slid down my face. He took my jaw in his hand and wiped the tear away with his thumb.

I pulled away from Vidar, ripped my hand from his and turned my back on him, stomping a few paces away, my hands curled into fists at my sides. I breathed in deeply, my shuddering breath hissing through my clenched teeth, anger boiling in the pit of my stomach. My whole body trembled as my anger swelled into rage, burning through my entire body like fire.

Vidar's footsteps crunched in the grass as he neared me.

"Leave without me." I spat.

"*What?*" Vidar exclaimed.

I whipped around and glared at him.

"*Leave without me.*"

Our eyes locked unblinkingly, my body trembling with fury, Vidar's face blank with confusion.

"You know that's not going to happen." Vidar said, narrowing his eyes. "Why in all of Miðgarðr would you even suggest that?"

"This is my only chance to meet my brother." I growled. "I can't give up this opportunity!"

"And what of your duties in Denmark?" He asked. "You're Jarlkona of Aros *and* Roskilde now – you owe it to your people to return as soon as possible."

"I owe it to myself to meet my brother." I retorted. "I have spent the last twenty years under the impression that my whole family was dead. To find out Beric is alive ... I *have* to meet him! I can't leave until I have!"

"What of our home? Aros – Roskilde – our people?" Vidar demanded.

"*Leave without me.*" I hissed. "How many times must I tell you?"

Vidar shook his head, the shock on his face contorting into frustration.

"We vowed never to be parted from each other," Vidar said heatedly. "We have broken that vow once, and I never intend to break it again. I will *not* leave you in Britain alone, you are coming back to Denmark with me. I will not leave you!"

"Don't you understand what this means to me? This is my brother!" I snapped.

"Of course, I understand!" Vidar yelled. "I would do anything to see *my* brother again! But we have higher obligations, Aveline! You are Jarlkona and I am Jarl and we *must* return to our people!"

"They've survived a year without us, surely a few more days wouldn't matter?" I hissed.

"*Have* they survived?" Vidar rumbled. "Remember, I was absent for only a few days when Erhardt attacked and seized Roskilde – and stole *you* away! When we left Aros for Francia, we left our people at risk of attack from other Jarls and towns. We *must* return to our people as soon as possible! We are their leaders – we must make sacrifices to protect them, that is our *duty*!"

I gaped at Vidar, tears flowing freely down my face. My body shuddered violently, but I didn't utter a single sound. Vidar rubbed his face with both hands and sighed deeply, his expression softening. He stepped nearer to me, took my shoulders and pulled me closer to him, resting his forehead on mine.

"Give me a year," Vidar said softly. "We will return to Britain in a year. Let us return to Denmark tomorrow – let us fulfil our obligations as Jarl and Jarlkona of Aros and Roskilde, and in twelve months we will come back here, and we won't leave until we've found him."

I gazed into his icy eyes and let a small breath slip through my lips. Could we truly fulfil our obligations to both towns in just a year? Upon our return to Denmark, we would first travel to Aros and find out what has happened there during our absence, settle disputes between the people, ascertain whether the riches we'd seized from Francia were divided fairly, and hold a grand feast for our people for our return and to celebrate the lives of men we had lost who were surely now drinking in the great hall of Valhalla.

After that, we would need to travel to Roskilde, confirm Alvar's death and hold a *blót* in commemoration of him, a funeral though we didn't have his body; we would celebrate his life and his arrival into Valhalla, and that of all the Roskilde townsmen who had died in Francia. Then we would announce our inheriting of Alvar's jarldom. Should all go well, and our rule was accepted, we would settle disputes, get updated on the affairs of Roskilde, give gifts to the people, then travel to all the settlements under Alvar's control and do the same things with them. We would hold a grand meeting in Roskilde with all Alvar's retainers, followers, supporters and townspeople in attendance, for them to publicly vow their fealty to Vidar and me.

Could all of that truly be done in just a year?

Where would Beric be in a year? What if there was another Danish uprising, and he was killed? If I left Gipeswic, would I be forfeiting the only chance to see my brother again? Beric had no idea I lived in Denmark; what if he travelled all the way to Gipeswic only to find I was gone? Would he search the whole of Britain for me? Where would he be in a year? It had been hard enough searching for him in Gipeswic though he was supposedly stationed here, looking for him in twelve months' time would be impossible.

"Please, little fawn, give me a year." Vidar pleaded. "I won't leave Gipeswic without you, but we *must* leave."

"I know." I whispered.

"We will find Beric," Vidar vowed. "In twelve months, we *will* return – we will search through all of the Anglo-Saxon kingdoms and we won't leave until we've found him. Just give me a year, little fawn, and I promise we *will* return."

A heavy silence blanketed us. Thoughts and doubts swirled like a tempest in my mind. Vidar was right, we were obligated to our people, and now with two towns and so many settlements under Vidar's hold now, we needed to return, we needed to show our presence in Aros and Roskilde, we needed to be there to protect them, to lead them, to mourn the loss of so many men in the battle against Francia … We had no idea how the two towns had faired during our absence, and we had missed the crop sowing … Almost all of our forces had returned to Denmark and if we were gone for much longer, we could run the risk of Vidar's rule being challenged or even seized while we were away if we appeared to be neglecting our duties to our people for personal issues, especially so soon after being defeated by the Franks …

"Alright," I mumbled. "You have your year."

"*Þakka fyrir*, little fawn."

Vidar cupped my jaw in his hands and brought my face to his, pressing a kiss to my lips, and with that my body crumpled in his arms. I wept furiously in Vidar's embrace, soaking the front of his tunic with my tears. He squeezed me tightly, holding me firmly against him, his head rested on top of mine, his warm breath dancing gently on my chestnut curls.

Vidar's heartbeat drummed against my ear, unwaveringly rhythmic, *thump, thump, thump*. After a while my cries quietened, my rasping gasps calmed to steady breaths, transfixed by the cadence of his heart. I focussed on the sound, the consistent drum drawing me out of my hysterical sadness and back into reality. I inhaled deeply; the musky scent of Vidar's perspiration from walking for hours mingled with the faded smell of the soap he'd used to wash this morning filled my nostrils comfortingly. The solidness of his body wrapped around mine, his large, muscled arms enclosed around me, securing me against him. I felt … Safe.

"I love you, Vidar." I murmured.

"I love you, too." Vidar replied just as quietly, kissing the top of my head.

I slipped from his embrace and wiped the snot and tears away with my sleeve.

"You're so beautiful." Vidar sighed.

"Snot and all?"

"Snot and all."

"Liar." I offered him a small, embarrassed smile, dabbing at my eyes with my sleeve.

Vidar pulled me against him and pressed a kiss to my brow. I cupped his jaw in both my hands and leaned upwards, gently urging him to bring his lips to mine. We kissed softly, our tongues grazing, Vidar's arms curling around my body, bringing me tighter against him. Our breath quickened, my heart raced, our kiss deepened.

"Do you resent me?" Vidar asked, suddenly breaking our kiss, his voice faded and quiet.

"*Nei*, of course I don't." I replied, shocked.

Vidar stared at me silently, chewing his bottom lip.

"I don't resent you." I said firmly. "I – I dislike your decision, I wish you'd let us stay, *but* I understand ... I do not, have not and will never resent you. I love you, Vidar Alvarsson."

All of a sudden, Vidar's lips crashed against mine, he scooped me off my feet, my skirts falling over my hips, baring my legs. He stumbled over the grassy bank to a huge, aged oak. I groaned against Vidar's lips as he thrust me against the tree trunk, the rough, furrowed bark scratching my back through my dress. I arched my back away from the trunk, pressing my front against Vidar's chest, and crossed my legs around him. The balmy breeze drifted over my bared flesh deliciously, and Vidar's hands raced over every inch of me, caressing my legs, squeezing my breasts, gripping my buttocks.

Vidar drew his lips down my throat, tenderly kissing my neck, sending shivers rippling through me. He hurriedly swept some stray curls over my shoulder and continued nuzzling me. His lips grazed my collarbone as he drew them to the soft flesh where neck and shoulder meet, lightly nipping me there with his teeth. Another deep moan rolled from my throat, heat erupting inside me from his touch and attention.

"*Argh!*" I groaned, falling to the ground with a painful thud.

I winced, my buttocks aching, and quickly glanced about to see Vidar dragged away from me by two Anglo-Saxon soldiers, one blond, one brown-haired, in Wessex colours, hauling him towards a group of two other Wessex soldiers and five horses by the path. I gaped, my sore rear immediately forgotten, and jumped to my feet, but before I could do anything, a pair of large hands grabbed my shoulders and held me back tightly. I writhed in my captor's arms, attempting to break free, but the man held me back.

Vidar glanced between his captors, his brows high and jaw dropped. Upon sight of me, however, his face contorted with rage. He tried to rip himself free from the soldiers' grasp, twisting and thrashing, a low growl rolling from his throat like a wolf. Another soldier sprinted towards them, his hand gripped around his sword hilt, disgust and loathing clear on his face.

Suddenly Vidar yanked one of his arms free and, with a hard thrust of his shoulder, he sent the blond soldier flying to the ground. Before Vidar could do anything else, the brown-haired soldier balled up his fists and punched Vidar in the face with a sickening *crunch!* followed by a swift jab to his stomach. Vidar stumbled backwards, gripping his face, blood dripping from his nostrils. The blond soldier clambered to his feet and both Wessex men dived onto Vidar. Vidar smashed the armoured men with such force, I could hear the loud, thuds and thumps of his fists colliding with their bodies even from my distance away.

"Get off me!" I snarled.

"Calm yourself, woman! You're safe now – we have the heathen!" The soldier exclaimed.

The blond- and brown-haired soldiers hung from Vidar, sweat pouring down their red faces, breathlessly attempting to restrain Vidar and failing miserably. Vidar was almost a head taller than both of the soldiers, his brawny body pure strength and muscle from a lifetime of battle and fighting. Vidar kicked the brown-haired soldier in the stomach, spun around and punched the blond soldier in the face, roaring furiously. Free from their grips, Vidar immediately bolted towards me, his icy eyes flashing with fury, scowling at the Wessex soldier holding me.

The third soldier quickly caught up with Vidar. With a roar, the soldier dived and tackled Vidar from the back, sending both men flying to the ground. Pinning Vidar beneath him, the soldier pounded down on Vidar's back with his fists. Bellowing fiercely, Vidar tried to spin around, but the blond- and brown-haired soldiers appeared. Pinned to the ground by the soldier on top of him, Vidar squirmed and groaned with each strike of the soldier's fists. The blond- and brown-haired soldiers darted to them, vicious grins on their faces, spitting out insult upon insult at Vidar before kicking and stamping on his head, legs, arms and sides.

"No!" I roared.

Finally, I tore myself from the soldier's grasp. I sprinted towards the men, drawing *Úlfsblóð* from its sheath. The soldiers paused, turning to stare at me in confusion as I ran at them screaming. That brief moment was all the time Vidar needed; he spun around, flinging the soldier on top of him to the ground. Vidar — bloody and bruised, his face already swelling from the soldier's kicks — lunged at the blond soldier, punching him square in the jaw, a sickening crack ripping through the air, before the soldier fell to the ground, gripping his face and wailing in anguish.

The brown-haired soldier yelped, drew his sword, but before he could raise it, Vidar tackled him to the ground, beating the soldier in the face with his bloody fists. The soldier who had been tying up the horses ran towards us, his sword unsheathed, howling in fury. Beside them at last, I held my sword's hilt with both hands, the blond soldier moaning at my feet. I aimed at his throat, raised *Úlfsblóð* and—

With a resounding *oof!* I fell to the ground, the soldier who had restrained me at the tree tackling to me to the floor. Briefly, my vision turned to black and when it returned, all I could see were stars. I shook my head and glanced about for my sword — *Úlfsblóð* had flown to the ground, just out of arms reach. The soldier who'd tackled me leapt up, hauled me to my feet and pinned me against him with one hand. He wasn't much taller than me, but he was far stronger.

Vidar, staring my way, jumped off the Wessex soldier and stormed towards us. He grabbed the hilt of his sword, but he couldn't draw it – in various states of injury, the Wessex soldiers persisted; the four of them pounced on Vidar, disarmed him and restrained him. Two of them kicked the back of his knees, making Vidar's legs buckle, and sent him crashing to the ground. The two soldiers who weren't holding his arms back, pulled their swords and pointed them at Vidar's throat.

My captor threw me to the ground, pulled his seax knife from his belt and stormed towards Vidar. He grabbed Vidar by his hair, pressed the blade to his throat–

"Holt? Is that you?" Vidar gasped in Ænglisc.

The soldier froze. Vidar winced in pain from laughing so hard at the soldier before him. The four other soldiers glanced blankly between themselves. I scampered up to my feet, retrieved *Úlfsblóð* and dashed to Vidar and the strangers.

"Aveline! It's Holt!" Vidar grinned at me before facing the soldier again. "I wondered where you'd gone to, Holt!"

"Aveline?" The soldier whipped his head round to face me.

"Theodric?" I gasped.

"What's going on here, Holt?" One of the soldiers asked. "How does the Dane know you? Who's *Theodric*?"

Theodric, his face drained of colour, stumbled backwards, gaping at me.

"Why are you trying to save this Dane?" Theodric demanded.

"He's my husband!" I exclaimed, *Úlfsblóð* still steadily aimed at him.

"*Husband?*" He repeated. "But – but he's a Dane! A Dane who was attacking you?"

"I wasn't *attacking* her; I was trying to *make love* to her." Vidar smirked, blood (I didn't know whose) dripping from his jaw.

Theodric gawped at me, confusion painted across his face. Vidar laughed again, earning a swift kick from one of the soldier's restraining him.

"My name is Theodric Holt." Theodric said quietly, staring at me. "I'm known only as Holt here – Holt the Dane Slayer."

"When I owned you, you were known as Holt the thrall." Vidar sneered.

One of the soldiers smacked Vidar in the face. Vidar groaned and spat out a glob of bloody saliva. Theodric stepped closer to me; I lowered my sword. Slowly he reached out and brushed the hair from my face, gazing at me, our eyes locked for a few intensely long moments. In my peripheral, I could see Vidar struggling in his captors' grips, angered by Theodric touching my hair.

"I wondered why you were so familiar," Theodric said. "Your eyes are so striking, they're hard to forget ... I thought perhaps I'd seen your brother – maybe I was mistaking your eyes for his? But no. I remember you from Roskilde – you're the Danethrall."

I nodded slowly; my lips pursed into a tight frown.

"I remember you, you lived in the hall for a time ... Everyone in the town spoke of you – thralls and Danes alike. You were the Anglo-Saxon thrall who'd captured the heart of the most fearsome warrior in Roskilde, the Anglo-Saxon thrall whom the Jarl's son had fallen in love with."

"I was never a thrall." I whispered. "The warrior adopted me; I was his daughter."

Theodric dropped his hand from my face.

"I was owned by Hefni the farmer before the Jarl's son purchased me. Do you remember?"

A vision of the past flooded my mind; it was winter ... The day my Danish father, Birger Bloody Sword, set sail for the Kingdom of the East Angles to join the Great Army. I had been walking home; I'd paused at the fence line of Hefni's farm, where Hefni was punishing a thrall, who was dressed in rags and bleeding in the snow ... Vidar was there, talking to Hefni, convincing him to be less harsh on the thrall. Vidar managed to convince Hefni to sell him the thrall he was beating; after the coin had exchanged hands and the thrall officially belong to Vidar, Vidar had sent the thrall immediately to the hall to have his wounds examined.

"I do." I replied softly.

"I purchased you from the farmer." Vidar said loudly, pausing to spit out more bloody phlegm. "I had my thralls heal you, I gave you warm, fresh clothes, I fed you good food. You were *my* thrall; you worked *my* fields for years – then you ran away."

"I escaped!" Theodric hissed, turning away from me and stomped over to Vidar, pressing his seax against his throat. "You enslaved me! You kept me in a barn like an animal! I was beaten by the Danes and forced to toil in your damned fields!"

"Theodric, please," I begged. "Don't hurt Vidar."

"I saved your life, Holt – or *Theodric*, whichever name it is you prefer to be called." Vidar continued, ignoring the blade against his neck. "*You are indebted to me!*"

Theodric glanced over his shoulder at me. His anger melted away to … sadness? He turned back to Vidar, loathing dripping from his words.

"Release him." Theodric spat.

"But Holt–" One of his men tried to argue, but Theodric cut him off.

"Release him!" Theodric bellowed.

Bewildered, his men slowly unhanded my husband, sheathed their weapons and stepped away from him. Vidar, smirking, spat on the ground, wiped his mouth on the back of his hand and stood up, towering over the four soldiers.

"My debt is paid, Dane." Theodric snarled. "You saved my life, and I have spared yours. You would do best to leave this place – should I see you again, I will kill you."

"And I, you, *Dane Slayer*." Vidar growled.

As he passed him, Vidar shoved Theodric with his shoulder. Theodric's grip on his seax tightened and his other hand whipped to the hilt of his sword. Vidar strolled over to me, stopped in front of me and touched my chin with his bloodied fingertips.

"Are you hurt, little fawn?" Vidar asked softly in Norse.

"*Nei*, I'm fine, my love." I replied in Norse, looking passed Vidar to the Wessex soldiers. "Theodric–"

"Silence, woman!" Theodric thundered, glaring at me. "Had I known you were a Dane lover I never would have helped you find your brother! I questioned why you were so adamant about staying in a Danish inn, but I stupidly ignored my better judgement. Never again! You sicken me, woman; you're a traitor to your people! You would do well to follow your husband and never return to Britain."

RISE TO FALL

My heart sank at his words. Theodric sheathed his seax and strode towards the horses without a second glance in my direction. His four men huffed and grunted and turned their backs on us, grumbling amongst each other.

"Never thought I'd see him again." Vidar commented. "You didn't tell me that Theodric was Holt."

"I didn't realise he was." I said wistfully. "But for the day you purchased him, I don't remember ever seeing him."

I watched Theodric near his horse. When he was just a few paces away, I left Vidar's side and darted to the soldiers. Breathlessly, I stopped beside Theodric, grabbing his hand and holding it tightly with both of mine. The soldiers began drawing their weapons, but Theodric held up his free hand.

"Mount your horses, I'll be there in a moment." Theodric ordered, staring at our hands.

My heart pounded in my ears and a knot was wedged in my throat. The four soldiers did as Theodric ordered and mounted their horses, watching us intently.

"You said you *never would have helped me find my brother—*" I panted, gazing at him with round, pleading eyes. "Does that mean you found him?"

"I did." Theodric replied stoutly.

"Please tell me where he is. I know you hate me, but please! *Please* tell me!" I begged. "It's been twenty years since I last saw him."

"Beric has spent the last few weeks in Lundenne with his family, but he will be returning to Gipeswic this eve."

"Why didn't he ride with you?" I asked softly.

"He had some duties to complete," Theodric said. "He will report to me immediately upon his arrival in Gipeswic."

"Can I – can I meet him?"

"If you would like, I will arrange a meeting between the two of you, but be advised, you should meet on the Anglo-Saxon territory of Gipeswic, not the Danish." Theodric said stiffly. "You should come alone, not even with your children; Beric does not view Danes kindly."

"Oh." I said, letting my hands drop, but instead of letting go, Theodric held my small hands tightly.

"Do you want to meet him?"

"Yes, I do."

"At nightfall, meet me at the Boar and Hen alehouse. I'll wait for you there and introduce you to Beric." Theodric promised.

I wanted to throw my arms around him in gratitude, but I held back. I took a step closer to him and brought his hand to my chest.

"Thank you, Theodric." I whispered.

We gazed at one another for a few moments, my heart racing, his expression softening. Theodric opened his mouth to say something but closed it as I felt a hand rest on my hip; Vidar had appeared quietly behind me. Theodric's gaze turned from me to my husband, his expression hardening immediately. He snatched his hand from me and strode over to his horse and mounted it. Theodric held the reins tightly, his knuckles white, and directed his horse towards us.

"We are even now, Dane, I have paid my debt." Theodric glared down at Vidar. "I will give you until the morn' to leave. Should I see you again, I will kill you with no misgivings."

"Do what you must, Theodric Holt," Vidar growled. "For I will do what I want."

CHAPTER THIRTY-TWO

"I HATE THE idea of you going alone." Vidar said for what felt like the hundredth time.

"It isn't an idea, my love, it is what's happening. Apparently, Beric isn't fond of Danes." I replied for what also felt like the hundredth time.

"At least let me—"

"*Nei*," I glared at my husband. "I am going alone. I have *Úlfsblóð*, I have my knife."

"But, little fawn—"

"*Nei*, Vidar! *Nei*. It's far safer if I go anyway – I look like an Anglo-Saxon and I speak like an Anglo-Saxon. When we tried to speak with the patrols today, none of them would talk to us because of *you*. When I was alone, all the soldiers willingly helped me." I pointed out.

"Then let me hide. It will seem like you're alone, but I'll be there in case anything bad should happen." Vidar pressed.

I cupped his jaw in my hands and kissed his forehead.

"*Nei*. This is my brother, Vidar. I'm going to be fine. If all goes well, I'll meet you at the inn and introduce you to him."

"You're hopeful." Jan commented.

"Indeed I am." I smiled.

"Why do you trust Holt so much?" Jan asked. "He *did* try to kill your husband."

"He thought he was saving me." I said stiffly. "He thought I was being attacked, and he did the *honourable* thing and tried to save me."

Jan bristled.

"If he knew you were married to a Dane, he wouldn't have tried to save you." Vidar pointed out, wincing as he shifted in his chair.

"This has nothing to do with trust, it's to do with meeting my brother." I snapped. "I've walked these streets for weeks, the alehouse isn't far from here, and I have my sword should I need it. I can't give up the opportunity to meet my brother."

I gazed at Vidar. The bruises on his face were hideously bright, the maroon cuts dark and crusted. His body was stiff, swollen and aching, he couldn't move without wincing. I slipped into the chair beside him and took his hand gently, pressing my lips against it.

"I hate what they did to you." I whispered. "Even if I let you shadow me, you'd only get hurt should something terrible happen. I couldn't bear that."

"At least have Jan, Domnall or Hallmundr go with you." Vidar asked, his voice low, his eyes pleading.

I shook my head.

"I can't risk it. If I bring a Dane with me, then something terrible *will* happen. I look like an Anglo-Saxon," I held my arms out, presenting the simple blue Anglo-Saxon dress I wore – no beads or the turtle shell brooches in sight. "I sound like an Anglo-Saxon, I'm meeting an Anglo-Saxon. I'll blend in – unfortunately, they won't."

I nodded towards our three male companions. From their huge statures, long hair, full beards and tattooed skin, there was no doubt they were Danes. Anglo-Saxons were far smaller than Danes, their hair was always cut short, their faces shaved and their flesh unmarked.

"We will take vengeance on Theodric and his men, little fawn." Vidar warned.

"Yes, we will, I have not changed my mind." I agreed. "But after tonight, after I've met Beric."

After Theodric Holt and his four Wessex soldiers had galloped off on their horses, Vidar and I began the long walk back to the inn. There we met Domnall, Hallmundr and Guðrin, whose jaw dropped at the sight of my bloodied and bruised husband. Domnall and Hallmundr helped haul Vidar upstairs, for he was hurting so much from the beating he'd received and the terribly long walk back to the inn, he could hardly climb the inn stairs on his own.

In our room, I peeled Vidar's filthy clothes off him and bathed his wounds with a bucket of warm water and some rags the innkeeper had kindly given us, while Guðrin rushed to the market to buy honey for his wounds. The bruises on Vidar's ribs and legs were huge, his bottom lip was split open and there were some (thankfully shallow) cuts on his neck from where Theodric had pressed his seax knife. No bones were broken, thank the gods, but Vidar's body was aching and stiff. I tore one of my linen dresses into strips and, after cleaning his wounds and coating them in honey, I bandaged him with the strips. I stayed with Vidar until he finally fell asleep, his slumber hastened by the strong cup of yarrow tea Guðrin had procured for him.

A few hours later, Jan, Lars and Einarr – all three men smelling strongly of mead and ale – returned to the inn. They found Domnall, Hallmundr, Guðrin, and me sat together by the fire, Vidar and my four children and Domnall and Guðrin's son scattered about the room – the youngest two playing, the older three talking in hushed tones across the room. Jan immediately noticed Vidar's absence.

After I had filled the three in on the details, Jan flew into a rage, ready to hunt Theodric and his four soldiers down and kill them.

"*Nei*, Jan!" I shrieked. "Stop it! We will do *nothing*!"

"Nothing? He tried to kill Vidar!" Jan yelled, his sapphire eyes wide in disbelief. "He tried to kill *your husband* – we can't let him get away with that!"

"Jan, stop!" I growled darkly, glaring furiously at him. "I have made my decision! After I have met my brother, then you can do whatever you like to Theodric and the four soldiers, but until then you will do *nothing*!"

"The moment you return to the inn, I *will* avenge Vidar." Jan vowed.

"And you will do so with my full support," I said. "But first I must meet Beric."

The hours had passed, Vidar had woken, and Jan had helped him down the stairs and across the way to the alehouse for the evening meal. The night was falling, and my anxiousness was growing; I couldn't sit still in my chair, leaning over to glimpse the sky every time the alehouse door opened.

Finally, it was time.

I gently gave Einar, who was sleeping in my arms, to Guðrin, and stood up.

"May I come with you, *mumie*?" Æsa asked, her eyelids drooped with sleepiness.

"Not tonight, my heart, I think it's time for you to go to bed." I smiled. "Go to bed, sweet girl, I will bring you the next time – or perhaps I will bring your uncle Beric to meet you later on?"

"Will you wake me, so I can meet him?"

"Of course, I will." I beamed.

I kissed Æsa, bid her goodnight and watched her disappear up the stairs with Guðrin and little Einar.

"Be safe. I love you." Vidar said.

"I will. I love you, too." I kissed his lips gently.

I bid farewell to Young Birger, Sander, Yngvi and the men, before scurrying off to the door.

"*Mumie*, wait!" Sander yelped.

Sander threw his arms around me and held me tightly.

"I'm sorry for all the horrible things I said." He said. "I'm glad you found your brother."

I kissed his cheek and squeezed him against me, tears burning in my eyes.

"Oh, Sander! *Þakka fyrir*!" I cried. "I love you, sweet boy!"

"I love you, too," Sander said. "*Góða nótt, mumie* – and good luck!"

***

I STOOD OUTSIDE the Boar and Hen. The deep rumble of laughter sounded through the wooden door. I trembled, not from the cold but from anticipation. It was a relatively warm, clear night, the white orb of the moon was scaling higher in the black night sky, stars twinkled silver. It was beautiful, the eve I'd finally be reunited with my brother.

Some men, addled by mead and ale, stumbled toward me, squalling like a group of excited pigs. As they neared me, I noticed they reeked like pigs, as well. Unfortunately, they paused at the door, noticing me.

"Are you coming in for a drink, love?" One of them slurred, a ridiculous grin on his face.

"Not with you." I replied, wrinkling my nose at him.

"Don't be a snide bitch, come and have some fun!" The first man said.

"Come on love, I'll show you a good time." Another grinned as he staggered towards me.

"She said no." A voice growled from behind me. "I suggest you find a different alehouse for the night; *we're* attending this one."

I turned and found Theodric, still dressed in his scarlet uniform, the golden wyvern arching across the front of his tunic. The fierceness of his expression sent shivers down my spine, but I couldn't help but smile at the men; they seemed to shrink under Theodric's glare. They mumbled and muttered amongst each other as they stumbled away.

"She's not even that pretty!" One barked over his shoulder.

"Never mind them." Theodric said, glowering at the drunken gaggle of men as they stumbled away.

"I didn't think you would come." I said.

"I almost didn't," Theodric admitted stiffly. "But I promised I would reunite you and your brother, and I am a man of my word."

"I appreciate it beyond measure."

"Come on," Theodric said, striding to the door and grabbing the door pull. "Beric is waiting inside."

I swallowed hard and shuffled passed Theodric, my heart racing painfully fast in my chest. He closed the door behind us with a soft thump and followed me in. My feet were heavy, as though they were suddenly made of lead, and my body trembled with nerves. The Boar and Hen alehouse was packed full of people, from farmworkers to soldiers. I tried peeking passed the alehouse patrons, searching through the sea of faces, but there was too much hustle and bustle.

"This way." Theodric murmured, pointing to the left.

Theodric stepped forward into the throng and I scurried after him, snatching his hand and clinging to it. He paused, glanced at my hands, a light blush glowing on his cheeks, before beginning again. We weaved through tables and patrons, dodging drunken men and slipping passed a couple of women with loose hair and low necklines who attempted to drape themselves over Theodric, but he pushed them away. I snickered to myself at the sight of his ears, the tips had turned scarlet with embarrassment at the women's behaviour.

"Here," Theodric said, clearing his throat.

In a somewhat quiet corner of the alehouse, far from the fire but illuminated by fish oil lamps, was a small, aged table with a few rickety looking stools tucked about it. Upon one of the stools was a man dressed in Wessex colours. Luscious chestnut curls sprang from his head, he was pale like porcelain with a long face and sharp cheekbones. He was staring absorbed into his dark ale, which, by the looks of it, hadn't been touched.

"Beric," Theodric said. "This is Aveline."

Beric turned and stared at me, his amber eyes wide and shining. His pale skin seemed to whiten even further upon sight of me. Our identical eyes met; our jaws dropped in unison.

"Beric?" I whispered.

"Aveline?"

He leapt to his feet, sending the stool flying out from beneath him. He dived towards me and I dashed into his arms, embracing one another tightly. Tears poured down my cheeks, my heart pounded so fast I thought it might explode, so overwhelmed with shock and happiness.

"I can't believe it's you!" I wept.

"I thought you'd died!" Beric exclaimed, his words thick with emotion.

"All this time, I thought *you* were dead!" I laughed through my tears. "When Guthlac told me you were alive–"

"Guthlac?" Beric asked, glancing down at me.

"Yes!" I beamed up at him. "I found my way to Wisbece and met him there – it was he who told me you'd survived the Danish attack! *Oh, Beric*! I'm so glad he was telling the truth! I asked every soldier I found if they knew you, but they didn't – I was beginning to lose hope, but you're here! You're real! *You're alive*!"

"I never thought I'd see you again, either," Beric said. "Guthlac and I returned to Wisbece after the Danes left, but we couldn't find your body. We assumed the bastards had taken you?"

"They did," I said, cheer swiftly fading from my voice. I shook my head. "I'm back though, Beric. I'm here."

Beric pulled me against him and hugged me tightly.

"God, how I missed you, Aveline." He murmured. "We will rid Britain of the Danish scourge – they'll pay for what they did."

I glanced at Theodric. He offered me a lopsided smile. He hadn't told Beric about Vidar or my children – Beric had no idea I was married to a Dane or mother of four little Danes. Beric hated the Danes that much was obvious from the contempt in his voice when he spoke of them – but Theodric had warned me of this before. I hoped over the course of the night I could convince Beric to meet Vidar and my children with an open heart …

"Let's sit, here, I'll fetch you a drink. We have twenty years to catch up on." Beric grinned, releasing me from his embrace.

I grinned and nodded, dabbing my eyes with the sleeve of my dress as I sat down. Beric swiftly disappeared in the crowd to purchase a drink for me, leaving Theodric and me alone.

"I'll leave you two to reacquaint yourselves with one another." Theodric said.

"Wait – Theodric!" I called out, jumping to my feet.

He stopped and turned to me. I wrapped my arms around him and hugged him tightly.

"*Ic pancie pē.*" I said. "*Ic pancie pē* for reuniting Beric and me. I don't know how I'll ever repay you."

Theodric, hesitant at first, accepted my embrace and held me silently. I could hear his heart racing in his chest. A deafening clatter rang abruptly through the alehouse, followed by an eruption of cheer, laughter and shouting. We turned and found a drunken man lying on the floor laughing, the wreckage of a table beneath him, tankards and mugs scattered about him. At a guess, I assumed the drunkard had lost his footing and fallen onto the rickety table. We turned to each other and laughed warmly together.

Suddenly Theodric's smile disappeared, his mouth tightened, and his brow furrowed. Theodric released me and shoved me an arm-length away from him. I opened my mouth to say something, but he raised his hand to stop me.

"What's done is done," Theodric said gruffly. "I vowed to find your brother and I have. You must keep to your word and leave Gipeswic tomorrow and never return. You're an ally to the Danes; you're not welcome in these lands."

I gawped at him. Theodric glared back at me, his brow furrowed, and his mouth drawn in a tight line.

"Why did you keep your word to me?" I asked, disbelief softening my words.

"By the time I found out your treachery, it was too late; Beric expected to meet you. My hand was forced; my obligation was to *him* at that point, not to you."

"You could've told him I was married to a Dane – you said he hates them as much as you – surely he would have refused to meet me then? But you didn't – *why?*"

"I will not tell him of your betrayal, you must admit your own sins and face the consequences."

Theodric turned his back on me and stormed away.

"Theodric!" I darted after him and grabbed his hand, scowling at him as he turned to face me. "Why did you spend so much effort finding Beric for me? I was nothing but a stranger to you."

Theodric surveyed me for a moment. With a sudden tug, he freed his hand from my grip.

"Had I known you married a Dane, I wouldn't have." Theodric growled.

With that, Theodric left.

I stared after him, but he quickly vanished in the throng of patrons. Beric appeared instead, grinning, an ale in each hand.

"Where did Holt go to?" Beric asked.

"Theodric's gone." I replied distantly.

***

I WATCHED ONE of the alehouse slaves drift about the dark alehouse lighting fish oil lamps, globes of soft orange firelight glowing through the darkness. Beric and I sat in the Boar and Hen for hours, the large, sunken rectangular room was now swathed in shadow and black. Much of the din had calmed as many patrons had stumbled off home or had passed out about the alehouse floor and seating. There were a few groups of people awake and going strong, their speech slurred by alcohol. Beric and I had been lost in conversation, reminiscing of days when we were children, our beer and ale quite forgotten.

"You haven't changed at all, Aveline." Beric smiled. "You still have such a dark sense of humour, must unbecoming of a woman. Tell me, do you still shoot your bow and try to battle like a man, or have you grown out of that nonsense?"

"I certainly have not – and it's not *nonsense*." I declared. "I'm sure I could *still* outshoot you. In fact, I'd wager I'm a better swordsman than you now."

Beric stared at me with silent disbelief for a moment before bursting into laughter, earning us a few groans and angry glances from a pair of drunkards across the way from us who were trying to sleep curled up on the hard dirt floor in front of the firepit.

"I kill Danes for a living, Aveline. Fighting is all I do – I hardly expect you could defeat me in a fight. We're not children anymore." Beric snickered. "How did you even come upon a sword? Especially one as fine as that!"

"It was given to me because I know how to wield it." I grinned. "And you're right, we're not children anymore so I expect a much better fight out of you – I used to beat you so easily. Honestly, I never thought I'd see the day where *you* would be a soldier."

"Is that so?" Beric smirked.

"I thought you'd be a farmer." I said, sipping my beer.

I wrinkled my nose. The beer was disgusting; bitter and warm. How I craved a good horn of the cold, sweet mead we drank in Aros! Beric chuckled at the disgust on my face.

"Speaking of children, Guthlac said you're wed and have a family now?" I said.

Beric bristled. He shifted in his chair, darkness settling over his face, his mouth formed into a rigid grimace. Beric grabbed his tankard of ale and took a few deep gulps – the most I'd seen him drink all night. He roughly wiped the ale residue from his lips, his unsettled glance darting from the contents in his tankards to the surrounding area.

"I am married, and I have two children," Beric grunted. "They live in Lundenne."

"You stiffen every time I mention Guthlac," I commented, watching him intently. "Why is that?"

"Let's not talk about *him*." Beric said, glaring into his tankard again.

"Why not? It's because of him we're reunited." I pointed out.

"Guthlac is a traitor." Beric spat, scowling at me. "I haven't spoken to him in years. He associates with Danish filth – he allowed his daughter to marry one of the bastards!"

"Guthlac said the Dane saved his daughter's virtue?" I said. "He said she was being attacked by Anglo-Saxons, but before he could save her, the Dane–"

"I know what happened!" Beric growled. "He should have left it at that, but instead he befriended the damned heathen. He should have let the bastard die! It doesn't matter what the Dane did, he was still a Dane!"

"And that means he deserves to die, good deed or not?" I gasped.

"Exactly! The only reason I keep in contact with Somerhild's family is because they are as upset as me that Guthlac allowed Elfilda to marry a Dane and move to Denmark." Beric said, taking another deep swig. "Lord knows what's happened to the girl now!"

"She's happily married with children I hear," I replied stiffly. "Beric, why would you hold this against him? He's your closest friend!"

Beric rubbed his face with both of his hands and sighed deeply.

"He *was* my closest friend. He escaped certain death with me; we grew up together, depended on each other! Then he allowed his daughter to marry a heathen. He betrayed his people by befriending the monsters who murdered our families." Beric looked up at me. "I don't want to talk about him, anymore, Aveline. It saddens me to think of him. Please, tell me about you. What do you do now? Where do you live? Are you married?"

"I raise sheep." I smiled, ignoring his second question. "And I am married to the most kind, wonderful and loyal man I've ever met. We have four beautiful children together – three sons and a daughter."

Beric gazed at me, stunned.

"Even after twenty years, you're still raising sheep?" He teased, and I kicked his leg under the table. "God, I can't believe you're a mother, I can't believe you're married! It's like I'm in a dream, I never thought I'd see you again, and here you are – a woman, a mother, a wife! How I've missed out on your life!"

"A lot has changed over the last twenty years." I said.

"The Danes stole our family, our home. They stole the last twenty years from us …" Beric said, his shoulders curling in and his head dropping as he fell into his thoughts. "They stole so much from us …"

I watched Beric's hands twitch as he clutched his half-empty tankard so tightly his knuckles and fingertips had turned white. The shadows cast on his face lent him an unnerving eeriness, here and there the orange glow of the oil lamps highlighted the silvery scars of nicks and scratches, and the lines of age on his face seemed deeper.

"What happened to you, Aveline?" Beric asked, his voice no higher than a whisper. "What happened after they took you away? How did you survive? How did you escape?"

I stared at the deep golden beer in front of me, the foam just a skinny ring edging the tankard, most of the bubbles popped from sitting for so long. A tempest was swelling in the pit of my stomach and my heart was throbbing in my chest. My breath came in shallow, quickened bursts, my nostrils twitching. I crossed my arms over my chest as though I were trying to block my heart from exploding out of my chest. It was time.

"They took me to their lands, with a few other women and girls." I said quietly, turning my eyes from my beer to my brother. Our eyes locked, unblinking; I took a deep breath. "I was adopted by a Dane named Birger Bloody Sword. He gave me a new name, Aveline Birgersdóttir."

Beric's eyes widened, and he rolled his lips so tightly together, they were almost unseen, just a stark black line of shadow across his face. As he tried to comprehend what I was saying, his eyebrows knitted together, furrowing deep lines across his brow.

"*Adopted you?*"

I nodded.

"He looked after me, he raised me, he taught me their language, and how to read and write the runes. I loved Birger like a father." I admitted. "I had some *issues* with the Danes, but for the most part, I was cared for. They accepted me as one of their own – in fact, my husband, Vidar, and I–"

"*Vidar?* That's not an Anglo-Saxon name." Beric sputtered, his voice strangled with shock.

"He's not an Anglo-Saxon," I confessed. "He's a Dane. He and I rule as Jarl and Jarlkona of Aros. Recently we acquired the jarldom of Roskilde as well. We have many settlements under our rule, our people are happy – I'm happy. I want for nothing, I live well. We–"

Suddenly, Beric stood up and stormed through the alehouse. I stared after him, stunned, before jumping to my feet and chasing after him. He ripped open the door and thundered through it, slamming it behind him. The door banged loudly over and over as it bounced in its frame. Quickly I grabbed the iron door pull and slipped into the night. I raced after him, calling out his name, but he kept his back to me, charging off into the night.

"Beric! Where are you going? What are you doing?" I yelled breathlessly. "Beric!"

"I was wrong." Beric snarled, whipping around to face me.

"What?" I panted. "What are you talking about?"

Beric stomped towards me, his nostrils flaring.

"I was wrong. My sister died twenty years ago."

"No, Beric–"

"Yes! Aveline is dead!" Beric snarled. "Had I known you were a traitor like Guthlac, I never would have met you. Leave this place and never return, do you hear me? Otherwise, you'll be killed like your Danish kin!"

CHAPTER THIRTY-THREE

I WATCHED BERIC turn his back on me and disappear into the darkness, his words ringing in my ears, my breath caught in my throat. *Aveline is dead* ... Searing pain shot through my chest then, like a boiling kettle overflowing, a wave of heat crashed through my body and tears poured down my face in cascades. A raw, wracking shriek ripped from my throat and my swaying legs gave way. I collapsed to the ground and pounded the hard dirt with my fists, my body aching, shuddering violently as I sobbed and gasped for air that wasn't there.

"Little fawn?"

Shakily I looked up and found Vidar gazing down on me, biting his bottom lip, his eyes silver in the darkness, shining with sympathy and sadness.

"Come to me, little fawn." Vidar whispered, opening his arms to me.

I scrambled to my feet and flung myself into his embrace. Vidar physically winced as my body crashed into his, his body still tender from his wounds and bruises. I tried to pull away, but he held me tightly, pinning me against him, choosing to comfort me over his pain. Too weak to fight and yearning so desperately for his touch, my heart bursting with love for him, I buried my face into Vidar's chest and wept.

The moon was at the highest point in the sky by the time my body stopped quivering and my wails had quietened to whimpers. I found my security, the song of his heart soothing me into calm. My cheeks stung, and my throat was sore from crying, but slowly I found my voice.

"You're not meant to be here." I murmured, my voice thick with grief. "You were meant to stay at the inn."

"You know I wasn't going to do that." Vidar said quietly, his voice husky and low.

"Where were you?" I whispered.

"In the shadows," Vidar replied. "I was there with you all the time."

I gently stepped back, slipping my hands down to his and clutching his long fingers in my own. I peered through the darkness; his hair was down, covering the shaven sides and tucked under the neck of his tunic. He wore a long-sleeved tunic and a thin cloak, a brooch pinning the cloak closed on his shoulder. Vidar winced as he pulled the deep hood over his head, his movement stiff, veiling his face completely with shadow.

"Thanks to my beloved wife teaching me Ænglisc, I managed to hide perfectly well." Vidar winked, tugging the hood back down. "Luckily the Anglo-Saxons aimed to get drunk rather than fight Danes."

I smiled at Vidar and embraced him again, slipping my arms around his waist and pressing my ear against his heart to hear its reassuring song.

"Let's go back to the inn," I said softly. "I want to be ready to leave at first light. I want to go back home with you."

***

SCREAMS TORE THROUGH the air. I opened my aching eyes, blurred by sleep, and glanced around the room. More screams. Vidar and I leapt up and dashed to the children lying at the foot of our bed. Sander was sleeping – *that boy could sleep through anything!* – but Æsa and Einar were already awake, their faces panic-stricken as louder and louder the screaming rang.

"Stay here." Vidar ordered, snatching up our swords.

Vidar laid my sword on the floor beside me, stumbling and cursing under his breath, but he scurried up as quickly as he could. Without a second glance, Vidar vanished through the bedroom door, closing it behind him.

"*Mumie*," Æsa whispered. "I'm scared."

"Come here, my heart. There's nothing to fear, I'm here."

Einar and Æsa crawled onto my lap and clung to me. I sat on the floor with bated breath, leaning against the straw mattress they had shared during our stay in Gipeswic. The young children were still, holding me tightly, listening to the screams, the shouts, the clanging and banging grow louder.

We flinched as Vidar, Jan and Hallmundr burst through the door, shields and weapons in hand. Lit by the orange glow of the oil lamps in the open room behind them, I watched Young Birger, Einarr, Lars, Domnall, Yngvi and Guðrin, weapons in hand, dash down the stairs.

"Where's Young Birger going?" I demanded.

"He's going with the others to get Storm-Serpent. We have to leave." Vidar said hurriedly. "Forget the trunks. The Anglo-Saxons are attacking the Danes; they're burning all the homes in the Danish district and moving their way to the marketplace."

"Let me hold you, *mumie* needs one arm free." Jan said to Einar, setting his shield down and taking my son from me.

Einar stared at me fearfully but burrowed deep into Jan's embrace, his eyes as round as coins, his small thin lips pulled down in a heart-breaking frown. Jan picked up his shield and held it with the arm he carried Einar, hiding Einar almost completely behind the shield. Æsa's body tensed. I scrambled to my feet, holding her tightly with one arm. Vidar snatched up my sword and shield and thrust them into my hands; I held my shield like Jan did, covering and protecting Æsa.

"Wake up child!" Vidar hissed, shaking Sander roughly. "Wake up!"

Sander lifted his head, his eyes still closed, and murmured something unintelligible. Hallmundr grabbed the boy, blankets and all.

"Let's go." Hallmundr said.

We rushed down the stairs of the inn, the lower floor completely empty of people. Vidar yanked the door open, revealing the chaos on the streets. Crowds of people rushed to the harbour, presumably Danes, screaming and howling and splashing into the river and climbing the ships. In the distance, we could hear the gurgling, raw screams of those being slain and the roar of battle – the clang of steel and the thudding blows on wooden shields.

"We have to get to Storm-Serpent!" Vidar exclaimed.

The sky was a deep indigo; the sun hadn't crested the horizon yet, but it was light enough for us to see where we were going. It was also light enough to see black plumes of smoke billowing upwards from all the buildings set afire, the air thick and reeking pungently of burning, I could taste the ash on the back of my tongue.

"Follow me!" Vidar ordered.

Before my mind could adjust, my legs began to move. Æsa wailed in my arms as I joined the throng of terrified Danes streaming to the shore, following close behind Vidar, who groaned as he shoved the crowd in front of us, forcing a path through the horde. As we were buffeted by the people, I scanned the waters for Storm-Serpent. *There!* Cast black by shadow, I watched the dark lines of the oars rise and dip into the waters, most stations manned by the looks of things. I hoped to all the gods in Asgard that Young Birger, Lars, Einarr, Yngvi, Guðrin and Domnall had assembled the crew, and Storm-Serpent wasn't being stolen.

Fires erupted in the marketplace as alehouses and inns were set alight. Anglo-Saxons led by soldiers in the reds of Wessex and Kent stormed towards the fleeing Danes. The clanging of steel weapons and the clatter of wooden shields sounded all around us. Tossed about like a ship on a stormy sea, I managed to draw *Úlfsblóð* and cross it over my front, using it to propel people away from me. I shoved and elbowed my way through the crowd, holding my crying daughter closely, but her body slipped in my grip.

I tried to shift Æsa higher up, ordered her to hold me tightly, to wrap her arms around my neck, which she tried desperately to do, but she was only five years old and wasn't strong enough to take the battering of the crowd and hold on to me while her body quaked with fear. The press gave way on the shore as people rushed across the docks and splashed into the water and Æsa dropped to the sand. I stumbled over her wailing body and fell on top of her.

Vidar whipped around and pulled me up, scooping Æsa from the ground and kissing her brow.

"I've got you!" Vidar soothed. "We're close to the ship – we'll be safe soon."

Æsa, weeping dreadfully, threw her arms around her *faðir*. Vidar winced but held her tightly, breathing words of comfort to her. I sheathed Úlfsblóð.

"Are you okay?" I gasped.

Vidar nodded. His brow was dripping with sweat and the colour had vanished from his face. He looked as though he was going to collapse. I took Æsa from Vidar; with two hands I was able to hold her securely against me, my shield covering her. With a nod to Hallmundr, who still carried Sander, we dashed across the shore. Ships bobbed in the harbour with gangplanks and rope ladders lowered so the helpless Danes could climb aboard.

A roar sounded behind me. I whipped my head around to see a wave of Anglo-Saxon freemen and Wessex and Kentish soldiers racing towards us. Three Wessex soldiers headed the horde. Hallmundr quickly set Sander on the ground, and the boy stumbled towards me. No soon had Sander's feet touched the ground when Hallmundr lunged towards the Anglo-Saxons, meeting one of the soldiers' lances with his shield. A crack ripped through the air as the lance skidded across the painted surface of his round shield. Hallmundr swung his axe and smashed the curved blade into the head of the soldier, who wore no helmet. Immediately the soldier dropped, blood spurting from the gash in his skull.

Sander flung himself at me and clung desperately to my leg. I wrapped an arm around him. Vidar dashed passed me, bellowing, his swollen face contorted in rage. Side-by-side, Vidar and Hallmundr fought the Wessex soldiers, swinging their weapons, ramming the soldiers with their shields, flesh tearing, blood jetting from wounds.

A soldier's seax was buried inside Vidar's shield. The soldier snarled at him as he tried to free his weapon. Vidar smashed his head into the soldier's face, who tumbled backwards, releasing the seax. Vidar thrust his sword into the soldier's chest and the soldier fell to the ground. Vidar stomped on his chest, yanked his sword from the soldier's corpse and glanced over his shoulder at me, Sander and Æsa.

"Get to Storm-Serpent!" Vidar shouted, panting.

"Come on!" I hissed at the children, grabbing Sander's hand.

He hesitated, glancing from me to Vidar.

"Come on!" I repeated, tugging his hand.

Sander made no move to run – instead, I bolted breathlessly towards Storm-Serpent, which was thankfully floating beside a dock, my arms aching, dragging my son along with me. I glanced back, watching Vidar exhaustedly battle Anglo-Saxon after Anglo-Saxon. He parried each strike, but his movements were slow and his face was contorted with exhaustion and pain.

"We can't leave *faðir*!" Sander howled.

"We're not – look, he's coming!"

Einarr, Domnall and few Danes I didn't recognise charged to Vidar and Hallmundr's aid, beating, striking and slashing the Wessex soldiers from the back. Thankfully the Danes seemed to get the upper hand on the Anglo-Saxons, surrounding them, trapping them and beating and cutting them down with their weapons and shields.

"Aveline!"

I whipped my head this way and that, trying to find the voice that had shouted my name. There! In the distance beside the dock, I spotted Jan waving one arm at me, the other holding Einar against him. Einar screeched my name, *Mumie! Mumie!*, waving both of his hands at me. Immediately, Æsa stopped weeping. I ran towards them, dragging poor Sander alongside me. As Danes hastily ran down the dock to climb aboard Storm-Serpent, I spotted a figure shoving through them, headed towards us. I reached Jan and set Æsa on the ground and gasping for air.

"Young Birger!" I cried as my eldest son threw his arms around me.

We embraced briefly, I kissed his face and squeezed him tightly. His bow was slung over his back and he had a quiver of arrows at his hip. Einar whimpered, and Jan quickly passed the wriggling child to me.

"We've got a crew. We need to get the children on board." Jan said.

I held Einar, kissing his cheek over and over, Æsa wrapped her arms around my leg and Sander clung to my dress, staring at Vidar as he ran to us from the shore, blood splattered across his shield, his sword dripping. Vidar swayed on his feet, his clothing ripped, new wounds and old oozing with blood. Beneath the purple bruises and red cuts, his bronze skin had faded to grey. The children gaped in horror at the sight of their *faðir*, but Vidar offered them the warmest smile he could muster. Unfortunately, Vidar's smile was twisted as he winced in pain. Sander threw himself at his *faðir*, embracing him tightly.

"I love you, my children." Vidar panted. "You must get on the ship. The Anglo-Saxons won't let up."

"I want to stay with you, *faðir*!" Sander argued.

Hurriedly, I pulled the utility knife from my belt and gazed at Sander. He turned to me, releasing Vidar, staring at me with pain-filled eyes. I thrust the knife into his hands and closed my hands over his.

"Get on the ship," I said gently. "I need you and your brother to protect the little ones."

Sander looked from the knife to my face and nodded; he was pale, his eyes were wide, and his mouth pursed shut. Young Birger had already taken his bow in hand, an arrow knocked in place.

"Stay on Storm-Serpent." Vidar urged, awkwardly bending to kiss each of his four children in turn. "We'll be going home soon."

"Where are you going?" Sander demanded. "You're too hurt to fight!"

"I'm never too hurt to fight." Vidar winked. "I've got to help Hallmundr and the others. Hurry, get on the ship – I'll be with you soon!"

Vidar grabbed me quickly and pressed a hasty kiss to my lips.

"I'll be with you soon, we can't leave Hallmundr." Vidar said.

"I'm fighting by your side, Vidar," I said firmly. "For as long as you're on the battlefield, I will be too."

Vidar smiled at the fierceness on my face.

"Get the children on Storm-Serpent then fight beside me, little fawn." Vidar kissed me again.

Vidar ruffled Einar's fair hair, kissed his brow and ran back to the shore, Jan charging beside him. Young Birger lunged passed me and loosed arrow after arrow at the Anglo-Saxons charging to meet Vidar and Jan. As Young Birger covered his *faðir* and Jan, the younger children and I ran up the dock. I spotted Lars ushering passengers aboard, Guðrin behind him. We bolted across the gangplank, but I didn't climb on board. I kissed Einar before thrusting the boy into Guðrin's arms, the poor young child screaming and writhing in her arms.

I lifted Æsa, kissed her and passed her to Lars.

"Stay with me, *mumie*, please!" Æsa wept.

"I'll be back shortly, I promise!" I cried, tears brimming in my eyes. I turned to Sander, trying hard to ignore my two youngest children's sobs. "Do you still have the knife?"

"*Já.*" He nodded, presenting it to me.

"Good," I said, bringing him to my chest and kissing his fair head. "Protect your brother and sister, my love!"

"Let me fight with you!" He begged, gazing up at me.

"You need to protect your brother and sister." I chided.

He rolled his lips together and nodded reluctantly.

"Be safe, *mumie*, I love you." He whispered.

"I love you, too, sweet boy!" I couldn't stop my tears from falling.

We embraced each other before Sander released me, wiping his face on his sleeve as he scurried onto Storm-Serpent. Young Birger appeared behind me.

"*Faðir* and Jan – where are they?" I asked.

"*Faðir* told me to board the ship." Young Birger said quickly. "I must cover them from the stern."

I nodded and kissed his cheek. I gazed at each of my children briefly, a knot abruptly forming in my throat.

"I love you, my sweet children!" I swallowed hard and, with sword and shield in hand, I dashed down the gangplank.

When I had fought in Francia, the children had been safely tucked away at camp. There had been order, we had control of our surroundings, there were many trusted persons there to watch and protect the children. Though we had lost that long battle, the children had been safe in the camp. Here in Gipeswic there was nothing but chaos and insanity, in the blur of panic I couldn't tell Danish ally from Anglo-Saxon enemy. Storm-Serpent was the safest place the children could be, but we needed to leave, we needed to row down the river and make it into the channel.

The sun had breached the horizon, its white rays piercing through the deep blue remnants of night, and still the battle ensued. Wessex soldiers slaughtered unarmed men, women and children upon the shores. Danes fought back, wild and frenzied, there was no order or discipline, they fought to kill, to get their families to safety – they fought to survive.

I scanned the shore and caught sight of Vidar. He was ducked behind his shield as a Wessex soldier beat down on it with an axe. Vidar lunged and fought with none of his usual skill and lustre. His body was stiff and sore from the attack he'd suffered just the day before. Vidar's handsome face was contorted with rage and agony; he was pale as a spirit, his own wounds and bruises invisible beneath the layers of dripping blood his exhausted body was drenched in.

The soldier smashed Vidar's shield with his axe so hard the shield shattered. The soldier lifted his axe up high, my heart leapt into my throat, blood pounded in my ears. Thankfully Vidar was faster, even in his current state – he swung his sword, slicing open the soldier's stomach, his guts and innards spewing out of the gash. Screeching, the soldier dropped his axe and tumbled to the floor clutching his innards, his face pallid and blood-spattered. Quickly Vidar plunged his sword through the Anglo-Saxon's throat, silencing his shrieks. Vidar snatched up a discarded shield, spun and blocked a blow from his right.

Suddenly my vision went dark and my head spun. The wind had been knocked out of me, I found myself on the ground, gasping for air, a hot pain in my belly. I rubbed my eyes on my arm, blinking hard to rid my vision of stars, my head throbbing from hitting the wooden dock. I briefly glanced at my hand and stomach – no blood, I must've run into a shield or person. A blur of red and gold stumbled upwards. My vision cleared somewhat, I squinted at the man, reaching for *Úlfsblóð*.

"You! It's because of you this has happened!" The man roared, standing above me, a shield in one of his hands, his sword pointed directly at me.

"Theodric?" I wheezed.

"This is your fault! Beric began an attack on the Danes in the early hours!" Theodric hissed, lowering his sword. "He's furious at you for betraying our people!"

"Why didn't you try to stop him?" I demanded, fumbling to my feet, sword in hand.

"You must leave." Theodric growled.

"Why didn't you stop him?" I repeated.

"Get on your ship, Aveline." Theodric snarled. "I vowed to you and your husband that if I saw you again, I'd kill you both – I'm giving you a final chance to leave!"

"Why are you like this?" I hissed. "Are you my friend or foe?"

"Leave!" Theodric spat.

"This is the way it's going to be?" I scowled.

Theodric didn't answer. He glowered darkly at me for a moment, spat on the ground and turned his back on me, running across the shore. Vidar had disappeared from my sight, waylaid by the Anglo-Saxons. I spotted Jan and fiery-haired Domnall, both men as tall as mountains, raging through a troop of soldiers and plainly dressed Anglo-Saxons. I stumbled towards them, squeezing the leather strap of my shield so hard it dug into my flesh.

The stench of smoke mingled with the filthy reek of shit, sweat and the tang of the river. Sweat stung my eyes as it dripped from my brow. I panted as I ran, my mouth dry, tasting the copper of blood, the hot pungent ash from the fires and dust from the sand as it kicked up beneath so many feet. Weapons clashed together, bodies lunged and toppled and fell; a whirlwind of madness, disorder and violence surrounded me. I didn't pay attention to whom I was fighting; I rammed my shield, slashed with my sword, dodged and rolled from attacks, blindly forcing my way through the crowds in search of Vidar. I didn't care who I killed or injured, I just wanted to find my husband.

"Take care, Aveline!" Jan bellowed, narrowly dodging my blade.

Woken from my daze, I realised Jan, Einarr and Domnall surrounded me. In front of us were five Anglo-Saxons, and one was locked in battle with Hallmundr. With a vicious snarl, Hallmundr smashed the Anglo-Saxon with his shield, knocking the enemy to the ground. Roaring like a bear, Hallmundr battered the Anglo-Saxon with the edge of his shield, the cracking and shattering of his skull ripping through the air, his face turned to indecipherable pulp.

We fought the four remaining Anglo-Saxons. They were armed with nothing more than clubs and aged farming equipment. My body was tiring, shaking with exhaustion, but so were my enemies. One of the Anglo-Saxons bypassed my shield and slammed my arm with his club, sending a horrendous tremor through my body, like I'd been struck by lightning. I shrieked with pain, reeled around and swung my sword at him, striking him in his side with the sharp edge of the blade. *Úlfsblóð*'s strike was smooth, ripping through his flesh with ease. The steel blade halted when it struck his rib, sending a tremor through the blade to my arm. I pulled *Úlfsblóð* free and stabbed him in the stomach, cutting through him effortlessly. He fell to the ground, dead.

"We've got to get to Storm-Serpent!" Domnall panted.

"Where's Vidar?" I demanded.

"Here, little fawn!"

Vidar staggered over to me and collapsed on the ground.

"Get up!" I cried grabbing his shoulder and trying to pull him up, but he was too heavy. "We have to go."

"Is everyone here, little fawn?" Vidar rasped.

"*Já*, come on now, let's go! Get up!"

Jan picked Vidar up, dragging him to his feet. Vidar held one arm around Jan's waist, gripping his tunic, the other arm draped around my shoulders. I tossed my shield to Einarr and haphazardly shoved *Úlfsblóð* in its sheath before arranging my arms around my husband. I held his waist with one hand, gripping his hand with my other. Vidar squeezed my hand in reassurance and rested his head on mine.

"Let's go home." Vidar wheezed.

We stumbled across the shore to the dock, panicked faces watching us from onboard Storm-Serpent. I spotted Sander hanging on to the centre mast, his face obscured by shadow as the sun slowly scaled the sky. Domnall and Hallmundr covered our backs while Einarr ran in front of us, leading us to Storm-Serpent.

Seagulls screeched above us; scavengers of the sky ravenous to feast on the bodies of the dead. Icy tendrils of fear skittered down my spine and my heart stopped at the sight of two ravens soaring above in the cloud of gulls – Odin's messengers scanning the battle for news to take to their master in Valhalla.

"Argh!" Jan bellowed, tumbling to the ground, dropping Vidar.

The three of us landed on the dock. I jumped up to my feet, glaring at Jan. A wrenching shriek rolled from my throat at the sight; there was an axe buried in Jan's shoulder. Jan groaned, reached to his shoulder and grazed the iron blade with his trembling white fingertips. Jan dragged his fingers up the blade, reaching the wooden haft the axe head was fixed to. With a deep breath, Jan yanked the axe free, a dreadful decision; blood poured from the wound in copious amounts, soaking his tunic in red.

Bolstered by a surge of rage and an unquenchable thirst for vengeance, Vidar leapt to his feet, spinning around and quickly finding the one who'd thrown the axe.

"Dane Slayer!" Vidar bellowed.

Theodric Holt glowered at Vidar, ripping his sword from his sheath and aiming it at him. Vidar snatched my shield from Einarr, ripped his sword from his sheath and stormed towards Holt, roaring in unrelenting fury. Vidar's ice-blue eyes radiated with bloodlust, blazing through the mask of blood and gore drenching his face.

Frozen to the spot, I watched Vidar and Holt's blades clash. In the corner of my eye, I noticed Domnall and Hallmundr easing Jan to his feet between the two of them.

"Wait." Jan rasped.

All faces watched Vidar and Holt. Shield smashed against shield, iron boss rammed iron boss. Their swords clashed; the clang of steel colliding rang through the air. The wooden shields splintered and crunched, cracking under duress. Sweat poured from both men. Sweeping and thrusting, charging and circling, leaping upwards and rolling across the ground. Vidar and Holt were like wildcats, agile and swift, but they were tiring quickly. I gaped at the scene before me, wanting to run but fixed to the spot, my heart racing, holding my breath. Vidar was winning.

With another monstrous slam, Vidar shattered Holt's shield beyond use. Panting, Holt tossed the remnants to the ground, glowering at Vidar. Even from this distance, I could see the smirk on Vidar's face. His chest rose and fell quickly as he gasped for breath, but, as cocky as ever, Vidar tossed his shield to the ground too, infuriating Holt.

Holt held the hilt of his sword with two hands and lunged at Vidar. Though Vidar was still aching, though his body was stiff, the rush of battle flowed through him. Vidar brought his sword to meet Holt's with such force, he knocked the blade from Holt's hands, sending it flying through the air and slamming to the ground far from Holt's reach.

Defenceless and without a weapon, panic spilt over Holt's face. Both men were breathless, exhausted, and the end was near. Vidar brought his sword down upon Holt. Fatigued from pain or from fighting for so long – or maybe the fright of death spurred Holt on – Vidar's strike was too slow. Holt caught Vidar's sword arm, grabbing his wrist and clinging onto it with desperate determination.

Vidar released a loud rasping "Ha!", eyeing Holt's fingers wrapped around his wrist. Holt grabbed the hilt of Vidar's sword and brought his knee up into Vidar's stomach, the smirk vanishing from Vidar's face. Grimacing, Vidar stumbled back, his grip still firm on the sword. Vidar headbutted Holt in the face and drove him to the ground.

Holt clung to the sword and Vidar's wrist with all the strength he could muster. He tried to flip Vidar, tried to force him off, but Vidar was bigger, Vidar was heavier, Vidar was stronger. Vidar cocked his fist back and slammed it onto Holt's face over and over. Holt released the hilt of the sword, covering his face with one hand.

Vidar was tiring fast. His punches slowed, becoming long, heavy blows instead. Holt was weakening quickly. His hand dropped from his face and fell to the ground, twitching madly. Finally, Holt released Vidar's wrist. Vidar held the sword hilt with both hands, raising it into the air with exhausted, shaking arms–

"*No!*" I shrieked.

Holt whipped up from the ground, thrusting a knife into Vidar's stomach. His hand wasn't twitching, it was searching for a blade!

I ran.

Jan ran.

Holt stabbed Vidar again.

Vidar fell to the ground.

Jan was faster than me. With the axe Holt had hurled at him in his hand, Jan reached Holt first. As Holt flipped himself onto his hands and knees, the knife in his fist, Jan buried the axe into the back of Holt's skull.

Holt dropped to the ground.

"Vidar!" I cried, falling to the ground beside him.

"Little fawn," Vidar said weakly.

Beneath the blood and bruises, Vidar's flesh was terrifyingly grey. I eyed his body, registering the wretched state of him, blood pouring from the stab wounds in his gut. I pressed my trembling hand on Vidar's wound, tried to stop the blood, but the scarlet liquid continued to stream, soaking my hand, hot and unremitting.

Vidar placed his hand upon mine.

"Are the children safe?" He rasped.

"They're on Storm-Serpent – we must get you on the ship too, I need you to stand–"

"Kiss me, little fawn." Vidar breathed, waves of sweat pouring from his every pore.

"We have to get you on the ship!"

"You need to hold me, little fawn," Vidar said as firmly as he could. "Kiss me."

Tears rushed down my face, dripping onto Vidar's cheeks as I pressed a quivering kiss to his lips. Distraught, I buried my face against Vidar's chest and wept.

"Do you remember on our wedding night, when I shattered the ceiling beam with my sword?" Vidar's voice was soft and hollow. "I wondered whether it signified the end of our marriage, and you said perhaps it meant our struggles weren't over ... It looks like we were both right."

"I also said we would be married for a long time." I glared at him. "We've only been married for seven years; we still have a lifetime together yet! You must get on the ship!"

"The only thing that will end our union is death ..." Vidar said, quoting yet more words I had spoken on our wedding night.

"You're not going to die! You vowed to me we'd never be parted – if you die, you'll break that vow! You cannot die, Vidar Alvarsson! You cannot leave me! You cannot leave our children!"

"Vidar—" Jan exclaimed, his eyes widening at the sight of Vidar's wound.

"Get him up! We have to get him on Storm-Serpent!" I hissed, spying a new wave of Anglo-Saxons storming towards the harbour. "Help me!"

Hallmundr, Einarr, Domnall and Jan stood over us staring at Vidar with wide, devastated eyes. Jan knelt beside Vidar and took his free hand, gripping it tightly.

"You fought well, *bróðir*." Jan said.

"Jötunnson, my friend, my *bróðir*, you must take care of Aveline," Vidar said. "You must take care of my children; you must love them as I do. Protect them! Take them home for me, Jötunnson."

"I promise," Jan vowed, tears slipping down his cheeks. "Make sure there is a full horn waiting for me at Odin's table – I will see you again!"

"*Nei*, don't talk like that!" I snarled. "Carry him to the ship!"

"Little fawn," Sadness and pain cracked Vidar's words. "You must go, little fawn. You must go back to Aros. Take the children to safety. We will not win here."

"I'm not leaving without you!" I cried.

"I don't want this either, little fawn. I want to be with you, but the Norns have chosen my time." Vidar replied, tears slipping from the corners of his icy blue eyes.

"Damn the Norns!" I wept. "You must live! Please, Vidar!"

"Take my sword, take my knife, take my bow, take my arm bands and give them all to my sons. Give Æsa my Mjölnir pendent." Vidar whispered, reaching the hammer-shaped amulet hanging around his neck with a heavy, shaking hand. "Kiss our children for me – tell them how proud I am of each of them; tell them I love them."

I nodded; no words able to pass the knot in my throat.

"I love you so much, little fawn. Since the day we met in the woodshed sixteen years ago, I have loved you." Vidar smiled, reaching his shaking hand out to me and grasping the back of my neck. "Thank you for giving me our children and thank you for being my wife."

"Sixteen years has not been long enough. I want to spend a lifetime with you, Vidar!" I wept.

"I wish we could've, but I treasure every moment I had with you – they were the greatest moments of my life. I love you, little fawn."

"I love you, Vidar."

Vidar pulled me down to him and pressed my lips to his. I kissed him desperately, my tears cascading over his face, touching his jaw with trembling fingertips. Suddenly Vidar's lips fell still, and his hand dropped.

Vidar was dead.

CHAPTER THIRTY-FOUR

JAN GRABBED MY shoulders, repeating over and over we had to leave. I ignored him, weeping uncontrollably over my husband, his skin still warm to my touch. Wretched screams billowed from my throat like smoke issuing from the burning Danish homes and alehouses. Suddenly Jan scooped me from the ground and carried me off, running towards Storm-Serpent. I writhed in Jan's arms, reaching out to Vidar, screaming his name, lost in hysteria. The scenery passed by in a blur of colour, my sight focussed only on Vidar's lifeless body. I didn't want to leave my husband; I didn't want to leave his body there on Anglo-Saxon land, but Jan followed Vidar's last wishes, taking me away to Storm-Serpent, to safety.

Exhausted, I wept but stopped flailing in his arms. Jan carried me over the dock and across the gangplank. He held me in his arms, and I screamed and cried, but he held me tightly, silently, on Storm-Serpents hard-wooden floor. Einarr, Hallmundr and Domnall's footsteps jolted the ship as they rushed onboard, then Storm-Serpent moved, cutting through the water quickly. I scrambled out of Jan's grip and dashed to the stern, watching Gipeswic quickly fade as the crew rowed Storm-Serpent away.

I found Vidar's body quickly and stared at it. Two ravens settled on top of him, cawing raucously. My heart stopped, my breathing halted, my tears ceased. As though I was carved out of stone, I sat still and watched Vidar's body disappear from my sight.

"*Mumie?*"

I turned to Young Birger, his icy blue eyes gazing at me, bloodshot, his cheeks stung red from tears. He held Einar in one arm, his other hand rested on Æsa's shoulder, the poor girl clinging desperately to his fingers with one hand, her other hand clutching Sander, who huddled beside her.

Wordlessly, I opened my arms to my children and the four of them collapsed onto me. I held them tightly, and we wept together in a huddled mass on the floor of Storm-Serpent, mourning Vidar.

***

"JARLKONA?" EINARR MURMURED.

I looked up at him. In his hands, he held Vidar's sword and belt, the pouches and utility knife hanging from them. He had retrieved them to give to my children, just as Vidar had requested.

"*Þakka fyrir.*" I murmured.

Gently Einarr placed Vidar's belongings on the floor beside me. All four children had fallen asleep in a bunch together on the ship's floor, fatigued from weeping. Slumber was the best thing for them, an exit from the painful reality of Vidar's death. Without saying another word, Einarr returned to his bench. I stared at Vidar's sword and a shuddering sigh fell from my lips.

Night had fallen, and Storm-Serpent drifted over the calm waves of the channel, the black sky stretched around us, glittering with silver stars. The moon wasn't whole, but it was bright. I don't know how long I had been staring at Vidar's sword before Jan appeared with furs in his arms and a cloak about his shoulders. Beneath his cloak he didn't wear a tunic, the bandages wrapped around his chest and shoulder were visible. Scabs and crusted over wounds were etched in his torso, but he smelled of sweet honey and strong soap – one of the women had cleaned him and dressed him in fresh linen bandages.

Jan carefully laid two of the furs over my four children before holding the last one out to me.

"You're shivering." Jan said.

I didn't answer. He laid the fur on me and eased himself to the floor beside me, wincing as he did so, his body rigid and aching from his wounds.

"The gods work in mysterious ways–"

"*Nei*, Jan–"

"I don't know why he had to die, but he's in Valhalla now–"

"Stop!"

"Aveline?"

"Damn your gods, Jan Jötunnson. First, they took my daughter and now they've stolen my husband from me!"

"Aveline—"

"*Nei*," I hissed. "Why do you turn to them? Why do you put your faith in them when they are so unkind to you? They took *all* your children and both your wives! They cursed you, they took everyone you loved – they took your mother, your older brother and now they've taken Vidar!"

Jan stopped. My heart hammered painfully in my chest and fresh tears brewed in my eyes, a few slipping down my cheeks. Silently Jan pulled a ring from his finger and handed it to me, dried blood flaking off the simple silver band.

"It's Vidar's." I gasped, turning the ring in my fingers.

"Hallmundr, Domnall and Einarr retrieved the things he wanted you and the children to have before Storm-Serpent left the harbour." Jan explained softly.

"*Þakka fyrir* ..." I whispered, closing my hand around the ring and holding it against my heart.

"I wish Vidar didn't die, Aveline." Jan murmured.

I leaned my head against his shoulder, clutching the ring tightly. Jan rested his head on mine and we stopped talking. I felt Jan's body shudder with silent tears, but no words passed our lips. I slipped the fur over his lap to keep him warm. We sat together in sadness; our tears hidden by the black night sky.

***

I DIDN'T SLEEP at all during the night. The sky was bright with pink, orange and blue as the sun rose from the horizon. I gazed at the waves as they eddied about us, the rhythmic rise and fall of the ship on the water as though Storm-Serpent rested upon the chest of a gigantic sleeping creature. The winds were strong – fine winds for sailing. If they stayed like this, we would get to Aros quickly.

In the distance, the sound of cawing reached my ears. I scanned the sky for the raven I knew was calling me. There, in the distance, high above the ship, was the black silhouette.

"Why Vidar?" I whispered.

Suddenly the memory of the raven who had flown into our bedroom replayed inside my mind. The raven had swooped into Vidar and my hall from the smokehole in the sleeping area roof. We had run out with the children and closed the bird off inside the room. Jan had arrived and agreed to help get rid of the bird. The moment Vidar opened the sleeping area curtains, the raven had swooped out and attacked him, before settling on Jan.

The raven had warned me long ago of Vidar's death ...

I sighed deeply. Jan would survive his wounds. The Allfather had received his seventh sacrifice. I would return to Aros in just a few days, not as Jarlkona, but as Jarl. I would announce Vidar's death to the people of Aros; we would hold a *blót* in commemoration of him, a funeral though we didn't have his body; we would celebrate his life and his arrival into Valhalla, and that of all the Danes who had died in Francia and Gipeswic. Then I would announce my inheriting of Vidar's jarldom ... Should all go well, and my rule was accepted and not challenged or objected to, I would settle disputes, be updated on the affairs of Aros, give gifts to the people, then travel to all of the settlements under Vidar's control and do the same things with them. I would hold a grand meeting in Aros with all of Vidar's retainers, followers, supporters and townspeople in attendance, for them to publicly vow their fealty to me. Then I would travel to Roskilde and do the same thing for Alvar and his people ...

I curled my hands into fists, my nails digging into my palms, and a whimpering cry fell from my lips. None of that mattered to me. I didn't care to be jarl; I didn't care about retainers or supporters or fealty or rule. I wanted Vidar, I wanted my husband, I wanted my daughter Alffinna, I wanted my family to be whole again. But it wasn't, and it never would be.

Since that fateful day when the Norsemen of Roskilde had sacked my village in the Kingdom of the East Angles and

RISE TO FALL

kidnapped me, a nine-year-old child, I realised that peace did not last forever. My past had proven that I would always rise to fall.

With Vidar's love, I had risen.

With Vidar's death, I fell.

AUTHOR'S NOTE

RISE TO FALL is the sequel novel to DANETHRALL. Historically inspired, RISE TO FALL is primarily a fiction and I hope any historical inaccuracies that may be found in these pages will be recognised as creative licence; forgiven and appreciated for their use in propelling this story.

Set mainly in ninth century Denmark, I have tried to remain as faithful to the period as possible but have taken advantage of creative licence to a certain degree. The language spoken in ninth century Denmark was Old East Norse, but you may find some Danish and Icelandic words amongst the Old Norse scattered throughout the book.

Most characters in this story have period-specific Old Norse names, but for a few characters I preferred to not be as strict. Therefore, in these pages you will find a handful of characters with Icelandic names; modern, traditional or Old Scandinavian names; names that weren't first used until well after the ninth century, etc. I have used the anglicised or 'younger version' of names here and there (for example, Vidar is the younger version of the old Norse Viðarr).

In a few chapters you will see the words 'seax' and 'sax' mentioned. No, there are no typos, 'seax' is the Old English word for a form of knife/dagger and 'sax' is simply the Norse version.

In chapter sixteen, Young Birger is considered an adult at the age of ten. Throughout my research the age of adulthood for Viking boys ranged between ten and sixteen, so I decided ten would be the age I would go with in my story.

For more information on *seiðr*, the siege of Paris, and the Old Norse, Ænglisc and Old French words used in this book – and a lot more – please visit my website, **gskterry.com**.

Regardless of inaccuracies and creative licence, I do hope this story was as exciting and enjoyable for you to read, as it was for me to write.

Gwendoline SK Terry